BOOKS BY HARRY CREWS

The Gospel Singer
Naked in Garden Hills
This Thing Don't Lead to Heaven
Karate Is a Thing of the Spirit
Car
The Hawk Is Dying
The Gypsy's Curse
A Feast of Snakes
A Childhood: The Biography of a Place
Blood and Grits
The Enthusiast
Florida Frenzy
Two
All We Need of Hell
The Knockout Artist
Body
Scar Lover

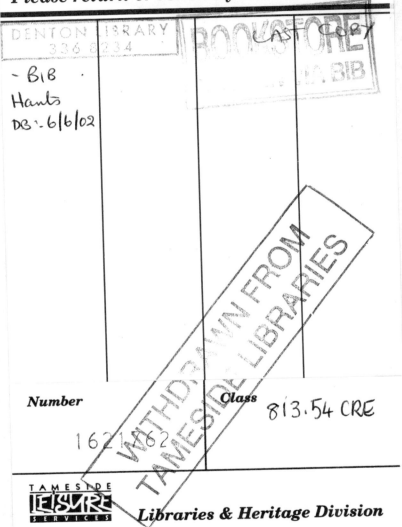

CLASSIC CREWS

A Harry Crews Reader

Harry Crews

GORSE

GORSE
231 Portobello Road
London W11 1LT
UK

British Library Cataloguing in Publication Data.
A catalogue record for this book is available from The British Library.

The right of Harry Crews to be identified as author of this work has been asserted by him in accordance with the Copyrights, Designs and Patents Act 1988.

First published in 1993 by Poseidon Press, an imprint of Simon & Schuster, New York.

"Fathers, Sons, Blood" first appeared in *Playboy*.
"The Car" and "Climbing the Tower" first appeared in *Esquire* .

Printed and bound by The Guernsey Press Co. Ltd., Guernsey.

*This book is dedicated to Huntley Johnson and Melissa Miller,
attorneys both, whose collaborations have often been brilliant
(Item: they've never yet allowed the sun to set on me while I
was locked in a jail cell), but their most beautiful collaborative
miracles to date have been Huntley III, age three, and
Cameron June, age six months. I am honored to have them
treat me as blood kin, for it is as blood kin that I think of them.*

Contents

Introduction

IN 1968, right at a quarter of a century ago, I called my mama in South Georgia, and before she could say hello, I blurted out, "I did it, Mama! I by God did it!"

"Don't cuss," she said. "You in trouble?"

"No mam, I'm not in trouble. Just the opposite."

"Son, you not making a lot of sense, and we long distance."

She had led a hardscrabble life, scratching for every penny she ever had, and she was always acutely aware of carelessly wasting money.

"Mama, I sold a novel."

There was a long moment of silence on the line. I could almost hear her thinking, perhaps even disbelieving.

"One of them novels, you say?"

"Yes mam. It's called *The Gospel Singer*."

"That's the one you just been working on," she said.

"That's the one."

There had been others. God knows there had been others. She had watched me ever since I got out of the Marine Corps trying to teach myself to write, watched me working night and day, snatching an hour here, a half-a-day there, denying myself, denying my family, while I pecked at the typewriter. I had written five novels and a roomful of short stories and I had made a hundred dollars. The *Sewanee Review* had bought a short story for that amount. And that was it. The total. But that had happened when I was still in college. Everybody had forgotten all about it by now. Except me. Publishing one story in the oldest literary quarterly in America for a hundred dollars had been a lifeline to hang on to in the high seas I'd been floundering in. And I had clung to it as such.

"You still there, Mama?"

"I was just thinking," she said.

"Thinking what?" I said.

"That novel you say you sold," she said, "you didn't pass it off as the truth, did you?"

"They know I made it up."

"You mean they taken and given you good money for something they known to be a lie?"

When I told her that was what they had done, she said: "It's a lot in this old world I don't understand, and I know I won't ever understand that."

But she was wrong. She has come to understand it. She had never read a novel until I wrote one, and it takes her about as long to read a novel as it does for me to write it, but when she's through, the print's read right off the page. She came to understand that all the best fiction is about the same thing: people doing the best they can with what they've got to do with, sometimes acting with honor, sometimes not, sometimes with love and compassion and mercy, and sometimes not.

Thank God, she had never had to listen to people who talk about fiction as though it were a complicated code that had to be broken before it could be understood. To her a novel is only people doing things with and to other people in a place and time according to their own best lights. They have their own good (at least to them good) reasons for what they do. Consequently, nobody is a villain in his own heart.

I was born June 7, 1935, at the end of a dirt road in Bacon County, Georgia. My father died when I was a baby and my mother, with a simple courage born and sustained by desperation and a lack of alternatives, raised my brother and me.

It must seem curious to the few people who might have thought about it for as long as thirty seconds why a boy who was born and raised in the rickets-and-hookworm belt of South Georgia and who moved nearly every year of his life from one framed-out piece of dirt to another so his family could rent out their backs and sweat as sharecroppers on somebody else's land, why such a boy should grow up determined to be a writer. It is more than curious to me; it is an ultimate mystery. But I had been asked about it so much as an adult that when I sat down to write the memoir of my childhood, I tried to address the question as best I could. I believe what I wrote then to be true as far as it goes. But it does not go very far. I could only point to the place and circumstances in which the notion of being a storyteller was planted in me as solid as bone.

My closest friend and constant playmate was a little boy named Willalee Bookatee. We lived sixteen miles from the nearest town and a distance much too far to walk from another farm. Whether it was out of necessity I cannot say, but we were as close as brothers and at times very nearly as vicious to one another as brothers. His family was sharecroppers, too. Whatever games and toys we had were games and toys of our own devising. I cannot remember how it got started, but Willalee Bookatee and I spent an incredible amount of time with the Sears, Roebuck catalogue. In those days everybody got such a catalogue whether he ordered anything out of it or not.

We looked at the men and women and children on the brightly colored pages and gave them names and personalities and histories and hopes, and in excruciating detail we established how all of them were related one to the other. Before we were through we had established feuds that had been running between families for years. We married men and women and we gave them children, some who died and some who did not. And blood! God, was there an extraordinary amount of blood splashed over those pages.

No man or woman or child in the catalogue was exempt from becoming a member of one of the several extended families we fabricated innocently and viciously, thereby keeping ourselves entertained all the days and weeks and months until the next catalogue came and we would begin again. I had never found anything before nor have I found anything since that gave me such an overwhelming sense of well-being and profound power. Because no matter what else the storyteller may or may not be, inside the boundaries of his story he is omniscient and omnipotent, godlike. I was seduced to the making of worlds that had never existed, and seduced also to contriving a tissue of lies that was —at least to me—truer than anything that had ever happened.

When the Korean Conflict came along, I went down and joined the Marine Corps. My brother, who is four years older than I, was already in

Korea fighting. Being good, southern, ignorant country boys, we did the good, southern, ignorant country thing: we volunteered as quickly as possible, anxious as we were to go and spill our blood in the good, southern, ignorant country way.

It was very nearly the best thing I ever did. As far back as I could remember, I had longed and lusted for an unlimited supply of books. I was weary of the catalogue and the Bible, the only two books I had ever seen in any sharecropper's house. When I got to my first duty station and walked into the base library, it was like throwing a starving man a turkey. I did my time in the Corps with a book always at hand. And since reading, like water, seeks its own level, I went from reading the novels of Mickey Spillane (all of which I read) to reading the novels of Graham Greene (all of which I read). Greene remains the writer to whom I owe the greatest debt, because in the best tradition of literature I stole everything I could possibly steal from his work. And most important, whatever else Graham Greene did, he always told you a story. And that is all I have ever tried to do: tell a story.

With the G.I. Bill I went to the University, not because I thought anyone there might teach me to write fiction, but because I thought someone there might teach me how to make a living while I taught myself to write fiction. At the end of two years, however, choking and gasping from Truth and Beauty, I gave up on school for a Triumph motorcycle. Going to the University had caused a nasty rash of boredom to break out in my world. I felt like I was swimming in a sea of gumdrops. Everything was so orderly, so safe. Everybody seemed to be so certain of his future, so satisfied with what he knew, that it bored the living hell out of me. And on the list of things I cannot bear, boredom is right at the top. Do anything to me but don't bore me. In the face of boredom, a demon rises in me and screams: "Do something, *anything*, even if it's wrong!" I can't get any closer to explaining it than simply to say that the demon is there, and when he rises and screams, I have to go. I headed west one bright spring morning with seven dollars and fifty-five cents in my pocket and a sleeping bag rolled up behind me on the motorcycle, and without the slightest notion of where I was going or how long I'd be gone. Money was the least of my concerns. If you can cook and tend bar you can work just about any day in any city in the country. At least you could when I was on the road. I worked all kinds of jobs, but mostly I pulled drafts, poured shots, and flipped burgers. I never made much money but I got along. And I flat-out covered some territory.

There was much good and much bad in the trip. I thought that the good was important enough to suffer the bad. I still do. As I traveled I kept a journal called *There's Something About Being Straddle of a Thing*. Riding a motorcycle that far under conditions you can imagine, and some that you can't, is as close as anybody is likely to come to knowing what it feels like to free-fall two thousand feet out of a light aircraft without actually making a jump. All my senses were reborn. The world was made new. An ordinary tree was a miracle, and my own place in the world was miraculous. On that long, good and bad ride, there were moments that opened onto mysteries very nearly unutterable.

I hooked up with a carny and worked for a while as a caller for the ten-in-one show. In the world of carnivals, the ten-in-one is the freak show. I was especially fond of the Fat Lady and her friends there under the tent. I think I know why, and I know I know when, I started loving freaks. I had been able to rent a place to sleep from a freak man and his freak wife and I woke up one morning looking at both of them where they stood at the other end of their trailer in the kitchen. They stood perfectly still in the dim, yellow light, their backs to each other. I could not see their faces, but I was close enough to hear them clearly when they spoke.

"What's for supper, darling?" he said.

"Franks and beans, with a nice little salad," she said.

And then they turned to each other under the yellow light. The lady had a beard not quite as thick as my own but about three inches long and very black. The man's face had a harelip. His face was divided so that the top of his nose forked. His eyes were positioned almost on the sides of his head and in the middle was a third eye that was not really an eye at all but a kind of false lid over a round indentation that saw nothing. It was enough, though, to make me taste bile in my throat and cause a cold fear to start in my heart.

They kissed. Their lips brushed briefly and I heard them murmur to each other and he was gone through the door. And I, lying at the back of the trailer, was never the same again.

I have never stopped remembering that as wondrous and special as those two people were, they were only talking about and looking forward to and needing precisely what all of the rest of us talk about and look forward to and need. He might have been any husband going to any job anywhere. He just happened to have that divided face. That is not a very startling revelation, I know, but it is one most of us resist because we have that word *normal* and we can say we are normal because a psychological, sexual, or spiritual abnormality can—with a little luck—be safely hidden from the rest of the world. But if you are less than three feet tall, you have to deal with that fact every second of every day of your life. And everyone witnesses your effort. You go into a bar and you can't get up onto a stool. You whistle down a taxi and you can't open the door. If you're a lady with a beard, every face you meet is a mirror to give you back the disgust and horror and unreasonableness of your predicament. No matter which corner you turn on which street in which city in the world, you can expect to meet the mirror. And I suppose I have never been able to forgive myself the grotesqueries and aberrations I am able to hide with such impunity in my own life. It was a painful and wondrous moment of self-knowledge, one I might never have had if I had not taken the bike on the road, looking for something I knew I'd recognize only when I saw it, looking for the limit—ultimately, looking for the edge.

During that year and a half I was jailed in Glenrock, Wyoming; was beaten in a fair fight by a one-legged Blackfoot Indian on a reservation in Montana; washed dishes in Reno, Nevada; picked tomatoes outside San Francisco; had the hell scared out of me in a YMCA in Colorado Springs, Colorado, by a man who thought he was Christ; and made friends in Chihuahua, Mexico, with a Mexican airline pilot who made a fetish of motorcycle saddlebags. I limped back into the University, purified and holy, ready to absorb whatever was left of Truth and Beauty.

There was not, of course, any more Truth and Beauty at the University when I returned than there was when I left. But at least I still had the good government tit to suck on. If I carried a full load of courses and maintained a C average, I got three hots and a cot and more time than I needed to read and continue my efforts to learn to write.

That learning to write was taking so long did not surprise or discourage me. At least I tried not to let it. No one knew better than I how hit-and-miss my learning had been. But I remained convinced in my belief that all anybody needed to develop as a writer was access to a good library and the willingness to play fast and loose with his life, because make no mistake about it, by the time a person even moderately masters any art form, it is almost always too late to do anything else. I certainly expected it to be too late for me. And I knew there was not a mother's son or daughter in the world who could tell any apprentice artist, no matter how much potential and willingness to work the apprentice had, whether he would in fact catch the brass ring or spend the end of his days just as he spent them in his youth: floundering and flopping about and still failing.

My compulsive need to look for the edge and live on it has marked me in more ways than I would want to know or try to explain. Never mind the marks it has left on my skin, let me go straight to the bone. Drag out the X rays. Take a quick look. Broken neck, left cheek crushed, nose broken, collarbones broken, ribs on both sides . . . But that's enough. That's too much. I've had some experience with *too much*, and I know what it looks like. The record I have left in my legs alone is *too much*. I have knees that would make a grown man cry, and my feet are strange.

The little that I have learned about the world, and, more important, that I have learned about myself, has been absurdly expensive, but I have always thought it more than worth the price. There is no other way. The miracle of the world, the miracle of a rebirth of the senses, the miracle of an accepting heart can only be paid for with blood and bone. No other currency has ever been acceptable.

"*We are the sum of all our moments*," Thomas Wolfe said. Thank God, I believe that. Nothing is wasted on a writer. If you are lucky, somewhere in the work there will be a place for the unspeakable and the unendurable. Somewhere the bad will fit seamlessly with the good. In my work, nowhere is this truer than in the memoir I wrote of my early years.

When I sat down to write A *Childhood: The Biography of a Place*, my dead father and his brother, who was also my father, haunted me and lived in my dreams, dreams that were an inseparable mix of the unendurable and unspeakable, the good and the bad. There was too much I did not understand. I wanted to understand it so I could stop thinking about it. I thought if I could relive it and set it all down in detailed, specific language, I would be purged of it. I wrote A *Childhood* in the most specific and detailed prose I could summon and relived it all again. It almost killed me, but it purged nothing. Those years are still as red and raw and alive in memory as they ever were. So much for good ideas.

The novel *Car* would, I think, be a better book if the automobile outraged me less. I hate its stifling presence and abhor the sheer stupidity of the automobile industry. Consider this question: How much sense does it make for a 113-pound housewife to get into 4,000 pounds of machinery and drive 2 blocks for a 13-ounce loaf of bread? That question and others like it made writing the book *Car* inevitable.

Once when I was a young man and a long way from home, I knew a man who suffered from the Gypsy's Curse. The Curse drove him to despair and the despair drove him to suicide. Because he was a good man and my friend, I brought him back with language, and with language I changed him and his world into something else. Given who he was, and who I am, I don't think there was a chance to do otherwise.

I had a son named Patrick. Circumstances collaborated to kill him. I got over it and wrote "Fathers, Sons, Blood." I hate myself for getting over his death. But I did, I got over it.

I wrote "The Car" to show that as a young man I loved cars with a deep, impossible, and idiotic lunacy. Anybody surprised by that? I did not think so.

In "Climbing the Tower" I wanted, as best I could, to take the reader through the process of what it is like for me as a writer when I feel myself start to slip out of my own skin and my own world and into the world and skin of someone else. It is a sometimes nasty but always necessary part of being a fiction writer. I don't think anybody anywhere, including the editors at *Esquire*, where I first published the piece, understood what I was trying to do. That happens. And I know now that I did not do what I was trying to do. But I like "Climbing the Tower" very much. That happens too.

A CHILDHOOD

The Biography
of a Place

Survival is triumph enough.
—DAVID SHELLEY, IN CONVERSATION.

I

One

MY first memory is of a time ten years before I was born, and the memory takes place where I have never been and involves my daddy whom I never knew. It was the middle of the night in the Everglades swamp in 1925, when my daddy woke his best friend Cecil out of a deep sleep in the bunkhouse just south of the floating dredge that was slowly chewing its way across the Florida Peninsula from Miami on the Atlantic to Naples on the Gulf of Mexico, opening a route and piling dirt for the highway that would come to be known as the Tamiami Trail. The night was dark as only a swamp can be dark and they could not see each other there in the bunkhouse. The rhythmic stroke of the dredge's engine came counterpoint to my daddy's shaky voice as he told Cecil what was wrong.

When Cecil finally did speak, he said: "I hope it was good, boy. I sho do."

"What was good?"

"That Indian. You got the clap."

But daddy had already known. He had thought of little else since it had become almost impossible for him to give water because of the fire that started in his stomach and felt like it burned through raw flesh every time he had to water off. He had thought from sunup to dark of the chickee where he had lain under the palm roof being eaten alive by swarming mosquitoes as he rode the flat-faced Seminole girl, whose name he never knew and who grunted like a sow and smelled like something shot in the woods.

He had not wanted her, but they had been in the swamp for three years. They worked around the clock, and if they weren't working or sleeping, their time was pretty much spent drinking or fighting or shooting gators. So since he could not have what he wanted, he tried to want what he could have, but it had been miserable, all of it because of the way she sounded and the way she smelled and the mosquitoes clotted about their faces thick as a veil and the heavy black flies that crawled over their legs.

"It weren't all that good," daddy said.

"No," said Cecil, "I don't reckon it's ever *that* good."

Gonorrhea was a serious hurt in the days before they had penicillin, and the hurt was compounded because daddy had resisted getting any treatment or even telling anybody until the pain finally forced him to do it.

"I don't know what I'm gone do."

"I do," Cecil said. "We gotta get out of the swamp and find you a doctor."

Cecil felt some obligation to help, not only because they had been friends since childhood but also because it was Cecil who had left Bacon County first to work on the trail and was later able to get his buddy a job working with him. It was all in the best tradition of "If you git work, write." And when Cecil wrote that there was steady work and good pay to be had in the Everglades, Ray had followed him down there.

He got on one of the gangs cutting right-of-way and in less than two years worked his way into the job of dredge operator. He was then not yet twenty and it was a sweet accomplishment for a boy who had no education, who was away from the farm for the first time in his life. But the clap soured the whole thing considerably.

Cecil was waiting for him when he came out of the doctor's office in the little town of Arcadia, Florida. It was the third doctor daddy had seen, and this one agreed with the other two. The word was final.

"He says I got to do it."

"Jesus," Cecil said.

"It's no other way."

"You gone do it?"

"I don't see no other way. Everyone I seen says I got to have one taken off. I guess I do if it ain't no other way."

"Jesus."

On the long drive back to the swamp in Cecil's Model T Ford in the shimmering heat of early summer, they didn't talk. Daddy did say one thing. "I won't ever have any children if they take it off. That's what the doctors said. All three of'm said it."

Cecil didn't say anything.

Did what I have set down here as memory actually happen? Did the two men say what I have recorded, think what I have said they thought? I do not know, nor do I any longer care. My knowledge of my daddy came entirely from the stories I have been told about him, stories told me by my mother, by my brother, who was old enough when he died to remember him first hand, by my other kin people, and by the men and women who knew him while he was alive.

It is demonstrably true that he went to work on the Tamiami Trail when he was seventeen and worked there until he was twenty-three. He did get the clap down there and he did lose a testicle because of it in the little town of Arcadia. He came back to Bacon County with money in his pocket and a gold watch inscribed on the back: "To Ray Crews, Pioneer Builder of the Tamiami Trail." Cecil got such a watch, as did several of the men who saw the job through from start to finish. Those are facts, but the rest of it came down to me through the mouths of more people than I could name. And I have lived with the stories of him for so long that they are as true as anything that ever actually happened to me. They are true because I think they are true. I, of course, had no alternative. It would have been impossible for me to think otherwise.

Jean-Paul Sartre in his autobiography *Words*, when writing about a man's tendency to smother his son, said his own father sired him and then had the decency to die. I've always thought that because my daddy died before I could ever know him, he became a more formidable memory, a greater influence, and a more palpable presence than he would have been had he lived. I'm not sure precisely what that says about me, but surely it must say more about me than it does about my daddy or his death. It also says a great deal about the people and the place I come from. Nothing is allowed to die in a society of storytelling people. It is all—the good and the bad—carted up and brought along from one generation to the next. And everything that is brought along is colored and shaped by those who bring it.

If that is so, is what they bring with them true? I'm convinced that it is. Whatever violence may be done to the letter of their collective experience, the spirit of that experience remains intact and true. It is their notion of themselves, their understanding of who they are. And it was just for this reason that I started this book, because I have never been certain of who *I* am.

I have always slipped into and out of identities as easily as other people slip into and out of their clothes. Even my voice, its inflections and rhythms, does not seem entirely my own. On journalism assignments during which I've recorded extended interviews with politicians or film stars or truck drivers my own voice will inevitably become almost indistinguishable from the voice of the person with whom I'm talking by the third or fourth tape. Some natural mimic in me picks up whatever verbal tics or mannerisms it gets close to. That mimic in myself has never particularly pleased me, has in fact bothered me more than a little.

But whatever I am has its source back there in Bacon County, from which I left when I was seventeen years old to join the Marine Corps, and to which I never returned to live. I have always known, though, that part of me never left, could never leave, the place where I was born and, further, that what has been most significant in my life had all taken place by the time I was six years old. The search for those six years inevitably led me first to my daddy's early life and early death. Consequently, I have had to rely not only on my own memory but also on the memory of others for what follows here: the biography of a childhood which necessarily is the biography of a place, a way of life gone forever out of the world.

On a blowing March day in 1927, just before his twenty-third birthday, my daddy started back home with his friend Cecil in the Model T Ford. They had been down in the swamp for six years, though, and they were in no particular hurry. With a bottle of whiskey between them on the floorboard, it took nearly three weeks to make the 500 miles up the coast of Florida on U.S. Highway 1, a blacktop double-lane that followed the edge of the ocean up from Miami to Fort Pierce to Daytona and on to Jacksonville. From Jacksonville, they cut up toward the St. Marys River, which divides Florida from Georgia. The air went heavy with the smell of turpentine and pine trees as they drove on north through Folkston and Waycross and finally through Alma, a town of dirt streets, a cotton gin, a warehouse, two grocery stores, a seed and fertilizer store, and a doctor, who had—besides a cash register—some pens out back to hold his fees when they came in the form of chickens and goats and hogs.

In the car with him as they drove, there was a shoebox full of pictures of my daddy with five or six of his buddies, all of them holding whiskey bottles and pistols and rifles and coons and leashed alligators out here in the rugged dug-out sea of saw grass and mangrove swamp through which they had built the Tamiami Trail.

As I work, I have those pictures, yellowed now, still in a pasteboard shoebox where they have always been kept. For better than four decades, when the old shoebox wore out every year or so, the pictures have gone into a new shoebox. I once put them in a heavy leather album, the better to keep them, I thought. But after a week or so, I took them out again. The album seemed wrong. I did not like to look at them caught in the stiff, protected pages. I gave no thought to why I didn't like to see them there, but I believe now it was because a worn and vulnerable pasteboard box more accurately reflected my tenuous connection with him whom I never knew but whose presence has never left me, has always followed me just out of reach and hailing distance like some vague, half-realized shadow.

Looking at them, I think I see some of what my daddy was and some of what I have become. He was taller than I have ever grown, being as he was six feet two and weighing always about 170 pounds. Everything about him—the way he stands, his every gesture—suggests a man of endless and exuberant energy, a man who believes in his bones that anything worth doing is worth overdoing. His is the gun that is always drawn; his is the head that is turned back under the whiskey bottle. He has already had enough trouble and sickness and loss in his short life to have broken a lesser man, but there is more often than not a smile of almost maniacal joy, a smile stretched around a mouthful of teeth already loosened by pyorrhea, a disease which would take the two front teeth out of the top gum before he died shortly after my birth.

They made their way up the coast of Florida, stopping here and there, staying at one place in Jacksonville for nearly a week, drinking and being rowdy in the best way of young men who have been on a hard job and now have money in their pockets, always talking, rehashing again what they had done and where they had been and where they were going and what they hoped for themselves and their families, even though my daddy carried with him the sure and certain knowledge that he would never have any children.

"It ain't the worst thing that could happen," Cecil said. "You ain't but a partial gelding."

"That ain't real funny, Cecil."

"I reckon not. But it still ain't the worst thing."

They were on the St. Marys River in a rented rowboat, drifting, drinking, ignoring the bobbing corks at the ends of their lines, not caring whether they caught anything or not after six years in a swamp where fish had been as plentiful as mosquitoes.

Daddy said: "If it ain't the worst thing, it'll do till the worst thing comes along."

Cecil gave his slow drunken smile, a smile at once full of kidding and love. "The worst thing woulda been to let that old man and his boy eat you alive."

"They'd a had to by God do it."

"Oh, they'd a done it all right. They'd already et several before they started looking at how tender you was."

"I guess. Dying cain't be all that hard though. Without thinking about it at all, people drop dead right and left."

Cecil said: "It's one thing to drop dead. It's sumpin else to have your head pulled off."

These were not violent men, but their lives were full of violence. When daddy first went down to the Everglades, he started on a gang that cut the advance right-of-way and, consequently, was out of the main camp for days, at times for more than a week. When he almost got killed working out there on the gang, Cecil almost killed a man because of it. Daddy's foreman was an old man, grizzled, stinking always of chewing tobacco and sweat and whiskey, and known throughout the construction company as a man mean as a bee-stung dog. He didn't have to dislike you to hurt you, even cripple you. He just liked to hurt and cripple, and he had a son that was very much his daddy's boy.

Because my daddy was only seventeen when he went out there, the full fury of their peculiar humor fell upon him, so much so that once it almost cost him a leg in what was meant to look like an accident when a cable snapped. If it had only been some sort of initiation rite, it would have one day ended. But daddy was under a continual hazing that was meant to draw blood.

When he got back to camp, he found Cecil over by the mess wagon. When he'd finished eating, daddy said: "I'm scared, Cecil. That old man and his boy's gone kill me."

Cecil was still at his beans. "He ain't gone kill you."

"I think he means to."

Cecil put his plate down and said: "No, he ain't cause you and me's gone settle it right now."

Cecil was six feet seven inches tall and weighed between 250 and 275 pounds depending upon the season of the year.

"Cecil, that old man don't know how strong he is his own self."

"He's about to find out. You just keep his boy off me. I'll take care of the old man."

They found the old man and his boy on the dredge and the fight was as short as it was brutal. They locked up and went off the dredge into the mud, the old man on the bottom but with his hands locked on Cecil's throat. He would have killed him, too, if Cecil had not thought to provide himself with a ten-inch steel ringbolt in the back pocket of his overalls which he used to break the old man's skull. But even with his head cracked, it took two men to get his hands from around Cecil's throat.

The old man was taken out to a hospital in Miami and his boy, whom daddy had managed to mark superficially, a cut across his forehead and another down the length of his back, went with him and nothing more was heard of the matter. At least for the moment. But a little over two months later word came into the swamp that the old man and his boy were coming back.

"Me and Luther's comin back to settle. We gone take the biguns one by one and the littluns two by two."

Cecil sent word back on a piece of ruled tablet paper. "If you and that boy come out here for me and Ray, have your boxes built and ready. You gone need'm before you git out again."

For whatever reason, the old man and his boy did not come back into the swamp. The matter had been settled. Surely not to everybody's satisfaction, but settled nonetheless. They had done it themselves without recourse to law or courts. That was not unusual for them and their kind.

Up in Jeff Davis County, just about where I was born and raised, a woman's husband was killed and she—seven months pregnant—was the only witness to the killing. When the sheriff tried to get her to name the man who'd done it, she only pointed to her swelling stomach and said: "He knows who did it, and when the time comes, he will settle it." And that was all she ever said.

In Bacon County, the sheriff was the man who tried to keep the peace, but if you had any real trouble, you did not go to him for help to make it right. You made it right yourself or else became known in the county as a man who was defenseless without the sheriff at his back. If that ever happened, you would be brutalized and savaged endlessly because of it. Men killed other men oftentimes not because there had been some offense that merited death, but simply because there had been an offense, any offense. As many men have been killed over bird dogs and fence lines in South Georgia as anything else.

Bacon County was that kind of place as they drove into it finally toward the middle of March in 1927. There were very few landowners. Most people farmed on shares or standing rent. Shares meant the owner would supply the land, fertilizer, seed, mules, harness, plows, and at harvest take half of everything that was made. On standing rent, you agreed to pay the landowner a certain sum of money for the use of the land. He took nothing but the money. Whether on shares or on standing rent, they were still tenant farmers and survival was a day-to-day crisis as real as rickets in the bones of their children or the worms that would sometimes rise out of their children's stomachs and nest in their throats so that they had to be pulled out by hand to keep the children from choking.

The county itself was still young then, having been formed in 1914 and named for Senator Augustus Octavius Bacon, who was born in Bryan County and lived out much of his life in the city of Macon. Bacon County is as flat as the map it's drawn on and covered with pine trees down in the bottomland near running creeks. Jeff Davis and Appling counties are to the north of it, Pierce and Coffee counties to the east, and the largest county in the state, Ware, joins its southern border.

There was a section of Bacon County famous all over Georgia for moonshining and bird dogs and violence of one kind or another. It was called Scuffletown, not because it was a town or even a crossroads with a store in it, but because as everybody said: "They always scuffling up there." Sometimes the scuffling was serious; sometimes not.

About a month before my daddy drove back into the county, Jay

Scott opened his mouth once too often to a man named Junior "Bad Eye" Carter. He was called Bad Eye because he was putting up wire fence as a young man and the staple he was driving into the post glanced off the hammer and drove itself deep into his right eye. He rode a mule all the way to Alma, where the doctor pulled out the staple, but the eye was gone forever. Having only a left eye gave him an intense, even crazy stare. Talk was that he could conjure with that unblinking, staring left eye.

For a long time there had been bad blood between Bad Eye and Jay Scott over a misunderstanding about some hogs. Bad Eye was chopping wood for the stove when Jay walked up. The woodpile was just inside the wire fence that ran along the public road. Jay stopped in the road and for a long time just watched him. But finally, watching wasn't enough.

"Watch out, old man, a splinter don't fly up there and put out that other eye."

Bad Eye kept on chopping, the strokes of the ax regular as clock ticking. He never even looked up.

"Splinter in that other eye, we'd have to call you Bad *Face*."

Ruby, Bad Eye's wife, saw the whole thing from the water shelf on the back porch of the house where she was standing. Jay saw Ruby on the back porch and said, loud enough for her to hear: "Why don't you git your old woman out here? They tell me she does most of the ax work for you anyhow."

That was when Bad Eye looked up, a big vein standing in his forehead. "You stand out there in a public road and talk all you want to. But don't come over the fence onto my land. Don't reckon you'd have the stomach for that, would you?"

Jay came across the ditch, put one foot in the wire and one hand on top of the fence post, getting ready to climb up and swing over. But he never did. That was as far as he got. Bad Eye, who had started chopping again, never missed a stroke, but drove the blade of the ax through Jay's wrist and two inches deep into the top of the post. Ruby said she bet you could hear him scream for five miles. Said she bet somebody thought they was slaughtering hogs, late in the year as it was.

Jay tied off his arm with his belt and then fainted in the ditch. When he woke up, Bad Eye was sitting on the woodpile with the bloody stump of a hand.

"This here hand belongs to me now, sumbitch. Found it on my land."

Jay fainted again. Two of Bad Eye Carter's kinsmen were killed in the fight to get the hand back. Jay wanted to give it a Christian burial. They never did get it back, but Bad Eye went fishing one day and didn't come back. They finally found him floating in Little Satilla River. His blue and wrinkled body had raised the fifty pounds of rusty plow points tied about his ankles.

It was this part of the county that my daddy and his people came from, back up in what's known as the Forks of the Hurricane, not far from Cartertown, which was not a town either but simply a section of the county where almost every farmer was named Carter. The Forks of the Hurricane was where two wide creeks rose in Big Hurricane Swamp and flowed out across the county, one creek called Little Hurricane and the other Big Hurricane. I was a grown man before I realized that the word we were saying was *hurricane* because it was universally pronounced harrikin.

So daddy came back to the home place, where his own daddy, Dan, and his mama, Lilly, lived with their family, a family which, like most families then, was big. His brothers and sisters were named Vera, D. W., Bertha, Leroy—who was crippled from birth—Melvin, Ora, Pascal, and Audrey.

Daddy's granddaddy had once been a slave owner and a large landholder, but his family, like most families in that time and place, had fallen on evil days. They still owned the land they lived on, but they had to constantly fight the perpetual mortgage held by the bank. There was a place to put your head down and usually enough to eat, but when daddy came home from the swamp, farmers were saying there wasn't enough cash money in the county to close up a dead man's eyes.

Daddy proceeded to do what so many young men have done before him, that is, if not to make a fool of himself, at least to behave so improvidently that he ran through what little money he'd been able to get together working in Florida. Cecil drove off to live in the mountains of North Georgia, so daddy bought himself a Model T Ford and he bought his mama a piano and he bought himself a white linen suit and a white wide-brimmed hat. I don't know how he could have managed it after the car and the piano, but he may have bought himself several of those white suits, judging from the number of pictures I have of him dressed in one. In the first flower of his manhood, he was a great poser for pic-

tures, always with a young lady and sometimes with several young
ladies.

I lift the lid off the shoebox now and reach in. The first picture I see
is of him, his foot propped up on the running board of his Model T
Ford, standing there with a young lady wearing her bonnet, the sun in
their faces, smiling. And looking into his face is like looking into my
own. His cheekbones are high and flat, and a heavy ridge of bone casts a
perpetual shadow over his eyes. There is a joy and great confidence in
the way he stands, his arm around the girl, a cock-of-the-walk tilt to his
pelvis. And along with that photograph there are others: him sitting
under a tree with another young lady, she short-haired and wearing a
brimless little hat almost like a cap; him leaning against the front fender
of the Model T, still in that immaculate white linen suit with yet another young lady; him standing between two girls in their Sunday
frocks on the bank of a river, probably the Little Hurricane.

There is no doubt that in that time he was, as they say in Bacon
County, fond of lying out with dry cattle. Maidens, or at least those
young ladies who had never had a child, were called dry cattle after the
fact that a cow does not give milk until after giving birth to a calf. An
unflattering way to refer to women, God knows, but then those were
unflattering times.

He was also bad to go to the bottle, as so many men have been in the
family. He drank his whiskey and lay out with dry cattle and stayed in
the woods at night running foxes and talking and laughing with his
friends and was vain enough to have it recorded as often as he could
with somebody's camera. It must have been a good time for him then, a
time when he did not yet have a wife and children or the obligations
that always come with them.

Because of the stories I've heard about him, his recklessness, his tendency to stay up all night and stay in the woods when he probably
should have been doing something else, and his whiskey drinking, I
have often wondered if in some way that he could not or would not
have said, he felt his own early death just around the bend. He had been
an extremely sickly child and Granddaddy Dan Crews had never
thought that he would raise him to manhood. When daddy was three
years old, he got rheumatic fever and from it developed what they called
then a leaking heart. After he developed the trouble with his heart, apparently from the fever, his kidneys did not work the way they should

and he would swell up from fluid retention and spent much of his childhood either sitting in a chair or half reclining on a bed.

The doctors in Baxley and Blackshear and even as far away as Waycross—about thirty-five miles—had been unable to help him. Granddaddy Dan in desperation mailed off for some pills he saw advertised in the almanac. Daddy's brother, Uncle Melvin, told me that when the medicine came, the pills were as big as a quarter, the size you might try on a horse. Granddaddy Dan took one look at them and decided he couldn't give them to his boy as little and sick as he was. So he put them on the crosspiece up over the door and forgot about them. But daddy, then only five years old, but already showing the hardheaded willfulness that would follow him through his short life, began to take the pills without anybody knowing about it. Whether it was the pills or the grace of God, the swelling began to go down and within a month he was able to get out in the field and hoe a little bit and in the coming weeks he gradually got better.

But he always had that murmur in his heart. Mama says she could hear it hissing and skipping when she lay with him at night, her head on his chest, and it was that hissing, skipping heart which eventually killed him. That and his predisposition to hurt himself. There seemed to be something in him then and later, a kind of demon, madness even, that drove him to work too hard, to carouse the same way, and always to be rowdier than was good for him.

Maybe it was his conviction that he would never have children that was hurting him, doing bad things in his head and making him behave as he did. He had to have thought of it often and it had to give him pain. Families were important then, and they were important not because the children were useful in the fields to break corn and hoe cotton and drop potato vines in wet weather or help with hog butchering and all the rest of it. No, they were important because a large family was the only thing a man could be sure of having. Nothing else was certain. If a man had no education or even if he did, the hope of putting money in the bank and keeping it there or owning a big piece of land free and clear, such hope was so remote that few men ever let themselves think about it. The timber in the county was of no consequence, and there was very little rich bottomland. Most of the soil was poor and leached out, and commercial fertilizer was dear as blood. But a man didn't need good land or stands of hardwood trees to have babies. All he needed was balls and the inclination.

And in that very fact, the importance of family, lies what I think of as the rotten spot at the center of my life or, said another way, the rotten spot at the center of what my life might have been if circumstances had been different. I come from people who believe the *home place* is as vital and necessary as the beating of your own heart. It is that single house where you were born, where you lived out your childhood, where you grew into young manhood. It is your anchor in the world, that place, along with the memory of your kinsmen at the long supper table every night and the knowledge that it would always exist, if nowhere but in memory.

Such a place is probably important to everybody everywhere, but in Bacon County—although nobody to my knowledge ever said it—the people understand that if you do not have a home place, very little will ever be yours, really *belong* to you in the world. Ever since I reached manhood, I have looked back upon that time when I was a boy and thought how marvelous beyond saying it must be to spend the first ten or fifteen years of your life in the same house—the *home* place—moving among the same furniture, seeing on the familiar walls the same pictures of blood kin. And more marvelous still, to be able to return to that place of your childhood and see it through the eyes of a man, with everything you see set against that long-ago little boy's memory of how things used to be.

But because we were driven from pillar to post when I was a child, there is nowhere I can think of as the home place. Bacon County is my home place, and I've had to make do with it. If I think of where I come from, I think of the entire county. I think of all its people and its customs and all its loveliness and all its ugliness.

Two

BEING as impermanent as the wind, constantly moving, I lost track for thirty-five years of my daddy's side of the family. I remember nothing specific of my paternal grandparents, and my paternal aunts and uncles remained strangers until I was grown. It was not their fault, nor was it mine or anyone else's. It just happened that way.

I saw a good deal of the kin on my mama's side. My Uncle Alton, her brother, was as much as any other man a father to me. He's dead now, but I will always carry a memory of him in my heart as vivid as any memory I have.

I was sitting on the steps of his front porch just after I got out of the Marine Corps in 1956, when I was twenty-one years old, watching him smoking one hand-rolled Prince Albert cigarette after another and spitting between his feet into the yard. He was so reticent that if he said a sentence ten words long, it seemed as though he had been talking all afternoon.

He was probably the closest friend of the longest standing that my daddy ever had. And I remember sitting there on the steps, looking up at him in his rocking chair and talking about my daddy, saying that I thought the worst thing that had happened in my life was his early death, that never having known him, I knew that I would, one way or another, be looking for him the rest of my life.

"What is it you want to know?" he said.

"I don't know what I want to know," I said. "Anything. Everything."

"Cain't know everything," he said. "And anything won't help."

"I think it might," I said. "Anything'll help me see him better than I see him now. At least I'd have some notion of him."

He watched me for a moment with his steady gray eyes looking out from under the brim of the black felt hat he always wore and said: "Let's you and me take us a ride."

He started for the pickup truck parked in the lane beyond the yard and I followed. As was his way, he didn't say where we were going and I didn't ask. It was enough for me to be riding with him over the flat dirt roads between walls of black pine trees on the way to Alma. He lived then about three miles from the Little Satilla River which separates Bacon from Appling County and very near two farms that I had lived on as a boy. We drove the twelve miles to the paved road that led into town, but shortly after we turned into it, he stopped at a little grocery store with Pepsi-Cola and root beer and Redman Chewing Tobacco and snuff signs nailed all over it and two gas pumps out front in the red clay lot where several pickup trucks were parked.

We got down and went in. Some men were sitting around in the back of the store on nail kegs and ladder-back chairs or squatting on their heels, apparently doing nothing very much but smoking and chewing and talking.

One of them came to the front where we had stopped by the counter. "How you, Alton?" he said.

Uncle Alton said: "We all right. Everything all right with you, Joe?"

"Jus fine, I reckon. What can I git you?"

"I guess you can let us have two of them cold Co-Colers."

The man got two Cokes out of the scarred red box behind him and Uncle Alton paid him. We went on back to where the men were talking. They all spoke to Uncle Alton in the brief and easy way of men who had known each other all their lives.

They spoke for a while about the weather, mostly rain, and about other things that men who live off the land speak of when they meet, seriously, but with that resigned tone in their voice that makes you know they know they're speaking only to pass the time because they have utterly no control over what they're talking about: weevils in cotton, screwworms in stock, the government allotment of tobacco acreage, the fierce price of commercial fertilizer.

We hadn't been there long before Uncle Alton said casually, as though it were something that had just occurred to him: "This is Ray Crews' boy. Name Harry."

The men turned and looked at me for a long considered time and it again seemed the most natural thing in the world for them to now begin talking about my daddy, who had been dead for more than twenty years. I didn't know it then and didn't even know it or realize it for a long time afterward, but what Uncle Alton had done, because of what I'd said to him on the porch, was take me out in the truck to talk with men who had known my father.

Maybe the men themselves knew it, or maybe they simply liked my father in such a way that the mention of his name was enough to bring back stories and considerations of people who were kin to him. Without making any special thing out of it they began to talk about those days when daddy was a boy, about how many children were in his family, and then about how families were not as big now as they once had been and from that went on to talk about my grandma's sister, Aunt Belle, who had fourteen children, all of whom lived to be grown, and finally to the time one of Aunt Belle's boys, Orin Bennett, was killed at a liquor still by a government man.

"Well," one of them said, "it's a notion most people have nowadays moonshinin was easy work, but it weren't."

"Moonshinin was hard work. Real hard work."

"Most men I known back in them days," said Uncle Alton, "made moonshine because it weren't nothing else to do. They'as working at the only thing it was to work at. I feel like most folks who make shine even today do it for the same reason."

"I'll tell you sumpin else," Joe said. "I never known men back then makin shine that thought it was anythin wrong with it. It was a livin, the only livin they had."

One of them looked at me and said: "It wasn't much whiskey made in your daddy's family, though. I don't know the ins and outs of how Orin come to be killed up at that there still. But your granddaddy didn't hold with none of his own younguns making whiskey or bein anywhere around where it was made. Not ole Dan Crews didn't. He'd take a drink, drunk his full share, I'd say, but he never thought makin it was proper work for a man."

"I've made some and I've drunk some, and I'd shore a heap ruther drink it than make it."

Just as natural as spitting, a bottle of bonded whiskey out of which about a quarter had been drunk appeared from somewhere behind one of the chairs. The cap was taken off. The man who took it off wiped the neck of the bottle on his jumper sleeve, took a sip, and handed it to the man squatting beside him. The bottle passed. Uncle Alton, God love him, didn't have any of the whiskey. Even then his stomach, which finally killed him, was beginning to go bad on him.

The man who had done most of the talking since we came in finally looked up at me and said: "It'll take a lot of doing, son, to fill your daddy's shoes. He was much of a man."

I said: "I didn't think to fill'm. It's trouble enough trying to fill the ones I'm standing in."

For whatever reason they seemed to like that. One of them took a hit out of the bottle and leaned back on his nail keg and said: "Lemme tell you a story, son. It was a feller Fletchum, Tweek we called'm, Tweek Fletchum, and he musta been about twenty-seven years old then, but even that young he already had the name of makin the best whiskey in the county. Makin whiskey and mean enough to bite a snake to boot." He stopped long enough to shake his head over how mean ole Tweek was and also used the pause to bubble the whiskey bottle a couple of times. "Me and you daddy was hired out plowin for Luke Tate and one evenin after we took the mules out we decided to go on back there to Tweek's place to where his still was at. We weren't nothing but yearlin boys then, back before he went off to work down in Flardy, we couldn't a been much more'n sixteen years old, but we *would* touch a drop or two of whiskey from time to time.

"We didn't do a thing but cut back through the field and cross the branch and then up Ten Mile Creek past that place your daddy later tended for one of the Boatwright boys. When we got to Tweek's, his wife, Sarah, pretty thing, a Turner before she married Tweek, she seen us comin and met us at the door and said Tweek was back at the still and me'n your daddy started back there to where he was at. Tweek didn't keep nothin at his house but bonded whiskey an that was just for show in case some government man come nosin around, so we went on back to the still and while we'as kickin along there in the dust, we decided to play us a little trick on Tweek. I cain't remember who thought it up, but it seem like to me it'as your daddy because he was ever ready for some kind of foolishness, playin tricks and such. That ain't sayin a thing agin him, it was just his nature. Coulda been me, though, that thought it up. Been known for such myself.

"Anyhow, that still of Tweek's was set right slap up agin Big Harrikin Swamp. Out in front of the still was the damnedest wall of brambles and briars you ever seen in your life. Musta been twenty acres of them thins, some of'm big as a scrub oak. And it was that suckhole swamp in

back of the still. Brambles in front and waist-deep swamp full of moc-
casins in back, with a little dim woods road runnin in from one side and
then runnin out the othern.

"Your daddy went around and come up the woods road from one side,
and I went around and come up the other. Everybody was having trouble them days with that govment man come in here from Virginia or
sommers like that and given everybody so much trouble before Lummy
finally killed him, but in them days, Tweek and everybody else was having trouble with 'm, so when I was sure your daddy had time to git on
the other side, I got up close to the still in a clump of them gallberry
bushes and cupped my mouth like this, see here, and shouted into my
shirt: 'STAY RIGHT THERE!'

"Tweek he was stirrin him some mash, but when I hollered, he taken
and thrown down the paddle and jerked his head up like a dog cuttin a
rank spoor in the woods. He tuck off runnin down the road the other
way, his shirttail standin out flat behind him. I didn't do a thing but cup
my mouth agin like this here and holler: 'HEAD'M OVER THERE!'
And a course he was runnin straight at your daddy. He waited till ole
Tweek got real close and then hollered: 'I GOT'M OVER HERE!'

"Tweek come up slidin soon's he known the road was closed on him
at both ends and he tuck him a long look at the Harrikin Swamp behind him and then he tuck'm a long look at them brambles in front of
him. And I got to credit ole Tweek, it didn't tak'm but about three seconds to make his mind up. He put his head down and charged them briars and brambles.

"We heard'm screamin and thrashin around out there for what musta
been fifteen minutes. It was as funny a thing as I ever hope to see, and
damn if me and your daddy didn't bout break a rib settin there sippin
some mash Tweek'd more'n likely run off that mornin, all the time lis-
tenin to Tweek out there screamin and tearin through the brambles.

"Got through and went on back up there to the house and Sarah
said, 'No, Tweek ain't come in,' so we set down on the front porch swing
to finish off that little mason fruit jar of shine we'd taken from the still.
Well, it was damn night dark and we'd moved into the kitchen where
we'as settin at the table, a kerosene lamp between us, eatin sausage and
syrup that Sarah given us, when what do we hear but this te-nine-see
scratchin at the back door.

"Sarah opened it and I could see Tweek standin down in the yard, but he didn't see us. He was cut from lap to lip, nothin but blood and scratches on his face and neck.

" 'Sarah,' says Tweek, 'put a little sumpin in a sack to eat. Goddamned govment man's after me.'

"She says, 'Tweek that weren't no govment man. Them's just Ray and Tom that. . . .'

"But we didn't hear the rest of it cause we heard him beller like a bull and seen he was going for the shotgun. Onliest thing that saved us was he had bird shot in it and maybe on account of it was gittin on toward black dark. But he thrown down on us as we'as goin out the fence gate. Your daddy didn't catch none of it, but I'm carryin sign to this day."

He unbuckled his galluses and pulled up his work shirt. His back was full of little purple holes, like somebody had set it afire and then put the fire out with an ice pick.

Uncle Alton and I stayed around for three or four hours talking and drinking—or at least I was drinking a little—and listening to stories and talking about my daddy and his people.

I'd heard the moonshine story sitting around the fireplaces of a dozen different farms. This was the first time I'd ever heard that daddy was there when Tweek had two years of his growth scared out of him, but this was also the first time I ever had the storyteller lift his shirt and show me the sign of the bird shot. Wounds or scars give an awesome credibility to a story.

Listening to them talk, I wondered what would give credibility to my own story if, when my young son grows to manhood, he has to go look-ing for me in the mouths and memories of other people. Who would tell the stories? A few motorcycle riders, bartenders, editors, half-mad karateka, drunks, and writers. They are scattered all over the country, but even if he could find them, they could speak to him with no shared voice from no common ground. Even as I was gladdened listening to the stories of my daddy, an almost nauseous sadness settled in me, knowing I would leave no such life intact. Among the men with whom I have spent my working life, university professors, there is not one friend of the sort I was listening to speak of my daddy there that day in the back of the store in Bacon County. Acquaintances, but no friends. For half of my life I have been in the university, but never of it. Never *of* any-where, really. Except the place I left, and that of necessity only in mem-ory. It was in that moment and in that knowledge that I first had the

notion that I would someday have to write about it all, but not in the
convenient and comfortable metaphors of fiction, which I had been doing for years. It would have to be done naked, without the disguising
distance of the third person pronoun. Only the use of *I*, lovely and ter-
rifying word, would get me to the place where I needed to go.

In the middle of the afternoon, Uncle Alton and I left the store and
drove out to New Lacy, a little crossroads village where Uncle Elsie and
Aunt Gertie lived with their house full of children until Uncle Elsie died.
Aunt Gertie was my mama's sister and Uncle Elsie spoke in tongues.

We sat on a little porch with a man who must have been old when
daddy died. His eyes were solid and cloud-colored, and his skin so wrinkled and folded it looked like it might have been made for a man twice
his size. His mouth was toothless and dark and worked continuously
around a plug of tobacco as he told us about chickens with one wing
and chickens with one leg gimping about over the first farm my daddy
worked on shares.

"Mule was bad to bite chickens," he said, sending a powerful stream
of tobacco juice into the yard, apparently without even stopping to
purse his old wrinkled lips. "Been your daddy's mule he mought woulda
killed it. Horse mule, he was, name of Sheddie."

The old man had withered right down to bone, but his mind was as
sharp as a boy's.

"Workin shares like he was, Sheddie come with the crop. But he was
bad to bite chickens like I said. Chicken'd hop up on the feed trough to
peck a little corn and Sheddie'd just take him a bite. Sometimes he'd git
a wing, sometimes a leg. Sometimes the whole damn chicken."

He began to cough and he stopped to spray the porch with black spit.

"Ray he got tired of seein all them chickens hobblin about the place
with a wing or a leg missin. So he cured that Sheddie, he did."

Daddy, the old man said, killed a chicken and hung it up to ripen.
When it was good and rotten, he blindfolded Sheddie, put on a halter
with a jawbreaker bit, and fastened that stinking chicken to the bit with
hay wire. It was a full day before the chicken came completely off the
bit it had been wired to. Sheddie was never known to bite again. He had
lost his taste for chicken.

Before we got through that afternoon, Uncle Alton and I had been
all over Bacon County and never once had he said to anybody: Here is

Ray Crews' son and he never knew his daddy and he wants to hear about him." And yet, somehow, he contrived to have the stories told. We finally went back to his house a little after dark and he never mentioned that afternoon again to me nor I to him, but I'll always be grateful for it.

It was through his friendship with my Uncle Alton that daddy first took notice of my mama, whose name is Myrtice. I suppose it was inevitable that he eventually should, because in the same shoebox with his pictures—the pictures of him playing the dandy with half the girls of the county—is a picture of mama just before she turned sixteen. She is sitting in a pea patch, wearing a print dress. And even in the faded black-and-white photograph, you can tell she is round and pink and pretty as she smiles in a fetching way under a white bonnet.

As pretty as she was, though, God knows there were enough children in the family for her to get lost in the crowd. Besides Uncle Alton and mama there was Dorsey, who died when he was four years old from diphtheria. Then there was Aunt Ethel and Aunt Olive and Leon, who died of pneumonia when he was two, and Aunt Gertie and Uncle Frank and Uncle Harley and Aunt Lottie and Aunt Bessie. Grandma Hazelton, whose name was the same as Grandma Crews, Lilly, gave birth to children over a period of twenty years. Nine of them lived to be grown and married. As I write this today, three are still living.

I think he really noticed her for the first time the day her daddy, Grandpa Hazelton, almost killed a man with his walking stick. My daddy had come over to their place for the very reason that he knew there was going to be trouble. He could have saved himself the trip because as it turned out, Grandpa handled the whole thing very nicely and with considerable dispatch.

Uncle Alton, who had just turned seventeen at the time, had managed to get in a row with a man named Jessup over a shoat hog.

"Pa," Uncle Alton said, "Jessup says he's coming over here today and he's gone bring his friends with him."

Grandpa Hazelton was never a man to talk much, probably because he didn't hear very well. He said: "He ain't comin on the place and causin no trouble."

But they did, later that day, three grown men. They stood in the dooryard and called Uncle Alton out, saying they had brought a cowwhip and meant to mark him with it.

Grandpa Hazelton said: "You men git off my place. You on my land and Alton here ain't nothing but a boy. You all git off the place."

Daddy and Uncle Alton were standing on the porch with Grandpa when he said it. The three men, all of whom had been drinking, said they'd go when they got ready, but first they had business to take care of and they meant to do it.

There were no other words spoken. Grandpa Hazelton came off the porch carrying the heavy hickory walking stick he always had with him, a stick he carried years before he actually needed it. He hit the man who had spoken between the eyes with the stick, hit him so hard that his palate dropped in his mouth.

The two men carried their friend, his dropped palate bleeding and his tongue half choking him, to the wagon they had come in and headed off toward town for the doctor. Grandpa followed them all the way to the wagon, beating them about the head and shoulders with his stick.

He stood in the lane shaking with rage and told them: "You come back on the place, I got some buckshot for you."

In that time, a man's land was inviolate, and you were always very careful about what you said to another man if you were on his land. A man could shoot you with impunity if you were on his property and he managed to get you dead enough so you couldn't tell what actually happened. The sheriff would come, look around, listen to the man whose land the killing took place on, and then go back to town. That was that.

In the commotion of the fight, the whole Hazelton family was finally on the porch, and there—daddy's blood still high and hot from watching the old man's expert use of his stick—was my mother standing pink and in full flower under her thin cotton housedress. In that moment, any number of lives took new and irreversible direction.

Once he saw her, he didn't waste any time. Four months later, in November, they were married. She was sixteen, he twenty-three. Immediately there took place in him a change that has been taking place in men ever since they got out of their caves. As soon as he got himself a wife, he took off that white linen suit and put on a pair of overalls. He got out of that Model T Ford and put it up on blocks under Uncle Major's cotton shed because he didn't have enough money to drive it. He drove a mule and wagon instead. And he went to work with a vengeance. More than one person has told me that it wasn't his heart that killed him, that he simply worked himself to death.

Still, he must have cut a fine figure that blustery, freezing day in November of 1928, when he took my mother down to Ten Mile Missionary Baptist Church and married her in a small service attended only by blood kin. They were joined together by Preacher Will Davis, who two years earlier had baptized my mother in Ten Mile Creek, which is just down behind Ten Mile Missionary Baptist Church. They went to the church that day in a mule and wagon, as did most of the other people who came, and after they were married, they spent their wedding night at Uncle Major Eason's house. Uncle Major would one day own the livestock barn in Alma and become known as one of the best mule traders in Georgia. Uncle Major's first wife had died early and he was then married to my mama's sister Olive.

After spending the night under Uncle Major's tin roof in a deep feather bed, with the ground frozen outside, they got up the next morning and, still in a mule and wagon, went to the first farm they were to live on. Daddy had gone from being a young dandy in a white suit driving a Model T Ford to a married man in overalls sharecropping for a man named Luther Carter. They framed the place on shares, which meant Luther Carter furnished the seed and the mules and the fertilizer for them to make the crop and at the end of the year they kept half of what they made.

In that little sharecropper's house of Luther Carter's they lived with Uncle John Carter and Aunt Ora, who was daddy's sister. Uncle John Carter was no kin to Luther Carter, but they were in Cartertown, where most people had that last name. The house had a wooden roof that leaked badly, no screens and wooden windows. There were two ten-by-ten bedrooms and a shotgun hall that ran the length of the kitchen, and Uncle John and Aunt Ora had one room to live in and the use of half the partitioned kitchen. Daddy and mama had the same arrangement on their side. Mama had a Home Comfort, Number 8, wood stove to cook on. There was a hot-water reservoir and four eyes on the cast-iron top of the stove, but it was a tiny thing, hardly more than three feet wide and two feet deep.

They brought to the house as wedding presents: a frying pan, an iron wash pot, four plates and as many knives and forks and spoons, an iron bedstead complete with slats and mattress, four quilts, four sheets, and a pillow. Daddy built everything else: a little cook table, a slightly larger table to eat off of, with a bench on each side instead of chairs, a chest of drawers, and an ironing board made from a plank wrapped in striped bed ticking. It was almost a year before they got two flatirons, one of which would be heated on the hearthstone while the other was being used.

The farm had sixty acres in cultivation, and so Luther Carter furnished Uncle John and daddy each a mule. Thirty acres was as much as one man and one mule could tend, and even then they had to step smart from first sun to last to do it. They had no cows or hogs and no smokehouse, and that first year they lived—as we did for much of my childhood—on fatback, grits, tea without ice, and biscuits made from flour and water and lard.

It was on the Luther Carter place that mama—with a midwife in attendance—lost her first child in the middle of August 1929, the year following their marriage. The baby was not born dead, but nearly so, its liver on the outside of its body. Its life lasted only a matter of minutes and mama didn't look at it but once before it was washed and dressed in a cotton gown and put in a coffin not much bigger than a breadbox and hauled in a wagon to Ten Mile Missionary Baptist Church, where it was buried in an unmarked grave. I don't know how wide the practice was or how it originated, but if a child was lost in miscarriage or born dead, or died nearly immediately from some gross deformity, there was never a marker put at its head.

I've tried to imagine what my daddy's thoughts must have been when the child was lost. He had told mama what happened down in the Everglades and in the town of Arcadia, and I know the death of his firstborn son must have hurt him profoundly. It was commonly believed then in Bacon County, and to some extent still is, that a miscarriage or a baby born dead or deformed was the consequence of some taint in the blood or taint in the moral life of the parents. I know daddy must have keenly felt all over again the crippled pleasure of that night so many months before under the palm-thatched chickee with the Seminole girl.

Maybe such thoughts are what drove him to work so hard. The sun always rose on him in the field, and he was still in the field when it set. He worked harder than the mule he plowed, did everything a man could do to bring something out of the sorry soil he worked, but that first year the crop failed. What this meant was that in August at the end of the crop year, he got half of nothing. They stayed alive on what they could borrow against the coming crop and what little help they could find from their people, who had not done well that year either.

Nearly everybody in the county had done worse that year than any of them could remember in a long time. Part of the reason, and probably the most important, was tobacco. Tobacco had come into the county as a money crop not many years before, and though eventually it turned into a blessing of sorts, for a long time it brought a series of economic disasters. It was a delicate crop, much dependent upon the weather. Most of the farmers were not yet skilled enough in all that was necessary to bring in a good crop: sowing the seeds in beds, transplanting from the beds to the field at the right time, proper amounts of fertilizer (too much would burn it up), suckering it, worming it, cropping it, stringing it, and cooking it in barns so that it turned out golden and valuable instead of dark and worthless.

Before tobacco came into Bacon County, the farmers were self-sufficient in a way they were never to be again. In the days before tobacco they grew everything they needed and lived pretty well. Since they were too far south to grow wheat, they had to buy flour. But almost everything else they really wanted, they could grow. Grandpa Hazelton even grew rice on a piece of his low-lying land that had enough water to sustain that crop.

But tobacco took so much of their time and energy and worry that they stopped growing many of the crops they had grown before. Consequently, they had to depend upon the money from the tobacco to buy what they did not grow. A failed tobacco crop then was a genuine disaster that affected not just the individual farmer but the economy of the entire county.

Even if the tobacco crop was successful, all it meant, with rare exceptions, was for one brief moment at the end of summer they had money in their hands before they had to give it over to whoever supplied the fertilizer to grow the tobacco and the poison to kill the worms, and to those who helped harvest and cook it, and a hundred other expenses that ate up the money and put them right back in debt again. Tobacco money was then and is now an illusion, and growing tobacco became very quickly an almost magical rite they kept participating in over and over again, hoping that they would have a particularly good crop one year and they would be able to keep some of the money and not have to give it all away.

But the tobacco crop was not successful that first year on Luther

Carter's place or anywhere else in the county, and daddy, along with everybody else, was desperate for money. On top of money worries, there was great pressure from Grandpa and Grandma Hazelton for daddy and mama to move back to the home place and live with them. Daddy didn't want to do it out of simple pride. Even though he was already a sharecropper, he didn't want to move in with and work for his wife's parents. He had never gotten along very well with Grandpa Hazelton, a man who liked to give much advice and do little work.

Grandpa spent most of his time reading the three newspapers he subscribed to, newspapers brought by the mailman. It didn't bother him that the newspapers were always two or three days out of date; he read them all from the first page to the last, staying up until the small hours of the morning with a kerosene lamp beside him, all the while taking little sips out of a mason fruit jar full of moonshine which he kept on the mantelpiece over the fireplace. He didn't get drunk; he just liked to have little sips while he was awake.

He stopped only long enough to look about now and then to see if anybody was about to do something. If they were, he would explain in great and careful detail just how they should do it. He would do this whether he knew anything about the task at hand or not. Then he would go back to his newspaper.

Daddy was too proud and stubborn and independent for such an arrangement to work. But his wife was the youngest child of the family, still only seventeen years old. She had just lost a baby and the crops had failed, and so, against his better judgment, he went to live with his in-laws.

It was a total and unrelieved disaster that came to the point of crisis, strangely enough, over biscuits one night when they were all sitting at the supper table. Daddy looked up and saw Grandpa Hazelton smiling down the table at him.

Daddy said: "Something the matter?"

Since the old man was bad to bristle and bark himself, he said: "Is it look to be something the matter?"

"What you laughing at?"

"I ain't laughing."

"I seen it."

The old man said: "A man cain't tell me in my own house I was laughing."

Daddy said: "You was. And it was because of them biscuits."

"I don't laugh at biscuits, boy. I ain't crazy yet, even if it's some that think I am."

"You was laughing at how many I et. Was you counting, too?"

Daddy didn't have a very thick skin, and one of the things he was touchy about was how much he ate. Just a little over a month before his run-in with the old man, he was at a church picnic and Frank Porter, a boy from Coffee County, said something about him being Long Hungry, which to the people in that time was an insult. To be Long Hungry meant you were a glutton. A hog at the trough. So Daddy invited Frank Porter—since they were at a church and couldn't settle it there—to meet him the next day on a scrub oak ridge separating Coffee from Bacon.

The next morning at sunup the two men met, daddy and the man who had insulted him, up in the middle of a little stand of blackjack oak on a sandy ridge full of gopher holes and rattlesnake nests. They had each of them brought several of their friends as overseers of the fight, or rather their friends had insisted on coming to make sure that no knives or axes or guns got in the way and resulted in one or both of their deaths.

They set to and fought until noon, quit, went home, ate, patched up as best they could, and came back and fought until sundown. They didn't fight the whole time. By mutual consent and necessity, they took time out to rest. While there were resting, their friends fought. Those that were there said it had been a real fine day. A little bloody, but a fine day. For years after the fight, time was often measured by farmers in both counties by the day the fight took place.

"*It weren't no more'n two months after Ray and Frank met up on the line.*"

"*That girl of mine was born three months to the day before Frank and Ray had the fight.*"

And sitting there now at the supper table still smarting from being called Long Hungry and still carrying sign on his back and chest and head from the fight with Frank Porter, he could not bear what he knew he saw in grandpa's face.

He stood up from the table and said to mama: "Myrtice, git your things. We leavin."

Grandpa said: "Where you going to?"

Daddy stopped just long enough to say, "I don't know where I'm going. It's lots of places I could go. What you don't understand, old man, is if I didn't have anyplace to go, I'd go anyway."

But he had a place to go and he knew it. Uncle Alton had recently been married to a lady named Eva Jenkins and they were sharecropping themselves for Jess Boatwright. Summer was coming on and all the crops had been laid by, which meant they'd been plowed the last time and all that remained was the harvest. Daddy put mama on the wagon seat beside him and started the long slow ride over the dirt roads in the dark to offer Uncle Alton a proposition which in his heart he didn't believe Uncle Alton would take. Since he was sharecropping for grandpa, he meant to trade crops.

"We got to swap," he said when Uncle Alton came to the door.

"Swap what?" Uncle Alton said.

"You take my crop and I'll take yours. You and Eva go and live with your daddy, cause I cain't stand it. Me and Mytrice'll come live here."

Daddy told him what had happened, and Uncle Alton never questioned it, knowing as he did how his daddy was. Also, daddy was his best friend and mama his baby sister. He knew daddy would never consent to going back after leaving in the middle of the night that way. They had to live somewhere. There were no options.

"We'll swap even," Uncle Alton said.

"I ought to give you something to boot," daddy said. "You got ten acres more'n me."

Uncle Alton said: "We'll swap even."

And they did. It made quite a noise in the county. Nobody had ever heard of such a thing. Some of the old folks still talk to this day about that trade, about how daddy and mama moved into the house on the Jess Boatwright place and Uncle Alton and Aunt Eva went over to live with Grandpa Hazelton.

Daddy never set foot in grandpa's house again as long as he lived. He would allow mama to go and visit and after my brother and I were born to take us with her.

After they finished gathering the crop, which was good enough to let them get far enough out of debt to borrow on the next crop, they rented the Jess Boatwright place for one year. But as the world seems to go sometimes when a man's got his back right up against the wall, the tobacco crop that year was so sorry daddy couldn't even sell it, and he ended by putting it in the mule stable instead.

Cotton that year was selling for three cents a pound and you could buy a quarter of beef for four cents a pound. It was 1931. The rest of the country was just beginning to feel the real hurt of the Great Depression, but it had been living in Bacon County for years. Some folks said it had always been there.

But in that year two good things did happen. On the ninth of July, mama gave birth to a healthy baby, who was named after daddy, Ray, but who has always been called Hoyet. The other thing that happened was that daddy somehow managed to buy a mare. A mare, not a mule. Her name was Daisy, and she was so mean that daddy was the only one in the county who could put a bridle on her, much less work her to a plow or wagon. It was the first draft animal he'd owned, and he was almost as proud of the mare as he was of his son.

As mean as she was, Daisy pulled a fine wagon and even a better plow if you could control her. As it turned out, daddy could control her. He had her respect and she had his. They knew what to expect from one another. He knew dead solid certain that she would kick his head off if she got the chance. And she knew just as surely that he would beat her to her knees with a singletree—if she did not cooperate.

It sounds like a terrible thing to talk about, hitting a mare between the ears with a piece of iron, but it was done not only out of necessity but also out of love. A farmer didn't mistreat his draft animals. People in Bacon County always said that a man who would mistreat his mules would mistreat his family. But it was necessary for daddy and Daisy to come to some understanding before they could do the work that was proper to both of them. And whatever was necessary to that understanding had to be done. Without that understanding, there could be no respect, to say nothing of love. For a man and an animal to work together from sunup to dark, day in and day out, there ought to be love. How else could either of them bear it?

Still, it was unusual for him to have a mare instead of a mule. Horses and mares were playthings. Mules were the workers. Mules bought the baby's shoes and put grits on the table.

I never remember seeing anybody plow a horse in Bacon County, and it wasn't because mules were cheaper than horses. They weren't. Daddy got Daisy for $60. A good young mule even in the depth of the Depression would have cost him $200. So it was not because of cost that farmers plowed mules instead of horses; it was because horses have no stamina in front of a turnplow breaking dirt a foot deep. Worse, a horse doesn't care where he puts his feet. A mule puts his foot down exactly where he means to put it. A mule will walk all day, straight as a plumb line, setting his feet down only inches from young corn, corn that might be less than a foot high, and he'll never step on a plant. A horse walks all over everything. Unless, that is, you can come to some understanding with him, which most men did not seem to be able to do. But daddy made a sweet working animal out of Daisy, and she was ready, if not always willing, to do whatever was required of her. In the shoebox of pictures, there is one of my brother when he was only four years old sitting on Daisy bareback. Nobody is holding her rein and she is standing easy as the lady she became under my daddy's firm, gentle, and dangerous hand.

Maybe it was because of the crops failing or the trouble they'd had with Grandpa Hazelton, but mama remembers the house at the Jess Boatwright place as the worst they ever lived in. It was made out of notched logs, but instead of being mud-sealed, it was board-sealed, which meant the wind had a free way with it in the winter. My brother had a case of double pneumonia that year and almost died. There was no smokehouse, so the little bit of meat they could come by was cured by hanging in the sun during the day and then putting it in the shed at night. They also put some of it in stone jugs of brine to preserve it, but while meat never spoiled in a jug of brine, it took real courage and a certain desperation to eat through all that salt.

But luck fortunately comes in two flavors: good as well as bad. And some good luck came their way at the end of the second year on the Jess Boatwright place. My Grandma Hazelton gave them 120 acres of land. What wealth there was in the Hazelton family at that time came through my grandma. Grandpa Hazelton brought very little to the marriage and what little he brought got away from him somehow while he read his three newspapers every day. But Grandma Hazelton's daddy left her a big piece of land and they—she and grandpa—built the house they lived in out of the sale of part of it. But there was a good bit left, and because mama was the youngest in the family, and because of the tragic circumstances of her firstborn child, and maybe also to try somehow to make up for daddy and mama having to trade crops with Uncle Alton and move out of the house in the middle of the year, she made the land a gift outright, and they went to live on it.

But even good luck rarely comes made out of whole cloth, and theirs had several pretty ragged places in it. For starters, none of the land was in cultivation. It was nothing but pine trees and palmetto thickets and stands of gallberry bushes and dog fennel. Worse than that, if there can be anything worse than a farmer with no land he can farm, there was no house on it, no building of any kind. There was nothing for daddy to do but build one.

And he did. Uncle Randal Jordan and one of my daddy's good friends, Cadger Barnes, helped him. Daddy paid them a wage of a quarter a day. None of the trees on the land they'd been given were big enough to use, so Cadger, who had a heavy stand of big pine on his land, gave daddy enough trees to build the house. And the three of them, using crosscut saws, felled the trees and snaked the logs over to the place with Daisy, and then they cut the trees into lengths they could split for boards. There was no money for a sawmill, so with wedges and mallets and axes they split the pine by hand into boards.

Once it was finished you could smell the turpentine out of that green pine house from a mile away. The whole house cost $50 to build. Mama planted a cedar tree out in the front yard the day they moved in. It was the house in which I would be born. The house is gone now, but I stood in the shade of that cedar tree four months ago.

The first year they were there daddy cleared ten acres for cultivation. The second year he cleared another ten. He and mama did it together with an ax and a saw and a grubbing hoe and Daisy. Daisy pulled what she could from the ground. What she couldn't pull out, mama and daddy dug out. What they couldn't dig out, they burned out. There were a few people, very few, who could afford dynamite to blow stumps out; everybody else dug and burned, burned and dug. An oak stump might cost a man a week of his life.

All through the winter of that second year, the hazy smoke of burning stumps floated over them as they picked up roots and grubbed palmetto and gallberry. Mama had been growing pinker and rounder and seemingly stronger every day with her third and what would prove to be her last pregnancy. She didn't quit going to the field until May, and on the seventh of June, 1935, Daddy got on Daisy and went over to get Emily Ahl, who came racing back behind his galloping mare in her midwifery buggy in which she had gone to farmhouses all over that end of Bacon County.

In the late afternoon, Miss Emily, wearing her black bonnet and black, long dress, a dress and color she considered proper to her calling, cut me loose from mama and tied me off. She was a midwife of consummate skill, and my entrance into the world was without incident.

I am compelled to celebrate the craft and art of the lady who did everything that was required of her so competently. Not only did she make a lovely arrangement of my navel when she cut me free, but she also left me intact, for which I have always been grateful.

Since they had no land to tend while they were taking in the new ground, daddy rented thirty acres from the land bank, a federal agency that controlled a lot of land and let it to farmers at a cost they could afford, which meant practically nothing. In his spare time, when he wasn't farming the acreage he'd rented from the land bank or pulling stumps or working on the stable for Daisy, he hired out to plow for other people. Mama would pack him some biscuit and fatback and maybe a vegetable she might have put up the previous summer, along with a little cold grits; she'd put it all in a tin syrup bucket, and he'd leave the house before sunup and come back after dark, bringing the empty syrup bucket and twenty-five cents for his day's work.

By the time I was born he'd put up a mule barn and a notched log smokehouse sealed with mud. Just when he got the place looking pretty good, he had the chance to sell it at more than he'd thought he'd ever be able to make out of it again, and at the same time the chance to buy a place cheap that he'd been looking at a long time. So he sold out and bought the Cash Carter place, which had a little better than 200 acres of land—about 40 of it in cultivation. He got it at a good price because the land had been allowed to lie fallow until it was rank with weeds. Most of the fences were down, there was no mule lot or smokehouse or tobacco barn, and the dwelling house was nearly as sorry as the one they'd lived in at Jess Boatwright's. But it was 200 acres of land, and daddy knew, or thought he knew, that he could make it into a decent farm on which he could support his family. It wouldn't be easy and it wouldn't be quick, but given five or ten years, he would do it and he would do it right.

Three

In early December 1935 daddy loaded us up in the wagon with Daisy between the shaves. He put the mattress and bedsteads and table and benches and the Home Comfort, Number 8, stove—put it all in the wagon with me, six months old at the time, and my brother, who was four years old, up on the mattress bundled in quilts, and mama beside him on the crossboard and started down the six miles of washboard road to the Cash Carter place.

Cash Carter didn't own it; it just went by his name. If the house were still standing today, it would still go by his name. A farm in Bacon County took a man's name, not always the first man who owned it, but some man's name, and once the name was taken, it held the name as long as it stood, no matter who lived there. It was a tradition that gave direction to the county. Farmers as a rule didn't move around much, but subsistence farmers—tenants out on the fringe of things—moved a lot, much more than most people would imagine, moved from one patch of farmed-out land to another, from one failed crop to a place where they thought there was hope of making a good one. Because they moved, it helped for the farms to hold the same name forever. It gave people's lives points of reference.

When we got there, daddy had to start building all over again. He worked from very early in the morning until very late at night, usually for as long as he and Daisy could see. During that first year he built a log tobacco barn and a lot for Daisy, and in the fall of the following year he managed to put up a little tenant house himself and move widow Ella Thomas into it with her three boys, ages ten, fourteen, and sixteen. They worked with daddy and mama, hoeing and weeding the forty acres in cultivation, helping with the turpentine timber, and taking in new ground. He paid the family fifty cents a day in wages.

It pleases me that right after daddy moved to the Cash Carter place he became good friends with the sorriest man in the county, Pete Fretch. Pete's affectionate name for his wife was "nigger." She was a thin, starved gray thing who moved about quiet as a shadow on her bare feet. Her mouth, nearly toothless, was always stained by the cud of snuff caught between lip and gum. Pete, when he wasn't busy telling lies and stealing, used to spend his time whipping his wife with a four-plait cowwhip.

Anybody in that part of the county who had something stolen would just go on over to Pete's little tar-paper shack and say: "All right, Pete, where's my wheelbarrow?" or "Where's my singletrees?" or "Where's my shoat hog?" And Pete, if he had whatever was missing, and he usually did, would give it up, always with a marvelous and convoluted excuse about how the hog had just wandered up to his place, or how he'd been walking down by the Harrikin four days ago to go catfishing and happened to find the singletrees in a ditch. He'd say he wondered at the time who them singletrees belonged to and how come they were in the ditch.

But if the notion struck him, and it almost never did, Pete could do just about anything there was to do. He could build a good drawing chimney, a chimney that would never back up and smoke the house, or he could butcher a hog quicker than a blink (no doubt from long practice of butchering other people's hogs in the woods and making off with the meat before he was caught) or make the best sausage meat in South Georgia or build anything: houses or barns or lots, the boards of which were true as a plumb line and tight as if they'd been made of brick.

In 1936, he built a wash trough for mama. She washed clothes in that trough for as long as we farmed. It was made out of a tree three feet thick and twenty feet long. He dug out one end of it for a place where mama could wash her clothes and dug out the other end for a place to rinse. He made it using a chisel and an ax and a drawing knife and fire. He chopped and hewed and chipped and burned it deeper, smoothed it out with litered knots. Finally, he flattened off the bottom so it would stand steady. When he finished, it was so symmetrical it might have been calibrated on a machine.

Daddy tried to give him a quarter for his work. Pete refused it. This strange, sorry, violent man would not spend one minute of his life doing anything for anybody for cash money. But he would do anything for a friend and *always* refuse money for it. Since there was hardly anybody who could stand him as a friend, the question of whether or not to work rarely came up.

Daddy had worked progressively harder since the day he got married. He was having a lot of trouble with his heart, and it wasn't unusual for him to fall in the field. He might fall anywhere, doing anything, and sometimes it was as much as an hour before he could move about freely again. But as soon as he could, he went directly back to the task at hand. He had also lost the two front teeth out of his top gum from pyorrhea, and his weight was down to 155 pounds. He had, as they said, gone to nothing but breath and britches. But he insisted on working as hard as ever. It was his custom to get up in the morning and build a fire in the stove, leaving mama and my brother and me in the bed asleep and get out to the lot, bridle and harness Daisy, and get to the field and work there until mama took a hammer and beat on an old plow point hanging up on the front porch.

When he heard the ringing plow point, he would come to the house, eat his breakfast, and go directly back to the field. The same thing was repeated at dinnertime in the middle of the day and again at night. It was an unusual day when he didn't go back to the field if it was light enough to see after he had eaten supper. If it was too dark to go back to the field, he worked on the mule lot or on the tenant house or on Daisy's harness, which he managed to hold together with baling wire.

His color had gone bad. There was a wildness in his eyes, but he resisted going to the doctor. Doctors meant money, and the little he had he desperately needed to keep everything together: the farm, his wife and babies.

It was during this time when daddy was working himself to death, practically living in the field, that something happened that will forever epitomize the experience of my people. It was a bright, hot summer day. It had not rained in nearly a month. The crop was doing well that year. Mama had been cleaning house since daylight and was scrubbing the floor of the last room, using homemade lye and a scrub brush made out of cornshucks.

It was midafternoon, and as she worked, she could see daddy through the open, screenless window out in the field. He was spraying the tobacco for cutworms. While she scrubbed, I was in the doorway leading into the room in a little playpen daddy had built for me.

They had done better than usual the first year there on the Cash Carter place and had managed to buy two yearling cows, the first they had ever owned. She looked up from her work and saw the two yearlings

walking along the fence row toward the barrel of lead poisoning daddy
had in a turpentine barrel on a sled. Mama knew they were going to
drink out of the barrel, and if they did, they would die right where they
were standing because the poison daddy was putting on the tobacco
was deadly.

She leaned out of the window and hollered for him, but he was down
between the tobacco rows with the sprayer, a long metal cylinder that
was filled with air pressure using a hand pump. The sprayer was
strapped to his back, and the hissing air and blowing spray made it impossible for him to hear her. So she threw down her shuck scrub brush
and ran out of the house toward the field.

Halfway there, she heard me scream and knew immediately what had
happened. When she got back to the house, I had turned over my
playpen and crawled into the room where she had been working. Some
of the pieces of lye had not melted, and I was sitting on the floor
screaming, holding a lump of raw lye in each hand, and worse, I had put
some of it in my mouth. Blood was running from my lips and tongue.
She snatched me up and ran for daddy, who put Daisy to the wagon,
and they galloped the eight miles to town to Dr. Sharp's office.

It turned out not to be as bad as it looked. I had not swallowed any of
the lye, and the burns in my mouth and on my hands were not serious.

When they got back home, the yearling cows were dead, lying already
stiff by the barrel of lead poisoning.

Daddy strapped the sprayer on and went back to work in the tobacco. He worked until it was so dark he couldn't see, and then he
hitched Daisy to the only two cows he'd ever owned and dragged them
off behind the field for the buzzards to eat. He was afraid to butcher
them because of the poison.

Ever since mama first told me that story of the day they lost the cows
I have thought a great deal about my daddy in that time, of how tragic
it was and how typical. The world that circumscribed the people I come
from had so little margin for error, for bad luck, that when something
went wrong, it almost always brought something else down with it. It
was a world in which survival depended on raw courage, a courage born
out of desperation and sustained by a lack of alternatives.

When the crop was finally gathered and sold, daddy took most of the
money he had made that year, sold the turpentine rights to his timber,

and paid off the mortgage that the bank held on the place. In spite of all that had happened, things were looking pretty good for him. He owned a little over 200 acres free and clear, and he had enough money to start his next crop.

But that same year on April 17, 1937, it all caught up with him, and he went down. They had a particularly bad winter, and even in mid-April it was still cold. All of us were sleeping in the same bed that night. Mama woke up shortly after dawn and was surprised to see him still in the bed beside her. No fire in the stove, none in the fireplace. And daddy still in bed where the light of day never found him. But he had butchered hogs not long before that and prepared the smokehouse to cure the meat, all of which is exhausting work, and she thought he was just tired out from it all and had overslept. She got quietly out of bed, got a fire going in the stove, and made breakfast.

About the time she got the grits bubbling and the biscuits in the oven and the water heated in the reservoir and the kitchen warm from the stove, my brother, who was then five years old, came walking in, yawning, wearing his cotton gown. Mama told him to go in and wake up his daddy. He went back into the bedroom and stood beside the bed watching his daddy and watching me, then twenty-one months old, sleeping at his side. Hoyet thought to play a trick on his daddy, an affectionate little-boy trick, and he reached over and twisted his daddy's nose to wake him up, twisted it gently, and then harder, and finally harder still. But daddy didn't move.

He went back into the kitchen and said: "Daddy won't wake up and his nose is cold."

He was dead, had died sometime in the night in his sleep of a massive heart attack, so massive and so sudden that he didn't move enough to wake his wife, who was sleeping with her head on his arm.

She screamed and ran into the yard. She stood there for a long time mindlessly screaming in a terror for her husband's death. Her screaming brought widow Ella Thomas out of her little tenant house, and then her three children, and finally the house that day was filled with her people and daddy's.

The door was taken down, as it usually was in those days, for a cooling board, and the body placed upon it. Ordinarily the women of the family would have gathered and washed the corpse and dressed it and closed its eyes and combed its hair and shaved it for burial. But mama,

for reasons she cannot now name, but which I have always thought of as
a statement of her love and respect for her husband, had an embalmer
come from Waycross, thirty miles away.

When daddy was drained of blood, the blood was buried out behind
the house in a deep hole but not deep enough to keep a dog we had
then, a hound dog whose name was Sam, from knowing what was
buried there. Sam lay on the buried blood and howled all night and continued to howl for three days and nights running until he was almost
dead himself from exhaustion because he would take no food or water.

Even the coffin was not built by the men of the family, as it customar-
ily would have been. Rather, it was brought from the Mincy Funeral
Home, the same place the embalmer came from in Waycross. Daddy
was dressed in the only suit of clothes he had and placed in his box. The
entire expense for the coffin, having it brought from Waycross, and the
job of work done by the embalmer was just under $60.

Two days later, on April 19, 1937, the coffin was loaded onto the
wagon he bought with the money from the sale of the Model T Ford
that he'd put up on blocks all those years ago. Daisy was hitched to the
wagon, and other wagons drawn by mules carrying members of the family set off for Corinth Freewill Baptist Church ten miles away. One of
the men riding the second wagon with his wife, Dinah, was daddy's
older brother Pascal. Eight months later, in December, Pascal would be
divorced from Dinah and mama would marry him.

They went the long slow way to the graveyard there behind a tiny
white clapboard church and put daddy in the ground with a wooden
marker at his head. Later mama would find the money, $150, for a slab
and headstone of Georgia marble. The same man who had baptized her
when she was fourteen and later joined her and daddy in marriage,
Preacher Will Davis, said the last words over the open grave on that day
unlike April at all, but rainy and blustery and still cold.

The two closest graves to the one daddy lies in today are the graves
of babies. One died in 1927 and the other in 1928. They were both
Smith babies. The first one had lived to be ten months old, the other
eight months old. For reasons I cannot name, it has always seemed profoundly right to me that two babies lie there so close to him who cared
so much for babies and who had been told so early that he would never
have any and who, once having them, lost them not because they died,
but because he himself went down so early.

The night after the day daddy was buried, somebody went in the smokehouse and stole all the meat that had been cured and hung there before he died. There were nine middlings of meat hanging, and sausage in boxes, and headcheese in muslin cloth, and somebody took it all, everything but one little piece about as big as a man's hand hanging in the back of the smokehouse.

Mama knows who got the meat, not because she has any hard proof, but because in her heart she knows, and I know too, but the one who got it is himself lying in the same graveyard daddy's in and I see no reason to name him.

He was one of my daddy's friends. I do not say he was *supposedly* or *apparently* a friend. He *was* a friend, and a close one, but he stole the meat anyway. Not many people may be able to understand that or sympathize with it, but I think I do. It was a hard time in that land, and a lot of men did things for which they were ashamed and suffered for the rest of their lives. But they did them because of hunger and sickness and because they could not bear the sorry spectacle of their children dying from lack of a doctor and their wives growing old before they were thirty.

II

Four

IT has always seemed to me that I was not so much born into this life as I awakened to it. I remember very distinctly the awakening and the morning it happened. It was my first glimpse of myself, and all that I know now—the stories, and everything conjured up by them, that I have been writing about thus far—I obviously knew none of them, particularly anything about my real daddy, whom I was not to hear of until I was nearly six years old, not his name, not even that he was my daddy. Or if I did hear of him, I have no memory of it.

I awoke in the middle of the morning in early summer from the place I'd been sleeping in the curving roots of a giant oak tree in front of a large white house. Off to the right, beyond the dirt road, my goats were trailing along in the ditch, grazing in the tough wire grass that grew there. Their constant bleating shook the warm summer air. I always thought of them as my goats although my brother usually took care of them. Before he went to the field that morning to work, he had let them out of the old tobacco barn where they slept at night. At my feet was a white dog whose name was Sam. I looked at the dog and at the house and at the red gown with pearl-colored buttons I was wearing, and I knew that the gown had been made for me by my Grandma Hazelton and that the dog belonged to me. He went everywhere I went, and he always took precious care of me.

Precious. That was my mama's word for how it was between Sam and me, even though Sam caused her some inconvenience from time to time. If she wanted to whip me, she had to take me in the house, where Sam was never allowed to go. She could never touch me when I was crying if Sam could help it. He would move quietly—he was a dog not given to barking very much—between the two of us and show her his teeth. Unless she took me somewhere Sam couldn't go, there'd be no punishment for me.

The house there just behind me, partially under the arching limbs of the oak tree, was called the Williams place. It was where I lived with my mama and my brother, Hoyet, and my daddy, whose name was Pascal. I knew when I opened my eyes that morning that the house was empty because everybody had gone to the field to work. I also knew, even though I couldn't remember doing it, that I had awakened sometime in midmorning and come out onto the porch and down the steps and across the clean-swept dirt yard through the gate weighted with broken plow points so it would swing shut behind me, that I had come out under the oak tree and lain down against the curving roots with my dog, Sam, and gone to sleep. It was a thing I had done before. If I ever woke up and the house was empty and the weather was warm—which was the only time I would ever awaken to an empty house—I always went out under the oak tree to finish my nap. It wasn't fear or loneliness that drove me outside; it was just something I did for reasons I would never be able to discover.

I stood up and stretched and looked down at my bare feet at the hem of the gown and said: "I'm almost five and already a great big boy." It was my way of reassuring myself, but it was also something my daddy said about me and it made me feel good because in his mouth it seemed to mean I was almost a man.

Sam immediately stood up too, stretched, reproducing, as he always did, every move I made, watching me carefully to see which way I might go. I knew I ought not to be outside lying in the rough curve of root in my cotton gown. Mama didn't mind me being out there under the tree, but I was supposed to get dressed first. Sometimes I did; often I forgot.

So I turned and went back through the gate, Sam at my heels, and across the yard and up the steps onto the porch to the front door. When I opened the door, Sam stopped and lay down to wait. He would be there when I came out, no matter which door I used. If I went out the back door, he would somehow magically know it and he would be there. If I came out the side door by the little pantry, he would know that, too, and he would be there. Sam always knew where I was, and he made it his business to be there, waiting.

I went into the long dim, cool hallway that ran down the center of the house. Briefly I stopped at the bedroom where my parents slept and looked in at the neatly made bed and all the parts of the room, clean, with everything where it was supposed to be, just the way mama always kept it. And I thought of daddy, as I so often did because I loved him so much. If he was sitting down, I was usually in his lap. If he was standing up, I was usually holding his hand. He always said soft funny things to me and told me stories that never had an end but always continued when we met again.

He was tall and lean with flat high cheekbones and deep eyes and black thick hair which he combed straight back on his head. And under the eye on his left cheek was the scarred print of a perfect set of teeth. I knew he had taken the scar in a fight, but I never asked him about it and the teeth marks in his cheek only made him seem more powerful and stronger and special to me.

He shaved every morning at the water shelf on the back porch with a straight razor and always smelled of soap and whiskey. I knew mama did not like the whiskey, but to me it smelled sweet, better even than the soap. And I could never understand why she resisted it so, complained of it so, and kept telling him over and over again that he would kill himself and ruin everything if he continued with the whiskey. I did not understand about killing himself and I did not understand about ruining everything, but I knew the whiskey somehow caused the shouting and screaming and the ugly sound of breaking things in the night. The stronger the smell of whiskey on him, though, the kinder and gentler he was with me and my brother.

I went on down the the hallway and out onto the back porch and finally into the kitchen that was built at the very rear of the house. The entire room was dominated by a huge black cast-iron stove with six eyes on its cooking surface. Directly across the room from the stove was the safe, a tall square cabinet with wide doors covered with screen wire that was used to keep biscuits and fried meat and rice or almost any other kind of food that had been recently cooked. Between the stove and the safe sat the table we ate off of, a table almost ten feet long, with benches on each side instead of chairs, so that when we put in tobacco, there would be enough room for the hired hands to eat.

I opened the safe, took a biscuit off a plate, and punched a hole in it with my finger. Then with a jar of cane syrup, I poured the hole full, waited for it to soak in good, and then poured again. When the biscuit had all the syrup it would take, I got two pieces of fried pork off another plate and went out and sat on the back steps, where Sam was already lying in the warm sun, his ears struck forward on his head. I ate the bread and pork slowly, chewing for a long time and sharing it all with Sam.

When we had finished, I went back into the house, took off my gown, and put on a cotton undershirt, my overalls with twin galluses that buckled on my chest, and my straw hat, which was rimmed on the edges with a border of green cloth and had a piece of green cellophane sewn into the brim to act as an eyeshade. I was barefoot, but I wished very much I had a pair of brogans because brogans were what men wore and I very much wanted to be a man. In fact, I was pretty sure I already was a man, but the only one who seemed to know it was my daddy. Everybody else treated me like I was still a baby.

I went out the side door, and Sam fell into step behind me as we walked out beyond the mule barn where four mules stood in the lot and on past the cotton house and then down the dim road past a little leaning shack where our tenant farmers lived, a black family in which there was a boy just a year older than I was. His name was Willalee Bookatee. I went on past their house because I knew they would be in the field, too, so there was no use to stop.

I went through a sapling thicket and over a shallow ditch and finally climbed a wire fence into the field, being very careful of my overalls on the barbed wire. I could see them all, my family and the black tenant family, far off there in the shimmering heat of the tobacco field. They were pulling cutworms off the tobacco. I wished I could have been out there with them pulling worms because when you found one, you had to break it in half, which seemed great good fun to me. But you could also carry an empty Prince Albert tobacco can in your back pocket and fill it up with worms to play with later.

Mama wouldn't let me pull worms because she said I was too little and might damage the plants. If I was alone in the field with daddy, though, he would let me hunt all the worms I wanted to. He let me do pretty much anything I wanted to, which included sitting in his lap to guide his old pickup truck down dirt roads all over the county.

I went down to the end of the row and sat under a persimmon tree in

the shade with Sam and watched as daddy and mama and brother and
Willalee Bookatee, who was—I could see even from this distance—
putting worms in Prince Albert cans, and his mama, whose name was
Katie, and his daddy, whose name was Will, I watched them all as they
came toward me, turning the leaves and searching for worms as they
came.

The moment I sat down in the shade, I was already wondering how
long it would be before they quit to go to the house for dinner because I
was already beginning to wish I'd taken two biscuits instead of one and
maybe another piece of meat, or else that I hadn't shared with Sam.

Bored, I looked down at Sam and said: "Sam, if you don't quit eatin
my biscuit and meat, I'm gone have to cut you like a shoat hog."

A black cloud of gnats swarmed around his heavy muzzle, but I
clearly heard him say that he didn't think I was man enough to do it.
Sam and I talked a lot together, had long involved conversations, mostly
about which one of us had done the other one wrong and, if not about
that, about which one of us was the better man. It would be a good long
time before I started thinking of Sam as a dog instead of a person. But I
always came out on top when we talked because Sam could only say
what I said he said, think what I thought he thought.

"If you was any kind of man atall, you wouldn't snap at them gnats
and eat them flies the way you do," I said.

"It ain't a thing in the world the matter with eatin gnats and flies," he
said.

"It's how come people treat you like a dog," I said. "You could probably come on in the house like other folks if it weren't for eatin flies and
gnats like you do."

That's the way the talk went until daddy and the rest of them finally
came down to where Sam and I were sitting in the shade. They stopped
beside us to wipe their faces and necks with sweat rags. Mama asked if I
had got something to eat when I woke up. I told her I had.

"You all gone stop for dinner now?"

"I reckon we'll work awhile longer," daddy said.

I said: "Well then, can Willalee and me go up to his house and play
till dinnertime?"

Daddy looked at the sun to see what time it was. He could come
within five or ten minutes by the position of the sun. Most of the farmers I knew could.

Daddy was standing almost dead center in his own shadow. "I reckon so," he said.

Then the whole thing had to be done over again. Willalee asked his daddy the same question. Because my daddy had said it was all right didn't mean Willalee's daddy would agree. He usually did, but not always. So it was necessary to ask.

We climbed the fence and went across the ditch and back through the sapling thicket to the three-track road that led up to the shack, and while we walked, Willalee showed me the two Prince Albert tobacco cans he had in his back pockets. They were both filled with cutworms. The worms had lots of legs and two little things on their heads that looked like horns. They were about an inch long, sometimes as long as two inches, and round and fat and made wonderful things to play with. There was no fence around the yard where Willalee lived and the whole house leaned toward the north at about a ten-degree tilt. Before we even got up the steps, we could smell the food already cooking on the wood stove at the back of the house where his grandma was banging metal pots around over the cast-iron stove. Her name was Annie, but everybody called her Auntie. She was too old to work in the field anymore, but she was handy about the house with ironing and cooking and scrubbing floors and canning vegetables out of the field and berries out of the woods.

She also was full of stories, which, when she had the time—and she usually did—she told to me and Willalee and his little sister, whose name was Lottie Mae. Willalee and my brother and I called her Snottie Mae, but she didn't seem to mind. She came out of the front door when she heard us coming up on the porch and right away wanted to know if she could play in the book with us. She was the same age as I and sometimes we let her play with us, but most of the time we did not.

"Naw," Willalee said, "git on back in there and help Auntie. We ain't studying you."

"Bring us the book," I said.

"I git it for you," she said, "if you give me five of them worms."

"I ain't studying you," said Willalee.

She had already seen the two Prince Albert cans full of green worms because Willalee was sitting on the floor now, the lids of the cans open and the worms crawling out. He was lining two of them up for a race from one crack in the floor to the next crack, and he was arranging the rest of the worms in little designs of diamonds and triangles in some game he had not yet discovered the rules for.

"You bring the book," I said, "and you can have two of them worms."

Willalee almost never argued with what I decided to do, up to and including giving away the worms he had spent all morning collecting in the fierce summer heat, which is probably why I liked him so much. Lottie Mae went back into the house, and got the Sears, Roebuck catalogue and brought it out onto the porch. He handed her the two worms and told her to go on back in the house, told her it weren't fitting for her to be out here playing with worms while Auntie was back in the kitchen working.

"Ain't nothing left for me to do but put them plates on the table," she said.

"See to them plates then," Willalee said. As young as she was, Lottie Mae had things to do about the place. Whatever she could manage. We all did.

Willalee and I stayed there on the floor with the Sears, Roebuck catalogue and the open Prince Albert cans, out of which deliciously fat worms crawled. Then we opened the catalogue at random as we always did, to see what magic was waiting for us there.

In the minds of most people, the Sears, Roebuck catalogue is a kind of low joke associated with outhouses. God knows the catalogue sometimes ended up in the outhouse, but more often it did not. All the farmers, black and white, kept dried corncobs beside their double-seated thrones, and the cobs served the purpose for which they were put there with all possible efficiency and comfort.

The Sears, Roebuck catalogue was much better used as a Wish Book, which it was called by the people out in the country, who would never be able to order anything out of it, but could at their leisure spend hours dreaming over.

Willalee Bookatee and I used it for another reason. We made up stories out of it, used it to spin a web of fantasy about us. Without that catalogue our childhood would have been radically different. The federal government ought to strike a medal for the Sears, Roebuck company for sending all those catalogues to farming families, for bringing all that color and all that mystery and all that beauty into the lives of country people.

I first became fascinated with the Sears catalogue because all the people in its pages were perfect. Nearly everybody I knew had something missing, a finger cut off, a toe split, an ear half-chewed away, an eye clouded with blindness from a glancing fence staple. And if they didn't have something missing, they were carrying scars from barbed wire, or knives, or fishhooks. But the people in the catalogue had no such hurts. They were not only whole, had all their arms and legs and toes and eyes on their unscarred bodies, but they were also beautiful. Their legs were straight and their heads were never bald and on their faces were looks of happiness, even joy, looks that I never saw much of in the faces of the people around me.

Young as I was, though, I had known for a long time that it was all a lie. I knew that under those fancy clothes there had to be scars, there had to be swellings and boils of one kind or another because there was no other way to live in the world. And more than that, at some previous, unremembered moment, I had decided that all the people in the catalogue were related, not necessarily blood kin, but knew one another, and because they knew one another there had to be hard feelings, trouble between them off and on, violence, and hate between them as well as love. And it was out of this knowledge that I first began to make up stories about the people I found in the book.

Once I began to make up stories about them, Willalee and Lottie Mae began to make up stories, too. The stories they made up were every bit as good as mine. Sometimes better. More than once we had spent whole rainy afternoons when it was too wet to go to the field turning the pages of the catalogue, forcing the beautiful people to give up the secrets of their lives: how they felt about one another, what kind of sicknesses they may have had, what kind of scars they carried in their flesh under all those bright and fancy clothes.

Willalee had his pocketknife out and was about to operate on one of the green cutworms because he liked to pretend he was a doctor. It was I who first put the notion in his head that he might in fact be a doctor, and since we almost never saw a doctor and because they were mysterious and always drove cars or else fine buggies behind high-stepping mares, quickly healing people with their secret medicines, the notion stuck in Willalee's head, and he became very good at taking cutworms and other things apart with his pocketknife.

The Sears catalogue that we had opened at random found a man in his middle years but still strong and healthy with a head full of hair and clear, direct eyes looking out at us, dressed in a red hunting jacket and wading boots, with a rack of shotguns behind him. We used our fingers to mark the spot and turned the Wish Book again, and this time it opened to ladies standing in their underwear, lovely as none we had ever seen, all perfect in their unstained clothes. Every last one of them had the same direct and steady eyes of the man in the red hunting jacket.

I said: "What do you think, Willalee?"

Without hesitation, Willalee said: "This lady here in her step-ins is his chile."

We kept the spot marked with the lady in the step-ins and the man in the hunting jacket and turned the book again, and there was a young man in a suit, the creases sharp enough to shave with, posed with his foot casually propped on a box, every strand of his beautiful hair in place.

"See, what it is," I said. "This boy right here is seeing that girl back there, the one in her step-ins, and she is the youngun of him back there, and them shotguns behind'm belong to him, and he ain't happy."

"Why he ain't happy?"

"Cause this feller standing here in this suit looking so nice, he ain't nice at all. He's mean, but he don't look mean. That gal is the only youngun the feller in the jacket's got, and he loves her cause she is a sweet child. He don't want her fooling with that sorry man in that suit. He's so sorry he done got hisself in trouble with the law. The high sheriff is looking for him right now. Him in the suit will fool around on you."

"How it is he fool around?"

"He'll steal anything he can put his hand to," I said. "He'll steal your hog, or he'll steal your cow out of your field. He's so sorry he'll take that cow if it's the only cow you got. It's just the kind of feller he is."

Willalee said: "Then how come it is she mess around with him?"

"That suit," I said, "done turned that young girl's head. Daddy always says if you give a man a white shirt and a tie and a suit of clothes, you can find out real quick how sorry he is. Daddy says it's the quickest way to find out."

"Do her daddy know she's messing round with him?"

"Shore he knows. A man allus knows what his youngun is doing. Special if she's a girl." I flipped back to the man in the red hunting jacket and the wading boots. "You see them shotguns behind him there on the wall? Them his guns. That second one right there, see that one, the double barrel? That gun is loaded with double-ought buckshot. You know how come it loaded?"

"He gone stop that fooling around," said Willalee.

And so we sat there on the porch with the pots and pans banging back in the house over the iron stove and Lottie Mae there in the door where she had come to stand and listen to us as we talked even though we would not let her help with the story. And before it was over, we had discovered all the connections possible between the girl in the step-ins and the young man in the knife-creased suit and the older man in the red hunting jacket with the shotguns on the wall behind him. And more than that we also discovered that the man's kin people, when they had found out about the trouble he was having with his daughter and the young man, had plans of their own to fix it so the high sheriff wouldn't even have to know about it. They were going to set up and wait on him to take a shoat hog out of another field, and when he did, they'd be waiting with their own guns and knives (which we stumbled upon in another part of the catalogue) and they was gonna throw down on him and see if they couldn't make two pieces out of him instead of one. We had in the story what they thought and what they said and what they felt and why they didn't think that the young man, as good as he looked and as well as he stood in his fancy clothes, would ever straighten out and become the man the daddy wanted for his only daughter.

Before it was over, we even had the girl in the step-ins fixing it so that the boy in the suit could be shot. And by the time my family and Willalee's family came walking down the road from the tobacco field to-ward the house, the entire Wish Book was filled with feuds of every kind and violence, maimings, and all the other vicious happenings of the world.

Since where we lived and how we lived was almost hermetically sealed from everything and everybody else, fabrication became a way of life. Making up stories, it seems to me now, was not only a way for us to understand the way we lived but also a defense against it. It was no doubt the first step in a life devoted primarily to men and women and children who never lived anywhere but in my imagination. I have found in them infinitely more order and beauty and satisfaction than I ever have in the people who move about me in the real world. And Willalee

Bookatee and his family were always there with me in those first tentative steps. God knows what it would have been like if it had not been for Willalee and his people, with whom I spent nearly as much time as I did with my own family.

There was a part of me in which it did not matter at all that they were black, but there was another part of me in which it had to matter because it mattered to the world I lived in. It mattered to my blood. It is easy to remember the morning I found out Willalee was a nigger.

It was not very important at the time. I do not know why I have remembered it so vividly and so long. It was the tiniest of moments that slipped by without anybody marking it or thinking about it.

It was later in the same summer I awoke to a knowledge of myself in the enormous, curving oak roots. It was Sunday, bright and hot, and we were on the way to church. Everybody except daddy, who was sick from whiskey. But he would not have gone even if he were well. The few times he ever did go he could never stand more than five or ten minutes of the sermon before he quietly went out a side door to stand beside the pickup truck smoking hand-rolled Prince Albert cigarettes until it was all over.

An aunt, her husband, and their children had come by to take us to the meeting in their car. My aunt was a lovely, gentle lady whom I loved nearly as much as mama. I was out on the porch waiting for my brother to get ready. My aunt stood beside me, pulling on the thin black gloves she wore to church winter and summer. I was talking nonstop, which I did even as a child, telling her a story—largely made up—about what happened to me and my brother the last time we went to town.

Robert Jones figured in the story. Robert Jones was a black man who lived in Bacon County. Unlike any other black man I knew of, though, he owned a big farm with a great shining house on it. He had two sons who were nearly seven feet tall. They were all known as very hard workers. I had never heard anybody speak of Robert Jones and his family with anything but admiration.

" . . . so me and Hoyet was passing the cotton gin and Mr. Jones was standing there with his wife and . . . "

My aunt leaned down and put her arm around my shoulders. Her great soft breast pressed warmly at my ear. She said: "No, son. Robert Jones is a nigger. You don't say 'mister' when you speak of a nigger. You don't say 'Mr. Jones,' you say 'nigger Jones'."

I never missed a stroke in my story. " . . . so me and him was passing the cotton gin and nigger Jones was standing there with his wife . . ."

We were all dutiful children in Bacon County, Georgia.

I don't know what difference it ever made that I found out Willalee Bookatee was a nigger. But no doubt it made a difference. Willalee was our friend, my brother's and mine, but we sometimes used him like a toy. He was always a surefire cure for boredom because among other things he could be counted on to be scared witless at the mention of a bull. How many afternoons would have been endless if we couldn't have said to one another: "Let's go get Willalee Bookatee and scare the shit out of him."

It didn't take much encouragement or deception to get Willalee out in the cornfield with us just after noon, when it was hot as only a day can be hot in the middle of an airless field in Georgia.

Hoyet turned to Willalee Bookatee and said: "You ever seen this here bull?"

"Which air bull?" Willalee rolled his eyes and shuffled his feet and looked off down the long heat-distorted rows of corn, the corn so green it seemed almost purple in the sun.

"The bull that stays in this field," I said.

My brother said: "To hook little boys that won't tote a citron."

Willalee was out in the middle of a twenty-acre field of corn, equidistant from all fences, brought there by design by Hoyet and me to see if we could make him carry a heavy citron to the gate. A citron is a vine that grows wild in the field, and it puts out a fruit which is also called a citron and looks in every way like a watermelon except it's slightly smaller. Its rind was sometimes pickled and used in fruitcakes, but by and large, it was a worthless plant and farmers did everything they could think of to get rid of them, but they somehow always managed to survive.

"Hook little boys," said Willalee.

It wasn't a question; it was only repeated into the quiet dust-laden air. There had been no rain in almost two weeks, and when you stepped between the corn rows, the dust rose and hung, not falling or blowing in the windless day, but simply hanging interminably between the purple shucks of corn.

"No siree, it's got to be bigger than that one," I said when Willalee rushed to snatch a grapefruit-sized citron off the ground. "That old bull wants you to tote one bigger'n that."

Willalee was scared to death of bulls. He had been trampled and caught on the horns of one when he was about three years old, and he never got over it. At the mention of a bull, Willalee would go gray and his eyes would get a little wild and sometimes he would get out of control with his fear. Willalee was struggling with an enormous citron, staggering in the soft dirt between the corn rows.

"That's better," I said. "That's a lot better. That old bull will never touch you with that in your arms."

Willalee couldn't have weighed more than about sixty-five pounds, and the citron he caught against his skinny chest must have weighed twenty pounds.

"How come it is you ain't got no citron?" said Willalee.

My brother and I walked on either side of him. He could hardly see over the citron he was carrying.

"We already carried ourn," I said. "That bull don't make you tote but one. After you tote one citron, you can take and come out here in the field anytime you want to and that bull don't pay no more mind than if you was a goat."

Willalee was a long way from the gate, and he had already started crying, soundlessly, tears tracking down through the dust on his cheeks. That citron was hurting him a lot.

"But you ain't toted your citron yet," I said, "and that big bull looking to hook into your ass if you put it down, that bull looking to hook him some ass, some good tender little-boy ass, cause that the kind he likes the best."

"I know," whispered Willalee through his tears. "I know he do."

And so Willalee made it to the fence with his citron and felt himself forever safe from the bull. He didn't hesitate at the fence but went right over it, still carrying his citron in case the bull was watching, and once over it, he didn't say anything but took off in a wild run down the road.

Five

BUT Willalee was not entirely helpless, and he gave back about as good as he got. He once took a crabapple and cut the core out of it, put some cow plop down in the bottom of the hole, and then covered it over all around the top with some blackberry jam his mama had canned.

"Jam in a apple?" I said.

"Bes thing *you* ever put in your mouth," he said.

My brother, who had seen him fix the apple, stood there and watched him offer it to me, did in fact encourage me to take it.

"Had one myself," he said. "That thing is some gooooood eatin."

"I ain't had nair one with jam in it," I said.

"Take you a great big bite," said Willalee.

I not only took a great big bite, I took *two* great big bites, getting right down to the bottom. Anybody else would have known what he was eating after the first bite. It took me two. Even then, I did not so much taste it as I smelled it.

"I believe this thing is ruint," I said.

"Nawwwww," said Willalee.

"Nawwwww," said my brother.

"It smells just like . . . like . . ." And then I knew what he had fed me.

Willalee was laughing when he should have been running. I got him around the neck and we both went into the dust, where we wallowed around for a while before my brother got tired of watching it and pulled us apart. No matter what we did to one another, though, Willalee and I never stayed angry at each other for more than an hour or two, and I always felt welcome at his family's house. Whatever I am, they had a large part in making. More, I am convinced Willalee's grandma, Auntie, made the best part of me. She was thin and brittle with age, and her white hair rode her fleshless face like a cap. From daylight to dark she kept a thick cud of snuff working in her caving, toothless mouth, and she was expert at sending streams of brown spit great distances into tin cans.

The inside of their tiny house was dark on the brightest day and smelled always of ashes, even in the summer. Auntie did not like much light inside the house, so most of the time she kept the curtains drawn, curtains she had made from fertilizer sacks and decorated with bits of colored cloth. Bright light was for the outside, she said, and shade—the more the better—was for the inside.

I ate with them often, as often as mama would let me, and the best thing I ever got from their table was possum, which we *never* got at home because mama would not cook it. She said she knew it would taste like a wet dog smells. But it did not. Auntie could cook it in a way that would break your heart. Willalee and I would stand about in her dark, ash-smelling little kitchen and watch her prepare it: She would scald and scrape it just like you would scald and scrape a hog, gut it, re-move the eyes, which she always carefully set aside in a shallow dish. The head, except for the eyes, would be left intact. After she parboiled it an hour and a half, she would take out the teeth, stuff the little body with sweet potatoes, and then bake the whole thing in the oven for two hours.

The reason mama would never cook a possum, of course, was because a possum is just like a buzzard. It will eat anything that is dead. The longer dead the better. It was not unusual to come across a cow that had been dead in the woods for three or four days and see a possum squeezing out of the swollen body after having eaten a bellyful of rotten flesh. But it never occurred to me to think of that when we all sat down to the table and waited for Willalee's daddy to say the only grace he ever said: "Thank the Lord for this food."

The first possum I ever shared with them was in that first summer in my memory of myself, and with the possum we had fresh sliced toma-toes and steamed okra—as well as fried okra—and corn on the cob, butter beans, fried pork, and biscuits made out of flour and water and lard.

Because I was company, Auntie gave me the best piece: the head. Which had a surprising amount of meat on it and in it. I ate around on the face for a while, gnawing it down to the cheekbones, then ate the tongue, and finally went into the skull cavity for the brains, which Auntie had gone to some pains to explain was the best part of the piece.

After we finished the possum, Willalee and Lottie Mae and I stayed at the table sopping cane syrup with biscuits. Will and Katie had gone out on the front porch to rest, and we were left alone with Auntie, who was already working over the table, taking plates to the tin tub where she would wash them, and putting whatever food had been left over into the screen-wire safe.

Finally, she came to stand beside where I sat at the table. "Come on now, boy," she said, "an ole Auntie'll show you."

"Show me what?" I said.

She was holding the little shallow saucer with the possum's eyes in it. The eyes were clouded in a pink pool of diluted blood. They rolled on the saucer as I watched.

"Nem mind," she said. "Come on."

We followed her out the back door into the yard. We didn't go but a step or two before she squatted down and dug a hole. The rear of the house was almost covered with stretched and nailed hides of squirrels and rabbits and coons and even a fox which Willalee's daddy had trapped. I would find out later that Auntie had tanned the hides by rubbing the animals' hides on the flesh side with their own brains. It caused the hair to fall out of the hide and left it soft and pliable.

"You eat a possum, you bare its eyes," she said, still squatting beside the little hole she had dug.

I motioned toward Sam where he stood at my heels. "You gone bury it," I said, "you better bury it deeper'n that. Don't he'll dig it up. You might as well go on and give it to'm now."

"Won't dig up no possum's eyes," she said. "Sam's got good sense."

Sam did not, either.

"Know how come you got to barum?" she said.

"How come?" I said.

"Possums eat whatall's dead," she said. Her old, cracked voice had gone suddenly deep and husky. "You gone die too, boy."

"Yes," I said, stunned.

"You be dead an in the ground, but you eat this possum an he gone come lookin for you. He ain't ever gone stop lookin for you."

I could not now speak. I watched as she carefully took the two little clouded eyes out of the dish and placed them in the hole, arranging them so they were looking straight up toward the cloudless summer sky. They seemed to watch me where I was.

Auntie smiled, showing her snuff-colored gums. "You ain't got to think on it, boy. See, we done put them eyes looking up. But you gone be *down*. Ain't never gone git you. Possum be looking for you up, an you gone be six big feets under the ground. You gone allus be all right, you put the eyes lookin up."

Auntie made me believe we live in a discoverable world, but that most of what we discover is an unfathomable mystery that we can name—even defend against—but never understand.

My fifth birthday had come and gone, and it was the middle of the summer, 1940, hot and dry and sticky, the air around the table thick with the droning of house flies. At supper that night neither my brother nor I had to ask where daddy was. There was always, when he had gone for whiskey, a tension in the house that you could breathe in with the air and feel on the surface of your skin, and more than that, there was that awful look on mama's face. I suppose the same look was on our faces, too, worried as we all were, not knowing what the night would bring, not knowing if it would be this night or the next night, or the morning following the second night, when he would come home after a drunk, bloodied, his clothes stinking with whiskey sweat.

We sat at the supper table, eating quietly, nobody saying a word, and when we finished, my brother and I went just as quietly into the fire-room and sat in ladder-back chairs, staring into the cold hearthstone where there had been no fire for two months. By the time mama came in to sit with us we had already brought in the foot tub full of water. The only thing we seemed to wash for long periods of time on the farm was our face and hands at the water shelf on the back porch and our feet in front of the hearthstone.

That night as we sat silently together, everybody thinking of daddy, thinking of where he was and how he might come home, I—for reasons which I'll never know—turned to mama and said: "I want to preach."

She immediately understood that I didn't mean that I wanted to be a preacher or to become a preacher, but rather that I wanted to preach right then. She said: "Well, son, if you want to preach, just get up there and preach to us."

She was always open and direct with us, always kind and loving, even though she was always strict. She believed that if a child did something he knew was wrong, had been told was wrong, he had to be whipped. And she did throughout my childhood throw some pretty good whippings on my brother and me. But she never whipped us when we did not know that we deserved it and, more, when we did not expect it.

Mama and my brother sat there in front of the cold fireplace while I got up and turned my ladder-back chair over and got the crocheted doily off the pedal-driven Singer sewing machine to cover the chair with. The chair covered with the doily made a fine altar from which to preach. I took hold of it with both hands, looked out at them, and started my sermon.

I said: "We all of us made out of dirt. God took Him up some dirt and put it in his hands and rolled it around and then he spit in the dirt and roll it some more and out of that dirt and God spit, he made you and me, all of us."

That is the way my preaching began. I don't remember how it ended, but I know it went on for a long time and it was made pretty much out of what I had heard in church, what I had heard the preacher say about hell and God and heaven and damnation and the sorry state of the human condition. Hell was at the center of any sermon I had ever heard in Bacon County. In all the churches, you smelled the brimstone and the sulfur and you felt the fire and you were made to know that because of what you had done in your life, you were doomed forever. Unless somehow, somewhere, you were touched by the action of mercy and the Grace of God. But you could not, you must not, count on the Grace of God. It probably would not come to you because you were too sorry.

I was exhausted by the time it was over, and I was asleep the moment my head touched the pillow. But I heard the pickup truck when it came in. And I heard daddy come through the front gate, the plow points banging and his own drunk-heavy feet on the steps and the front door slamming, and then I heard, as I already knew I would, querulous voices as mama and daddy confronted each other there beyond the thin wall. Finally, their voices raised to shouts and even screams, but since there was nothing breaking, no pots hitting the wall, no glass splattering on the floor, no furniture turning over, I could stand lying in my bed if I concentrated on hell and damnation. This was nothing compared to the eternal fires of hell that God might someday demand that I endure. With my whole self firmly immersed in hell, I could usually go back to sleep.

I woke up sometime in the middle of the night. An enormous and brilliant moon shone over the cotton field where I was standing, still in my gown. It was not a dream and I knew immediately that it was not a dream. I was where I thought I was, and I had come here by walking in my sleep. I came awake that night the way I always have when I've gotten up in my sleep and walked. Terrified. Terrified almost beyond terror because it had no name and was sourceless. My heart was pounding, and my gown was soaked with sweat and sticking to my freezing skin. My mouth was full of the taste of blood where I'd chewed my lips.

The cotton bolls were open all about me. As far as I could see, all the way to the dark wall of trees surrounding the field, was a white sheet of cotton, brilliant and undulating under the heavy moon. I stood there for a long time, unable to move. Off there to the left was the enormous oak tree that I had slept under that morning, it, too, brilliant in the moon, and behind the tree was the house, dark in its own shadow. I did not know what to do. I did not cry and I did not scream. I did not think that I could go back there to the dark house where my family slept. I somehow knew they would not receive me. I knew that I was guilty of something neither man nor God could forgive. But it would always be so when I walked in my sleep.

I stood utterly still and waited because I knew if I waited long enough, the terror would find a source and a name. Once it had a name, no matter how awful, I would be able to live with it. I could go back home.

Gradually, the terror shapes itself into a school bus. I can see it plainly. It is full of children. Stopped by the side of a road. I am in the ditch by the side of the road. They do not see me. It is broad daylight and many of the children are looking right at me. But they don't—they can't—see me. I have something in my hand. I do not know what it is. I cannot tell what it is. I come slowly out of the ditch and touch the school bus with the thing in my hand. The moment contact is made, the whole bus disintegrates in my eyes. There is no explosion, no sound at all. The disintegration is silent as sleep. When I can see again, the bus is on its back, broken children hang from open windows, and some—the ones toward the back—are drenched in gas from the ruptured tank and they are frying, noiselessly frying. I can smell them frying. And I am terrified at the probable consequences that will follow what I have done, but I am glad I have done it.

Now I can go home, and I start off in a dead run between the rows of cotton toward the dark house beyond the oak tree.

When I got to the door, I opened it quietly and went down the hall to the little room where I knew daddy was sleeping on a pallet. It was where he often had to sleep when he came in drunk and out of control and mama would not let him into their room. He lay, still dressed, curled on the quilt spread across the floor under an open window through which bright moonlight fell. I sat down beside him and touched his face, traced the thick scar of perfect teeth on his flat high cheekbone. The air in the room was heavy with the sweet smell of bourbon whiskey. Sweat stood on his forehead and darkly stained his shirt.

"Daddy," I said. He made a small noise deep in his chest, and his eyes opened. "Daddy, I'm scared."

He pushed himself onto one elbow and put an arm around me and drew me against him. I could feel the bristle of his beard on my neck. I trembled and tried not to cry.

"Sho now," he whispered against my ear. "Everybody's scared now and then."

"I was in the cotton field," I said. "Out there."

He turned his head, and we both looked through the window at the flat white field of cotton shining under the moon.

"You was dreaming, boy," he said. "But you all right now."

"I woke up out there." Now I was crying, not making any noise, but unable to keep the tears from streaming down my face. I pushed my bare feet into the moonlight. "Look," I said. My feet and the hem of my gown were gray with the dust of the field.

He drew back and looked into my eyes, smiling. "You walked in your sleep. It ain't nothing to worry about. You probably got it from me. I'as bad to walk in my sleep when I was a boy."

The tears eased back. "You was?" I said.

"Done it a lot," he said. "Don't mean nothing."

I don't know if he was telling the truth. But hearing him say it was something that he had done and that I might have got it from him took my fear away.

"You lie down here on the pallet with your ole daddy and go to sleep. Me an you is all right. We *both* all right."

I lay down with my head on his thick arm, wrapped in the warm, sweet smell of whiskey and sweat, and was immediately asleep.

Willalee's daddy did not drink and almost never left the farm. In fantasy I often thought of Willalee as my brother, thought of his family as my family. His daddy was always there, and everybody in the family had a place and a purpose, all of them integrated into the business of making a living in a way that my family was not. My own daddy was easy to love, but he was often drunk and often gone. Willalee's daddy was easy to love, too, because everywhere about the farm he was there, always steady, never raising his voice, making you feel good to be with him. He never told anybody to do anything. He asked for your help in a way that made you feel as though you were helping him out of a tight spot he could not get out of by himself.

"Reckon you boys could bring Sam and help me doctor a cow?"

Willalee's daddy had stopped us in the lane between the house and the mule lot. We were in a little two-wheeled buggy pulled by Old Black Bill, the boss goat of the herd we kept. Willalee sat beside me holding two blackbirds we had just taken out of a trap down behind the field.

"Harry got to put up these 'er buds," said Willalee.

"That be fine," Will said. "I be in the lot."

Willalee and I had been down to my bird trap that Saturday afternoon in late July and found the two blackbirds in it. Sometimes the trap would take a whole covey of quail, as many as thirteen or fourteen birds at one time. My Grandma Hazelton taught me how to make it out of tobacco sticks. Those are the sticks, about six feet long and one inch square, that the tobacco is strung on to be hung in the barn and cooked. To make the trap you lay the sticks down, one on top of another with the ends overlapping like the walls of a log cabin. When the four sides of the trap are about eighteen or twenty inches high, you cover it straight across the top, leaving about an inch between the sticks. Now you've got a cage six feet square that admits the sun well enough for it to be nearly as light inside as it is outside. For good reason. Birds won't enter a dark trap.

You dig a hole—a rather large hole—under one side of the square of tobacco sticks. Sprinkle meal or broken corn around the front of the trap, some more down in the hole you've dug under one side, and still more inside the trap itself. Birds will come along, eat a little outside, scratch and feed into the hole, and finally go up into the trap where most of the food has been placed. When they get ready to leave, they will never once think of the hole right there at their feet. They could walk out the same way they came in, but when they get ready to go, their only thought is flight.

It always took some doing to get the birds out of the trap, and that morning was no exception. You had to be really careful when you were working with a trap that big or your birds would get away. After a half hour of false starts, we finally got the two blackbirds out and we were taking them up to the house to turn them loose in the little room at the back of the house mama had given over to my brother and me. The room had always been empty except for a couple of broken chairs and half a bedstead, so my brother and I asked her one day if we could have it to keep birds in, and to our complete amazement, she said yes.

Birds, particularly wild birds, are a little crazy when you turn them loose in a room. But if there are other birds already resting quietly in the room, they don't fly blindly about, bashing into walls and windows. The floor was ankle deep in straw and leaves and twigs and moss for the birds to build nests with in the dead, branching limbs I had nailed around the room. A pair of redbirds I caught built a nest, laid eggs, and hatched them out.

After we turned the blackbirds loose, I was about to put down meal and corn and peas and fresh water when I saw that my brother had already done it. We never had gotten the ownership of the room straight. He said it was his because he took care of the birds. I said it was mine because I took care of the birds. Mama said it belonged to us both and that neither one of us took care of the birds.

When we had gotten rid of the birds, Willalee and I went back out to help Will with the cow that had screwworms. He had her penned behind the corncrib and he was waiting for us there, squatting on his heels in the shade of the fence, watching the cow. She was so poor you could hang your hat on her hipbone. Her lifeless hide cleaved to her ribs and hung in folds down to her widened, shriveled udder which had been torn on one side and was now alive with worms. She backed into a corner of the lot when she saw us, head lowered, showing us the points of her long sweeping horns.

Sam had come with us, and it was up to him to take her down so we could clean her out. If we didn't, the screwworms would very likely kill her. Screwworms are gone now, but when I was a boy, they were just about everywhere. If any animal got a cut on it from something like barbed wire or in any other way managed to tear its hide in the hot months of the year, a blue-bellied fly about half as big as a man's fingernail would blow eggs into the wound. From the eggs would come tiny worms, hundreds, sometimes thousands of them. The worms could, and often did, kill whatever animal they got into. The only two things on a farm I never saw screwworms in were chicken and people.

Will left the shade of the fence and came to stand between us. He put his left hand on his son's shoulder and his right hand on my shoulder. I could feel it thick and strong and warm through my shirt. I thought of that morning when my own daddy had put his hand, the same kind of strong, thick hand, on my shoulder. But with his other hand he had wiped his forehead and I'd watched the sweat drip from the ends of his fingers. He had laughed when he said: "Boy, that's pure bourbon whiskey running off my hand." But I had not laughed as I watched him get in the pickup truck and drive off. And now I pretended the hand on my shoulder was his.

"I don't know what that ole cow'd do if you boys didn't help me doctor'er." He sucked his lips and clucked to Sam, his voice coming now low as a whisper. "Sic'er. Take'er down, Sam."

Sam was as good a catch dog as anybody ever saw work. He circled to the cow's left, cautiously, growling but not barking. He had to first get her out of the corner, if he was to catch her. We backed out of the lot into the space between the stables and corncrib.

Almost gently, and without seeming effort, Sam soon had the cow trotting round and round, then running as fast as she could given the tight circle she had to make in the lot. He was running right beside her, step for step, when he lunged and caught her high in the right ear. As soon as he had a firm hold, he drew his big body upward. His weight pulled her head down and he went between her front feet. The cow was thrown in a single solid *thump* onto her back. Stunned, the breath partially knocked out of her, she lay as still as if she were dead.

Sam was a choke dog as well as a catch dog. On command, he would attempt to catch anything, even a mule. But once he took hold there were only two ways to get him off. He always kept his eyes tightly shut, and he seemed to go stone deaf as soon as he caught. Then it was either take him by the throat and choke him off or else pry his mouth open with a little spoon-shaped piece of wood whittled from a shingle.

Will twisted her head until he could brace against her top horn with his leg. He poured the Benzol into the wound, and it worked alive with squirming worms, boiling them out onto the hide. Then he took a fork that was kept with the Benzol and carefully cleaned out the V-shaped wound. The last thing that was applied was a thick, black, turpentine-smelling paste that sealed the hide so it would not be reinfected.

"I reckon she'll live," he said.

We untied the cow's legs and stood back as the cow got shakily to her feet. Will's shirt was soaking wet halfway to his belt, and sweat ran on his forehead and dripped from his chin.

When we had finished with the cow, Will took us back down to the tenant house, where we cut a watermelon and sat on the front porch eating it while Auntie banged around in the kitchen making supper.

Six

THE first real illness of my life came on the night of August 7, 1940, exactly three months after my fifth birthday. The day will always be fixed firmly in memory because it was the day the Jew came. He came into our little closed world smelling of strangeness and far places. Willalee and I had just come up from his house when we saw him far off down the road coming steadily and slowly, dust rising behind his wagon in the heat-distorted distance. My brother came out to join us where we stood under the oak tree.

The Jew traveled in a covered wagon pulled by a pair of mismatched mare mules. One of the mules was normal-sized, but the other one was small enough to be a pony, although she was not. The tiny mule had a cast in one eye and her left ear had been split all the way down to her head so it made her look like she had three ears.

The Jew, whose name I never knew, always dressed in black, and on even the hottest days he wore heavy black pants and a black coat and a little black cap right on top of his head. He traveled a regular route through Appling County and Pierce County and Jeff Davis County and Bacon County. People said you could set your watch by where he was on any given day of the month, so regularly did he travel his route.

The inside of his wagon was better than anything Willalee and I could make up, filled as it was with spools of thread and needles and thimbles and bolts of cloth and knives and forks and spoons—some new, some used—and a grinding stone of a special design so that he could sharpen anything, and mule harness, and staples, and nails, and a thousand other things.

He did business almost exclusively with women, and whatever they needed, they could always find in the Jew's wagon. If they didn't have the money to pay for what they needed, he would trade for eggs or chickens or cured meat or canned vegetables and berries.

He had a water barrel strapped to the back of his wagon, and hanging from the sides of the canvas cover and from the sides of the wooden body of the wagon were frying pans and boiling pots and even washtubs and cast-iron washpots. He had also contrived to wire mason fruit jars onto the side of his wagon, wire them in such a way that when they swung they would not strike each other and break.

I can never remember anybody saying anything bad about him or anybody treating him badly. But he *was* different from the rest of us. When he spoke, he did not sound like us. For that reason he was mysterious and often used to scare the children with. People in the county would sometimes say to an unruly child: "If you don't behave, youngun, I just might let you go on off with the Jew. Just let'm have you." It was at least as effective as a whipping.

He came slowly into the lane in front of the house and stopped his wagon under the oak tree. Willalee, my brother, and I stood in the dust watching him. He had longer hair than we had ever seen on a man and a long dirty-white beard. The fingers on his hands were badly twisted. We wanted very badly to speak to him, to talk to him, but we were afraid. After the dust had settled under his wagon and he had been sitting there a long quiet time, he slowly turned his head, looked at us, nodded his head in the smallest of movements, and got stiffly down by stepping over onto the hub of the wheel.

Mama came out of the house with a pair of scissors in her hand. He stood by his wagon, and when she was near, he moved his head forward in a slight, stiff bow instead of taking off his hat as other men might have done. He did not speak.

"I got these for you to sharpen," mama said.

He took the scissors from her and turned them slowly in his hands. Then: "For maybe a quarter?" he said, looking up from the scissors through his heavy eyebrows.

"I thought a dime," mama said.

"For less than fifteen cents I couldn't," he said.

"I guess it's worth that to me," said mama.

"In the wagon," he said, "I have some very good cloth. A nice bright print."

"I ain't got the money," mama said, but she turned her eyes toward the back of the wagon.

"Let me show you," he said. "It does no harm to look."

"It don't do no good neither, if you ain't got the money," she said.

But he was already starting for the back of the wagon, and she followed him. He opened one flap on the back and pulled a thin bolt of thin, brightly colored cloth halfway out and spread a small length of it over his hands.

"Feel it," he said. "A very nice cloth."

"I ain't got the money," she said. But she felt the cloth anyway, slowly, letting it trail through her fingers.

"Maybe some corn for my animals," he said, "and a little hay."

"We didn't make much hay this year," she said. "We ain't got nigh enough for the stock on the place now."

"You wouldn't miss fifty ears of corn and two bats of hay," he said. "For that much, I could maybe let you have three yards. It's very good cloth."

"It ain't worth fifty ears and that much hay to me," she said. "We didn't make much hay this year."

"Fifty-five ears then," he said, "and one bat of hay."

"I might could see my way clear to let you have forty-five ears and a bat," she said.

"It is very little for such nice cloth," he said. He looked into the darkness of covered wagon for a moment as if expecting to find some answer in there. "But for you, why not a bargain?"

The expression on his face never changed while they talked. Mama left the scissors with him and went back into the house. He took his team out and led them to the lot and watered them at the trough. We followed him and watched as he put the corn and hay into a burlap sack. He did it all very slowly and with great deliberation. He never seemed sad and he never seemed happy. He did not speak to us, nor we to him. He spoke only when he was trading and then only so much as was necessary to business. He did all that he did in seeming exhaustion, but with utter patience.

We watched him wash his face and hands in the water trough at the lot, and then we watched as he put his team back to the wagon. His twisted hands worked quickly and surely over the scissors at his grinding stone. Mama came back out and watched him cut the bolt of cloth with the scissors he had sharpened. When he finished, she silently took two brown chicken eggs out of her apron and gave them to him. Just as silently he took them and stood holding them in his hand as though weighing them.

"I thought you might could use them," she said.

He nodded silently and then turned and slowly reached deep into the back of his wagon and finally came out with three tiny peppermint balls. He opened his hand to Willalee, my brother, and me. The candy lay in his palm unwrapped and dusted with confectionery sugar.

"For you, and you, and you," he said, giving each of us a candy.

He turned to my mother, gave his slight, stiff bow, and climbed over the wheel and onto the seat board of his wagon. When he lifted the lines, his pair of mismatched mules leaned into their collars and he was moving away. With the candies melting on our tongues, we stood and watched him go, feeling as though we had ourselves just been on a long trip, a trip to the world we knew was out there but had never seen.

That night I woke up with a burning fever. Mama, as was her custom when treating toothache, fever, sore throat, earache, eye strain, or headache, sent my brother down to the tenant house to get some wool. When my brother knocked on Auntie's door in the middle of the night, she would know immediately what he was there for, and without turning on a light she would stand in her gown in the doorway lighted bright as day by the moon and with a pair of heavy scissors cut two thimble-sized pieces out of her hair.

Mama said the wool from Auntie's head kept our ears warm and the oil from it eased the pain. Sometimes it seemed to help, sometimes not. This time it did not. The next morning the wool was still in my ears tighter than ever because she had pushed them deeper into my head every hour or two, but I still had the fever and my legs had begun to draw up. They were bent at the knees, and the ligaments were slowly drawing my heels closer and closer to the cheeks of my buttocks. It felt like both legs were knotted from hip to heel. The pain was enough to make me chew my lips and the inside of my mouth.

Daddy got home, sick himself and seriously hung-over, just in time to drive to the only farm I knew of in the county that had a telephone. The man who owned it didn't really farm the way the rest of us did. His farming was done in the woods. He had a big turpentine distillery and a good-sized village of blacks living on his place. The blacks cut V's into the faces of pine trees and nailed tin cups under the V's to catch the raw turpentine when it drained out. They collected the turpentine in buckets, which they poured into barrels, which eventually found their way, usually on mule-drawn sleds, to the distillery.

Daddy called Dr. Sharp, who arrived at about noon looking starched and powerful as God as he always did, dressed in his black coat and carrying his black bag full of magic. It wasn't long though before he looked as I had never seen him. He had determined with pins that there was feeling in both legs. But that was about as far as he got, which he freely admitted. He scratched his head and poked here and pulled there and finally said he didn't know for sure what I had, but he thought it was infantile paralysis.

He left something for the pain and said he would be back out the next day. By the time he got back my legs were drawn as tight as they were going to get—as tight as they *could* get, with the heels pulled all the way up until they touched the backs of my thighs. Dr. Sharp even had Dr. Branch to come over from Baxley. But he was as baffled as Dr. Sharp. I got a few shots for the pain, and both Dr. Branch and Dr. Sharp said I would never walk again. It was a time of great grief for mama and a time of sheer terror for me because I could not imagine what in God's name I would do for the rest of my life with my legs drawn up that way.

As it happens, about four days later, a band of gypsies came through in their wagons. It was not uncommon to see them traveling about the countryside, doing whatever they were allowed to do: repairing pots and pans and tubs, trading, doing a little carpentry—mostly roofs of barns and lots. But mostly they stole. At least most of the farmers were convinced they did.

Like the Jew, they dressed differently from the way we dressed, and they spoke to us in voices full of accents different from our own, at times spoke a language amongst themselves that made as much sense to us as the greaseless squealing of a wagon wheel. And because of their language and the way they dressed, we thought they had powers we did not have: powers for curses, potions, and various miraculous cures that could be had for a little money or a few chickens.

The head of the tribe, a very old man who looked strangely like the Jew even though he was not bearded and wore a bright cloth on his head instead of a black cap, had heard that I was sick and asked to be taken into the house to see me. He said he might be able to help me, said he might have something in his bag that could kill the disease, attack it and kill it. He had a bag just like the doctor's, except the old gypsy's was made out of the hide of a goat from which the hair had not been removed.

While the old man was looking at me, touching my legs and head in a tentative way, stopping now and again to search through his goatskin medicine bag and eventually selling a bag of herbs for $10—a sizable amount of money then—while he was doing that, the rest of the band went out to the lot and stole a brood sow. A theft we did not discover until the next morning.

I drank those herbs boiled in tea for ten days, but when I had finished, my heels were just as tight against my ass as they had ever been. We were out $10 and a brood sow.

Following the gypsy came a great parade of people: aunts and uncles and cousins and even Grandpa and Grandma Hazelton, who didn't get out of the house much anymore because they were full of years and had the miseries; and people from neighboring farms; and after them, total strangers from other counties, all of them come to stare at me where I lay in a high fever and filled with the most awful cramps, come to stare at my rigid legs. I knew that they were staring with unseemly intensity at my legs, that they wanted most of all to touch them, and I hated it and dreaded it and was humiliated by it. I felt how lonely and savage it was to be a freak.

Sometime later, the fourth or fifth day of my illness, after Dr. Sharp and Dr. Branch both had come and after both of them had said they did not know for sure what was wrong but thought (the thought voiced in front of me) that I would never walk again and after my uncle had come—the one who spoke in tongues—after he had fallen on me in a fit of glossolalia, which did not seem to affect me one way or the other, there appeared at my bedside a faith healer brought in from another county, Jeff Davis. He stood by my bed for what seemed to me a very long time. He was a small man with an upper lip so long that you could not see his top teeth and very few of his lower ones. The flapping upper lip made him appear toothless, and he never took his hat off.

He seemed to me the most objective of men. What he knew he knew with the certitude of science. When he spoke of what he could do, it sounded like the recitation of fact. It did not trouble him in the least if you did not believe he could do what he said he could do. Such doubts were met with a numbing indifference.

"I can cure the thrash out of a youngun's mouth," he said, still look-ing at me.

"He ain't *got* the thrash," daddy said, a raging unbeliever at the foot of the bed.

"It is red thrash and yeller thrash and black thrash," he said. "Yeller thrash is the worst."

"It's a God's pity that ain't what he's got," daddy said.

"God," he said quiet as a whisper but full of fact. "God? Did you say God? It's the way I do it. With the help of the Lord. With the help of the Lord. I couldn't do no healing without the help of the Lord."

Daddy snorted. He had a way of making it sound just like a horse does after he's had a run. I had heard him and mama arguing about whether or not to bring the faith healer. The argument was resolved when he found out it was not going to cost anything. "Labor deserves its hire," he would say, "but them sumbitches don't do nothing."

When somebody said in his presence that a preacher had made a good sermon on a particular Sunday, he would invariably say that he could make a good sermon, too, if somebody would give him a week's wages to do it. "Purty goddamn good wages for a hour's work."

Mama brought a ladder-back chair to the side of the bed and then re-treated into the shadows beyond the reach of the kerosene lamp. The faith healer sat down in the chair and carefully adjusted his hat until it was squared to his satisfaction. Now that he was sitting, the baggy, fold-ing trousers and the heavy coat did not look as if there was really a body in them, only maybe a lot of old coat hangers. Also, I now saw that he was a little walleyed, but as best he could, he still fixed me with a steady stare. I remember thinking (thinking in anger, which in turn came out of fear) that if he was a healer, the first thing he ought to do is go look in a mirror and heal that wandering eye. But of course, I said nothing about it.

I did not know this man, not his name (although it was mumbled to me), nor his work, and more than that, he was not from our county, which amounted to making him not only a stranger but a foreigner as well. I had had my legs stared at now for days by a seemingly endless pa-rade of people, and I had been probed and pulled and finally pummeled by Dr. Sharp and Dr. Branch, and I was still as bad off as ever. Nothing inspired me with any confidence, and certainly not this little toothless, starved, and wrinkled man. He must have known that I had no hope of him curing me because he sat and talked to me for a long time in his flat, matter-of-fact way about himself and his powers.

"I can draw far and I can stop blood," he said. "Why, it was one time, Tom, Tom's my middle youngun, Tom he got cut on the laig with a crosscut saw. They was a cuttin tobacker wood and he got cut on the laig with a crosscut saw and he was a bleeding bad. An when they come to me to go back down there in the woods where he was at cause he was hurt that bad, so bad he couldn't come back up to the house, when they come for me and I went down there, I just took one look at it.

"Didn't do a thing but look at it and said that verse out of Ezekiel. I said that verse and got that blood to stop right there where it was at.

"They'd been a puttin spider webs and I don't know what all up in that cut there trying to get it to stop. But it didn't stop till I got there, but when I got there and said the words, it stopped right away, youngun.

"Now the thing about far is you don't want to drive it no deeper. That's how come it is doctors cain't do no good with burns is they drive the far deeper. But me, what I do is draw it out, draw that far right on out of there. But a doctor he will most gently drive that heat right down to the bones, drive it even to the holler of the body. That far gets in the holler of the body, it'll jest cook an burn till it ain't nothin else to burn up anymore before it goes out. Which time you usually dead."

I could hear the rage mounting in my daddy's breathing at the foot of the bed. When the little man paused for breath, he said: "What about legs? Git to the part about legs."

Daddy's voice was full of helplessness and sarcasm and unbelieving, but if the faith healer heard the quality of the voice, he never let on that he did.

"You take them laigs of yorn right there," he said, pointing, as if there were some question as to which legs we were there to consider. "I can't say as I ever seed laigs jest like them. but them is the Lord's laigs and He's seed them laigs and He's laid His hand on them laigs and He knows, so it don't bother me none that I ain't seed'm."

Daddy could not contain himself. "Then git to it," he shouted.

The little man turned his trowel-shaped face in the lamplight, and his steady voice, coming counterpoint to daddy's shout, seemed less than a whisper. "I already got to it. I'm through."

"Then why the hell ain't his legs done nothing?" asked daddy. "His legs is jest like they was."

"No, they ain't. They jest look like they was. I said the verse out of Ezekiel an now it is between me and that boy and the Lord. An it ain't any way his laigs is the way they was. Never be again, neither."

A long-drawn silence followed his words, and I felt, as well as saw, my daddy trembling as he watched my legs, watched them as if he expected them to suddenly and miraculously loosen and straighten. Insects fluttered through the screenless windows and burned instantly crisp against the lampshade as the room wavered in the guttering light. I was the focus of their attention, the little man's and mama's and even daddy's, as I realized that in his grief and however temporary, he was a believer.

As the silence stretched on, I was humiliated all over again because the action of mercy had not come down from God and touched my legs and made them well. They were just as bent and just as white and just as full of pain as they had ever been, and I thought about how it would be not only to suffer the whole world to look at how I was and find me freakish and unacceptable, but also to suffer the knowledge that God Himself would not intercede.

"His legs ain't done a goddamn thing," daddy said.

The little faith healer said, matter-of-factly: "You standin in danger of hellfire blasphemin when Ezekiel's spoke by mouth or mind."

Daddy did not say so much as sang in a lilting grief, his voice soft, the fight gone out of him: "My boy is crippled. A cripple."

The faith healer stood up. "He won't always be," he said, and without looking at me again left the room. Finally, from down the hall, his thin, tiny voice came floating back to us: "It mought be today, or it mought be tomorrow. Whatever it is God will allow."

That night, when all the lights were out and I was dozing fitfully, daddy came into the room and lay down beside me. I could see well enough to see he was crying, crying in the open way that I had never seen a man cry.

"You want to sleep on your old daddy's arm, boy?"

When I slept with him, I always slept with my head on his arm. I lifted my head to his arm, and for the first time since the sickness started, I felt good.

"Why don't you tell me about the boy in the swamp?" I said.

It was a story he had told me many times before, always told in a different way from the way it had ever been told before but always about a boy who lived in a swamp and swam and fished and lay in the sun all day and had a best friend that was an alligator. I went to sleep trying to pretend that surely in the morning I would wake up and find my legs straightened. I tried to pretend that the last thing the faith healer had said from the hall had helped me to believe. God might not cure me that night, but tomorrow He would make it so I could walk again. And if not tomorrow, the next day. For a whole week I woke up every morning expecting my legs to be straight, expecting to be able to swing over to the side of the bed and stand up and go out and get my goat and Willalee Bookatee and the wagon. But it did not happen.

Finally, I quit believing that it would. Right there, as a child, I got to the bottom of what it means to be lost, what it means to be rejected by everybody (if they had not rejected me, why was I smothered in shame every time they looked at me?) and everything you ever thought would save you. And there were long days when I wondered why I did not die, how I could go on mindlessly living like a mule or a cow when God had obviously forsaken me. But if I was never able to accept my affliction, I was able to bear it and finally to accept the good-natured brutality and savagery in the eyes of those who came to wish me well. Mainly because of Auntie's sheer wisdom and terror. She made me see that in this world there was much more to worry about than merely being crippled.

After about a week, when it became clear that no miracle was going to save me from my bed, Willalee's grandma came up to the big house to take care of me. Getting Auntie to stay with me all of the time was the best present anyone could have given me.

All of us children, although none of us would have been able to say it, knew that Auntie was too strange—weird even—for the big people. She belonged with children, being as she was, full of the most fantastic stories and marvelous comments upon the way of the world and all things in it, whether of the earth or air. A lot of grownups had seen me by myself or with Willalee Bookatee making stories out of the Sears, Roebuck catalogue, but none of them had ever offered to join us. Not so with Auntie.

She didn't like anything better than to get right in the Sears, Roebuck catalogue with us and fix once and forever how it was between the people smiling out of the slick pages. In great detail, she told us various powers they had and about the painful curses they laid, one upon the other. She knew more about their hidden but afflicted skins than Willalee Bookatee and I had ever been able to imagine.

Somehow all of us knew that Auntie behaved as she did because she
had got way beyond just being grown-up. She had grown up and up and
up until she got to the very top, as high as you could go. Then she
started down, and having been on the downhill side of growing for such
a long time, she had got right back to where we were, but with an imagination more fecund and startling than any we had ever encountered.

Late in the night, when I could not sleep for the cramps in my legs,
she would sit up with me sometimes for hours, talking in her old, soft,
mother's voice of a world I had never heard anybody else even hint at.
She loved to talk about anything with snakes in it. And even though
the ring of truth that informed her voice made my skin go to goose
pimples, at the same time I somehow knew that hers was a fine inven-
tion. I listened, hardly breathing, while she told me how her lifetime
preoccupation with snakes had been set early for her.

"I weren't even a yearlin gul," she would say. "I was jest a little bitty
thing, big as your thumb." Long, scary pause. "An I seen him in the
ditch."

I had heard the story before, but I would shiver with a delicious horror. Because I had heard it before did not mean it held any less mystery
for me.

"Jest walking along and this snake I seen in the ditch had a white
man's head. It was the marsah's head on the snake in the ditch."

Auntie had been born in the time of slavery. She had told me all
about it a long time ago, but it never meant very much to me. It was
hard to imagine what a slave might be, and it was impossible to think of
people like my daddy and mama owning people like Willalee's daddy
and mama. It still is.

"The bluest eyes," she said. "An marsah had the bluest eyes and that
snake with marsah's head on it had them eyes and them eyes looked at
me. Stopped me right where I was walkin. One foots down an one in the
air and couldn't move. That snake done struck me stone still and dumb
as a rock. Couldn't even holler. And he come over to me where I was
still standin with my foots in the air. What he done was he come up on
me and say he hongry an says I gots to haf my vittles with him, bring'm
haf ever day there in the ditch and I say I will. Say I will do anything if
he jest take them blue eyes off me an let me go. He did and I did."

"Did what, Auntie?" I said. I wanted the details. Details were everything.

A CHILDHOOD

"I *did* go back to the house and I *did* commence to start to haf up my vittles with that snake in the ditch. I took him on out there a biscuit with a hole in it. I took him on out there some of that fried poke. I took him on out there some rice, and I took him on out there vegetables when I could. An right from the first I commenced to get sick a little, chile. Didn't know jest what, but I was feelin poorly, full of the miseries, an commenced to lose flesh off my body. So one day when my Uncle Ham was to the house, I axe if he ever heard tell of anybody or other feedin a snake."

"What did he say? What?" I asked, knowing already what he said.

"Chile, he say. It was a youngun no biggern you up the other side of Lanter and she commenced to lose flesh. She was poor folks jest like us, but her mama and daddy taken vittles from their own plate an given it to that chile, given her all the syrup on all the clabber, tryin to build up that chile where she losin that flesh. Then something passin strange happen. Youngun say she got to eat by herself. She so sick, she got to have a long time and a slow time when she eat, else her stomach she know gone come up on her. She say the only thing to do is go out behind the lot to eat. So they kept on givin that gul the best they had on the table and she keep totin it all out behind the lot where she say she can have a long time an a slow time. One day her daddy followed her on out there to the other side of the lot an he find her out there *sharin* them vittles they'd taken an given her. *Sharin with a snake.* Her daddy jest went ahead on an killed that snake." She stopped and regarded the far dark window and sucked her teeth in a contemplative, satisfied way. Then, almost as an afterthought, she turned back to me and said: "His gul was dead fore he could git her back to the house."

Her voice had gone flatter and flatter, but it was coming faster, and she moved on the hard ladder-backed chair where she sat and I moved with her in my bed at the horror of it all.

"Chile, that how I got away from that blue-eyed snake with the marsah's head. When I hern tell about that gul taken and died after her snake was kilt, I known the same thing gone happen to me I keep goin out there. God in His power and mercy taken and given me the strength to leave that snake in the ditch. I ain't been sorry, neither. Naw, naawww, I *ain't* been sorry."

Late at night she would tell me about coachwhip snakes, snakes that could wrap themselves around your leg and whip you on the back and

shoulders with their platted tails, running you until they ran you to
death. Then they would eat you.

And she told me about hoop snakes, snakes that had spiked tails and
could form themselves into a hoop and roll after you, up hills and down
hills. When they caught you, they'd hit you with the spiky end of their
tails and kill you. If the spike missed you and hit a tree instead, the tree
would be dead in fifteen minutes, with all the leaves on the ground because that spiky tail held killing poison.

She especially liked to talk about joint snakes, which she sometimes
called glass snakes. They were pretty and seemed to be one of the few
things in her world that was not deadly. When you hit or touched a
joint snake, it would break into pieces about as long as a joint of your
finger. It would stay that way until you left and then join itself back together. It didn't hurt the snake to be knocked apart, and it lived forever.

Perhaps most of all, she loved to talk about her daddy, dead these
many years, dead so long that she had forgotten his name, calling him at
various times Mr. William or Mr. John or Mr. Henry. Of all the names,
though, and there were others, she favored Mr. William. He had never
been bitten by a snake even though he had walked freely among them.
He could just raise up his hand and tell the snakes to lie down and they
would press themselves flat against the earth.

"Git down you snakes," Mr. William would say. "An them snakes'd lie
down flat like they weren't no more'n a dog. I axe him how he did that
and he said he didn't know how he did that but he thought anybody
could do that ifn they thought they could do that but he didn't his own
self know how he did that."

In the middle of the night, when the rest of the family had gone to
bed and had long since been asleep, she would talk of much more than
snakes. The entire world for her was aberrant and full of shadows, but
she understood the aberrations and the shadows, knew all about them
and never seemed to find it strange that so little of her world was what
it appeared to be. One night after I had been crippled in the bed for
nearly two months, she was rubbing my legs with liniment, as had become her habit. She rubbed and kneaded the fleshless, wasted bones,
talking while she worked. Suddenly, she stopped, cocked her head, and
seemed to listen.

"Now them birds," she said.

"Birds," I said.

"I tol you bout them birds, chile."

"No," I said. "You ain't told me bout no birds."

"Did," she said. "Did, too."

She sometimes got terribly excited if you argued too much with her in the middle of the night. I didn't want her thrashing about, falling over the furniture, getting the house up, so I just lay there shaking my head but without ever saying no to her again.

"Youngun, you oughten to have them birds in the house," she said. "A house ain't no place for no birds. Birds need to be shot. Need it bad. A wild bird oughten to be in your hand. In your house. A house is for folks. Trees and the sky yonderway for birds. I tol you bout the birds."

Auntie was not just right in the head, and I knew it. She was, as they said in Bacon County, *that way*. You couldn't go crazy in Bacon County; you were just *that way*. She was a little, frail thing who had an amazing strength in her spidery hands. Under the voluminous skirts she always wore, her bones seemed as brittle as a bird's. She was born, she was quick to tell you, a slave. But she did not know how old she was. If you asked her, she would say, "Round about a hundret." More than once mama had told me Auntie was *that way* because of her age.

In a deliberately whining voice I knew she could accept, I said, "I wish you'd *tol* me bout the birds, Auntie."

Her head cocked again, listening. "You know a bird can go ahead on a spit like a snake," she said. "Spit jest like a snake. I know you know that."

I didn't know a bird could spit like a snake, but once she said it, it sounded marvelously, horribly right to me. After the words came out of her old shrunken mouth that had known everything and said everything, it was hard for me to imagine a bird *not* spitting like a snake. And never mind that I had no idea how a snake might spit.

"Birds spit like a snake and never hit you but in one place," she said, pausing, holding the silence like a measure while she looked at me expectantly. Then, when it was obvious I didn't know: "Right in the mouf."

She got out of the chair and came to the bed and stooped for me. She took me out of the bed like my daddy might have done, in spite of the fact that wasted as I was, I must have weighed as much or more than she did. She took me out of the room and through the long shotgun corridor running down the middle of the house to the room where the birds were kept.

At the screen door giving onto the bird room, she stopped, and we stood looking in. There was enough light from the moon falling through the two tall windows for us to see the outlines of the nests where they were built on little tree limbs nailed into position on a counter along one side of the room and see the birds themselves, grown restless now, their wings fluttering and their heads bobbing silhouetted in the moonlight.

"Look in there, youngun," she said. "Look in there and *bleve*. A bird mought take you to hell. Mought take you anywhere at all. Me, I been grieved more than some, you up here in the house with them birds. Them spittin like snakes, lookin to hit you all up in your mouf. One hit you—an one *gone* hit you—that bird own you, own all of you. Now you look in there an *bleve*."

Her old soft voice got sharp when she demanded that I believe. But she could have saved it; I'd been a righteous believer in the deadly accuracy of bird spit long before we came down the hall.

"Bird spit mix all up with your spit, and then your spit is his and he's you. You listening, chile? Listen good to ole Auntie cause I think a bird . . . a bird moughta . . . a . . ."

She could not seem to go on and turned, still holding me against her thin, bony breast, and went back down the darkened hallway to the room and put me in my bed. She sat again in her chair and was quiet a long time before she could speak. I waited because I knew there was more to come and she had scared me pretty good back there in the dark with the birds moving against the moonlit windows. Her mouth moved silently over some words.

"I think a bird is . . . spit in you mouf, chile."

I struggled to sit up but couldn't against my drawn legs, so I was reduced to getting as far away from her as I could on the other side of the bed. I was terrified. I could hear the house through the night settling around us, making all the night noises that an old house can make, beams creaking, boards popping, all of it settling deeper into its foundation.

Then in a hushed, scared voice she described in great detail how she had seen me come down the road toward the tenant house one night late, climb the fence, and start off into the cotton field. I had been wearing, she said, my gown and I had gone out into the cotton field and walked in one great circle before finally stopping and looking up into the sky at the moon for a long, long time. She had been at the window and had seen it all, and it scared her bad because she knew right off a bird must have been at my mouth and that I was not in control of what I was doing. It had been the doings of birds.

She sat a long, still time before she finally said: "Chile, if the bird done got you, don't hex on old Auntie."

She laughed in a startled kind of way. It sounded like real craziness, but she came over and tickled me. I didn't laugh with her but lay like something dead because sleepwalking had been such a mysterious, unanswerable horror, had terrified me so profoundly that I was perfectly willing to believe that I was possessed by birds, had been guided to the field by them. She kept chuckling and clucking, but when I would not respond, she went back and sat in her chair.

"Jest two things," she said. "Don't you hex and don't you conjure on Auntie. Not on ole Auntie."

I was too afraid to look at her, but when I did find the courage after a while, she had her eyes fixed upon me, and they were no longer the eyes of the little old lady I had played with and laughed with in the pages of the Sears, Roebuck catalogue. They were the eyes now of a long-caged ancient stinking monkey, crazed with some unknowable outrage.

She said: "Won't do no good conjurin on me." She leaned forward out of her chair. "I be a conjure woman, too."

I knew even then what a conjure woman was, knew that it had to do with the bones of chickens and the stomachs of goats and hair and pins and fire and sickness and death.

When I could finally speak, I said: "Ain't no bird spit in my mouth. I may be afflicted, but I ain't no bird. Nothing in here but me."

We never spoke of it again. Several times I tried unsuccessfully to work up the nerve to do it. But I *did* let the birds out of their room the next morning. Or rather I told mama to do it.

"Turn out the birds," I said when she came in with my breakfast.

"Turn'm out?" she said.

"All of'm," I said. "Don't leave one in the house."

She did not understand, but as sick as I was she would probably have done anything to keep from upsetting me. She didn't understand, but I did. I had already learned—without knowing I'd learned it—that every single thing in the world was full of mystery and awesome power. And it was only by right ways of doing things—ritual ways—that kept any of us safe. Making stories about them was not so that we could understand them but so that we could live with them. A part of me knew that, at best, I had no right to keep flying birds in a closed room, and at the same time, another part of me knew that if there were no birds in the house, one could not spit in my mouth. It all made perfect sense to me. Fantasy might not be truth as the world counts it, but what was truth when fantasy meant survival?

Seven

I was in the bed for six weeks with my legs drawn up, and I never expect to spend a longer six weeks in my life. The visits by the doctors became fewer and fewer, and finally, they did not come anymore. They
had done all they knew to do. I think I was an embarrassment to them.

The fever was gone. There were cramps still in the middle of the
night, but about all that could be done for them was to have Auntie rub
my legs, which she did. The uncle who spoke in tongues came back and
fell across my bed several times. Even that did not cure me.

For reasons nobody ever knew, toward the end of September my legs
had loosened up a little and I was able to sit on the porch for a while
every day if I wanted to. I was on the porch when the last load of cotton
was hauled off to Blackshear in the back of the pickup truck, on the
way to a huge open-sided warehouse where the buyers would walk
among the high-stacked bales, followed by the farmers, many of them
wearing new overalls and new brogans, their ancient black hats pulled
low over their grim faces as they listened to the buyers tell what a year
of their sweat and worry was worth.

Sam sat beside me on the porch, but he too was in a bad way. Old age
had dropped on him sudden as a stone. He had lost the sight in both
eyes within a period of less than a week, and he had started to bleed
from his ears. The bleeding was not continuous, just a kind of spotting
that left an irregular and inconstant blood spoor wherever he went.

Because my legs were loose enough to allow me to be carried about
over the farm to the tobacco barn, out to sit under the oak tree, down
to the abandoned barn to see my goats in the afternoon, I got to see the
last catch Sam ever made before he had to be taken down behind the
field and killed with a shotgun. Sam and I were taking the weak fall sun
on the front porch one morning when daddy came walking up from the
mule lot. He carried his left arm hooked up at the elbow, his hand held
up in front of him. His hand was bloody, and blood had run down over
the sleeve of his shirt.

He stopped at the edge of the porch and said: "Son, I believe I'm gone have to borry your dog. Will and me been trying to load that old brood sow and damned if she ain't bout bit my finger off here."

He took me off the porch, and Sam fell in behind us, following, as he had to do now, the sound daddy's feet made over the dry sand down to the lot where the enormous sow stood grunting and snorting in the corner of the fence. Her eyes were red, and a light white froth fringed her snout. They opened the gate for Sam and whistled him inside. Once he was in the lot with the sow, daddy spoke softly to him.

"Git'er, Sam. Sic'er."

Sam's great solid head rose and his nostrils flared and his pointed ears struck forward on his head. Once he got a fix on the sow from the sound she was making backed in the corner, he did not hesitate but charged blindly. When he and the sow collided, he took a deep hold on one of her long, thick ears, and using all his weight, managing at the same time not to get caught on the tusks curling out of her mouth, he threw and held her fast, she squealing like the end of the world. Will and daddy went in and got an ear twist and nose twist on her and, after choking Sam off, led her like a lamb into the pickup truck which had high wooden livestock sides on it.

There was a snap in the air now and the winds every day grew higher than the day before and the leaves were beginning to thin on the oak tree. By the first of October I was able to ride around the farm in my goat cart pulled by Old Black Bill. Willalee Bookatee was not allowed to ride with me but had to walk alongside the cart instead. I felt very keenly how being a cripple had ruined our play, ruined all the things we used to do. That knowledge made me miserable and bad company. If Willalee minded it, he never said anything about it as he followed my cart around the fields in early fall.

We watched them bank sweet potatoes in pyramid-shaped mounds of earth and straw in such fashion that they would keep all winter long, and we watched them take the Irish potatoes to the cotton house (which would not be used again to store cotton for nearly a year) and spread them out in a single layer over the entire floor. And when the air got sharp enough, we watched daddy castrate twenty shoats in a single morning, watched him as he stood straddle of the pigs, one foot on their heads, their legs spread and he, bloody up to his elbows, reached and made two neat delicate incisions, removed the shoats' gonads, first one, and then the other, and finally tossed them into a pan where later they would be deep-fried in a flour batter. With such skill and grace and precision did he move that the entire operation seemed a single movement.

Then the ride ended one day because mama decided it was too cold even though I was bundled up nicely there behind Old Black Bill. I felt relief as much as anything else, grateful as I was to get inside where nobody else could see me. More than one mule and wagon passing on the high road had stopped while a gaunt farmer and his wife—sometimes with a wagon bed full of children—stared at me. Looking the way I did, I knew it was inevitable that the county begin thinking of me not as a cripple but as "that way." And I desperately did not want to be *that way*.

So I had to go back to my bed, which had been moved by the fireplace in the living room. But I didn't have to stay in the bed all the time. My heels were no longer drawn up tightly against me. I could crab about over the house in surprisingly quick lateral movement.

One of my favorite places to be was in the corner of the room where the ladies were quilting. God, I loved the click of needles on thimbles, a sound that will always make me think of stories. When I was a boy, stories were conversation and conversation was stories. For me it was a time of magic.

It was always the women who scared me. The stories that women told and that men told were full of violence, sickness, and death. But it was the women whose stories were unrelieved by humor and filled with apocalyptic vision. No matter how awful the stories were that the men told they were always funny. The men's stories were stories of character, rather than of circumstance, and they always knew the people the stories were about. But women would repeat stories about folks they did not know and had never seen, and consequently, without character counting for anything, the stories were as stark and cold as legend or myth.

It is midmorning, and the women have been sewing since right after breakfast when the light first came up. They are quilting, four women, one on each side of a square frame that has been suspended from the ceiling to hold the quilt. When they are through for the day, the frame can be drawn up to the ceiling out of the way, but for now the needles and thimbles click over the quiet, persistent drone of their voices.

I sit on the floor, and with me are two white-haired children, brightly decorated with purple medicine used for impetigo, and we sit there on

the floor, the three of us, sucking on sugar tits, trying to avoid the notice of our mothers, who will only stop long enough to slap us if the
noise of our play gets in the way of the necessary work of making quilts.

The sugar tits we are sucking on are to quiet and pacify us through
the long day. They could not have worked better if they had been opium
instead of flour soaked with syrup or sometimes plain sugar wrapped in
a piece of cloth. We chew on the cloth and slowly the melting sweetness
seeps onto our tongues and it puts us into a kind of stupor of delight,
just the mood to receive the horror story when it comes.

"The Lord works in mysterious ways."

The needles click; the heavy, stockinged legs shift almost imperceptibly.

"None of us knows the reason."

They start talking about God. We know the horror story's coming.

"But it is a reason."

"Like the song says: Farther along we'll understand why."

"In heaven it'll be clearer, but here on earth He works in mysterious
ways His many miracles to perform."

"It's no way to understand how things can sometimes be so awful. We
jest got to take the good with the bad."

"I reckon."

"A week ago tomorrow I heard tell of something that do make a body
wonder, though."

Nobody asks what she heard. They know she'll tell. The needles click
over the thimbles in the stretching silence. Down on the floor we stop
sucking and have the sugar tits caught between our teeth.

Here it comes.

"You all member Bernice's next to youngest girl, Flo?"

"Is it the one with that pretty yeller hair saved at Ten Mile Baptist
Church when Reverend Harvey was in to preach?"

"That's the one, always smart as a whip and they sent her to Waycross, all the way there, after graduation to college, took a business
course and she's been working with Dr. Barnes in Almer since she had
to quit school when that youngest of theirs was born. Anyway, I was
over there a week ago tomorrow when Flo come in from work—got a
real good job answering the telephone and typing up things. She took
the typewriter in college, you know. She come on in from work and told
me and Bernice the whole thing."

She stopped to draw a long good breath, and the clicking needles hesitate while the breath is drawn and then click furiously, faster than ever.

"A womern come in off the street and set down. Flo didn't know her but thought she might could have been a Woodbine womern, course it could a been any of 'm at all or somebody else from down in there. Dr. Barnes, you know, done a lot of charity in Woodbine. Didn't give her name to Flo, that is one of Flo's jobs to git their names, but the womern didn't give it or nothing, jest set down there and Flo seen blood running down her laig.

"Said the womern looked in her face like she was asleep or something, not crying or moaning, and all the time blood—an I don't mean a little blood but I mean blood everywhere—was puddling in the floor like you'd taken and cut a hog's throat and it was coming from under this woman's dress and a running down her laig."

And us there on the floor thinking, Merciful God, we'll all drown in blood before this is over.

"Flo didn't do a thing but go back there and tell Dr. Barnes it was a womern out there a setting in the chair a bleeding. Course, Dr. Barnes, he went right and got her and tuck her in his little room and it weren't but a minute before Flo said she heard screaming and she known right off what it was and she run back there and opened the door to that little room. It was then that she seen it."

Under the frame we can see all movement leave the stockinged legs, the knees tense, flex—all except the legs of the woman telling the story. Hers move in a timely, monotonous rhythm with the sound of her voice. And then the voice stopped, I remember her legs never missing a beat in the curious little dance she is doing.

"What Flo seen was the doctor had bent the womern over a table and had her dress flung up over her head and from between. . . ."

Here a nervous glance at us, sitting rigid now against the wall, our teeth caught in the sugar tits in a spasm of horrors.

". . . between her cheeks—and I'm talking about the aner—out of her very aner came this little arm with a little hand on the end of it.

"It was a little baby arm. Flo said she couldn't breathe, talk, or do nothing but just stand there staring at that little arm with that little hand on the end of it. Flo said them little fingers commenced to move, wrinkled as prunes, and them little fingers seemed like they was a beckoning at Flo. Them's her very words: *a beckoning*.

"Flo said she felt like she was gone faint, but before she could do it, the doctor took hold of that little arm, and when he did, that womern taken and given another scream and jumped from where he had her flung over the table and run out of the room. Flo almost fainted, she said, but she didn't till she saw how it all come out. The doctor run after her and it taken three men to catch her in the street and hold her while the doctor taken and given her a shot."

Down on the floor I would have sucked all the sweetness out of the sugar tit and by then eaten most of the sacking that held it.

At night it was a different story. Since I had become sick, we had a lot of company, especially at night. The people in the county had never seen such legs as mine. The first thing they had to do was inspect my legs, staring at me where I lay, often wanting to touch me, sometimes actually doing it, ten or twelve people in a row.

Then some of them would leave and some would stay to sit by the fireplace late into the night, listening to the men talk, staying so late now and then they would end up staying all night, particularly if it was a weekend.

Because the only fireplace was in the living room where I lay, everybody gathered there after supper to watch the fire and eventually wash their feet and go off to bed. If it was a very cold night, they would carry a heated quilt from the fire to put over the icy sheets.

The stories start early in the night when the fire is as big as the hearth will hold, making its own sucking roar counterpoint to the roar of the wind under the shingled eaves of the house. Men and women and children sit in a wide semicircle, faces cast red and hollow-eyed by the fire. Auntie, who still stayed with me at night, floats into and out of the room, sometimes settling by my bed, sometimes going back to the kitchen to get something for me. Now and again, a woman or young girl will rise from her chair, back up to the hearthstone and discreetly lift her skirt from behind to receive the fire. My legs have loosened now to the point where I could, if I really tried, sit in a chair, and the doctors have begun to revise their original opinion and say that, yes, there was a real chance that I might walk again.

The galvanized foot tub, holding perhaps two and a half gallons of water, captures the light on its dull surface. It is sitting in front of the first man in the semicircle. The water is getting hot. At some time dur-ing the evening, the man in front of whom it sits will slip his feet into the tub and wash. Then he will slide it to the person sitting next to him, maybe a woman, or a young girl, and that person will wash.

While the men talk, the tub makes its way around the line of people warming from the fire. After the last person washes his feet, it is only minutes before the other children will have to go off to bed and leave their daddies and uncles and older brothers to sit and talk late into the night. But I, safely in my fireroom bed, am privileged to hear whatever is said.

"Well, he was always like that."

"Had to happen like it had to happen."

"He jest had to win."

"He *would* win."

"Kill him to lose, jest kill'm is all."

"I remember. . . ."

Here the man would lean back and chew on a kitchen match, and the skin would draw tight around his eyes. He might not say anything for several minutes, but those of us sitting there, watching him chew on the match stick, didn't care how long he took to start the story because we knew that he was about to make what had been only gossip before personal and immediate now. The magic words had been spoken: "I re-member. . . ."

"I remember the day it happened. I wasn't sitting more than five or six feet from them when they got started talking on it. But I guess it was meant to happen. Both of them doing the same kind of work and him being like he was, it was bound to come to blood sooner or later.

"The hell of it was they liked each other. Nearabout like brothers as two people who ain't blood likely to git. It's how come them both to git on the same job at the same time climbing and topping trees for the REA right-of-way. They was both good at it, too. Jest about the god-awfulest climbers you ever seen. Like monkeys nearabout where climb-ing was concerned.

"First time I notice them talking about it, they was eating out of their dinner buckets, and I heard Leroy say, 'You cain't beat me at nothing. That's what you can beat me at, Pete, *nothing.*'

"What they was arguing about was which one of them could climb the fastest, and Leroy, of course, right away said it was him, said there was nobody in the state of Georgia could climb a tree or nothing else as fast as him, Leroy, could. Leroy's face was all red, the veins standing out in his neck, and he was kind of slobbering like a dog. You remember, he was bad to slobber. Oh, he was hot about it, he was.

"Pete musta said he could climb faster than Leroy—I didn't hear it, but that musta been what he said—and now Leroy was inviting him out to see which one of them was the best at it. You see, we'd put up light poles down the middle of the right-of-way we'd cut, but it weren't no insulation knobs or crosspieces on them yetawhile.

"Nothing wouldn't do Leroy, soon as Pete said he could climb faster'n him, but the two of'm go on out there and both of'm git at the bottom of two different poles and somebody else git between the two poles to start'm climbing by clapping his hands. First one to the top could be the winner. Leroy wouldn't have it no other way.

"Pete tried to back out of it three times, but Leroy said: 'No, goddammit, you ought not to a gone and said I couldn't do it. Said I was slower'n you. Now we got to see whose ass is the blackest.'

"That boy had a bad mouth, he did. Always had one, jest like his daddy. Anyway, they got up from their dinner buckets and put on their climbing rigs: big thick safety belts that loop around the pole, then inch-and-a-half climbing jack-spikes buckled to their boots. Leroy walked off down the line and got at the bottom of one of them lectric poles and Pete, he got on the nigh pole. On account of I was the closest one to him, they said: 'You get in the middle there, Bob, and do it for us. You clap the third time, we go.'

"Well, I didn't want to do it cause I was afraid Pete might somehow beat him, and if he did, Leroy might kill somebody, maybe hisself. He was crazy about winning. At anything. I'd heard him myself say he'd jest as soon die as lose. Nothing wouldn't do him, though, but I git in the middle and start them off, which I did.

"They had the wide safety belts looped around the poles and their spikes set when I clapped my hand. They started climbing, and I seen right away that Leroy didn't have nothing to worry about. It made me feel better that nobody was gone git hurt, and I stood back to watch the climb.

"Before his spikes hit the pole six times, he was already a foot higher than Pete was. What he was doing, see, was going for it, gonna win or bust.

"He was holding onto the safety belt that went around the pole with both hands and he was a climbing, puffing, his feet working, hitting that lectric pole with them spikes, driving up it, and when his feet would come up to take a fresh hold, he'd flip that leather belt with both hands and he was looking down, straight down between his pumping knees, and never looking up and flipping that belt and driving with his feet, and when he got to the top of the pole, well, bless Pat, he didn't do a thing but flip that leather belt right over the top of that pole and come sailing back down on the back of his head and broke his neck. Dead fore we could git there. Damn boy'd do anything to win. It was so smooth, it looked like a goddamn trick. It mighta been, too."

Eight

GRADUALLY, very gradually, I got more and more use of my legs, and finally, they were completely straight. I could straighten them all the way out so that the knees locked. My bed was taken out of the fire-room, and I myself was put out by the fence to hold onto the wire and walk around the house and around the house, despite the fact that from hip to heel my legs were nothing but bone loosely covered with dimpled, wrinkled skin, so ugly that nobody short of your God or your mama could have any faith in them.

I did not particularly want to walk around the house holding onto the fence. It was painful and boring and more than a little hopeless, but mama gently encouraged me and would sometimes walk along with me. If she wasn't with me, Willalee and blind Sam was nosing at my heels out there by the fence. Willalee was as depressed by my legs as I was. My being crippled had changed his life nearly as much as it had changed mine. And Sam was sick in a way he had never been before. The bleeding in his ears was not as bad as it had been, but he had started losing his teeth. Within a month of the time he had lost the first one, nearly all of them were gone. With our loving him as we all did, it was getting very close to the place where it would be unbearable.

One day Willalee's daddy, Will, came to me out by the fence. I knew right off it was going to be bad when he took my arm and helped me to the porch. Then he sent his boy home while he talked to me.

"Your daddy sent me to talk to you," he said.

"What about?"

"He woulda come hisself, but he wanted me to do hit. He thought I better do the talking."

"Do what?" I said, but I already knew. I'd known it was coming and that it wouldn't be long.

He looked out at the brown, cut-over fields under a lowering fall sky. The stalks had been cut already, cotton stalks and corn stalks and to-bacco stalks, and the landscape had that butchered quality peculiar to

Bacon County just before winter comes down in earnest.

"I got to take Sam off yonder behind the field," he finally said.

I didn't say anything.

"I got to do hit today." Then after a long pause: "Now."

"I reckon," I finally said.

"It ain't right to leave him like this," he said. "Sam been too good a dog. Him blind, he won't even know about hit."

"I don't reckon," I said. I was trying to keep from crying, not because Will was there, but because I felt how useless and silly it was to cry. If you couldn't cure an animal, you killed it. And nobody ever cured anything of old age. If constant and unrelievable pain was the alternative, death was right. There wasn't anything to talk about.

I could feel Sam breathing there where he stood in the dust by the porch. I didn't call his name, and I didn't look at him.

"All right," I said.

Will took a short lead rope out of his back pocket and dropped a loop around Sam's neck. Sam followed him off down the lane, his huge square head down, his wet tongue hanging out of the side of his mouth.

Later, when I was back by the fence, walking, I heard the single shot-gun blast in the woods behind the house. That was when I cried.

By late January I was able to walk all the way out to the lot by myself and watch them as they sheared the mules with hand clippers. The mules would grow a thick coat of hair as winter came on to keep them warm. But when the farmers started breaking ground in early February, or as soon as the ground thawed, the mules carried so much hair that they couldn't stand to work in front of a turnplow all day unless they were clipped.

I never knew any mules that liked to have their hair cut. That busy steel mouth chewing away over their hides brought them to the place of blasted nerves and blasted bowels. The problem was solved by putting on a nose twist, a simple loop of plowline over the mule's upper lip with a stick through the loop so that it could be twisted tight enough to bring a little blood, not much, but a little blood down from the upper lip, tracing a thin line over the gum and teeth.

When the blood began to show, I began to cry. At first it was only a whimper with a few tears, but before Will, who held the twist, and daddy, who did the clipping, had finished with the third mule, I was nearly in hysterics. It embarrassed me terribly and embarrassed Willalee, too, who was there with me in the corner of the lot, but I could not help it. I do not know whether it was from my long stay in the bed with paralysis or whether it was from the increasing violence in the house at night—the shouting and screaming and sounds of breaking dishes and splintering chairs—brought on by daddy's bouts with whiskey, but I had been crying more and more as the winter deepened, crying as I had never done before, over anything or nothing. Sometimes when I was right by myself, tears would burst from my eyes.

Daddy tried to get me to go to the house, but I would not, and because I had been so sick for so long, he did not make me get out of the lot, as he might otherwise have done. They put off clipping the fourth, and last, mule until a time when they could do it without me being aware of it. And still I cried. Every time I looked up and saw the three trembling, naked mules, a bloody foam at their mouths, I fell into a louder fit of crying.

Daddy, who had been holding me in his arms, trying to comfort me, finally asked in a desperate voice—for he could not bear my tears—how I would like to go in the wagon with Will to Mr. John Turner's farm, a place about six miles away. Willalee could go, too. Since I almost never got off the farm, and had not been anywhere since I got sick, not even to church, I snuffled and hiccuped and was finally quiet.

When mama found out about it, she was immediately against it, which threw me instantly back into hysterics, and she relented. We left the farm, Willalee and I, in the bed of the wagon, wrapped up together with just our heads showing, and Will up front on the crossboard, driving the only mule on the place that still had his hair.

Will was on his way to Mr. John Turner's place to help a horsing mare couple with a jack. Will was known throughout the county as a man successful in such matters, a man who could, with his hands and voice, gentle down jacks and mares and, consequently, keep their breeding from being any bloodier than it had to be.

When we got to Mr. Turner's lot, Willalee and I climbed up on the top board of the fence and watched the mare loping around the lot, agitated, her wild eyes rolling, her tail lifted, and her jaws working around a light froth that bubbled from her mouth. We did not have to be told that she was horsing, that is to say, that she was ready to receive a male, either a stallion or a jack. From a stallion, Mr. Turner could expect a horse or mare colt in the spring; from a jack—a male donkey—he could expect a mule. In this instance, he was looking for a mule, and the jack was already there, haltered and hitched, waiting outside the lot. The jack was about half as tall as the mare, and no more than a third her weight, but he had already smelled her and his huge ears were pitched forward and his mouth, too, was champing and foaming. He was ready to work.

Will went in the lot and got a loop of plowline around the neck of the charging mare, and then a halter. While she rolled her eyes and grunted and slobbered—all the while pulling Will around the lot, dust swirling at their feet—Will talked to her in a low, unhurried voice. They let the jack in, and without hesitation he galloped across the lot on his stubby, ugly little legs and bit the mare on the rump. She, just as quickly, kicked him twice in the chest. The jack's eyes shot with blood, and he wheeled and kicked her in the side with both feet. As they pitched and rared and bit and kicked, Will—still talking on in his soft and soothing voice—was working the mare to the hole dug in the middle of the lot. He had to get the mare backed down into the hole or the little jack would never be able to mount.

On the lot fence, I had begun to whimper, not as badly as I had done earlier at the clipping, but tears were beginning to form nonetheless. There was obviously no reason to cry because nobody was doing anything to the animals; they were doing whatever hurt was being done to each other. But still the tears were about to come.

"You know how come it is," said Willalee, "mules cain't do it an git little mules like goats do it and git little goats or hogs do it?"

"No," I said. I knew it was true, but I didn't know why. I had never thought to wonder.

"Well," said Willalee, "in the time of Jesus. . . ."

While his daddy got the mare into the hole to receive the jack, Willalee Bookatee told a story he'd got from Auntie about how it was a mule that had carried the beams out of which Jesus' cross was made and for that reason the mule had forever after been deprived of the joy of coupling with his own kind.

Just as the little jack was driving the mare to her knees with his final, savage thrust, Willalee was saying in his wisest voice: "It also how come mules have to work so hard at the plow, on account of what all they done in olden time. Auntie say so."

All of us grew up in Bacon County surrounded by sexual couplings of every kind. Nobody ever tried to keep such matters from us. It would have been impossible anyhow. Even though I was only five years old at the time, in some vague, unconscious way I knew that people must do the same thing as animals, more or less, but it had never occurred to me that *I* might be expected to try it. Therefore, it was a real jolt when my brother sidled up to me one day and said: "It's time you got yourself a little piece, boy."

I knew very well what he meant, but I resisted it. "A piece of what?" I said.

He told me.

"Naaawww," I said.

"Yep," he said with chilling finality.

I told him I did not know anything about it, nothing at all. He proceeded to tell me all about it, in much greater detail than I wanted to listen to. He told me how it was done and where I was to do it—under the house—and further that I should put the girl on top of an old dishpan that he had already thoughtfully stored under there for me.

"On a damn dishpan?" I said. When I was away from grownups, I had recently begun to see how all the curse words I knew would fit my mouth.

"Ain't nothing bettern a dishpan," he said. "Put her up on that dishpan when you lay'er down and it'll turn that thing up to you like a fried egg."

I didn't know why I wanted it turned up like a fried egg, but Hoyet said I would see how it all worked once I got started. More than that, I didn't really want to do it because I couldn't see any sense in it, but my brother clinched it for me when he said: "It always comes a time in a man's life when he's got to do it. Purvis says it's sure as death." Purvis was a boy who worked for one of our uncles, but he was already old enough to come home drunk and bloody at daylight, for which we greatly admired him. If it was good enough for Purvis, it was good enough for me. Lottie Mae was the girl.

It was cold enough to crack your eyeballs, and Lottie Mae and I were bundled up in clothing. But I worked at her shivering, buttoned-up little body as best I could and finally got her out of her clothes there where I had her under the house that sat up about two and a half feet on blocks made out of brick. We were trembling, both us naked as babies, as I struggled to get her up on the dishpan. To get her square-legged, home-made drawers off I had to promise she could play with me and Willalee in the catalogue.

She didn't know any more about it than I did, and at first she thought I wanted to see her pee. When she did begin to see what I had in mind, she thought I was crazy.

"It ain't *no* way to do that," she said. "Ain't gone *do*. Try if you wants to, but I know it won't do."

I carefully explained to her what my brother said we should do, and while I talked, I watched her eyes grow rounder and rounder and her mouth go slack, and even though she shook her head the whole time I was saying it, she did not balk at the dishpan and I finally had her on it, both of us full of chill bumps from the cold. Just as I was about to mount, to do God knows what, because in the wind I was rapidly forgetting my brother's instructions, I heard something behind me, and when I looked over my shoulder, I saw mama's stout legs, those knees flexed and ready.

"Come out from under there, youngun," mama said. And I did. I came out quickly, head already contritely down heading for the place where she would catch and hold me while she violently shredded a peach tree switch over my upturned bottom, stung by the cold, cheeks red already.

Never a word about my crippled legs and never a word about the months in bed, so recent I still had small sores the size of fever blisters on my back. It was the first whipping I'd had since I got sick, and I knew that I was well and whole again.

Nine

As winter grew deeper and we waited for hog-killing time, at home the center was not holding. Whether it was because the crops were in and not much work was to be done or whether it was because of my having just spent so long a time crippled in the bed, daddy had grown progressively crazier, more violent. He was gone from home for longer and longer periods of time, and during those brief intervals when he was home, the crashing noise of breaking things was everywhere about us. Daddy had also taken to picking up the shotgun and screaming threats while he waved it about, but at that time he had not as yet fired it.

While that was going on, it occurred to me for the first time that being alive was like being awake in a nightmare.

I remember saying aloud to myself: "Scary as a nightmare. Jest like being awake in a nightmare."

Never once did I ever think that my life was not just like everybody else's, that my fears and uncertainties were not universal. For which I can only thank God. Thinking so could only have made it more bearable.

My sleepwalking had become worse now that I could get out of bed on my unsure legs. I woke up sometimes in the middle of the night in the dirt lane by the house or sometimes sitting in my room in a corner chewing on something. It didn't matter much what: the sleeve of my gown or the side of my hand or even one time the laces of a shoe. And when I would wake up, it was always in terror, habitually remembering now what Auntie had said about the birds spitting in my mouth. No, more than *remembering* what she had said. Rather, seeing what she had said, the image of a bird burned clearly on the backs of my eyelids, its beak hooked like the nose of a Byzantine Christ, shooting spit thick as phlegm on a solid line into my open and willing mouth. With such dreams turning in my head it came time for us to all help kill and butcher hogs. Daddy was laid up somewhere drunk; we had not seen him in four days. So he did not go with us to Uncle Alton's to help with the slaughter. Farm families swapped labor at hog-killing time just as they swapped labor to put in tobacco or pick cotton. Early one morning our tenant farmers, mama, my brother, and I walked the half mile to Uncle Alton's place to help put a year's worth of meat in the smokehouse. Later his family would come and help us do the same thing.

Before it was over, everything on the hog would have been used. The lights (lungs) and liver—together called haslet—would be made into a fresh stew by first pouring and pouring again fresh water through the slit throat—the exposed throat called a goozle—to clean the lights out good. Then the fat would be trimmed off and put with the fat trimmed from the guts to cook crisp into cracklins to mix with cornbread or else put in a wash pot to make soap.

The guts would be washed and then turned and washed again. Many times. After the guts had been covered with salt overnight, they were used as casings for sausage made from shoulder meat, tenderloin, and—if times were hard—any kind of scrap that was not entirely fat.

The eyes would be removed from the head, then the end of the snout cut off, and the whole thing boiled until the teeth could be picked out. Whatever meat was left, cheeks, ears, and so on, would be picked off, crushed with herbs and spices and packed tightly into muslin cloth for hog's headcheese.

The fat from the liver, lungs, guts, or wherever was cooked until it was as crisp as it would get and then packed into tin syrup buckets to be ground up later for cracklin cornbread. Even the feet were removed, and after the outer layer of split hooves was taken off, the whole thing was boiled and pickled in vinegar and peppers. If later in the year the cracklins started to get rank, they would be thrown into a cast-iron wash pot with fried meat's grease, any meat for that matter that might have gone bad in the smokehouse, and some potash and lye and cooked into soap, always made on the full of the moon so it wouldn't shrink. I remember one time mama out in the backyard making soap when a chicken for some reason tried to fly over the wash pot but didn't make it. The chicken dropped flapping and squawking into the boiling fat and lye. Mama, who was stirring the mixture with an old ax handle, never missed a beat. She just stirred the chicken right on down to the bottom. Any kind of meat was good for making soap.

By the time we got to Uncle Alton's the dirt floor of the smokehouse had been covered with green pine tops. After the pork stayed overnight in tubs of salt, it would be laid on the green pine straw all night, some-

times for two nights, to get all the water out of it. Then it was taken up
and packed again in salt for three or four days. When it was taken out of
the salt for the last time, it was dipped in plain hot water or else in a solution of crushed hot peppers and syrup or wild honey. Then it was
hung over a deep pile of smoldering hickory spread across the entire
floor of the smokehouse. The hickory was watched very carefully to
keep any sort of blaze from flaring up. Day and night until it was over,
light gray smoke boiled continuously from under the eaves and around
the door where the meat was being cured. It was the sweetest smoke a
man was ever to smell.

It was a bright cold day in February 1941, so cold the ground was still
frozen at ten o'clock in the morning. The air was full of the steaming
smell of excrement and the oily, flatulent odor of intestines and the heavy
sweetness of blood—in every way a perfect day to slaughter animals. I
watched the hogs called to the feeding trough just as they were every
morning except this morning it was to receive the ax instead of slop.

As little slop *was* poured into their long communal trough, enough to
make them stand still while Uncle Alton or his boy Theron went quietly
among them with the ax, using the flat end like a sledgehammer (shells
were expensive enough to make a gun out of the question). He would
approach the hog from the rear while it slopped at the trough, and then
he would straddle it, one leg on each side, patiently waiting for the hog
to raise its snout from the slop to take a breath, showing as it did the
wide bristled bone between its ears to the ax.

It never took but one blow, delivered expertly and with consummate
skill, and the hog was dead. He then moved with his hammer to the
next hog and straddled it. None of the hogs ever seemed to mind that
their companions were dropping dead all around them but continued in
a single-minded passion to eat. They didn't even mind when another of
my cousins (this could be a boy of only eight or nine because it took
neither strength nor skill) came right behind the hammer and drew a
long razor-boned butcher knife across the throat of the fallen hog.
Blood spurted with the still-beating heart, and a live hog would sometimes turn to one that was lying beside it at the trough and stick its
snout into the spurting blood and drink a bit just seconds before it had
its own head crushed.

It was a time of great joy and celebration for the children. We played
games and ran (I gimping along pretty well by then) and screamed and

brought wood to the boiler and thought of that night, when we would have fresh fried pork and stew made from lungs and liver and heart in an enormous pot that covered half the stove.

The air was charged with the smell of fat being rendered in tubs in the backyard and the sharp squeals of the pigs at the troughs, squeals from pure piggishness at the slop, never from pain. Animals were killed but seldom hurt. Farmers took tremendous precautions about pain at slaughter. It is, whether or not they ever admit it when they talk, a ritual. As brutal as they sometimes are with farm animals and with themselves, no farmer would ever eat an animal he had willingly made suffer.

The heel strings were cut on each of the hog's hind legs, and a stick, called a gambreling stick, or a gallus, was inserted into the cut behind the tendon and the hog dragged to the huge cast-iron boiler, which sat in a depression dug into the ground so the hog could be slipped in and pulled out easily. The fire snapped and roared in the depression under the boiler. The fire had to be tended carefully because the water could never quite come to a boil. If the hog was dipped in boiling water, the hair would set and become impossible to take off. The ideal temperature was water you could rapidly draw your finger through three times in succession without being blistered.

Unlike cows, which are skinned, a hog is scraped. After the hog is pulled from the water, a blunt knife is drawn over the animal, and if the water has not been too hot, the hair slips off smooth as butter, leaving a white, naked, utterly beautiful pig.

To the great glee of the watching children, when the hog is slipped into the water, it defecates. The children squeal and clap their hands and make their delightfully obscene children's jokes as they watch it all.

On that morning, mama was around in the back by the smokehouse where some hogs, already scalded and scraped, were hanging in the air from their heel strings being disemboweled. Along with the other ladies she was washing out the guts, turning them inside out, cleaning them good so they could later be stuffed with ground and seasoned sausage meat.

Out in front of the house where the boiler was, I was playing pop-the-whip as best I could with my brother and several of my cousins. Pop-the-whip is a game in which everyone holds hands and runs fast and then the leader of the line turns sharply. Because he is turning through a tighter arc than the other children, the line acts as a whip with each child farther down the line having to travel through a greater space and consequently having to go faster in order to keep up. The last child in the line literally gets *popped* loose and sent flying from his playmates.

I was popped loose and sent flying into the steaming boiler of water beside a scalded, floating hog.

I remember everything about it as clearly as I remember anything that ever happened to me, except the screaming. Curiously, I cannot remember the screaming. They say I screamed all the way to town, but I cannot remember it.

What I remember is John C. Pace, a black man whose daddy was also named John C. Pace, reached right into the scalding water and pulled me out and set me on my feet and stood back to look at me. I did not fall but stood looking at John and seeing in his face that I was dead.

The children's faces, including my brother's, showed I was dead, too. And I knew it must be so because I knew where I had fallen and I felt no pain—not in that moment—and I knew with the bone-chilling certainty most people are spared that, yes, death does come and mine had just touched me.

John C. Pace ran screaming and the other children ran screaming and left me standing there by the boiler, my hair and skin and clothes steaming in the bright cold February air.

In memory I stand there alone with the knowledge of death upon me, watching steam rising from my hands and clothes while everybody runs and, after everybody has gone, standing there for minutes while nobody comes.

That is only memory. It may have been but seconds before my mama and Uncle Alton came to me. Mama tells me she heard me scream and started running toward the boiler, knowing already what had happened. She has also told me that she could not bring herself to try to do anything with that smoking ghostlike thing standing by the boiler. But she did. They all did. They did what they could.

But in that interminable time between John pulling me out and my mother arriving in front of me, I remember first the pain. It didn't begin as bad pain, but rather like maybe sandspurs under my clothes.

I reached over and touched my right hand with my left, and the whole thing came off like a wet glove. I mean, the skin on the top of the wrist and the back of my hand, along with the fingernails, all just turned loose and slid on down to the ground. I could see my fingernails lying in the little puddle my flesh made on the ground in front of me.

Then hands were on me, taking off my clothes, and the pain turned into something words cannot touch, or at least my words cannot touch. There is no way for me to talk about it because when my shirt was taken off, my back came off with it. When my overalls were pulled down, my cooked and glowing skin came down.

I still had not fallen, and I stood there participating in my own butchering. When they got the clothes off me, they did the worst thing they could have done; they wrapped me in a sheet. They did it out of panic and terror and ignorance and love.

That day there happened to be a car at the farm. I can't remember who it belonged to, but I was taken into the backseat into my mama's lap—God love the lady, out of her head, pressing her boiled son to her breast—and we started for Alma, a distance of about sixteen miles. The only thing that I can remember about the trip was that I started telling mama that I did not want to die. I started saying it and never stopped.

The car we piled into was incredibly slow. An old car and very, very slow, and every once in a while Uncle Alton, who was like a daddy to me, would jump out of the car and run alongside it and helplessly scream for it to go faster and then he would jump on the running board until he couldn't stand it any longer and then he would jump off again.

But like bad beginnings everywhere, they sometimes end well. When I got to Dr. Sharp's office in Alma and he finally managed to get me out of the sticking sheet, he found that I was scalded over two-thirds of my body but that my head had not gone under the water (he said that would have killed me), and for some strange reason I have never understood, the burns were not deep. He said I would probably even outgrow the scars, which I have. Until I was about fifteen years old, the scars were puckered and discolored on my back and right arm and legs. But now their outlines are barely visible.

The only hospital at the time was thirty miles away, and Dr. Sharp said I'd do just as well at home if they built a frame over the bed to keep the covers off me and also kept a light burning over me twenty-four hours a day. (He knew as well as we did that I couldn't go to a hospital anyway, since the only thing Dr. Sharp ever got for taking care of me was satisfaction for a job well done, if he got that. Over the years, I was his most demanding and persistent charity, which he never mentioned to me or mama. Perhaps that is why in an age when it is fashionable to distrust and hate doctors, I love them.)

So they took me back home and put a buggy frame over my bed to make it resemble, when the sheet was on it, a covered wagon, and ran a line in from the Rural Electrification Administration so I could have the drying light hanging just over me. The pain was not nearly so bad now that I had for the first time in my life the miracle of electricity close enough to touch. The pain was bad enough, though, but relieved to some extent by some medicine Dr. Sharp gave us to spray out of a bottle onto the burns by pumping a black rubber ball. When it dried, it raised to form a protective, cooling scab. But it was bad to crack. The bed was always full of black crumbs, which Auntie worked continually at. When they brought me home, Auntie, without anybody saying a word to her, came back up the road to take care of me.

The same day Hollis Toomey came, too. He walked into the house without knocking or speaking to anyone. Nobody had sent for him. But whenever anybody in the county was burned, he showed up as if by magic, because he could talk the fire out of you. He did not call himself a faith healer, never spoke of God, didn't even go to church, although his family did. His was a gift that was real, and everybody in the county knew it was real. For reasons which he never gave, because he was the most reticent of men and never took money or anything else for what he did, he was drawn to a bad burn the way iron filings are drawn to a magnet, never even saying, "You're welcome," to those who thanked him. He was as sure of his powers and as implacable as God.

When he arrived, the light had not yet been brought into the house, and the buggy frame was not yet over my bed and I was lying in unsayable pain. His farm was not far from ours, and it was unlike any other in the county. Birds' nests made from gourds, shaped like crooked-necked squash with a hole cut in one side with the seeds taken out, hung everywhere from the forest of old and arching oak trees about his house. Undulating flocks of white pigeons flew in and out of his hayloft. He had a blacksmith shed, black as smut and always hot from the open hearth where he made among other things iron rims for wagon wheels. He could handcraft a true-shooting gun, including the barrel which was not smooth-bore but had calibrated riflings. He owned two oxen, heavier than mules, whose harness, including the double yoke, he had made himself. His boys were never allowed to take care of them. He watered them and fed them and pulled them now and again to stumps or trees. But he also had the only Belgian draft horse in the county. The horse was so monstrously heavy that you could hitch him to two spans of good mules—four of them—and he would walk off with them as though they were goats. So the oxen were really useless. It just pleased him to keep them.

He favored very clean women and very dirty men. He thought it was the natural order of things. One of the few things I ever heard him say, and he said it looking off toward the far horizon, speaking to nobody: "A man's got the *right* to stink."

His wife always wore her hair tightly bunned at the back of her head under a stiffly starched white bonnet. Her dresses were nearly to her ankles, and they always looked and smelled as if they had just come off the clothesline after a long day in the sun.

Hollis always smelled like his pockets were full of ripe chicken guts, and his overalls were as stiff as metal. He didn't wear a beard; he wore a stubble. The stubble was coal black despite the fact he was over sixty, and it always seemed to be the same length, the length where you've got to shave or start telling everybody you're growing a beard. Hollis Toomey did neither.

When I saw him in the door, it was as though a soothing balm had touched me. This was Hollis Toomey, who was from my county, whose boys I knew, who didn't talk to God about your hurt. He didn't even talk to *you*; he talked to the *fire*. A mosquito couldn't fly through a door he was standing in he was so wide and high, and more, he was obviously indestructible. He ran on his own time, went where he needed to go. Nobody ever thought of doing anything for him, helping him. If he wanted something, he made it. If he couldn't make it, he took it. Hollis Toomey was not a kind man.

My daddy had finally come home, red-eyed and full of puke. He was at the foot of the bed, but he didn't say a word while Hollis sat beside me.

Hollis Toomey's voice was low like the quiet rasping of a file on metal. I couldn't hear most of what he had to say, but that was all right because I stopped burning before he ever started talking. He talked to the fire like an old and respected adversary, but one he had beaten consistently and had come to beat again. I don't remember him once looking at my face while he explained: "Fire, this boy is mine. This bed is mine. This room is mine. It ain't nothing here that's yours. It's a lot that is, but it ain't nothing here that is."

At some point while he talked he put his hands on me, one of them spread out big as a frying pan, and I was already as cool as spring water. But I had known I would be from the moment I had seen him standing in the door. Before it was over, he cursed the fire, calling it all kinds of sonofabitch, but the words neither surprised nor shocked me. The tone of his voice made me know that he was locked in a real and terrible conflict with the fire. His hands flexed and hurt my stomach, but it was nothing compared to the pain that had been on me before he came.

I had almost dozed off when he suddenly got up and walked out of the room. My daddy called, "Thank you," in a weak, alcohol-spattered voice. Hollis Toomey did not answer.

When they finally got the buggy frame up, it was not as terrible as I at first thought it was going to be. I was, of course, by then used to the bed and that was no problem and the buggy frame gave a new dimension, a new feeling to the sickbed. With the frame arching over me it was a time for fantasy and magic because I lived in a sort of playhouse, a kingdom that was all mine.

At least I pretended it was a kingdom, pretended it in self-defense. I did not want to be there, but there was no help for it, so I might as well pretend it was a kingdom as anything else. And like every child who owns anything, I ruled it like a tyrant. There was something very special and beautiful about being the youngest member of a family and being badly hurt.

Since it pleased me to do so, I spent a lot of time with the Sears, Roebuck catalogue, started writing and nearly finished a detective novel, although at that time I had never seen a novel, detective or otherwise. I printed it out with a soft-lead pencil on lined paper, and it was about a boy who, for his protection, carried not a pistol but firecrackers. He solved crimes and gave things to poor people and doctors. The boy was also absolutely fearless.

I was given a great deal of ginger ale to drink because the doctor or mama or somebody thought that where burns were concerned, it had miraculous therapeutic value. This ginger ale was the store-bought kind, too, not some homemade concoction but wonderfully fizzy and capped in real bottles. Since Hoyet and I almost never saw anything from the store, I drank as much of it as they brought me, and they brought me a lot. I never learned to like it but could never get over my fascination with the bubbles that rose in the bottle under the yellow light hanging from the buggy frame.

But I was tired of being alone in bed, and since I was going into my second major hurt back to back, I decided I might as well assert myself.

Old Black Bill had sired several kids the previous spring, and one of them was himself black and a male, so I named him Old Black Bill, too, and he grew up with me under the buggy frame. No animal is allowed in a farmhouse in Bacon County, at least to my knowledge. Dogs stay in the yard. Cats usually live in the barn catching rats, and goats, well, goats only get in the house if they have first been butchered for the table.

But I had been scalded and I was special. And I knew even then that an advantage unused becomes no advantage at all. So I insisted Old Black Bill's kid be brought to my bed. I was only about three weeks into my recovery, and I thought that a goat would be good company.

They brought him in, and I fed him bits of hay and shelled corn under the buggy frame. We had long conversations. Or rather, I had long monologues and he, patiently chewing, listened.

The two tall windows at the foot of my bed opened onto a forty-acre field. Through the long winter days Old Black Bill and I watched it being prepared to grow another crop. First the cornstalks were cut by a machine with revolving blades, pulled by a single mule. Then two mules were hitched to a big rake, so big a man could ride on it. When all the stalks were piled and burned, the land had to be broken, completely turned under, the single hardest job on a farm for the farmer and his mules.

Every morning, when the light came up enough for me to see into the field, Willalee's daddy, Will, would already be out there behind a span of mules walking at remarkable speed, breaking the hard, clayish earth more than a foot deep. Sometimes daddy was out there plowing, too. Most of the time he was not.

Willalee's daddy would mark off an enormous square, fifteen acres or better, then follow that square around and around, always taking about a fourteen-inch bite with the turnplow so that when he went once around on each of the four sides of the square, the land still to be broken would have been reduced by fourteen inches on a side.

A man breaking land would easily walk thirty miles or more every day, day in and day out, until the entire farm was turned under. Even though the mules were given more corn and more hay than they were used to, they still lost weight. Every night when they were brought to the barn, they had high stiff ridges of salt outlining where their collars and backbands and trace chains and even their bridles had been.

With only my head out from under the buggy frame, continually dried and scabbed by the burning light, I watched the plows drag on through the long blowing days, Willalee's daddy moving dim as a ghost in the sickly half-light of the winter sun. Then after the longest, hardest time, the turnplow was taken out of the field, and the row marker brought in to lay off the lines in the soft earth where the corn would finally begin to show in the springtime. The row marker was made out of a trunk of a tree, sometimes a young oak, more often a pine, made by boring holes thirty-six inches apart and inserting a straight section of limb into each of the holes. Two holes were bored into the top of the log for handles and two holes in the front of the log for the shaves, between which the mule was hitched to drag the whole rig across the turned-under field, marking off four rows at a time.

Some farmers always had crops that grew in rows straight as a plumb line. Others didn't seem to care about it much, one way or the other. It was not unusual for a farmer bumping along in a wagon behind a steaming mule in the heat of summer to comment on how the rows were marked off on each farm he passed.

"Sumbitch, he musta been drunk when he laid them off."

"I bet he has to git drunk again ever time he plows that mess."

"I guess he figgers as much'll grow in a crooked row as a straight one."

For reasons I never knew, perhaps it was nothing more complicated than pride of workmanship, farmers always associated crooked rows with sorry people. So much of farming was beyond a man's control, but at least he could have whatever nature allowed to grow laid off in straight rows. And the feeling was that a man who didn't care enough to keep his rows from being crooked couldn't be much of a man.

In all the years in Bacon County, I never saw any rows straighter than the ones Willalee's daddy put down. He would take some point of reference at the other end of the field, say, a tree or a post, and then keep his eye on it as the mule dragged the row marker over the freshly broken ground, laying down those first critical rows. If the first four rows were straight, the rest of the field would be laid off straight, because the outside marker would always run in the last row laid down.

It didn't hurt to have a good mule. As was true of so many other things done on the farm, it was much easier if the abiding genius of a good mule was brought to bear on the job. There were mules in Bacon County that a blind man could have laid off straight rows behind. Such mules knew only one way to work: the right way. To whatever work they were asked to do, they brought a lovely exactitude, whether it was walking off rows, snaking logs, sledding tobacco without a driver, or any of the other unaccountable jobs that came their way during a crop year.

After the field was marked in a pattern of rows, Willalee's daddy came in with the middlebuster, a plow with a wing on both sides that opens up the row to receive first the fertilizer and then the seed. When all the rows had been plowed into shallow trenches, Will appeared in the field early one morning with a two-horse wagon full of guano, universally called *gyou-anner*. It was a commercial fertilizer sold in 200-pound bags, and Will had loaded the wagon before daylight by himself and brought it at sunup into the field where he unloaded one bag every three rows across the middle of the field.

Shortly after he left with the wagon, he came back with the guano strower and Willalee Bookatee. Willalee had a tin bucket with him. He plodded sleepily behind his daddy, the bucket banging at his knees. The guano strower was a kind of square wooden box that got smaller at the bottom, where there was a metal shaft shaped like a corkscrew and over which the guano had to fall as it poured into the trench opened by the middlebuster. The corkscrew shaft broke up any lumps in the fertilizer and made sure it kept flowing. Two little tongue-shaped metal plows at the back of the guano strower were set so that one ran on each side of the furrow. They covered up the thin stream of fertilizer the instant after it was laid down.

Willalee was out there to fill up the guano strower for his daddy, a bad, boring job and one reserved exclusively for small boys. Willalee would open one of the bags, fill the strower, and his daddy would head for the end of the row. As soon as he was gone, Willalee would go back to the sack, and since he could not pick up anything that heavy, he would have to dip the bucket full with his hands. Then he had nothing to do but shift from foot to foot, the fertilizer burning his arms and hands and before long his eyes, and wait for his daddy to come back down the row. When he did, Willalee would fill up the strower and the whole thing would be to do over again.

Ten

BY the time the field was covered with corn about an inch high I was able to do without the buggy frame and the constantly burning light. Dr. Sharp also said I could stay out of bed all I wanted to if the pain was not too bad.

Then two things happened in the same day: I saw my first grapefruit, and daddy went briefly crazy. I always remember the two things together. They got mixed and twisted in such a way that in the months to come, my nose would sometimes fill with the oily, biting smell of grapefruit.

My brother was going to the schoolhouse a half mile away on the same dirt road as our farm, and every other Thursday the federal government sent out a big truck filled with food of one kind or another, mostly in cans, for the children to take home.

"What all was it in the commodities truck?" I asked immediately upon seeing my brother's face when he came home from school.

"It was everything it ever was. And something else besides, too."

Mama had come in the room where we were. She stood wiping her hands on her apron.

"Did you git your commodity?" I asked, knowing he would never have come gloating into my room like that if he had not. But I'd really asked just so I could say the word *commodity*. All of us loved the word and put some pretty good mileage on it every other Thursday during the school year. I didn't have the slightest notion of what *commodity* meant. To me it meant: free food that comes on a truck. I've since managed to find the several definitions of the word, but in my secret heart I'll always know what commodity means: *free food that comes on a truck*.

"What did you git, son?" mama asked.

"Oh, I got my commodity," Hoyet said, drawing the whole thing out for as long as he could.

"You lost it. You lost your damn commodity," I said in a choked, accusing voice, hoping that saying he'd lost it would make him produce it.

Which he did. While mama scowled and warned me about cursing—a habit I'd developed with some vigor because my nearly mortal hurts made everybody spoil me, even mama—my brother whipped his hand from behind his back.

"Godamighty," I said. "Is it a orange or just what?"

"That commodity right there," said my brother in a voice suddenly serious as death, "is a grapefruit."

The words *grape* and *fruit* did not seem to me to cover it. We all stood silently staring at the round golden thing in his hand, so strange there in the tag end of winter, when everything in Bacon County was burned brown with cold and broken in the field. Then I began to smell it, *really* smell it, a smell full of the sun and green leaves and a sweet tongue and a delightfully cool bellyful of juice.

"See," he said. "We could have a can of Campbell's pork and beans or one of these."

"And you took this," I said.

"It don't look like pork and beans, do it?" he said. Then: "It's just like a orange, only bigger."

We knew all about oranges, or not all about them, but we did see them from time to time, little, shriveled, discolored things. But this was orange to the tenth power, which was precisely the way we thought about it even though obviously we could not have said it.

We all smelled it, pressing it against our noses, and felt it and held it longer than was necessary. Mama had brought the butcher knife from the kitchen.

"You reckon we ought to wait for daddy?" I said, a genuinely optimistic question since we hadn't seen him in almost a week.

"Ain't no use to wait," Hoyet said. His expression did not change. He raised the plump grapefruit to his face and peeled it back. Then we halved it and lifted off carefully and deliberately one slice at a time. The slices, which we called slisures, were dripping and yellow as flowers.

But I only had to touch my lips to my piece to know that something was wrong, bad wrong. "Damn if I don't believe my slisure's ruint," I said.

"Do taste a little rank, don't it?" Hoyet said.

Mama made me come over to her so she could hit me. She said: "Come over here so I can slap your head, boy. You cain't talk like that in my house." She liked to make you come to her to get your lick sometimes because she knew the humiliation made it worse. Soon as she had my head ringing like a bell tower she gently and sadly explained the bitter truth about certain grapefruit. "But they tell me," she said, "grapefruits is real good for you. Howsomever, to me they do taste a lot like a green persimmon."

We stood there in the room and gagged down that whole sour thing, slice by slice. It wouldn't do to let a commodity go to waste. The federal government had hauled it all the way to the schoolhouse, and Hoyet had deliberately chosen it over pork and beans and then brought it home in the empty syrup bucket with the wire bale on top he used to carry his lunch to school. That was why it had to be eaten, as mama carefully explained, while we chewed and swallowed, swallowed and chewed.

Finally, it was over. All that remained were a few seeds, a little pulp, and the skin. As soon as I could do it without either of them knowing, I went outside, leaned over the fence, and threw up. When I finally raised my head, I saw Willalee. His back was to me, down in the dirt lane by his house, too far to call him. It was the last time I ever saw him because that night daddy shot the mantelshelf off the fireplace with a twelve-gauge shotgun.

I heard the pickup truck and heard him when he came in and knew without thinking it was going to be a bad night. For about an hour, things were bad in the way they had been bad before: incredibly imaginative cursing between mama and daddy delivered at the top of their voices; pots and pans bouncing off the walls of the kitchen, where daddy had gone to feed the long bout he'd had with whiskey; dishes breaking; the dull unmistakable thump of flesh on flesh. The old house was shaking and I was shaking and my brother, who had started sleeping in the same bed with me again now that my burn had pretty much healed, my brother was shaking too.

Then the shotgun, the eye-rattling blast of a twelve-gauge, so unthinkably loud that it blew every other sound out of the house, leaving a silence scarier than all the noise that preceded it. The sound we had all waited for and expected for so long had finally come. It literally shattered our lives in fact and in memory.

We left in the dead of night, mama, my brother, and I, daddy behind us, silhouetted by the kerosene lamp and raving in the doorway. It had all happened quickly in confusion and fear, all of us rushing through the smell of gunpowder, putting something—I don't remember what—in a little pasteboard box for my brother to carry. Mama jerking me into my overalls and tying the string on a tiny straw suitcase at the same time.

Daddy had followed us about the house, alternately begging mama to stay and threatening to shoot something else if she did. There was no doubt in my mind that what he might shoot was me or all of us. But I still loved him. For all I knew, every family was like that. I knew for certain it was not unusual for a man to shoot at his wife. It was only unusual if he hit her. I had heard enough stories—many of them told by the same wife the shot had barely missed—to know that.

But this was the first time daddy ever fired the gun in the house, and certainly it was the first time mama—her face utterly pale except for her blue lips—had bundled us out in a chilly, moonless night to walk the half mile to Uncle Alton's house. My brother and I tried a few questions on the way, timid, unsure questions that brought no answer. My scalded legs were not hurting, but I was scared and unable to stop crying, so I said they were. I stumbled along in the deep ruts behind mama, following her in the dark by the sound of her strained, constricted breathing. In one long, strangled sob I told her that all my burns hurt and that my infantile paralysis hurt and that I wished I could go back home.

She never slowed or broke her stride, and I could tell by the muffled quality of her voice that she didn't even turn her head to look back at me when she said: "Wish in one hand and shit in the other. See which one fills up first."

It was not like mama to talk like that to a youngun exposed to the night air, and I knew once and forever that nothing in our lives would ever be as it had been again. So right there in the road, unable to see my hand in front of my face, I came apart a little more. The seams began to fray and unravel along all my joinings. Further, something that had never happened before, I began to feel myself as a slick, bloodless picture looking up from a page, dressed so that all my flaws whatsoever but particularly my malformed bones were cleverly hidden.

I knew that it was not true, that it was made up, and that also it was a kind of cheating to go about pretending you were what you were not. But there seemed to be no alternative. It only needed to be done with enough conviction to keep from going crazy. The only way to deal with the real world was to challenge it with one of your own making. For a long time after that, the next six months, from March to August, lived in my memory as a series of scenes, flashes of actions lit down to the most brutal detail under a blinding light.

We stood in the lane, not going near the yard gate while two cowering hounds bayed at us from under the front door step. Finally, we saw the flare of a match and then the steady light of a kerosene lamp. Uncle Alton, only one strap of his overalls gallus strapped over his longjohns, stood in the door with the lamp held high as he called to the hounds.

Mama marched across the yard and up the steps, stopping inches from Uncle Alton. Her face was turned up under the high-held light, showing her blue, unreal mouth. And when her lips moved, it was as though they were controlled by nothing so subtle as a mind but instead by something mechanical and arbitrarily calibrated like the strings of a puppeteer.

When finally she did speak, her voice held hate enough to break the backs of all the peoples of the world. "If I'd a been six inches taller, you'd be talking to my ghost. He taken the gun and shot the mantelshelf."

The next day in the afternoon we left Bacon County—packed onto the bus with two old suitcases and some stuff tied up with string and a shoebox full of chicken and biscuit on the road to Jacksonville, Florida, 100 miles away. I had not heard of Hitler's cattle cars then, but when I think of that trip, I remember it most often in that image. Tired people savaged by long years of scratching in soil already worn out before they were born. There was no talk in the crowded hot bus. When we had to slow down for traffic or for one of the little towns along the way where everything looked temporary, as though it might all be taken down during the night and hauled away, the greasy odor of burned fuel floated in through the open windows, choking us where we sat. But even on the straightaway, driving steadily between stunted forests of second-growth pine, an unbreathable, malodorous fog of combustion seeped up through the paneling at the bottom of the bus. Babies and little children moaned in their sleep when they breathed it.

Mama reached over and shook me gently where I sat by the window. "Wake up and look at that," she said. "It's the border keeping Georgia and Florida separate."

But I had not been asleep. I'd just had my forehead pressed against the window, which was not cool, but it was not as hot as everything else. It was after sundown, but there was plenty of light to see the river, and when mama touched me, I was already staring at its black surface, wondering what it would be like to fish from one of the little black boats I could see as the bus hurtled over the bridge, and wondering, too, about the marvel of the river, long and slow and snaky, pouring between banks of oak and black gum and sometimes cypress, pouring under bridges and on past little towns and maybe big ones—*all the time keeping everything that was Georgia away from everything that was Florida.*

It was a magic moment for me because I had always been fascinated with boundaries and borders—the Little Satilla, for instance, separating Appling County from Bacon, made me feel safe and good when I started to sleep at night, knowing that it was keeping all of us in and all of them out—but the St. Marys River was a border that went beyond fascination. Before mama spoke to me, I had recognized the river although I had never seen it before. I knew also it formed the border although I don't remember anybody ever telling me that it did. The vague shape of streets and houses and buildings and factories began to filter down behind my eyes. I knew I had never seen any of it before but if I concentrated, I could see all of it.

Still seeing the streets and buildings I had never seen before I suddenly shocked myself by saying: "We gone go right on over to the Springfield Section."

I knew absolutely, without knowing how I knew it, that something called the Springfield Section of Jacksonville was where all of us from Bacon County went, when we had to go, when our people and our place could no longer sustain us.

I was seeing the streets and houses and factories, and I knew we would go to the Springfield Section, because I had spent a lifetime hearing about the city. Jacksonville came up in conversations like the weather. Farmers' laconic voices always spoke of Jacksonville in the same helpless and fatalistic way. It was a fact of their lives. They had to do it. *Everybody* had to do it. Sooner or later everybody ended up in the Springfield Section, and once they were there, they loved it and hated it at the same time, loved it because it was hope, hated it because it was not home.

"It's some good, some bad, I reckon."

"A man *can* make a dollar there."

"And Godamighty, I tell you the truth being able to git up in the morning like that and turn you on some water or piss right there where you sleep, well Godamighty."

"Yeah, but I cain't get used to hearing the feller next door ever time he breaks wind."

"Or walk out the front door ever morning of your life and see right across the road that it's five or six other front doors looking dead at you."

"Still it *is* nice to give water in the house."

They loved *things* the way only the very poor can. They would have thrown away their kerosene lamps for light bulbs in a second. They would have abandoned their wood stoves for stoves that burned anything you did not have to chop. For a refrigerator they would have broken their safes and burned them in the fireplace, which fireplace they would have sealed forever if they could have stayed warm any other way.

But it seemed dreadfully unnatural to them to stand on their front porch and be able to talk to somebody else standing on *his* front porch. It sometimes happened back in the county that a man could *see* another house from his front porch, but not often. In the city, though, they were forever cheek to jowl. They felt like animals in a pen. It was, they said, no way for a man to live. But that was not the worst part of the city. In a way that was beyond saying, what they missed the most was their county's old, familiar smell: pine sap rising in trees, the tassels of corn topping out, the hard, clean bite of frost on dead and broken cotton stalks.

Everything everywhere in the city was tainted, however faintly, with the odor of combustion. To their country noses it seemed that a little oily gas had been added to everything. They could smell it vaguely in their clothes; they could taste it in the food. It got into the drinking water and onto their hair. It hung about over the streets, a blue fog, undulating and layered.

Finally, after a little while in the city they started to long for the society of animals. They caught themselves at odd moments thinking about hogs or goats or calves.

But there was nothing to be done for all that, and everybody knew it. The little shotgun row houses were waiting in the Springfield Section and the factories were waiting and they knew their time was coming— maybe there would be many times before it was over—for them to fill the houses and offer themselves up to the factories.

In a matter of hours after we got off the Greyhound bus mama had us settled into one of the shotgun row houses. The thing was about twenty feet wide, split down the middle with a narrow hallway on either side of which were tiny, criblike rooms, four of them, one of them a kitchen with a two-burner oil stove and a midget refrigerator into which the iceman would deposit a ten-cent cake of ice twice a week, and one a clothes-closet-sized bathroom jammed full of a foreshortened tub and a toilet that leaned dangerously to one side and a deep tin sink that had two faucets. I was immediately curious about the faucets.

"How come it's got two?" I wanted to know.

"It's some places in the world you can git hot water out of one and cold water out of the othern."

"*All* the time?" Of all the marvels I'd seen or heard, that seemed the finest.

"All the time," she said.

We stood out in the hall for a long time looking at the faucets before I finally said, "I don't reckon them right there's got hot and cold."

"I don't reckon," she said. "We ain't quite that grand yet."

But we were grand enough. It was a dizzying thought that the toilet was right in the house. Every morning on the farm underneath every bed there was a chamber pot. My brother and I took turns carrying them out. Here you just squatted in a little closet, cranked a handle, and then everything was gone in a rush of water.

The toilet was better than the telephone, but not as mysterious. The one in the Greyhound Station was the first telephone I'd ever seen. I'd heard about them, but I never believed what I heard and didn't believe it while mama called one of our relatives (one good thing about going from Bacon County to the Springfield Section of Jacksonville, some of your relatives would always be there, not always the same ones, but somebody would be waiting. On any day of my life, including the day I was born, I've had blood kin in Jacksonville. I do today) and the relative mama spoke to gave her another number to call and we took a long ride on a stinking city bus out Main Street to Eighth and east on Eighth to Phoenix Avenue, where on a narrow dark street the landlord's overseer (he could only be called an overseer, never a manager) met us on the porch of one of the shotgun houses. He got mama's money holding matches while she carefully counted it out of her purse.

Everything was new and grand, even the things that did not work, and that made up a little for daddy not being with us. Mama said that daddy was supposed to finish up the crop year and that Uncle Alton would manage to look after her things. Uncle Alton remains the most beautifully stoic and courageous man I've ever known. He inevitably found the time and the wherewithal to do whatever was asked of him. Years later, when mama got bone cancer and had to stay in bed a year in a full body cast, Uncle Alton took me in with his houseful of children, keeping me and loving me as one of his own.

Shortly after we were in the house, mama gave us one of her terse, elliptical explanations of how things were.

"Me and your daddy's separated," she said.

"Separated?" I said.

"Yes," she said.

"Separated from what?" I said.

"Each other," she said.

Well, hell, I knew they were separated from each other. Hadn't I just been on a bus for three hours? It would be awhile before I understood she was talking about more than distance.

In a little over a week daddy showed up in the middle of the night. My brother and I were sleeping in the same bed when we heard the banging at the front door. We knew immediately that it was daddy. He was doing some serious begging out there on the front porch. But mama's voice was coming low and hard and abrupt right behind his as he wildly tried to explain why he had shot the mantelshelf off the fireplace.

As soon as I knew he was sober and heard him *asking* to come through the door instead of kicking the door off its hinges, I went back to sleep. During the night I woke up several times and drowsily followed the course of the argument. Once he was squatted out in the moonlight, his hat pushed back on his head, singing an old Jimmie Rodgers song. He had one of those good country voices: part drunk, part hound dog, part angel. The next time I woke up he was whispering ninety miles a minute on the other side of the front door; on this side mama was whispering the same way. Just as I was falling asleep again, one of them giggled. Sometime just before day I woke up and found the little house shaking, the thin walls humming with a low, lilting croon, a lovely sound that put me happily and profoundly back to sleep.

We all ate breakfast the next morning jammed together in the kitchen. Daddy was silent and contrite. Mama was sullen and full of frowns, darkly muttering so that only a word or two came through to us now and then. Fascinated, we all listened to grumble grumble *shotgun* grumble grumble grumble *kill* grumble *never* grumble grumble *split his* grumble. Daddy's face went tighter and his mouth thinner, but he didn't say anything.

But he might as well have gone on and said whatever was on his mind, though, because mama ran him off again anyway before the day was half over. He went quickly and seemed to take pleasure in his going, the hot urgency of the night before considerably cooled. I don't know how long he might have got to hang around if she had not caught him bubbling a bottle of whiskey in front of the green wavy mirror in the bathroom. He dearly loved to drink in front of a mirror. I don't know why. He never said; I never asked. But mama had caught him more than once at the mirror. He was pretty helpless and easy to trap there, his head thrown back, his eyes walled and turned down, trying to see the bottle raised over his face. His vision would be blurred from watering eyes, his other senses warped and crippled from whiskey roaring in his blood. Which was a hell of a time to have somebody run right up his back. Which is exactly what mama would do. He could come home drunk and not catch much heat at all, but if mama caught him bubbling a bottle in front of the mirror, she went right up his back.

The sight of whiskey in her house drove her to inspired heights of outrage and violence, so much so that she would sometimes take daddy right off his feet with a broom handle or whatever she could lay hand to. He barely missed taking a plate in the ear as he went out the door this time, his bottle in one hand, his hat in the other. The tension and anger coming off the two of them like sparks off a stove brought the unmistakable smell of grapefruit into the house. It was the first time, but it was not to be the last.

Mama went straight to King Edward Cigar Factory for a job and got it. The women of the Springfield Section, at least the Bacon County women, all worked for King Edward. Women were thought to be defter and quicker at handling the various processes—filler, rolling leaf, packaging—and since the factory was right there in the same section of town where the Georgia women lived, they ended up working for King Edward almost exclusively.

Mama's job was to spread a single leaf of tobacco evenly on a metal plate of a machine which in turn rolled previously shaped filler into a finished cigar. She did piecework: the more cigars she rolled, the more money she made. I cannot remember how much she was paid, but it was little enough so that when help was offered to keep us fed, we were glad to accept it.

What little help there was came in the form of food baskets and secondhand clothing from various charitable agencies, including the Baptist Church. Sometimes it came on holidays, sometimes not. But whenever it came and whatever it was, it always looked good and felt even better.

That may seem strange to those who have a singularly distorted understanding of the rural Southerner's attitude toward charity. The people in the South I come from, those who knew what it meant to be forever on the edge of starvation, took whatever they could get and made whatever accommodations they had to make in their heads and hearts to do it.

Back in the county there was no charity. People gave things to each other, peas because they couldn't sell them or use them, same with tomatoes, sweet corn, milk, and sometimes even a piece of meat because it was going to turn rank in the smokehouse before they could eat it. But nothing was made out of giving or receiving. It was never called charity or even a gift. It was just the natural order of things for people whose essential problem, first and last, was survival.

They accepted what was offered them in Jacksonville the same way, as the natural order of things. We ate the food with relish and wore the clothes with pride. Farmers relocated from Georgia, most of whom had spent their lives working somebody else's land, felt right at home with overalls that were perfectly good except for maybe a rip in one knee and a section in the bib made rotten by bleach.

While mama went off to the cigar factory every morning at six and my brother went off to school at eight, I went out into the street with the other children too young for school. I was bigger than most of them because not only would I soon be six, I was also big for my age. Most of the shotgun houses were empty during the day. Everybody who was old enough to quit school was at work, women and men alike; the rest were in school, except for those of us too young for work or school and so spent the day trying to find odd jobs or stealing or pressing flesh in unthinkably erotic games of our own devising inside the empty shotgun houses.

My best friend was Junior Lister, who was not a junior in the sense that his name was the same as his father's. Junior, a particularly common name in Bacon County, was his real and only name.

"Shit no," he told me. "It don't stand for nothing. It ain't nothing else there. I ain't even got a damn initial."

Junior had a head as blunt as a snake's, with a broad, flat forehead, that he claimed he could break a brick with. I saw him butt through several things, including a door. And while I never saw him break a brick, I never doubted he could. His neck was as broad as his head so that the whole thing from his ears down drove right into his meaty little shoulders. He was bigger than I was, but then he was bigger than any of the other children who roamed the broken streets of the Springfield Section during the day. Junior had become six in January and hadn't been old enough to start school the previous year. So besides being a naturally big boy, who was already showing the arms and shoulders that would make him the terror of Bacon County a decade later, he was also older than any of the rest of us. He was meaner, too. He smoked cigarettes and cursed and ran down little girls, groping them right in the street, and was afraid of nobody, not even his parents, who periodically beat him savagely whether he had done anything or not, because as all our parents said, a beating will loosen a child's hide and let him grow.

It was a great thing in the neighborhood to become Junior's friend and wonderful beyond anything to be his best buddy, which I became shortly after I met him. I've never known precisely why it happened, but I suspect it was because it never occurred to me to question anything he said or did. He was seldom without a scheme, and I was always anxious to do what I could to help.

"Can you git out tonight for a little while?"

We were sitting on a curbstone on Phoenix Avenue. It was sundown, already an hour past the time when I should have been home.

"I reckon," I said.

"I got a place I can sell a set of hubcaps off a new Plymouth car," he said. "It's got to be set, though. Two or three won't do us a bit of good."

He never stole anything unless he knew where he could sell it. And if he saw something particularly nice that he knew he could steal fairly easily, he would go out and find somebody willing to pay. I found out later that was what happened with the hubcaps. He had seen some that were eminently stealable, and by asking around he heard that his older brother had a friend who was building a car that new Plymouth hubcaps would fit.

"What time?' I said.

"How bout nine?"

"Ma ain't gone let me out of the house at nine," I said. "We either got to do it by seven-thirty or else wait till leven."

Mama would be deep in an exhausted sleep by eleven and I could sneak out. There was no need to explain anything to Junior. We'd been through it all before. My brother, who slept in the same bed with me, wouldn't say anything about it, either. He didn't care what I did as long as I didn't want to do it with him. Boys from the farm didn't have anything to do much with their younger brothers, especially when there was as much as four years' difference in their ages, unless the older one was feeling especially violent and didn't have anybody else handy to beat.

"I'll meet you here at leven," Junior said. "It's over yonder by Eighth Street. We oughta be back in a hour."

It was easy enough to get out of the house, as I knew it would be. Mama was lying on the bed, one arm thrown across her eyes, when I came in.

"Where you been?" she said, without taking her arm down.

"We was playing marvels," I said. Two or three years later I would be shocked to find out that other people in the world pronounced the word *marbles*. "I didn't see how late it was gittin."

"You ain't got no marvels," she said.

That was true. I'd given up my marbles when I started to steal. The two didn't seem to go together.

"No, ma'am," I said. It wouldn't do to lie about anything she had direct knowledge of. Mama would get up and beat you no matter how tired she was for telling an obvious lie. "Junior let me borry some of hisn."

"You ain't been playing with Junior Lister again," she said.

"No, ma'am," I said. "He was just passing by where I was at."

"You ain't gone make it in life as a liar. You a sorry liar."

"Yes, ma'am," I said.

She didn't move on the bed, not even her arm covering her eyes, while she told me the stock was bad. Stock was the final leaf the cigar was rolled in. Mama's job was to spread that leaf out smoothly, nothing else, just that single spreading movement, about 6,000 times a day. If the leaves were soft and pliable, she came home carrying nothing more serious than exhaustion in her bones. But if the leaves were brittle and broken, if they resisted being spread on the metal plate, then you kept your mouth shut and walked softly around her. No strategy was too complicated if it kept you from being noticed. On days when stock was bad, you could easily end up paying the price for 6,000 broken leaves of tobacco, for 6,000 moments of frustration that had the effect of producing in her a crushing anxiety and paranoia.

Which is pretty much the same effect it had on the other women in the neighborhood. That was why I knew the stock had been bad that day before I got home. That's why I stayed out on the street as long as I thought I possibly could without getting my head caught between her knees. I'd seen kids being beaten and slapped about all afternoon in the Springfield Section by women you could smell as far away as you could see them. They smelled, stunk, of tobacco, their hair, their clothes, their skins, probably even their hearts.

"You gotta git another clock," Junior said when I met him at midnight.

"She had a headache," I said. "She couldn't go to sleep."

"That bad stock," he said. It was not a question but simple affirmation. He had caught a couple of licks from his own mama.

"Where is it at we're going?" I said when he headed off toward Eighth.

"Market," he said.

"That's a long ways," I said.

"All the time'll be walking over there and gittin back. The job ain't gone take but a minute."

When we'd got to Eighth, we went west to Market Street and then turned left. It was in the third block, a little confectionery store, not as long nor as wide as our house. A brand-new Plymouth was at the curb in front of the store.

"Old lady that runs the place lives in the back."

"You mean she lives right here."

"We ain't got nothing to worry about."

I was glad to hear it, but not entirely convinced, because the store was so short and the curb so close to the front door, I was sure she would hear us, and I told Junior so.

He didn't even look up at me as he squatted beside the right front wheel with a screwdriver. "You ain't been caught yet, have you?" he asked.

"What do you want me to do?" I said.

"Just cetch it when it pops off."

I did. We moved to the next one. He worked the screwdriver and another hubcap slid off into my hands. He'd had some practice at it, and he was good. Too good, because when he popped the third one, I hadn't yet got into position and it hit the pavement and rolled. Simultaneously with the hubcap hitting the pavement, a light came on in the rear of the store.

In a flat, inflectionless voice while he moved to the last hubcap, Junior cursed people who couldn't hold onto things.

"I give you the easiest goddamn part of it," he said.

But I was babbling by then. "A light's come on. They turned on a light. It's. . . ."

"You ain't got nothing to worry about. Shut up and squat down here."

Whether the light made him nervous and fumble-fisted, or whether it was stuck, Junior couldn't pop it right off. He was mumbling and prying at the hubcap when the front door of the store opened and an old, cracked, woman's voice floated out to us on the night air.

"Boys, please don't steal my hubcaps. Please don't. Ohhh, boys."

The old lady had turned on the lights in the front of the store, and we were very near where she sat now in her wheelchair sharply silhouetted in the door.

"Junior," I said. "She's in a wheelchair."

Junior looked up, his face radiant in the dim light from the store. "I know," he said. "She ain't even got a telephone neither." He stood up with the last hubcap, looked over casually at the old lady, who begged in a continuous broken voice. He kicked the tire a couple of times. "Too bad we cain't steal the whole car." He ambled off down the sidewalk, and I followed him.

Half a block away, I turned and called: "I'm sorry, lady."

Junior stopped and stared at me. "If you so sorry, it may be we oughta take'm back. Course Bernie's gone give us eight dollars cash money for'm."

"It didn't hurt to tell that poor old thing I was sorry," I said and kept on walking.

• • •

There were a few weeks in which we sold to the same man we stole from. The man owned a junkyard, three square blocks of parts of tractors and parts of cars and parts of washing machines, seemingly a little bit of everything in the world that was made of metal. He bought his own copper from us with great enthusiasm. He would buy any kind of metal, but he paid the most for copper. He was nuts about any kind of copper.

"I found out where they is some copper," Junior said to me one day at our place on the curbstone.

He had found out about the copper being piled up under a shed, which not only had no doors, it had no walls.

"We can just walk in there and git us some and then sell it back to'm. They like that pipe the best. If we can steal us a mess of them copper pipes, we'll be in high cotton."

And we did. We stole and we sold. The man we sold it to knew that it was stolen. How else could children our age, a couple of six-year-olds, get so much copper? But he didn't know where it was coming from and thought he didn't want to know. He didn't even want to know our names. He just beamed when we came in with his copper. He'd pay us—knocking down the price he would have had to pay anybody but children, which we knew—and happily send us on our way.

He was glad to be getting a cheap supply of copper, and we were glad to oblige his larceny. But it couldn't go on forever. Either Junior or I or maybe both of us had talked it around that we were stealing at the back door and selling at the front door. Somebody called the cops—probably a kid Junior had dragged down the street by his heels, he being habitually disposed to beat up on any child he could run down without too much trouble.

The cops came to his house but found nothing. They did, however, scare him witless. Both his mama and his daddy beat him, but he told me he was still so scared by the cops he hardly felt it and he had to concentrate to cry. His parents, like all the parents from Bacon County, used crying to determine when they should stop. It wasn't how loud the crying was, but a whole complexity of factors: how genuinely contrite did it sound, how hopeless, how agonized and full of grief, how well did the child understand that he was worthless and that only by the Grace of God and the slash of the whip, both administered for reasons of love, could he expect to get near people again, most of whom—he was given to understand—were his moral superior. That Junior was able to bring his voice to the proper sound after he'd just been visited by cops of a foreign country astounded me.

"If I don't cry when daddy whips me," Junior said, "if I don't git it right, he never will let up. There for a while when I couldn't git my mind on it, he had me down on the floor whoppin me hard as he could with that razor strop. He's beatin me across the head and everything, hard as he can swing, and all the time he's yelling: 'Don't play with me, Junior. Don't play with me.'"

It made a believer out of Junior. He said we ought to bear down and get us something regular to work at. Many of the children had jobs, an hour or two a day cleaning something up in a store or cleaning up the pen where the stores put their garbage, anything a kid could be trusted with doing, and doing quickly, since it was against the law to work them too long.

A few days later I was out in the end of Phoenix Avenue and I passed a little grocery store that had a butcher shop in the back. I went inside and convinced the man who owned it that he needed me to clean up the butcher shop. The day after I went to work for him I was in the back scrubbing down the butcher's block and sweeping up the sawdust on the floor, because it was only about twenty minutes until quitting time, when a man came into the store and sprinted down between the aisles to where I was working. Everybody in the store stopped to watch, such was the look in the man's face of raw, wild desperation. When he got to the back, he came right behind the counter and slid to a stop. He was wearing faded overalls, brogans, and a felt hat. His upper lip was weighted with a heavy, stained mustache. His wrists and hands seemed much too large for his emaciated body.

"Knife," he said to me.

"Knife," I said.

"Where?" he said.

"Butcher block," I said.

I was as motionless as a stuffed bird. Only my eyes moved, and they only moved to follow him. The customers from the store, including Mr. Joseph, who owned it, came rushing back to the meat counter. They were terrified as I was, and all we could do was watch as the man went to the butcher block and withdrew from a rack nailed into the side of it a very long knife, honed until the blade was thin and sharp as a razor. He brought the knife up and jammed it into his chest. Strangely it did not go in very deep. Everybody gasped and one lady fainted when he made that first plunge. He walked in a little circle like a dog looking for a place to lie down. He walked that way for a long time, making a little track in the sawdust. The lady who fainted came around and was led away. Then the man stopped in his circle. He held the knife steady with one hand and struck it with the other hand, palm down, driving the blade a little deeper.

"He's gone puncture his heart!" one of the ladies screamed. As if on signal they all ran out of the store. Mr. Joseph, who owned the place, called back over his shoulder that he was going for the police.

The man had started circling again, but he stopped. "How come that feller to go for the police?" He no longer looked angry or desperate, only very sad. The knife had calmed him down. I remember thinking it was like medicine. He'd run in here hurting, but he slipped that blade into his chest and the pain went away. "How come him to go?" His voice was little more than a whisper; his eyes wet and bright but calm.

"I don't think you allowed to do it," I said.

"What?" he said.

"Stick yourself."

When he spoke, his voice was subdued. "I reckon I shouldn't a come in here and taken his knife. That's near bout stealing." He casually raised his open hand and tapped the knife a little deeper. After he put another little bit of the blade in his chest, he almost smiled.

"The knife ain't how come him to go for the police," I said. "You cain't stick your own self in a store or out in the middle of the field or anywhere. It's agin the law."

"Law ain't studying me," he said, beginning to circle again.

"You from Bacon County?" I asked. It was the only thing I could think of to say.

He smiled at me as he turned in his circle. "Sho now, boy." He tapped the knife a little more. He was really bleeding now, his overalls full of blood all the way to his knees.

"I'm from Bacon County, too," I said, desperate to stop him.

"I'm a Pitfield," he said.

"I'm a Crews," I said.

"I mought know your people. I probly do."

"Myrtice is my mama and Pascal is my daddy," I said, watching the door, hoping for Mr. Joseph and the police.

"I don't know," he said. "I don't know. It is some Crewses up around the Harrikin I known."

"You don't need to do this," I said. "You can always just quit an go on home." I was a little beside myself to think of something to get him to stop.

"Home," he said in a quiet, bemused voice, addressing whatever came before his eyes as he turned the circle. "It ain't nair nail left in the world where my hat is welcome."

He turned his eyes toward me. "Come over here, boy." I stood where I was. "Come on over here." I stepped closer. He leaned just perceptibly. "You don't have to worry about this. I don't want you to worry about this." I didn't say anything. "You know why it ain't no reason for you nor nobody else to worry about this?"

"Why?" I said.

"The knife feels good."

"Godamighty," I said.

"It feels good."

He said something else, but I didn't hear him. I knew it was hopeless. I could not have said it then, but I knew in my bones that he was caught in a life where the only thing left to do was what he was doing. He had told himself a story he believed, or somebody else had told it to him, a story in which the next thing that happened—the only thing that *could* happen—was the knife. It was the next thing, the right thing, the only thing, and the knife felt good. If my life to that moment had taught me nothing else, it had made me understand exactly what he meant. Talking wasn't going to do any good.

He took another little slap at the top of the knife and seemed to relax all along his bones as the blade went deep. His face grew calmer still.

"Well, I'm through with it all now," he said. He hit the knife particularly hard, and he stopped in his circle as though he had run into a stone wall. "I'm through with it. Somebody else is gone have to look after it."

Like a folding chair closing, he sank slowly to his knees. He turned his face, the whitest face I'll ever see, toward me. "I've kilt myself," he said in a flat, matter-of-fact voice.

He stayed just that way, on his knees, his bloodless face turned to me, as Mr. Joseph came running through the store with a policeman. As they came around the counter, the man gave himself a little more of the blade and pitched forward on his face into a ring of blood-soaked sawdust.

The cop, red-faced and breathing heavily, walked over and turned his face out of the sawdust, glanced at it briefly, and stood up.

I went over to Mr. Joseph and gave him my apron. "Quittin," I said, and rushed out of the store.

Shortly after I quit my job in the butcher shop, we were evicted. Mama came home one evening and there was a notice nailed to the door explaining it. She glanced at it a moment and threw it in the garbage. The overseer came by four or five days later to inquire about our plans. But the stock had been bad that day and he never should have come.

"I seen it," mama said.

"You ain't got but four more days," he said.

"Four more days to what?"

"Move out."

"I ain't moving out," she said.

"We'll just have to start tearing the roof off then because the landlord's building something else here. He'll come down and talk to you hisself."

"Anytime he wants to," she said, and went back to the bed to lie down but not without first telling the overseer that he was the sorriest man ever to shit behind two shoes.

The landlord, a short, plump man with tiny feet and tiny hands, showed up two days later.

"It's just me and these younguns here, and we ain't got nowhere else to go," mama said.

"I'm very grieved to hear that," he said, "but I'm afraid we'll have to tear the roof off anyway."

He stayed around for another half hour and told mama he was very grieved about her life and what was happening in it. Finally, he waved as he was leaving and said over his shoulder in a pleasant singsong voice: "We won't put you in the sidewalk, Mizz Crews, if you don't make us. No sireeee."

Even though mama had never missed a rent payment, or even been late with one, when I came home later that same week from selling newspapers, a job I had got at the Jacksonville *Journal*, everything we owned, which was precious little because all the splintered, stick furniture belonged to the landlord, was piled out on the sidewalk. The doors and windows were nailed shut. It was just beginning to mist, but by the time mama got home from work it was raining hard. She was soaking wet after walking from where the bus let her off. Everything we owned was soaked. It was cold. My brother and I were sitting on the front steps of the boarded-up house. Mama had stopped by the store on the way home. The bag of groceries she was holding had split. A package of Spam was showing out of the bottom.

"Junior's mama said we could stay over with them," I said.

"I'm staying right here," she said, walking past my brother and me. She set the sack down on the floor and without any apparent difficulty ripped off the boards that had been nailed over the front door. "You two boys bring that stuff back in here."

My brother and I both were scared to death that the landlord or his man would show up that night. If they did, neither of us had any doubt that mama would attack. In her state after seeing her things pitched onto the sidewalk, she would have chewed their throats out. Fortunately, they did not come that night. But they did come the next day, and when we got home, all our stuff was on the sidewalk again. Mama sent word to Junior's mama that we would stay there until we found a place, if it was all right. In two days we had another house, identical to the one we had been forced out of.

The landlord never did get around to tearing down the house we'd been living in before, nor had we expected him to. Within the week another family was living there. If a landlord in the Springfield Section got an offer of $2 more than he had been getting, he'd throw one family out and let another family in. It was done all the time. With such regularity, in fact, that a pile of things—sheets and pillows and pans and maybe a chest of drawers and clothes—piled on the sidewalk turned nobody's head. Unless you happened to know and like the people who had been evicted. Then you tried to help. Usually, if it was not in your block, you ignored it.

Shortly after we had been evicted, daddy—not knowing we had moved—crawled in through one of the windows of the little house and ended up scrambling around in the bed with the man and woman who had moved in behind us, whom it nearly scared to death. It scared daddy pretty good, too.

"Scared my pony," he said. "Damn if I didn't think he meant to kill me."

He had come banging on our door at ten o'clock Saturday morning. Mama let him in because the stock had been good the past few days and also because it had been over two weeks since she had let him in the last time.

Daddy had been around pretty regularly of late. He had even *stayed* with us a few times. But generally it was swooning and crooning on the sidewalk and at the bedroom window, or whispering frantically through doors and walls. And then, once he was inside, it was a continual mad rush through the house, senseless and crazed.

But I never thought too much about it all, one way or the other. Certainly it did not cause me any shame. How could it when half the fathers and husbands at any given moment were swooning and crooning along the sidewalks and at the bedroom windows of the Springfield Section and later rushing madly about, senseless and crazed? Junior's own daddy, Leland Lister, almost never used any other entrance to his house except the side window after first giving himself a medium to heavy hurt with whiskey. He would immediately attack his family savagely until he had punched them all enough to make them listen. Then he would commence to say in a broken and poorly voice that he was doing the best he could, saying that it wasn't his fault. He always ended with: "I'm just like Godamighty made me." All the men of Springfield Section went about it pretty much the same way. Daddy was neither better nor worse than the rest. He was simply one of them.

But finally the night came when not only was the fight different from any I had heard before, it was the worst. It lasted longer, too, about five hours. It would stop for a little while and then start again. The other fights had risen straight to the top and exploded. This one rose and fell, rose and fell. When the screaming quit, a murderous murmuring started up.

Sometime toward the end of that exhausted night, daddy came into the room where I was alone on the bed. My brother had gone to the bathroom and stayed, because you could never be sure the fight would not spill over into whatever room you happened to try to hide out in.

Except the bathroom. For some reason the fighting never came into the bathroom after you.

Strangely, daddy was almost sober. His eyes were red as coals. He seemed to stand with a curious resignation, curious because when he had been drinking, he stood and walked like a bandit, a kind of strut that invited violence.

"Well," he said, "I reckon that about does it."

He did not sit down and left my door open, through which a wedge of dim light fell from the hall. He stood next to my bed but did not look at me.

"You all right?" I asked.

When he had been drinking, he sometimes thought there were men waiting outside to kill him. When he was like that, mama would always ask him if he was all right. The question popped out of my mouth because it scared me to have him come into my room like that in the middle of a fight. He'd never done it before.

"It ain't nothing the matter with me," he said.

But I'd heard him say the same thing when he was shaking with fear of the men outside armed with shotguns, men who were not outside at all.

"I ain't gone be by to see you no more," he said.

"Never?" I said.

"Never," he said.

I thought about that for a moment. It was clearly impossible. "Daddy," I said, "you *got* to come by."

"Cain't," he said. "Have the law on me I do. You ma's gittin a divorce. She got a peace bond on me now."

It didn't make sense to me. I knew what a divorce was well enough, but when he mixed it with a peace bond, the purpose of which I had no notion, and said too that he would never see me again, it only scared and confused me.

"I never was your daddy, but I tried to be one to you." He shook his head. "It just wasn't in me, though."

I felt myself burn all along my nerves. Was not my daddy? *Not* my daddy? Is that what I heard?

"What?"

I have lost most of the rest of whatever passed between us, lost it in the same way that I lost the fact that he was my stepfather. I must have known it, must have heard it somewhere, perhaps more than once, but if I did, I somehow managed to forget it.

But I remember clearly how it all ended.

"My daddy was who?"

"My brother."

"Brother?" I could only think of my own brother. It didn't make sense.

"I was your uncle."

"Uncle?" I could only think of Uncle Alton. It didn't make sense.

"I won't be by to see you no more," he said. "I won't be seeing you." I didn't for a second believe him because it made no sense.

But he was as good as his word, and it taught me not to give a damn for what makes sense. I didn't see him again until I was out of the Marine Corps and going to the University of Florida. I had not thought of him in years when I woke up one Saturday morning determined to do whatever was necessary to see him.

I found him in the Springfield Section of Jacksonville not far from where I lost him. He was sitting in the back of a tiny store, huddled beside a stove in a huge overcoat. He was very nervous. He did not want to talk. I left minutes after I got there. We never touched each other, not even to shake hands.

Eleven

IN the middle of summer, five months after we moved to Jacksonville, mama announced that we were moving back to the farm. She had managed to put a down payment on a little place about a quarter of a mile from where we used to live. It was not at all like the Williams place. The house was unpainted; the mule stable and corncrib were badly slanted. There was no tobacco barn because the place had no tobacco allotment. Many nights I got myself to sleep by seeing how many stars I could count through the shingles of the roof, and when things were slow during the day, I would fish for chickens. But I had to be careful that mama didn't find me with a fishhook tied to a piece of tobacco string and baited with a kernel of corn hanging through a crack in the floor down to where the chickens scratched under the house.

The farm was a little less than thirty acres in cultivation, and so we only had one mule, whose teeth showed him to be probably over twenty, which meant he was on the downhill side of his life. A mule man can always tell within a year or two how old a mule is. And if a mule is young enough, he can tell his age within a few months.

A mule has a full set of teeth when he's born. But when he is two years old, he sheds two of the teeth right in the front. A good mule man can tell if he's shed those two front teeth, in which case he is between two and three years old. A really good man can tell if those teeth have just grown back in or if they've been back in the mule's mouth for several months. The next year, when he's three, the mule sheds two more teeth, one on each side of the two he shed the year before. From then on the mule sheds two teeth a year until he's five years old. That's the last time he sheds.

Then you have to go to the cups to tell his age. Mules and horses have little trenches, called cups, in the top of each tooth. Eating corn and picking up sand when they graze on grass wear down those cups. Each year they become shallower, and by the time he's ten he becomes what farmers call smooth-mouthed. When the cups are entirely gone, the mule starts to get a noticeable overbite—buck-toothed. From the age of ten until the animal dies, it becomes progressively harder to get his age with much certainty. Unless you happen to be a real mule man. If you are, you can check the angle of inclination of the teeth and get his age within a year or two. About the time the mule is thirteen or fourteen, he has become about as buck-toothed as he's going to get. Then instead of looking in the mule's mouth, you get behind him, squat down so you have a low-angle vision of his legs and haunches, and have somebody lead him away from you so you can see how he tracks. The mule man wants to see how he walks. Does he favor a leg? Do his hindquarters "drag," that is, seem to be pulled along rather than offer the driving power they should have. Does anything on the animal seem to be sore, particularly his back?

After the first ten years, the rest of it depends upon the mule man's eye and his experience. Usually the mule traders who judge the age of very old mules are themselves very old men. They sometimes make bad mistakes, because some old mules will look very young, having a high sheen on their coats, smooth, tight-muscled bodies, and a spirit in their hearts that kept their heads high, kept them fast walkers and mean. An old mule usually will not kick you and he will not bite you. But there are exceptions, and it was on these exceptions that the best of traders sometimes got cheated.

But that wasn't the only way to get cheated. There were men—a few—who specialized in reconditioning a mule's mouth. And as is always the case, there was one man who was better at it than anybody else in the county. All the other men charged about $1 a head to work on a mule's mouth. But the man who was the recognized expert at it charged $5, and he was worth it. Nobody looked down upon these men for what they did. They had a special and perfected craft, and they exercised it for anybody willing to pay the freight.

What the mouth doctors did was to put the cups back into the teeth with an electric drill that had a bit about the size of a match stick. They just put a twist on the upper lip of the mule so he would stand still and then drilled a little trench in the top of each tooth. When that was done, they stained the trench so that it looked as it would if it were the original. All the mouth doctors had a special stain, and they would die and go to hell before divulging how it was made. It was common knowledge that the base of these stains came from green walnuts, but whatever the ultimate ingredients, the best stains could not be taken, not even with sandpaper. An old mule that's been recapped is allowed to stand in the lot for a week or two before he's taken to market. Any mule, no matter how old he is, that is not worked for a couple of weeks gets as frisky as a colt, his ears are always up, and he farts a lot. It is an act of faith in Bacon County that "a farting mule is a good mule." Such a mule will kick you, too. If it's all done right, it takes a good man not to get beaten in a trade for a mule whose mouth has been worked on by somebody who knows what he's doing.

We had no such trouble with the mule we bought when we got back to Bacon County. Every physical attitude, every aspect of the way he moved showed he had done his time between the trace chains and then some. He'd even gone gray in the head. As young as I was, I was glad Pete—that was his name—didn't know he'd been sold to us for $20.

Pete, with that old gray head and a mouth full of ground-down and bucked teeth, had also been cupped, which shamed Mr. Willis as much as if somebody had spit in his face. Mr. Willis was the hired man mama had got to come and live with us to tend the farm. He must have been fifty, but with his body still ropy with muscle, carrying almost no fat, so reticent that he rarely spoke unless spoken to, and never in a hurry. The house could have been burning down and he would have moved as slow as grass growing. Mama would sometimes say something to him about working a little faster, and he would stop completely, turn to her, and say in his grave, considered voice: "Mizz Crews, I ain't made of iron nor steel nor run by lectricity," then he would methodically resume whatever he was doing in his same slow way.

He'd been a hired hand all his life, but he was formal to the point of being courtly. I don't even remember his first name; everybody called him Mr. Willis. He was a man whose schedule was as regular as the ticking of a clock. The first thing he did in the morning was take his hat off the bedpost and put it on his head; the last thing he did at night was to take it off and put it back on the post. If you wanted to see him without his hat, you had to catch him asleep. Which nobody ever did because he got up with the chickens.

He slept with a tiny piece of tobacco in his mouth, about the size of a pencil eraser. After he got his hat on, he took out the chew he'd slept with, which he said with utter conviction kept a man's stomach free from worms, and replaced it with a half a plug of Day's Work, keeping it in his mouth all day except for meals. Sometimes, apparently forgetting to take it out, he would eat with the tobacco bulging like a tumor in his right jaw.

He was also—I think—the cleanest man I ever knew. I say I *think* he was the cleanest man I ever knew because like everything else he did, he made his toilet in absolute privacy. After his hat was on his head, he filled a syrup bucket full of water from the well, went off through the field to a little head of woods about a quarter of a mile away, carrying with him rags torn from worn-out bed sheets stuffed in his pockets. He would stay down there for an hour and come back carrying an empty bucket and no rags. My brother and I went back to where he washed and there were white rags hanging everywhere, from limbs of trees, from bushes, carefully spread out to dry. Several cakes of homemade lye soap would be wedged in the crooks of trees and wrapped in the rags he washed in. Eventually a quarter acre of woods was decorated with white, various-shaped rags. And yet every morning he would carry another pocket of rags with him. When he came to breakfast, his skin was red and scrubbed to glowing. In the year he farmed with us, I never remember him saying anything at breakfast. It was not in his schedule. He ate slowly, chewing slowly and with the precision of a metronome. He never drank anything while he was eating, but the moment his jaws stopped he lifted the quart of iced tea he insisted upon for every meal and drank it down slowly, without stopping. We always stopped to watch him do it, his throat pumping impossibly until it was all gone. Then he would abruptly set the jar down and leave the table to go to the lot to put the gear on Pete.

Later we would see him and Pete in the field, Mama, looking at him through the window, would say: "Damn, if you wouldn't have to set a peg out there to see if he's moving."

Pete would stop about every seventy yards, and Mr. Willis would stop with him, standing quietly between the handles of the plow until Pete would start up again in about five minutes. We had bought Pete from an eighty-year-old farmer, and Pete had learned to stop about every seventy yards so the old man could rest two or three minutes before going on. Pete had been doing it for twenty years or more, and Mr. Willis saw no reason to change Pete's ways.

Mama, short on patience as usual, suggested that Mr. Willis take a strap to Pete when he stopped for the rest periods. Mr. Willis thought about it for a minute and finally said: "Mizz Crews, Pete's as old as I am, turned as many rows as I have, and I ain't got it in me to beat this old man." Mr. Willis clucked and Pete leaned into his collar and the two of them moved off down the row at the same ambling gait for another seventy yards.

But all mules, young and old, had their ways. You got to know them like people, what they liked and what they didn't, what they would put up with and what they wouldn't. And you remembered them like people, just as vividly.

The most intense love affair I've ever known was between two mules we owned the year I finally left the farm for good. Doc, a big iron-gray horse mule, and Otha, a little red mare mule about 300 pounds lighter than Doc were matched mules. They had been broken together, trained to move in their harness with precision and smoothness.

Matched mules are nearly always the same weight because if they are not and they are asked to pull something really heavy, the bigger mule lunges into his harness, bellying down behind his collar and simply snatches the smaller mule back against the doubletree, an iron bar to which their trace chains are ultimately fastened, and, in effect, this loses all the pulling power of the lighter mule. It becomes a seesaw, with one mule lunging and then the other. The bigger mule isn't pulling *with* but *against* the one he's in double harness with.

Not so with Doc and Otha. Doc waited. He compensated. The two of them would, slow as breathing, tighten their traces together, leaning into their collars. When I've seen Doc turn—even in the middle of the worst kind of pull—and look at his fine little mare mule beside him giving all she had to give, I knew he was *thinking* how best to help her, how best to take whatever part of the load he could off her. I always knew he thought about her a lot. *Thought.* A deliberate word. I can't prove it's true, but then most of what I believe I can't prove.

We always had to take both Doc and Otha to the field even if we planned to work only one of them. We had to hitch the one not being worked so that they would never be out of sight of one another. If we took one out of the lot without the other, or for any reason made it so they could not see each other, they would literally rip themselves apart in an effort to get back together: knock down fences, go through barbed wire, cut their heads and chests slamming through stables.

I've never doubted the love between Doc and Otha. As everybody knows, mules are hybrids and cannot breed. Who, but a fool, though, would maintain that breeding is an indispensable part of love? Doc and Otha were the same age, both five-year-olds. One of them had to die first. I've always been grateful I was not there to see the one that was left.

I was unfortunate enough to see Pete almost die. We'd cut a lot of green grass and put it in the corncrib to dry. Somehow the door to the crib was left open, and Pete got in there with all that corn and green grass and just about ate himself to death as old mules will sometimes do. Mr. Willis came to the house and told mama she had better come out to the crib and see Pete.

"What ails'm?" she asked.

"Swol up," he said.

"Swol up?"

"That old man's foundered."

"Mr. Willis, for God's sake, spit it out. What is it you trying to say?"

What he was trying to say was that Pete was hideously swollen in the belly and legs and that he would very probably die, being as old as he was.

"Them old fellers cain't take it much. He was younger, he'd have a better chance."

"What are we gone do?" mama said.

"Best we can, I reckon," he said.

Mr. Willis' best was good enough as it turned out. I went with him down to the creek, walking very slowly, leading Pete, who waddled like a duck. Even Pete's face seemed swollen from eating all night. And he insisted on stopping every seventy yards or so to rest awhile even though he wasn't pulling anything.

Mr. Willis took Pete out belly deep in cool running water and hitched him there. "We'll just let that old man stand there in that water a few hours and see don't that help him some."

Pete stood in the water until sundown, and when Mr. Willis took him out of the water, he didn't look much different from the way he did when we put him in.

"Didn't go down much, did he?" said Mr. Willis.

"He don't look like he went down none," I said. Mr. Willis had taken out his pocketknife. "What you aim to do with that knife?" I asked.

"I'm gone bore some holes in'm and let that swelling out."

"You better ask mama before you go boring holes in the mule," I said.

His saying he was going to bore holes to let the swelling out scared me. I had an immediate vision of Mr. Willis up under Pete's swollen and drum-tight belly boring away with his knife, stabbing great gouty holes through the flesh, and black poisonous fluid pouring down over his head and shoulders as he did so. I was considerably relieved to see him bend to Pete's hooves.

"What you do is bore some holes down here where the hair meets the hoof." He grunted while he worked. "Let'm give a little blood."

"Will he be all right then?"

As was his way, he quit entirely with what he was doing, stood up, and turned to face me. "Well," he said, after he had considered the question for some time, "he might and he might not."

He put about five holes in each hoof while Pete, stunned from eating all night and standing in water all day, didn't even flinch as the blood started trickling over his hooves. Finally, he began to stamp and paw the ground.

"See, that right there smarts," said Mr. Willis, "and gits'm to stompin his feet. Now, he'll either die or he'll git better."

Pete must have bled two quarts before the wounds closed up. The next morning the swelling had gone down a lot, and in a few days Pete was back in the field working. Pete had all that land to break by himself, and it was a killer. The place had lain fallow for a year, so there were no stalks to cut and rake and burn, but there were weeds: cockleburs and coffee weeds and dog fennel. The fields had to be burned first and then disked with a plow we called a cutaway harrow. Only then could it be turned. But eventually it was done, because although both Pete and Mr. Willis were slow, they were steady.

After Pete was over his sickness from eating too much, I talked to Mr. Willis about the cure, something that had been bothering me.

"Didn't it hurt Pete to cut his feet that way?" I asked.

"I reckon so," he said.

"It was a awful thing to have to do to'm."

Mr. Willis thought about it for a little and said: "No, it weren't."

"It weren't?"

"Not awful as dying," he said. "Nothing else to do. Things git easy when it's nothing else to do. I known that when I weren't no biggern you are, boy."

When something was necessary, it was done, whether to a mule or to a child or to your own mother did not matter. People in Bacon County never did anything worse to their stock than they were sometimes forced to do to themselves. Mr. Willis was no exception. I never knew him to be sick (despite the fact that he bathed naked in the woods out of a syrup bucket in freezing weather), but he *did* have very bad teeth, perhaps from sucking on tobacco day and night. His reticence and courtly manner never left him except when the pain from his teeth was on him bad.

He lived in a shedlike room off the side of the house. The room didn't have much in it: a ladder-back chair, a kerosene lamp, a piece of broken glass hanging on the wall over a pan of water where he shaved as often as once a week, a slat-board bed, and in one corner a chamber pot, which he carried out every morning himself.

I slept in a room on the other side of the wall from him. One night after winter had come, I was asleep in my red gown Grandma Hazelton had made for me since we'd come back from Jacksonville, and Mr. Willis' mouth came alive with what had to be an unthinkable pain.

When I heard him kick the slop jar, I knew it was his teeth. I just didn't know right away how bad it was. When the ladder-back chair splintered, I knew it was a bad hurt even for him. A few times that night I managed to slip off to sleep only to be jarred awake when he would run blindly into the thin wall separating us.

He groaned and cursed, not loudly but steadily, sometimes for what seemed like half an hour. Ordinarily, mama would have fixed a hot poultice for his jaw or at least tried to do something. But she had learned he was a proud man and preferred to suffer by himself, especially if it was his teeth bothering him.

The whole house was kept awake most of the night by his thrashing and groaning, by the wash pan being knocked off the shelf, by his broken shaving mirror being broken again, and by his blind charges into the wall.

What was happening was only necessary. The dentist would not have gotten out of his warm bed for anything less than money. And Mr. Willis didn't have any money. Besides, the dentist was in town ten miles away, and we didn't have anything but a wagon and Pete, who, stopping every seventy yards or so to rest, would have taken half a day to get there.

I was huddled under the quilts, shaking with dread, when I heard him kick open the door to his room and thump down the wooden steps in his heavy brogan work shoes, which he had not taken off all night. I couldn't imagine where he was going, but I knew I wanted to watch whatever was about to happen. The only thing worse than my nerves was my curiosity, which had always been untempered by pity or compassion, a serious character failing in most societies but a sanity-saving virtue in Georgia when I was a child.

I went out the front door barefoot onto the frozen ground. I met Mr. Willis coming around the corner of the house. In the dim light I could see the craziness in his eyes, the same craziness you see in the eyes of a trapped fox. Mr. Willis headed straight for the well, with me behind him, shaking in my thin cotton gown. He took the bucket from the nail on the rack built over the open well and sent it shooting down hard as he could to break the inch of ice that was over the water. As he was drawing the bucket up on the pulley, he seemed to see me for the first time.

"What the hell, boy!" he shouted. "What the hell!"

His voice was as mad as his eyes, and he either would not or could not say anything else. He held the bucket and took a mouthful of the freezing water. He held it a long time, spat it out, and filled his mouth again.

He turned the bucket loose and let it fall again into the well instead of hanging it back on the nail where it belonged. With his cheeks swelling with water he took something out of the back pocket of his overalls. As soon as I saw what he had, I knew beyond all belief and good sense what he meant to do, and suddenly I was no longer cold but stood on the frozen ground in a hot passion waiting to *see* him do it, to see if he *could* do it.

He had a piece of croker sack about the size of a half dollar in his left hand and a pair of wire pliers in his right. He spat the water out and reached way back in his rotten mouth and put the piece of sack over a tooth. He braced his feet against the well and stuck the pliers in over the sackcloth. He took the pliers in both hands, and immediately a forked vein leaped in his forehead. The vein in his neck popped big as a pencil. He pulled and twisted and pulled and never made a sound.

It took him a long time, and finally, as he fought with the pliers and with himself, his braced feet slipped so that he was flat on his back when the blood broke from his mouth, followed by the pliers holding a tooth with roots half an inch long. He got slowly to his feet, sweat running on his face, and held the bloody tooth up between us.

He looked at the tooth and said in his old, calm, recognizable voice: "Hurt now, you sumbitch!"

His old teeth never hurt him again like that while he was with us. They hurt him bad enough to make him stomp around and break a few things, but never bad enough again to make him go into his mouth with a pair of pliers. And it was just as well, too, because things were dreadful enough without that. But he never complained as he kept his methodical but incredibly slow pace fixing up the fence to keep the stock out (we didn't have any to keep *in*), and putting in a big patch of collards and turnips—a winter garden that doesn't even taste really good until the first frost has fallen on them—and building a pen for the hundred tiny biddies ordered by mama and brought by the mailman.

After we got the biddies, my grandma came to live with us. She woke up one morning paralyzed in her leg and arm and the cheek of her face, so they hauled her over to us in a pickup truck. Uncle Alton took in grandpa, who had withdrawn more and more into the silence of deafness. He spent his days reading three newspapers and taking little sips of moonshine from a jar on the mantelshelf. Grandma rocked relentlessly, stared into the middle distance a lot, and drained her mouth of snuff into a can beside her chair. But she took what came her way without complaining. Her mind was alert and she liked to talk. We were all glad she was with us except that the house was not big enough to accommodate another child, much less an old crippled lady. She didn't eat as much as a bird, but we didn't have enough extra food to feed a bird, not even a small one. Hunger was already in the house when she got there. But we made do.

We were already beginning to go out to the pen Mr. Willis built and stare at the biddies. They were then about as big as good-sized sparrows. Each day we tried to calculate how much longer it would be before we could fry up some.

"We could do six, even ten," my brother said.

"Not now," mama said.

"They big as dove, some of'm," I said.

"But they ain't dove," she said. "They biddies."

"I reckon," said Mr. Willis. "Howsomever, I have seen'm split down the middle and cooked in two pieces."

It was late afternoon and we were standing in the backyard. Even

Grandma Hazelton. She carried her paralyzed hand in a sling from her neck and leaned heavily on a walking stick she held in her good hand. If she took her time, she got around pretty well in a kind of sliding, sidewise shuffle, dragging her bad leg. She had been helped down the steps when she came out with us to look at the biddies.

Just as we were about to go back in, a red-tailed chicken hawk glided low and fast over where we stood, taking a good look for himself into the pen.

"We gone have to git that hawk," she said. "Don't won't none of us be eating them biddies." She looked at me and winked her good eye. "You and me'll fix that gentleman tomorrow."

Mr. Willis said: "I don't believe it's a gun on the place."

"Won't need one," said Grandma Hazelton, turning to begin the long, slow shuffle back to her rocking chair.

She woke me up early the next morning. "We better git on out there an fix breakfast for that hawk," she said.

I got out of bed and, still wearing my gown, let her shuffle on down the hall to the backyard. She allowed me to help her down the three wooden steps, that being the only help she would accept. We went on back to the pen and stood looking in.

Chickens, as everybody knows, are cannibals. Let a biddy get a spot of blood on it from a scrape or a raw place and the other biddies will simply eat it alive.

"Git me that one out," she said, pointing. "The one bout half eat up."

I brought it to her. It was scabby, practically featherless, with one wing nearly pecked away. She took it into her old soft, liver-colored hands and stroked its head gently with her thumb until it settled down. Then she opened one of her snuff cans, and I saw it was a quarter full of arsenic. Calmly and with great care, she covered the biddy's head and raw neck, making sure none of the poison got in its eyes.

She handed it to me. "Put it out yonder by the fence. If it don't stay there, we'll have to tie it down with a string the hawk can break."

The biddy stayed where I put it though; it had been too brutalized by the other biddies in the pen to have much inclination to move around. And it wasn't long—still early morning—before the hawk came in low over the fence, its red tail fanned, talons stretched, and nailed the poisoned biddy where it squatted in the dust. The biddy never made a sound as it was carried away. My gentle crippled grandma watched it all with satisfaction. The hawk lit in a tree in a head of woods, and I could plainly see him tearing at the biddy on the limb.

I loved the old lady for all things she showed me and told me, but the time came when she got in the way of what I wanted to do, and I showed my true, little-boy colors. Mama had to go to Waycross, which was an overnight trip. Mr. Willis took the opportunity to visit some of his own connections over in Jeff Davis County. That left my brother and me to look after grandma and take care of things on the place. Mama cooked us some food and left it in the safe, and then caught a ride to town, where she could get the bus for Waycross. She told us to clean up after we ate—wash the dishes, put the food back in the stove—and, above all, not to leave the spoon in the gravy.

"You leave that spoon in the gravy and it'll be ruint sure. Taste just like tin."

She caught her ride, and everything went fine that first day until about sundown, when Ray came over on the mule. Ray was a friend of my brother's who lived on the next farm. He was going down the creek for some catfish and wanted us to come with him. My brother was all for it, and of course, I was too. But that left a problem. Grandma. I told her she'd be all right. She said she wouldn't.

"I'm scared," she said. "Don't leave me here all by myself."

"You'll have to stay," my brother said to me.

Who else? I was the youngest, and if anybody was going to stay home and do something dull and boring like look after an old crippled lady, it would have to be me.

"I don't want to," I said.

"She's scared," he said.

"Tell'm you ain't scared," I said. "If you don't, they gone make me stay."

"I'm scared," she said. They made me stay.

They made me stay, but as soon as they were gone, I started closing up the house, every door, every window.

"What you doing, son?"

I'd gone into a little room where she was lying down and where my own narrow bed was jammed into one corner. It was just getting on toward dark on one of those occasionally steaming days Bacon County sometimes has in late September just before it begins to cool into fall.

"I locked up everything," I said. "It's so many bad things out there in the dark, you cain't tell what's apt to come in here and git us."

Her old washed blue eyes watched me steadily in the light from a kerosene lamp I'd lighted on the little table beside her bed. She smiled uncertainly. "Ah, son," she said.

The room was tight and hot and smelled of dust. The liver spots grew almost black in her ivory skin, and sweat started on her thin blue temples.

"Please, son, please, a little air," she said. "Cain't we open one winder?"

"I think we better keep them winders closed," I said, "so we won't be scared."

I kept the dear old lady sweating, locked there in that steaming room, until my brother came back about four hours later. He immediately wanted to know what was going on. I told him. He, always being much more gentle-natured and decent than I, was not sympathetic.

"Boy, you gone git you tail beat bad when mama gits home."

I had already known that when I started shutting the house up. We both assumed grandma would tell on me, and maybe she would have if things had been different.

When mama got home the next day and went back to the kitchen, the first thing she saw was that gravy bowl. It had a spoon in it. My brother and I had followed her back to the kitchen, and we saw the spoon the same time she saw it. Both of us kind of hunkered down, shriveled where we stood. Grandma was in her chair between the back door and the wood stove and saw it all.

Mama turned slowly from the safe, her eyes blazing, and said in a calm, flat, terrible voice: "You the two sorriest boys that ever shit out of the gills of an asshole."

The skin over my heart went cold, and I could already feel the vise-like knees gripping my head. But it was not to happen.

"These boys been just as good as they could," grandma said. "They taken precious care of me." She was looking directly at me where I stood, guilt pouring over me like scalding water. "They *both* taken precious care of me."

I went to bed that night a very different boy than I had ever been before. Or at least with a different understanding than I had before. I don't know how much it affected whatever I've done since, but that moment between mama and grandma and me was fixed forever in my head and heart as if nailed there.

Twelve

DURING that year, partly because grandma was staying with us, I began to think of Uncle Alton as if he were my daddy. He had been keeping grandpa ever since grandma had her stroke and the old folks had to break up housekeeping. Uncle Alton would come down to our place to see his mama, and sometimes he would take grandma up to his place so she could get together with grandpa for a while.

From the beginning I loved him and wanted to be near him. It was never anything he said to me, but rather the way he treated me. He never treated me like I was a stump, as other people seemed to do. He noticed me. He acted like I might be somebody good to have around, somebody who could help a man with a job.

The first time I ever went cooning in Little Satilla River, he took me. I knew about cooning, but I'd never done it. And I was scared to death. Cooning is catching fish with your hands in the shallow sloughs off the river where the banks are a tangle of roots. You stick your hands up in the roots and trap fish there.

The notion of sticking my hands underwater and up into pockets of roots where I could not see made the hair get up on my neck. But if he noticed my fear, he never mentioned it.

"Git down here beside me, son," he said, "and help me with this fish. We got to be careful, though. I think it's a catfish. Mind you don't git finned."

He was waist deep in the creek, and I got in with him, up to my shoulders. The feel of his arm around my shoulders, and him saying *we* had to be careful, made me so happy I cried. He thought I had snagged a finger on a root, and I let him think it. The truth was, at that moment, I would have stuck my *head* under the water and into the roots if he had asked me to.

He took me squirrel hunting the first time I ever went, and he let me use his gun. He showed me how to whittle a trigger for a rabbit trap made out of a hollow log. He told me why the hair must not touch the meat when a goat is being skinned, and then showed me how to do it. But perhaps the best thing he ever showed me—made me *feel*—was that a man does not back away from doing whatever is necessary, no matter how unpleasant.

Our biddies were about half as big as a pigeon when the rooster began to get sluggish, walking about the yard with his head and tail feathers drooping. Everybody had noticed it—Mr. Willis first mentioned it—but Uncle Alton was the first to do something about it. He and I were on the porch with grandma, she in her chair, we on the doorsteps when the rooster came moping around the corner of the house.

"Alton," she said, "you ought to do sumpin about that rooster. He's lookin like, mama, I've come home to die."

"He ain't gone die, ma," he said.

"Will you don't do something?"

"I reckon Harry and me's gone help'm a little."

"You know what ails'm?"

"Yes, ma'am, I reckon I do."

That was another thing, which I understand imperfectly to this day: how mysteriously wonderful it was to be around Uncle Alton when he was with *his* mama. Here was a man old enough to be my daddy, and who I wished was my daddy, saying "Yes, ma'am," to his mama just like I said, "Yes, ma'am" to mine. With my life as broken, tenuous, and imperiled on every side as it seemed, knowing that we were the same blood, knowing that the blood went from that gentle, ruined old lady to Uncle Alton to me made me feel less alone, less helpless.

"Go over there and pick'm up, son," Uncle Alton said. "I don't reckon he's gone run much. I'll go in and git a few things from Myrtice."

Mama had the stove going, and so there was hot water in the reservoir. Along with the hot water, Uncle Alton found some turpentine, the only sterilizing agent we had, and some clean rags to wipe the turpentine off before it could blister, and some fishing line and a long curving needle used to repair harness. He brought it all out on the front porch, where I was holding the sick rooster. My brother was in the field with Mr. Willis, and mama, as soon as she found out what was going on, wanted no part of it. I kept calling for her to come and look while we worked, but she stayed in the kitchen.

"Now what it is, son," said Uncle Alton, when he had everything ready, "is he's crawbound. Feel right here." He took my hand and put it at the base of the rooster's neck. As young as I was, I had felt enough chicken's craws to know something was wrong. The rooster's was tight and solid as stone. "He'll be dead in a few days, maybe even tomorrow if we don't help'm. We got to clean out that craw."

I held the rooster on his back, and Uncle Alton cleaned the feathers off his craw and then shaved him down with his razor-sharp castrating knife, a spot about as big as a lemon. The rooster was too sick to care. But when Uncle Alton sliced open his craw, the rooster screamed with a sound a child might have made. Feathers and blood stuck to my hands. The thin, shivering body pulsed under my fingers. Uncle Alton was quick, and in his quickness showed every trust and confidence in me. It was a horrible and beautiful moment.

"Cut in a little deeper there, son," said grandma.

"Yes, ma'am," said Uncle Alton. "Son, git that turpentine swab right here."

"Yes, sir."

"Clean it down in the corner, Alton."

"Yes, ma'am," said Uncle Alton. "Son, I got the needle started, but I cain't git the end of it. See if you can."

"Yes, sir," I said. Uncle Alton's hand moved to take the rooster's feet, and my own fingers were suddenly deep in the wound, the living flesh slipping and throbbing.

The rooster lived to get his share of the biddies growing up in the pen back of the house. I never saw him walking around the yard that I did not remember that his blood had been on my fingers, and more, that I had touched his blood because Uncle Alton had treated me like a son he trusted. Just knowing Uncle Alton was in the world helped me deal with what was ahead of me that year.

What was ahead of me was God and little girls. The mystery and general scariness of both. As the year moved into winter, I went to wood sawings and peanut poppings for the first time. Families gathered all over Bacon County to saw logs that would be used to cook tobacco the following summer and to shell peanuts for seed. A farmer snaked up as many logs as he could cut, and then the night of the party all the men and the young bucks sipped a little moonshine and sawed themselves into a sweat. Sometimes eight or ten crosscut saws would be working at the same time, steam rising off the men's bodies in the cold air, their straining faces lighted by an enormous bonfire. Sometime later in the evening, a fiddler started and the sawing stopped. Peanut poppings were the same kind of party. A farmer would have saved back sacks of peanuts from the year before. If he wanted to plant ten or fifteen acres, an incredible number of peanuts had to be shelled by hand. Thirty-five or forty people, men, women, and children, sat around for three or four hours with peanuts in their laps, shelling as fast as they could. Finally, somebody began pushing furniture back and the first tentative squawks of the fiddle cut through the cold night air.

But mostly what went on at these parties was *walking out*. Walking out means just what it says: boys and girls walked out together into the darkness. They walked down the lane holding hands, and in a few minutes they came back, only to walk out again in a little bit. The mothers kept careful track of their daughters, how long they'd been out with a boy, and if a girl had been gone more than five or ten minutes, a mother might go sailing out into the dark, her apron flapping, to find her.

But for a child less than ten years old, walking out wasn't necessary. You could go at it in the backyard or anywhere, because nobody paid any attention to you. Perhaps that is why there was such tremendous pressure to do *it* and, consequently, a lot of hot, smarmy struggling of little, bony bodies in dark places about the house and the farm.

There was a boy my age named Bonehead whom I had got to be friends with at school who was forever at me to do *it*. A great many others were pushing me about the same thing, but Bonehead was the worst.

"You git any, boy?"

"Naw. I just about did, but I didn't."

"You got to git yourself some."

"I know," I said, in real dejection. "I know I do."

I knew that I did, that sooner or later I'd be minding my own business in some dark corner of the farmhouse or out in the lane and Bonehead would turn up with a little girl who had *it,* and there I'd be. I knew the details of the thing. Hadn't my brother explained it all and got me under the house with Lottie Mae? Hadn't I seen jacks and mares, bulls and cows banging away at each other? So I knew I had to get myself some, but the problem was that I didn't want any.

As long as I thought about cows and bulls, or even men and women, I was all right. But when I thought about *me* and. . . . Clearly impossible.

I had lots of little girls down on their backs in Springfield Section of Jacksonville, and it was fun—a little like wrestling—until it got too feverish. Then I would jump up and run.

The mystery of little girls stood at dead even with the mystery of God. See, little girls had *it*. None of the little boys had *it*. We had to go through all kinds of things—fights, gifts, lies, whatever—if we wanted *it*. And little girls could give us some of *it* if they wanted to. As well as being unpleasant, the whole thing was scary.

But then we had an evangelist come to the county to preach, and everything was all rolled into the same ball. Obviously, there was no walking out at church, but the boys and girls managed. At night services, they *did* manage. I don't know why it was so. But after the last service at night, if you could have heard the hymens popping it would have sounded like crickets in a field.

Bonehead was sitting on the aisle seat. I was next to him and pressed in on me from the other side was a boy named Alonzo. We were huddled in the Baptist Church, driven there by our parents against our wills, knowing what we were going to find.

Our own minister had prepared us for the evangelist, a man from Colorado, who continuously traveled about the country calling down the Wrath of the Living God on all unsaved heads. He also called down the Love, which sounded exactly like the Wrath, of the Living God on the same heads.

Hell came right along with God, hand in hand. The stink of sulfur swirled in the air of the church, fire burned in the aisles, and brimstone rained out of the rafters. From the evangelist's oven mouth spewed images of a place with pitchforks, and devils, and lakes of fire that burned forever. God had fixed a place like that because he loved us so much.

With a God like that on one side and a hell like that on the other, it was enough to make a little boy unaware of his loosening bowels, but even when I realized, I didn't care. What was filling my shoes compared to a God who might boil me *forever* (a word and a condition I could not imagine)? Worse, He was going to do it for reasons of love. He had—the evangelist said—sent His only son to be beaten with brambles and given vinegar to drink and finally even nailed to a tree for the same reasons of love.

I couldn't imagine such a being. But that didn't help a bit. It gave no comfort at all, because by now the man raging up there in the pulpit owned me, every cell—blood, bone, and hair. Faith had nothing to do with it. I was one with the voice and the vision of the God-crazed evangelist, standing six and a half feet tall in cowboy boots, joyous in his anger at my filthy life, with hands so enormous that as he buried me in the water later that night, his fingers wrapped my head as if it were an orange.

When a man like that told you God, by God, was coming soon, was probably on His way this very night to touch you with His Love if you didn't *come on home to Jesus right now!* you didn't argue about it, resist it, or even think about it. You just shit in your pants, stood up and staggered down the aisle toward the altar, blinded by tears and terror.

But I had always known I would someday have to do God. I had been watching people do Him all my life: fainting, screaming, crying, and thrashing about over the floor. My turn had come and I'd survived him. All that was left was *it* as I charged out into the night. I don't remember what I was thinking or if I was thinking anything. But as Bonehead kept watch for the little girl's older sister, whom their mother had sent to look for her, I got a little girl down on the dark back porch of the church, delirious, full of God and raging. I didn't know when it was over if she had given me *it* or not. But Bonehead and I were both pretty sure she had. She was crying because not only had I ripped her little cotton drawers, but I had thrown them in the yard and she didn't know what she was going to tell her mama.

For my part it was a great relief, getting on the right side of God and little girls all in the same hour. I went back to the farm that night and slept the sleep of one who is at peace with the world. It carried me nicely through the year while the turnips and collards grew green and marvelous in the winter and died in the spring, while the biddies grew up and scratched around in the yard with the rooster, and while Pete got another year grayer, another year slower.

From the beginning, though, I wanted somebody to tell about the girl and God, somebody grown. I don't know why I wanted to tell a grownup, maybe only to have what I had done confirmed as fine. Whatever the reason, as the weeks and months went by, the desire to tell somebody got stronger. I was no longer as certain as I had been. I wasn't sleeping as well. I woke up in the yard and in the fields more often sleepwalking.

Then the chance came. Mr. Willis was going to take corn to town to be ground at the mill into grits and meal. It was a sunup-to-after-dark trip, and I was allowed to go with him. We shelled out the corn, put Pete between the shaves, and eased out onto the road to Alma while it was still dark.

We were hardly out of sight of the house when I told Mr. Willis the whole story of God and the girl. It was a slow and tortuous telling. But it was easy enough to do. The burden had become too great to keep to myself. I was beginning to think that the girl had canceled out God. You don't git *it* from Him and run around to His back porch and git *it* from a girl. If in fact I had got *it* from either of them. I was no longer very sure.

Mr. Willis sat in a ladder-back chair in the bed of the wagon, looking straight ahead, while I told him all of it. The sun showed full above the wall of black pine trees when I finally finished.

He sighed and said matter-of-factly: "God an girls is just like farmin. You cain't ever git finished. Take sumpin out of the ground and it's time to put sumpin in again. Soon's you find out you ain't never gone git finished, you don't have to hurry or worry." He sent a long stream of tobacco juice over the traces. "If the grass is growing or *not* growing ain't sumpin a reasonable man oughta worry about. The grass is *gone* grow."

I didn't know what to say to him, so I said: "It's gone take a long time to git where we going."

He looked out over Pete's aged, bony withers and said: "Oh, it *always* takes a long time to git where you going."

In July of 1956 I was standing at the edge of a tobacco field with four of my cousins waiting for the sled to come from the barn. The month before I had been discharged from the Marine Corps after serving three years. I'd come back to Bacon County to visit my kin people. I had no plans to return to Georgia to live, although I thought someday I probably would. Thus far, twenty-two years later, I never have. But on that sweltering day in July, standing in the tobacco field, it felt as though I had never left. It felt good to be home again.

We'd worked since before daylight, cropping tobacco so it could be sledded to the barn where the leaves would be strung onto sticks and put into the barn to cook. My cousins were about my age, boys I'd grown up with, and as close to me as brothers. We'd had a good time that day working, although it had been hard, dusty, and hot. Particularly hot. It was early afternoon now, and I could feel the sun across my shoulders, where it lay like a weight.

The sled we'd been waiting for turned into the field. It was time to stoop to the stalks again, time to go between the rows of tobacco where no breeze ever reached. My cousins had been kidding me all day about getting bear-caught, by which they meant that I would probably go down from exhaustion and heat before we finished the field. And they were closer to the truth than they knew. Three years in the Marine Corps had not prepared me for a Georgia summer in a tobacco patch.

Looking at me, Edward said: "Boy, I believe I see the bear out yonder behind a tree."

"I believe he wants *you*," his brother Roger said, smiling.

The youngest boy, Jones, looked out into the woods bordering the field. "I believe he means to come in here and git on your back."

It had all got a little beyond joking to me, because I didn't know if I was going to make the rest of the day or not. I glanced up at the sky and said: "Goddamn sun."

As soon as I'd spoken, I knew what I had done. The four boys perceptibly flinched. When they turned to look at me, the joking and laughter were gone.

"Look," I said, "I . . . I didn't. . . . "

But there was nothing I could say. I had already done what, in Bacon County, was unthinkable. I had cursed the sun. And in Bacon County you don't curse the sun or the rain or the land or God. They are all the same thing. To curse any of them is an ultimate blasphemy. I had known that three years ago, but in three years I had somehow managed to forget it. I stood there feeling how much I had left this place and these people, and at the same time knowing that it would be forever impossible to leave them completely. Wherever I might go in the world, they would go with me.

Fathers, Sons, Blood

ON July 31, 1961, in Fort Lauderdale, Florida, I was sleeping late after writing all night when I heard my wife, Sally, scream above the yammering of children's voices. I didn't know what was wrong, but whatever it was, I knew instantly that it was bad. I sprinted down the hallway, and before I ever reached the front door, I had made out what the children, all talking at once, were trying to say.

"Patrick . . ."

" . . . can't . . ."

" . . . in the pool . . ."

" . . . get him out."

The only house in the neighborhood with a pool was two doors away. I didn't break stride going through the front door and over the hedge onto the sidewalk.

As I went through the open gate of the high fence surrounding the pool, I saw my son face down in the water at the deep end, his blond hair wafting about his head the only movement. I got him out, pinched his nose and put my mouth on his mouth. But from the first breath, it didn't work. I thought he had swallowed his tongue. I checked it and he had not.

I struggled to breathe for him on the way to the emergency room. But the pulse in his carotid artery had stopped under my fingers long before we got there, and he was dead. That morning, at breakfast with his mother, he'd had cereal. The doctor told me that in the panic of drowning, he had thrown up and then sucked it back again. My effort to breathe for him had not worked, nor could it have. His air passages were blocked. In a little more than a month, September fourth, he would have been four years old.

A man does not expect to be the orphan of his son. Standing by the open grave, returning to his room, taking his clothes out of the closet and folding them into boxes, sorting through the stuff that was his, taking it up from the place he last left it—all of this is the obligation of the son, not of the father. Not of the father, that is, unless some unnatural and unthinkable collaboration of circumstances and events takes the life of the son before that of the father.

Patrick had never gotten out of the yard before, but that morning, some neighborhood children, most not much older than he, had come by and helped him out, and he had gone with them. The family that owned the pool always kept the gate locked, but that day the gate was open. There, two doors away, somebody was always at home on Saturday, and certainly somebody was *always* at home when the gate was unlocked, but nobody was at home when Patrick sat down on the cement lip of the pool, took off his shoes and socks and slipped into the water, thinking, probably, that he was going wading.

As I worked through Patrick's things after the funeral, I could hear Byron, my other son, bubbling and gurgling across the hall. I quit with the Slinkys and the Dr. Seuss books and the stacks of wild crayon drawings and walked into Byron's room, where he lay on his back watching a mobile of butterflies dancing over his head in the mild breeze from the open window. He would be one year old in less than a month, on August 24, and he was a happy baby even when he had befouled himself, which he had managed to do only moments before I walked in. I unpinned his diaper and a ripe fog of baby shit floated up and hung about my face. I looked at his pristine little cock, standing at half-mast about as big as a peanut, and I thought of my own cock and of the vasectomy I'd had a month after his birth.

"It's just you and I now, Buckshot," I said, "just the two of us."

I thought then and I think now that two children make up my fair share. Sally and I had reproduced ourselves and, in a world drowning in a population problem, that was all we were entitled to. If I had it to do all over again, I'd do it the same way. It is not something I ever argue about with anybody. It's only what I believe; whatever other people believe is their own business. Fair share or not, though, I had lost half of the children I would ever have. And behind that fact came the inevitable questions. Who needs this kind of grief? Who needs the trouble that will surely come with the commitment to fatherhood? Isn't a son at times disappointing and frustrating to the father? And isn't he at all times an emotional and financial responsibility that could just as easily have been avoided? And the ultimate question: Is it worth it?

I've had that final question answered time and again over the past 20 years, and the answer has always been yes, it is worth it.

The answer has come in many forms, out of many circumstances. One of the answers was given to me a short time ago when I came in on a plane and Byron was there to meet me. I was dead tired from days of airports and motel rooms and taxi-cabs.

When I walked up to him, I said, "I'd kiss you, son, but I don't think I can reach you."

He smiled, put his hand on my shoulder and said, "Hell, I'll bend down for an old man."

And the baby, who was now in the first flower of manhood and 6'3" tall to boot, bent and kissed me.

What affected me so much was not what he said or that he kissed me. Rather, it was the tone of his voice, a tone that can be used only between men who are equals in each other's eyes, who admire and respect each other. It was the voice of men who have been around a lot of blocks together, who have seen the good times and bad and, consequently, know the worst as well as the best about each other. Finally, it was the voice of love, the sort of love that asks nothing and gives everything, that will go to the wall *with* you or *for* you. In my experience, it is the voice hardest to find in the world, and when it is found at all, it is the voice of blood speaking to blood.

Blood, begetting it and spilling it. In those nightmare days following Patrick's death, I inevitably thought long and hard, usually against my will, about the circumstances of his brief life and his death. Much of it came as incriminations against myself. It is part of the price of parenthood. And anybody who would keep you from the knowledge of that hard price is only lying, first to himself and then to you.

The boy had developed a hideous stutter by the time he drowned. The great pain it had given me while he was alive was only compounded when he was dead. Somehow I must have caused it. I must have been too strict or too unresponsive or too unloving or. . . . The list went on—just the sort of low-rent guilt that we heap upon ourselves where blood is concerned. Being low-rent, though, doesn't keep guilt from being as real as an open wound. But in my case, it got worse, much worse. Part of me insisted that I had brought him to the place of his death.

Sally and I had been married when I was 25 and a senior at the University of Florida. She was 18 and a sophomore. A year and a half later, when I was in graduate school, she divorced me and took the baby to live in Dayton, Ohio. I'm not interested in assigning blame about who was at fault in the collapse of our marriage, but I do know that I was obsessed to the point of desperation with becoming a writer and, further, I lived with the conviction that I had gotten a late start toward that difficult goal. Nobody knew better than I how ignorant, ill read and unaccomplished I was, or how very long the road ahead of me was to the place I wanted most to be in the world. Consequently, perhaps I was impatient, irritable and inattentive toward Sally as a young woman and mother. But none of that kept me from missing my son when he was gone, longing for him in much the same way I had longed for my father, who had died before I could ever know him. So out of love and longing for my son (selfishness?), I persuaded her to marry me again, come back to Florida and join her life with mine.

And my efforts to have Sally come back to Florida haunted me in those first hard days following the death of my son. If I had not remarried her, if she had stayed in Dayton, Patrick could not have found his death in that swimming pool in Fort Lauderdale, could he? But the other side of that question was yet another. If I had not remarried Sally, I could never have known and loved my second son, Byron, could I? The crazed interrogation with myself went on. Was there somehow a way to balance things there? Was there a way to trade off in my head and heart the life of one son for the life of another? Patently not. That was madness. But . . . ? Always another but.

Enter my uncle Alton, who was as much a father to me as any man could ever have asked for. When he heard that my son had drowned, he walked out of his tobacco field in south Georgia and drove the 500 miles to be with me. While neighbors and friends stood about in my house eating funeral food, Uncle Alton and I hunkered on our heels under a tree in the back yard, smoking. We'd walked out there together and, as I'd seen him do all my life, Uncle Alton dropped onto his heels and started making random markings in the dirt with a stick. And just as naturally as breathing, I talked to him about the questions that were about to take me around the bend of madness, questions that I had not talked about to anybody else before and have not told anybody since. It was a long telling, and he never once interrupted.

I finished by saying, "It feels like I'm going crazy."

His gray eyes watched me from under the brim of his black-felt hat.

He had only two hats, one for the fields and one for funerals. He was hunkered there in the only suit of clothes he owned. He couldn't afford this trip any more than he could afford to walk out of the field during the harvest of the only money crop he had on the farmed-out piece of south Georgia dirt he'd scratched a living out of for 40 years, any more than he could have afforded to give me a home when I was eight years old and had nowhere else to go. He needed another mouth to feed like he needed screwworms in his mules or cutworms in his tobacco. But he had taken me in and treated me the same way he treated Theron and Don and Roger and Ed and Robert, his other boys.

"You ain't gone go crazy, son," he said.

He had not responded until he had taken out a Camel cigarette and turned it in his hands, studying it, and then examining a long kitchen match the same way before firing it against his thumbnail. He was nothing if not the most reticent and considered of men.

"That's what it feels like," I said. "Crazy."

"Well, crazy," he said, acknowledging it and dismissing it at the same time. "What you gone do is the next thing."

"That's what the next thing feels like."

"I reckon it might. But it's some of us that cain't afford to go crazy. The next thing is lying in yonder in a crib. You ain't gone give up on blood, are you, boy?"

It was not a rhetorical question. He wanted an answer, and his steady eyes, webbed with veins from crying himself, held mine until I gave him one.

"No, sir, I'm not."

He put his hand on my shoulder. "Then let's you and me go on back in the house and git something to eat."

"You feel like a drink of whiskey?" I said.

"We can do that, too," he said. "I'd be proud to have a drink with you."

"Good," I said.

The two of us went into the back room where I worked and sat down with two whiskeys. As we drank, both of us heard the sudden furious crying of Byron from somewhere in the house. Funerals and death be damned; the baby was hungry. Uncle Alton lifted his glass toward the sound of the angry, healthy squalling, a brief smile touching his face, and said, "There it is. There it is right there."

And so it is. Part of the way I am bonded to my son is made up of the way I will always be bonded to Uncle Alton, dead now these many years, dead before Byron could ever know him. But no great matter. Blood is our only permanent history, and blood history does not admit of revision. Or so some of us believe.

I picked up a magazine not long ago in which a man was writing about his children. In the very beginning of the piece, he said, "The storms of childhood and adolescence had faded into the past." He would be the poorer for it if that were true. But it is not true, not for him or for any father. The storms don't fade into the past, nor do all the moments that are beautiful and full of happiness, the moments that quicken our hearts with pride. In early July of the summer Byron would turn 12, we were sitting on the top of Springer Mountain in Georgia. It was raining and we were soaked and exhausted to the bone, having made the long steep climb of the approach to the Appalachian Trail, which winds its way across the Eastern United States and finally ends on Mount Katahdin in Maine. Between us, embedded in the boulder on which we were sitting, was the metal image of a young hiker.

Byron put his hand on the stone and said, "Well, we made it to the beginning."

And so we had, but a hell of a beginning it had been. It hadn't stopped raining all day as we'd climbed steadily over broken rock. He was carrying a 20-pound pack and mine weighed 45, both probably too heavy, but we'd decided to pack enough with us so that we could hike for as long as we wanted to without getting out of the mountains to re-stock our supplies. I had put him in the lead to set the pace.

"Remember, we're not in a hurry," I called after we'd been going awhile. "This is not a goddamn contest."

I was forced to say it because he'd taken off over the brutally uneven trail like a young goat. He'd looked back at me for only an instant and kept climbing.

Then, as the mud and rock made the footing more and more unsure, I said, "You think we ought to find a place to wait out this rain?"

He stopped and turned for just an instant to look at me. "Did we come to by God hike or did we come to hike?"

He was smiling, but he'd said it with just the finest edge of contempt, which is the way you are supposed to say it, and I scrambled to follow him, my heart lifting. Byron had heard me ask him much the same thing many times before, because if you change a couple of words, the question will serve in any number of circumstances. And now, in great high spirits, he was giving it back to me. I would not be surprised if someday he gave it to his own son.

The question had come down to him through my own mouth from Uncle Alton. When he would be in the woods with me and his other sons hunting on a freezing November morning and one of us said something about being cold or otherwise uncomfortable, he'd say, "Did we come to by God hunt or did we come to hunt?" And the other boys and I would feel immediately better, because that was something men said to other men. It was a way a man had of reminding other men who they were. We had been spoken to as equals.

All of that is what I was thinking while we sat there in a misting rain on a boulder with the metal image of a hiker in it signaling the official beginning of the Appalachian Trail atop Springer Mountain. But it was not what he was thinking.

"Dad, you remember about the time with the rain?"

"The time about the rain? Hell, son, we been in the rain a lot together." I was wet and my feet hurt. I wanted to get the tent up and start a fire.

He cut his eyes toward me. Drops of rain hung on the ends of his fine lashes. He was suddenly very serious. What in the hell was coming down here? What was coming down was the past that is never past and, in this case, the past against which I had no defense except my own failed heart.

"We weren't in it together," he said. "You made me stand in it. Stand in it for a long time."

Yes, I had done that, but I had not thought about it in years. It's just not the sort of thing a man would want to think about. Byron's mother had gone North for a while and left me to take care of him. He was then seven years old and just starting in the second grade. I had told him that day to be home at six o'clock and we would go out to dinner. Truthfully, we'd been out to eat every night since Sally had been gone, because washing dishes is right up at the top of the list of things I won't do. It had started misting rain at midday and had not stopped. Byron had not appeared at six, nor was he there at 6:45. That was back when I was bad to go to the bottle, and while I wasn't drunk, I wasn't sober, either. Lay it on the whiskey. A man will snatch at any straw to save himself from the responsibility of an ignoble action. When he did come home at 7:15, I asked him where he'd been.

"At Joe's," he said. But I had known that. I reminded him of when we had said we were going to dinner. But he had known that.

"It was raining," he said.

I said, "Let's go out and look at it."

We went out into the carport and watched the warm spring rain.

"And you thought the rain would hurt you if you walked home in it?"

"It's *raining,* Dad," he said, exasperated now.

"I'll tell you what," I said. "You go out there and stand in it and we'll see how bad it hurts you."

He walked out into the rain and stood looking at me. "How long do I have to stand here?"

"Only until we see if it hurts you. Don't worry, I'll tell you when you are about to get hurt."

I went back inside. So far, pretty shitty, but it gets worse. When I went back inside, I sat down in a recliner, meaning to stay there only a minute. But I hadn't reckoned with the liquor and the rain on the roof. I woke with a start and looked at my watch. It was a quarter of nine. I went outside and there the boy stood, his blond hair plastered and every thread on him soaked. He didn't look at all sad or forlorn; what he did look was severely pissed.

"Come on in," I said. And then: "Where do you want to eat?"

"I don't want to eat."

"How do you feel?" I asked.

He glared at me. "Well, I'm not *hurt.*"

We sat there on the top of Springer Mountain and looked at each other with the rain falling around us. I'd forgotten entirely about my feet and the tent and the fire. My throat felt like it was closing up and I had to speak to keep breathing.

"I wanted to apologize, but I had done such a sorry-assed thing that I couldn't bring myself to do it. But at the time, it didn't seem like it'd do any good."

"It probably wouldn't have," he said. "Then."

"Well, I'm sorry. I was wrong. I should have said so, but. . . ." I'd run out of words.

He said, "I know. And I was only down the block. I've thought about it. I could have called. But, shit, I was only a *little* kid."

I loved that. I loved how he said he was only a little kid. "What were you thinking while you were out there? I mean, you had plenty of time to think."

He shook his head and laughed as though he couldn't believe the memory of his thinking himself. "I never thought but one thing."

"What was that?"

"I thought, That drunk fucker thinks I'm going to call and ask him to come in out of the rain . . . but I'm *not*." Then he laughed like it was the funniest thing in the world, and I laughed, too.

That was the first time I knew he was the kind of guy who could be put out on the street naked and he'd survive. The kid had grit in his craw. I thought it then and I think it now. But more than that, there on the mountain, the boy and I had been privileged to share a moment of grace that we could never have shared if I had not fucked up so badly all those years ago and if he had not had the kind of heart he has. But that moment is the privilege of blood.

Sons grow up, though. God knows they do in a New York heartbeat. Byron grew up running with me. By the time he was a teenager, we had a four-mile course full of hills laid out. But the very worst of the hills was the last one. On the four miles, we jogged and talked, nothing serious; but at the bottom of that last, long hill, we'd always turn to shout at each other, "*Balls!* Who's got 'em?" And then we'd sprint and I always won. Somehow, I thought I always would. But the day came at the beginning of his 14th year when he beat me by 20 yards. I shook his hand, but I was pissed. I don't like to lose at anything. But then, neither does he. And we always had the understanding between us—never, to my knowledge, spoken—that neither of us, whether playing handball or whatever, gave the other anything. If you wanted the point, you had to win it. As we cooled out walking, I began to feel better and then proud of him. But the only thing I said was, "There's always tomorrow."

He patted my back, a little too kindly, a little too softly, I thought, and said, "Sure, Dad, there's always tomorrow."

I never beat him on the hill again. But I still had the gymnasium. Lungs and speed may go, but strength stays. Well, it stays for a while. And I don't even have to tell you, do I?, that the day came when he was stronger on the bench and at the rack than I was. Strange feeling for a father. No, not strange; sad. Part of me wanted him to grow into manhood, but another part of me had a hard time accepting it. Maybe, in my private heart, I'll never be entirely able to accept it. If I live to be 70, he'll still be my boy at 40. I know; mushy, isn't it? I don't even like it myself. But I don't have to like it; all I have to do is live with it.

And out of the feeling of the father for the son comes the desire to save him from pain, knowing full well that it is impossible. But that in no way diminishes the desire. You want to save him from the obvious things, like broken legs or lacerated flesh; but more than that, you are at some trouble to see that he is not hurt by life. I am talking here about education. Maybe I'm particularly sensitive about that because nobody in the history of my family ever went to college except me, and I had to join the Marine Corps during the Korean War so I could get the GI Bill to do that. So imagine how I felt six months ago when I walked by Byron's apartment and, as we were talking, he told me that he was quitting the university after being there two years.

"What are you going to do, son?"

"Play guitar," he said.

The guitar has been his passion for years. It is not unusual for him to practice six hours a day for weeks running. And to give him his due, he is a righteous picker. But if he just continued in the university, he would. . . . But you probably know the kinds of things I tried to tell him. Father things. But he wasn't having any of it.

Finally, in exasperation, I said a dumb fatherly thing: "Byron, do you know how many boys there are in this country with guitars who think they're going to make a living picking?"

He only smiled and asked, "Dad, when you were my age, how many boys do you think there were in this country who owned typewriters who thought they were going to make a living writing?"

There it is. The father has his dream. The son has his. And a dream is unanswerable. All you can do for a man with a dream is wish him well.

"Do well, son," I said.

"I'll try," he said.

THE GYPSY'S CURSE

CURSE

A Novel

My favorite thing is to go where I've never been.
—DIANE ARBUS

I

One

FOR the record, call me Marvin Molar. I said to call me Marvin Molar because that's not my real name. It's only what I call myself. I don't know my real name. Nobody does. Actually, somebody does, but I don't know where they are. Al Molarski raised me and named me Marvin and his name is all I've got. But I dropped the "ski" part of it and just call myself Marvin Molar. I figured I had enough wrong with me without being a Polack, which is what Al is.

I lived upstairs in some rooms at the back of the Fireman's Gym with Al and a kid from Georgia named Leroy and a seventy-year-old ex-prizefighter with a bad brain named Pete who was a nigger. The kid kept the gym clean and pretended he was training for another fight. The nigger drove the car and talked to himself. I did the best I could nickle-and-diming at Rotarians' meetings and shopping malls and wherever else they wanted to see me do my act.

Al owned the gym, which had nothing to do with firemen by the way. It was just called the Fireman's Gym. It was probably always called that but I don't know for sure. Al didn't talk much. I had been there all my life—since I was a baby—but I didn't know much about how things got to be the way they were because Al hardly ever talked and I couldn't talk except with my hands or else write it out on a piece of paper so I was easy to ignore if you wanted to. But of course most people didn't want to ignore me. Most people paid too much attention to me, just about everybody except Al. He didn't talk much and you would be lucky if he looked at you. He would look near you. But he wouldn't look at you. One of his favorite tricks was to look at your left ear. He would just stare at it and it made him look kind of stunned, like his eyes were not focusing and like he might be a little crazy which he probably was. With the things that happened to him, he should have been crazy as a bat.

I had my reasons to be bitter, but I wasn't. And I wasn't as bad off as I sound either. Actually, in a lot of ways, I was pretty goddam bad off but not as bad off as I sound—or as bad off as I looked for that matter. One thing I do is read a lot. I'm not a dummy. Some people thought I was, but I wasn't. It's easy to think that a guy who can't talk or hear is a dummy but anybody who thought that about me was a long way from being right. The whole wall above my bed was filled with shelves of books. And I read'm too; they weren't just there for show. I wasn't like Pete and Al and the Georgia boy whose name was Leroy and who *was* a dummy from being hit on the head so much. I'm not as sharp as I'd like to be—who is?—but I'm pretty sharp for somebody who has every right to be bitter.

The day she called was Sunday and Sunday was a little different for me from the other six days in the week, but not a whole lot different. I didn't have to start my workout until nine o'clock instead of eight on Sundays. That's why I was still in bed. When I opened my eyes that morning I saw the same thing I saw every morning. The note my parents left with me.

It was in one of those gold-gilt cheapy frames that people buy out of Woolworth's to frame their kid's high school diploma in. And that was where Al got it, out of Woolworth's. The frame, not the note. And I read it that morning just like I did every morning. God knows I didn't have to read it. I had seen it on the wall ever since I'd been there, sixteen years. For the record, that's how old I am, sixteen. January twenty-first I'll be seventeen. We called January twenty-first my birthday. But that wasn't it. That was just the day my parents left me on the stairs leading up to the Fireman's Gym. The note was pinned to the blanket wrapped around me.

Al said it was a very nice blanket, not a cheapy at all. A first class blanket. And the note was typed, if you can believe that. I can't get over it, the note being typed. It had turned yellow behind the glass of the diploma frame, but you could still read it from all the way across the room. Here was what it said:

WE ARE YOUR NORMAL PEOPLE AND WE CAINT STAND IT. WE JUST CAINT STAND IT. WHOEVER YOU ARE, WE WOULD BE ABLIDGED IF YOU WOULD TAKE CARE OF THIS FOR US BECAUSE WE CAINT STAND IT ANY MORE.

THANK YOU
HIS PEOPLE

PS It caint talk.

And there I was under the blanket, a great big kid, probably three or nearly four years old already. I found that out from Al. Even though he doesn't talk much, I have managed to find out a few things in sixteen years. And one of the things I found out was that I was three or four already when he found me on the stairs. So off the record I'm not sixteen. I'm probably nineteen or twenty, but like I said, Al counted my birthday from when he found me. And if he said that was my birthday, what could I do? It would be easy to be bitter, but I'm not. I got better things to do with my time than be bitter. I did look at that note a lot though. It hurt my heart that those words were misspelled. Type up a note to abandon a baby and then misspell the words. Something in that rubs you the wrong way. They couldn't have been people who read much. They might even have been dummies like Leroy and the nigger. That hurt my heart but it might be true.

I remember when the telephone rang. I could feel it all the way across the room. It came through the floor from the little table by the door and up into the bed. Al was standing at the stove with his back to me cooking eggs and bacon for him and Leroy and Pete. I wasn't allowed to eat until after my morning workout. Even on Sunday. His back got still as a wall. He knew I could feel the telephone ringing. He slid the skillet off the fire and went to the little table by the door. After touching his cauliflowered ear with the receiver, he turned and stared at a spot just over my head somewhere in the first shelf of books. I watched his lips. But he didn't speak. He stood there looking stunned and distant. I took my hand out from under the covers and asked who was calling. I already knew and he knew I knew but I asked him anyway just to get him a little tight. I watched his mouth and finally he said, "Her."

"Ask her what she wants," I said.

He put his mouth to the receiver, and turned his head so that I could barely see the corner of his mouth. "He says to tell you he can't talk now."

I snatched down a book from the lowest shelf and threw it as hard as I could. It hit a picture of Al posing in a pair of swim trunks on the deck of a Navy battleship. Al slowly looked up and cut his old-man eyes at the picture where it lay on the floor. Then he stared at my left ear. He did it all real slow, like he did everything.

"If you're going to lie," I said, "turn your head all the way around."

"Did you say Al lies?" he said.

He always called himself by his name. I think he thought it made him sound scarier, which it does.

I said: "If you're going to lie, turn your head all the way around. I can read the corner of your mouth. I can even read the way your chin moves."

"Al don't lie," he said.

"I can talk, baby," I said to Al. "You know how I love to talk to you." Al said what I said into the phone, his eyes dead and steady now, lost among the curling mat of black hair on my fantastic chest.

I watched Al's mouth. It said: "You didn't come back last night."

"You know I would have if I could," I said.

"You coming down today?"

"Sure," I said. "Right after the workout. Pete'll bring me down."

Leroy had come in now and was standing just inside the door, squinting at us—Al and me—his beat-together eyes swinging from my hands to Al's face. He couldn't read lips or sign language or probably even writing although I don't know that for sure, but I do know he thought what we did was magic. I'd never seen him say it, but I knew that was the way he thought about it. Leroy was a little afraid of me and if he watched me and Al talk with our hands very long he started to turn gray like he might throw up. But I ignored him. I was zeroed in on Al's mouth, until it was Hester's mouth I was looking at. I could see her great little pointed tongue all wet with peppermint spit right there in Al's mouth.

"You like it, don't you?" she said.

"Don't I just about faint?" I said.

"You want it this afternoon?"

"Hot damn," I said.

"I'll make it good for you," she said.

"You always do."

Al and I stared at each other across the room. His eyes always got blank and flat when I talked through him on the phone. It was almost like he didn't listen in, even though it had to go through him. But I knew he did. Al didn't miss much.

Finally she said: "Did you ask him yet?"

"What?"

"Did you ask him?"

"We'll talk about it later," I said. "When I get to the beach."

"You didn't ask him."

"I have to go now," I said.

"Ask him before you come, you hear?"

"I have to go now, sweetheart. Good-by."

Al hung up the phone. He went over to the stove, his back still as a wall again, even though his arms were moving around over the pots. I threw another book, but this time I was careful not to hit anything. It wouldn't do to get Al too tight.

When the book hit the wall, Al waited about a minute before he turned around real slow and focused on my ear. He didn't say anything. Leroy was sitting at the table now, staring at my hands. He had only been living there a month and he watched my hands when I talked like they might turn into rabbits.

"Did she say good-by?" I asked.

He just stared at me. I could see the grease popping out of the skillet behind him on the stove, making little blue stars in the fire. Finally he said: "Yes."

"I want it," I said.

He turned back to the stove, shook the skillet, then looked over his shoulder and said: "Good-by."

"All right," I said, "good-by." But he already had his face turned away and didn't see it.

I sat up in bed, took the nylon strap down from its hook on the wall and began to bind up my legs. See, that's why the people—my parents, I guess, except I've never been sure of that or really able to believe it—why the people who left me on the steps of the Fireman's Gym didn't have to worry about me getting up and wandering off even though I was a great big kid. These legs I was born with shouldn't happen to a dog.

I could swim pretty good but I never did, ever since a boy about five years old standing by the pool one day told me I looked like a tadpole. My upper body doesn't sit on the back seat to nobody, but in the water my little legs trail along behind like, well, like a tadpole's, I guess. For the record, they're only three inches around and they look like they don't have any bones in them except they do. Bones but no feeling. I thought a couple of times about getting them cut off but I could never bring myself to do it. I mean they're my legs even if I can't do anything with them. I keep'm folded back and bound against the cheeks of my ass with a nylon strap and walk on my hands. My act is all hand-balancing stuff that Al taught me and I can do just about anything on my hands you can do on your feet. I mean my arms, hot, measure twenty inches around and I don't know how much you know about arms but a pair that tapes twenty inches'll stop people in the street.

I slid out of bed and went over to where the book I threw knocked Al's picture off the table. I rocked over into a one-hander and picked the picture up and put it back. Just about everywhere you look in the Fireman's Gym or in the rooms we live in, you see pictures of Al in swim trunks or wrestling tights, usually with four men hanging from each arm or a car running over his chest or him standing on a platform with a small cow hanging from a harness hooked into his teeth or something like that. When he was young he was wrestling champion of the United States Navy for six years and he never got over it. He spent the rest of his life tearing tennis balls in two, bending dimes between his mean fingers, twisting bridge spikes and generally scaring the shit out of everybody. Along with the pictures of Al, there were bridge spikes bent like pretzels, and decks of cards with a piece the size of a thumb torn out of one corner and U-shaped quarters lying all over the place. Al's hands and wrists were a nightmare.

After I put the books back, I went over and pulled myself up in a ladder-back chair. Al had the food on the table by then and Pete came shuffling in talking to two invisible seconds, telling them if they could stop the blood in his mouth that he would take the bum out in the next round. He choked on blood, coughed, and sat down by Leroy, who had a piece of bread in each hand and was batting the eggs back and to across his plate. Al's got a special place in his heart for boxers because you can fuck over their heads so easy.

God knows where he got Pete; he was here when I came here, looking just like he does now. But the Georgia kid, Leroy, walked in off the street a month ago. He was carrying a canvas bag and had on what looked like a railroader's cap. Al was sitting on the stool behind the wire cage where the towels and massage oil and Hoffman food supplements were kept. There was where Al sat mostly when the gym was open. Sometimes he wouldn't move off the stool for five or six hours. I was working on the Roman rings when the kid came in. He stopped at the top of the stairs and just stood there. He stayed there a long time watching the iron freaks pumping steel in the front part of the gym where the light was better. Then he saw Al sitting behind the screen wire. He walked over and stopped in the open door leading into the cage.

I hung in the rings and watched them.

"I'm a boxer. Name Leroy."

Al didn't look at him. He didn't say anything either.

"I thought to work out here," said the kid.

Al almost turned his back and looked down at the other end of the gym as though the thought of a boxer working out here had never come to him. But there was a ring down there where he was looking, and some heavy bags and a speed bag and skip ropes and stuff hanging on the wall.

"I got some money," the kid said.

He put his hand in his back pocket and took out a black change purse. He opened it and even from where I was on the rings I could see the bills folding out in a little roll. Al didn't look at the money or the purse or the kid.

"I come from Bacon County, Georgia," said the kid, "on the Greyhound today." He looked down at the canvas bag he was carrying. "I fight anybody," he said. "It don't matter."

He stood there shifting from foot to foot and I saw he had scar tissue in his eyebrows. I quit watching and dropped into an iron cross on the rings and held it until I saw black spots start to dance in the air and heard a high whistle that I hear when I'm about to pass out. I think it comes from the blood in my heart.

Finally, I looked back and the kid was saying: " . . . and on Sunday I'd hitch up the wagon and drive around from farm to farm fighting anybody that'd put on the gloves with me. Sometimes I'd git thirty, thirty-five fights, in just a Sunday." He paused and looked down at his bag and at his change purse he was still trying to show Al. "I fight anybody."

Now Al stood up and put his hand on the kid's shoulder. I remember how he flinched under that hand. Al's fingers were about eight inches long—you think I'm saying more than it was, but I'm not—they were about eight inches long. He can hold a medicine ball like an orange, and I remember how the kid cut his eyes to look at the hand on his shoulder like he'd found a rattlesnake there. But I saw too how the boy loved that hand, wished it was his. Hell, I can understand that.

Al still hadn't looked at him and still hadn't said anything, or at least I hadn't seen him say anything, and Al pointed to the back of the gym to the room where the lockers and showers were, where little clouds of steam were always coming through the door, and kind of pushed the boy toward it. The boy looked and mumbled something like—I couldn't make it out exactly—something like, "I 'preciate it," and started back, but Al held his shoulder tight and lifted the change purse out of his fingers. He took a long time looking down into the purse and then he emptied it, took all the money out of it, and sat back down on the stool and began to count it real slow. The boy watched him, and that was when Al looked at him for the first time. It was to hand him the empty purse back. The kid held it a moment and then walked on back to the lockers. After a while he came out wearing his railroad cap and dressed in a yellow bathing suit, black tennis shoes with black nylon socks. He punched the hell out of the heavy bag for the rest of the afternoon. I had to do my act that evening at the Springfield Shopping Mall and when the nigger drove me back after dark there was another bunk in the place where we live and the kid was in it with his face turned to the wall, fast asleep.

That was Al Molarski for you. He would take the last thing in the world you had and then give you a place to sleep.

They were about through eating now. Pete had carefully wiped his mouth and hands with the sleeve of his shirt and Leroy was hooking and jabbing the last piece of egg yolk around on his plate. Leroy hooked and jabbed about all the time. He slipped punches in his sleep too.

Al stood up from the table. The other two stood up with him. It was time for the workout and I was anxious to get it over with. The rest of Sunday was free if I didn't have to do my act anywhere and the only place I had to be was in the basement of the Baptist church at seven-thirty that evening to balance for some boy scouts, but the rest of the time was mine.

I slid off the chair onto my hands and followed the three of them down the hall to the steam room. I always take a little steam to warm up for a workout. I wasn't wearing anything but jockey shorts and I kept them on. Al held the door open for me and I went in and pulled myself up on a wooden bench. The steam hung in wavy layers under the yellow bulb in the ceiling. In a minute the three of them came in naked, one behind the other. Al and the boy were the same color, not white, but kind of an off gray, like they'd got that way from being mashed under something. The nigger was purple under the light, and steam beaded him like drops of oil. I rolled onto my back and Pete came to hang over me, rubbing my chest and pulling at me and gently pounding my shoulders. Hanging over me, his teeth were white on purple while he talked. He was his second and then his manager and then himself and then the ref and then the guy he was fighting and sometimes somebody I didn't know. Behind him, Al was leaning back with his eyes closed and he wasn't moving at all except for his hands feeling each other, soft and slow as a girl. The boy sat beside him, slipping punches and hooking. I couldn't read his nose, but I knew he was snorting.

"Wake to his body, wake to his body," Pete said. His old broken fists kept his boxer's rhythm as he worked to my stomach. "Wake to his body," he whined in a little song. "He come down, wake to his head, wake to his head."

"The nigger ain't got all that's coming to him, has he?" said Leroy.

Al kept washing his hands in the steamy air and didn't say anything.

"He waking to my head, he waking to my head," said Pete. "Got to slip, got to roll," he said, full of panic, being hurt bad. "You thumbing, you butting." As the referee, Pete was calm in the middle of the punches, and sweat and pain.

Leroy said: "That nigger ain't got all that's coming to him."

Leroy was scrambled bad by the last and only pro fight he ever had, came out of it punch-drunk, if he wasn't before. Punch-drunk at seventeen. That's how old he is, my age more or less, but I always thought of him as a kid because he was scrambled so bad. Everybody's got plenty of reason to be bitter.

Al's lips moved and I felt the little scratchy vibrations of his old ruined voice run in the tiles. "Al knows Pete," he said.

Leroy squinted through the steam. "Huh?"

Al's hands were still hanging on to each other. Not washing now, just hanging on. "Al knows Pete," he said.

I could see the kid's face struggling with that. "All right," he finally said.

Al's hands slipped into easy motion again. He would do that to you, either not answer you at all, or else answer so long after you spoke to him that you didn't remember what it was you were talking about.

Al had his head run over once. I found it out in the scrapbook in the little leather trunk he kept under his bed. All his other scrapbooks were lying around the gym, but not this one. This one had a big story out of the newspaper about how he got his head run over. And a picture too. He kept it hidden probably because he told everybody he got the cauliflower ear when he won the wrestling championship of the United States Navy. But he didn't. He got it from his head being run over.

See, he was supposed to have this car run one wheel up a big board he had laid over his chest, but the driver made a mistake, or was drunk, or maybe did it on purpose—there's a lot of that in the world too—anyway, whatever it was, there was old Al with his face squashed shut, mashed half into the dirt under the wheel of a Hudson Hornet. Some guy took the picture with the car right on top of his head. Al's mouth was open, but his eyes were shut. Jesus, he was screaming. I sneaked it out of that trunk under the bed sometimes and spent all afternoon just looking at that wheel up on Al's head.

"He be hurt. He be hurt," said Pete clinching with me, working to the solar plexus. "Now cut the ring on him. Now cut the ring in *two*."

His old nigger voice had a hard-on. It smelled blood. He'd been working to my arms. He loved those arms. Worked my arms good. I was loose and ready to go by then. I was warm and ready to work. He was finishing, finishing big.

"He hurt," said Pete.

Then: "I be hurt," Pete said.

"He going down," said Pete.

"I be going down," Pete said.

Then he was down. he was standing over himself, counting himself out.

"One," he said. "Two. Three . . . "

I didn't wait for him to finish, but rocked up on my fantastic ass. Directly across from me on the other wooden bench, Leroy faced me, dazed. His eyes were glazed. His mouth was slack, broken in pain. He had got lost in Pete's voice and been knocked out. It happened all the time. It was one of the reasons Leroy didn't like Pete. While I watched, Leroy's eyes gradually focused and he gave Pete a long sullen stare.

"Sumbitch ain't got all that's coming to him," Leroy said.

Al held the door for me and I went through and down the hall to the gym. It was the middle of July and there was no air-conditioning. A huge fan circled in the roof but nobody ever felt it do anything. It squeaked though. I could feel the squeak in the floor as soon as Al turned it on every morning. He only had it up there in the first place so he'd be able to point to it when somebody told him there was no air in the gym and that he ought to do something about it.

They came out behind me, wrapped only in towels, leaving a trail of water. Al took the stool out of the wire cage and sat on it. Pete and Leroy stood on each side of him. Pete's careful to stand a good ways from Leroy ever since Leroy got excited watching me work out one morning and hooked Pete to the heart, a shot that dropped him like he was dead and I thought he might be until I bent over Pete and saw his eyes were open and he was quietly telling himself to stay down and take eight and at the same time he was counting himself out.

I started working out like I always did, stacking the bricks. It looks pretty good. I got it in my act, but actually it just finishes the warm-up. What I do is stack two columns of bricks ten high. Besides the balance, all it takes is being able to press out of a one-hander. I walked over to the pile and took a brick in each hand and walked with the bricks to the place in front of Al and put the bricks about two feet apart on the floor. Then I went back and got two more and put these two on top of the first two. There's nothing to it until you get to about the fifth level, because Al doesn't just make me stack them, he makes me get on top of them. By the fifth one, I have to reach up from the floor, put my hand on top of the stack, and press into a one-hand handstand. It's about there that Leroy really starts to get excited. By the fifth brick, he's bobbing and weaving, a little spit hanging in one corner of his mouth. About every two minutes he'll throw that hook.

And the kid can punch. That's all he's got, the hook and a cast-iron head. It's what almost got him killed in the fight Al set up for him, or set him up for would probably be a better way to say it.

Leroy had been in the gym for five days, sweeping and straightening up after the iron freaks and working out on the heavy bag every afternoon in his yellow bathing suit and tennis shoes and still sleeping on the bunk in back, when Al came out of the cage about noon and told Leroy he had a fight Friday with Millard Fillmore.

Leroy looked like he'd just been told he had good sense. His eyes got bright and his hands moved in little nervous tics and when he tried to speak, he only ended up punching the nigger in the arm and saying, "Friday. Friday night."

It was Wednesday already, and that gives you some idea what kind of fight it was. I figured the guy scheduled to fight Millard Fillmore died or else they didn't think they'd be able to get him sober in time, and the Greek who owns the Catherine Street Arena had called Al, who always had his eye out and knew somebody who was willing to get beat up. If Leroy hadn't been in the gym, Al might've thrown the nigger in with the guy.

Christ, they had the same dressing room, Millard Fillmore and Leroy did. The first prelim, which is what Leroy was fighting, was supposed to start at eight-fifteen, and we left the Fireman's Gym at seven in the Dodge with Pete driving and me and Al in the back seat with Leroy. When we got there, we went through a back door and down a hall to a dressing room that was about fifteen feet long and very narrow. There was a table in it, and two ring stools.

Millard Fillmore was sitting on one end of the table with his back to us being taped by a guy that looked like he'd stumbled out of a novel by Budd Schulberg. He had a dirty felt hat cocked low on his forehead, and a cold cigar caught between some real bad teeth. He didn't look like he'd had anything to eat since winter. We stood in the door for a second but when they didn't look up, Al caught Leroy by the shoulder and kind of took him over and set him on the other end of the table. Leroy seemed a little dazed but his face was bright and he put his bag down and got his yellow bathing suit and tennis shoes out.

This was supposed to be a light heavyweight bout, but Leroy had never weighed more than a hundred and fifty pounds in his life and Millard Fillmore looked like he was pushing two hundred. That'll give you some idea of the Greek and his Catherine Street Arena. I found a ring stool and sat down by a broken locker. Al had one of Leroy's hands taped before Millard turned around and looked down the table. He looked at me the longest, so I told him to eat shit and die. There's satisfaction in talking with your hands sometimes. But not all that much actually. Millard pushed his manager away and got off the table. He was bowlegged, had a little belly, and walked mostly on his heels. His face was bluish with scar. He just stood looking at Leroy, which finally made Leroy blush.

"My name's Millard Fillmore," he said.

Al kept looking over Millard's shoulder at the far wall and didn't say anything. Leroy said: "Name Leroy Johnson."

"How many fights you had, kid?" said Millard.

"Oh," said Leroy, "I . . . a lot. I don't know."

Millard looked down the room at his manager, then back to Leroy. "You don't know?"

"See," said Leroy, "I used to hitch up the wagon and . . ."

Millard leaned forward almost in Leroy's face. "Hitch the fuckin' wagon? A wagon?" He looked at his manager. "Goddammit, George . . ."

George shifted his cigar. "He ain't had no fight."

Now Millard swung to look at Al. "The kid's first go, and you letting him in with me?"

Al's eyes flicked over Millard's face and he looked at the other wall. "Al knows what he's doing."

"He does, huh?" Millard said. "Who the fuck's Al?"

"He's Al," said Leroy, blushing again.

Pete, staring at the floor on the other side of the table suddenly started counting: "One, two, three, four . . ."

Millard looked back at his manager. "George, where do you find'm?"

George shrugged. "You take it where you can git it."

Millard rolled his head on his ropy neck and looked at the ceiling for a long time, then he said: "Look, kid, this is ham and eggs, right? I mean you can jest about eat breakfast on what we working for, O.K.? I had over a hunnert fights. *Ring* magazine had me tenth when I'm twenty-two years old, unnerstand. How old are you, anyway?"

"Seventeen," said Leroy.

"Jesus, George," said Millard. Then: "We gonna go out there and dance a six-round waltz, Leroy. You got what I'm saying? Just take it easy and we'll dance through it. It'll be all right."

Al pushed Leroy back on the table and started taping his other hand.

"Al's fighter don't dance no waltz," he said.

Millard, who was going back down to the other end of the table, stopped and looked over his shoulder. "And when you git outta here tonight, kid, do yourself a favor and unload those zombies."

"I train in his gym," said Leroy.

"I bet you do," said Millard Fillmore. "I bet you do do that."

Al and Leroy and the nigger were shouting and screaming. They always did that when I got to the part of the workout that really started to hurt. I didn't look at them, but I felt their voices humming up the walls of the gym and down the ropes of the Roman rings where I held myself in the iron cross. They were pretty quiet while I stacked the bricks and did my prone presses and even when I did the ten trips up and down the stairs of the gym they still didn't make much noise, but when I got to the place where I started doing the finger stuff, they usually started to mumble and then to talk and finally to shout. The only reason I could do the finger stuff in the first place is I'm so light. People can never believe I only weigh ninety. The girl who called me that morning outweighs me forty or fifty pounds, but she's got a twenty-two-inch waist and I've got twenty-inch arms. You think about that for a minute and it's easier to believe my finger stuff.

I would stand flat on my palms and then raise myself on the ends of my fingers. A ten-finger fingerstand. I let myself down and when my palms touched the floor again I would come off it in an eight-finger stand. Then a six. Then four. I'd press to the two, and the whole gym would shake with their voices. Finally I tilted to one side and up on my one incredible finger. It's the middle finger on my right hand and once I got the balance I'd start turning round and round on it slow and steady as a clock ticking. It drove'm crazy. On every turn, I saw them, upside down, Al and Pete and Leroy, screaming at me, Al off the stool and slobbering a little, all of them waving their arms and stamping their feet. And after that they never quieted down for the rest of the workout.

Even though I knew what he was saying, I looked down from where I was hanging in the Roman rings to the place where Al was standing right below me, his fists clenched, his face red and full of swollen veins.

He screamed: "Al loves you, Marvin! Son, Al loves you!" He would do that when you were in pain. I've never known him not to. Behind him, Leroy and Pete were sparring and screaming at each other. Millard Fillmore ruined whatever balance Leroy had left so Pete was slipping everything Leroy was throwing and at the same time coaching him. "Cross wif the lef! Cross wif the lef! Combination, combination!"

Al Molarski screamed: "Al loves you, Marvin! Son, Al loves you!"

Leroy yelled: "I'll fight anybody, it don't matter."

Pete begged: "Stick and move! Stick and move!"

Pete caught Leroy by the shoulders and spun him. Leroy, off-balance and lost, looked up at me on the Roman rings with the same dazed expression he'd had on his face when he came back to his corner after the third round with Millard Fillmore. The first round had been a waltz just like Millard said it ought to be. It was so slow that the audience booed in the same half-hearted way Leroy and Millard moved in the ring. A few people threw peanuts and beer caps. Leroy came back to the corner, his bright face smiling around his mouthpiece. Al put the ring stool through the ropes and Leroy sat down.

Al bent over Leroy and said: "Al don't like it."

"Huh?" said Leroy.

Al slapped him.

"You slapped me," said Leroy.

"Hardest you been hit tonight," said Al. "Al don't like it."

I was sitting on the apron of the ring watching Al's old wrinkled wrestler's face get closer and closer to the kid.

"Hurt him," said Al. "You got to hurt him bad." He reached out and took Leroy's ear and twisted it, twisted it hard. "Told Al you boxed. Said you fight anybody. You go out there and hurt him. Hurt him bad."

"Hurt him," said Leroy. It was not a question; he was just saying it over again.

They went out for the second round as slow as the first. I felt the vibrations of the same half-hearted booing. Millard Fillmore wasn't even paying attention. I think he was embarrassed at this finally happening to him, being in the ring with a semi–punched-out seventeen-year-old boy in a yellow bathing suit. The same thing came on me when I went once to balance for a ward full of paraplegic soldiers. It just shows what *might* happen to you in the world. So Millard wasn't even paying attention and got caught flat-footed by the best punch the kid had, his hook. Like I said before, Leroy had two things, a hook and a cast-iron head. It's a good thing he had that head, too, or Millard would have killed him instead of just scrambling him good. With Pete in the corner screaming, "Combination! Combination!" the first hook buckled Millard's knees and the second one busted his nose and caused the light to go out in his flat pinched eyes. Millard Fillmore clenched and turned Leroy into a corner and held him there while he shook his head. When he broke the clench, he turned Leroy out into the center of the ring and beat the living shit out of him for the next three rounds. Two or three times he was actually holding Leroy up with one hand and beating him with the other. But every time he stumbled back to his corner, Al poured water over his head and hugged him and cried: "Al loves you, Leroy!"

And Leroy would show his bloody mouthpiece in a dazed smile and squint at Al through the slit that was still open in his left eye. In the fifth round when Millard Fillmore turned Leroy's head three quarters of the way around with an overhand right, Al burst through the ropes and straddled Leroy where he lay on the floor and screamed down into his face, "Al loves you, Leroy! Son, Al loves you!"

We finally got Leroy on his feet but we could never get him to speak, not even on the ride back to the Fireman's Gym, and he went to bed still stunned, his cut and swollen face looking like a bloody cabbage.

I let myself out of the cross on the rings and hand-walked down a hemp rope to the floor. I lay on my back until my breathing was back to normal and then I told Al to tell Pete to bring the car around.

"You got to eat," Al said.

"I'll eat at the beach," I said.

"Al don't want you eating that bad shit."

"Well, it's Sunday," I said.

Leroy was staring at our hands.

"Al don't care," he said.

"Man does not live by bread alone," I said.

"Get meat," he said. "Bread's bad."

Al in many ways was a very stupid bastard, a real dummy.

"I'll get a steak," I said.

"Bring the car, Pete," said Al. "Marvin's going to the beach."

I rocked up on my hands and headed for the shower. I felt hot and tight and good from the workout. I wished I was at the Ocean Club right then, sitting in Hester's terrific lap.

Two

HESTER was a normal. As Leroy would say, she had everything that was coming to her, all the arms, legs, toes and so on, besides which she could talk and hear and see. But she tended to be bitter. Her mother and father were deaf mutes and her first language was fingers. She could lip-read as good as anybody, including me. But she tended to be bitter, and I probably wouldn't have started messing around with her in the first place if it wasn't for her terrific lap. She had one of the world's great laps and I couldn't leave it alone.

It was a bright day and I slipped on my sunglasses as we were leaving the causeway going from Clearwater to Clearwater Beach. You may have heard of Clearwater Beach. It's one of the best beaches—I think *the* best—in Florida. It's on the Gulf of Mexico side, just above Tampa, and you couldn't ask for a better piece of water. Only thing is, there's not much gash in that part of Florida, and what you are able to find is usually defective. Mostly old skins. I mean really old skins, eighty-five, ninety, like that. And while there's nothing wrong with an old skin now and then, a steady diet of it will depress you. Or does me, maybe you're different. I don't know if you know this or not, but this part of Florida—St. Petersburg, which is just down the road, and Tampa, and Clearwater—is all one big outdoor old folks' home. They're everywhere you look, dropping dead left and right. A few college kids wander in from time to time, but that's not something you can count on except at holidays. I don't care one way or another though, because like I said, I've got Hester, and Hester's got a lap that'll stop your heart.

When Pete pulled up just the other side of Clearwater Beach Hotel and stopped, there was nothing but oldy-goldies as far as the eye could see. I call them oldy-goldies because the only thing those old skins like to do is lie out in the sun and cook like bacon. They retire and come down here and have a contest to see who can get skin cancer first.

They're always waiting when I get there. They knew the car, and even though they couldn't see me in the back seat, when I opened the

door and came down to the sidewalk on my hands, their old heads lifted
off the blankets and swung in my direction like they spent all morning
practicing it. Every head raised, every neck twisted, and they held me
dead in their sun-bleached eyes while I came down across the sand. I
can't remember if I told you—I'm a great magazine reader, *Time*,
Harper's, *Atlantic Monthly*, like that—and lately I've been seeing a lot
about compulsory retirement, but I swear to God, you live around these
oldy-goldies and while you don't think about compulsory retirement,
you get to thinking about compulsory death. They just lie around in
their flaky skins littering the goddam beach. Jesus.

I walked down across the sand careful not to look at any of them because if you do they'll start talking to you. They're so goddam bored and
hungry to talk, they don't care if you can hear or not. And with their
old mouths caved in, their lips are just about impossible. That's one
thing about Al Molarski, he may be seventy-two years old but he's got
almost every one of his teeth. Probably from all those cows and one
thing and another he's had hanging hooked in his mouth.

The Ocean Club was only about a hundred yards down the beach and
before I was halfway there I saw Hester come out onto the porch. She
was sucking at a tall beer but when she saw me she set it on the railing
by the steps and came running across the sand toward me. I arched my
back a little more and shook the hair out of my eyes so I could watch her
run. I always had my hair cut short before I met Hester, but she liked it
long so I let it grow. It was all right sitting down, but it was a pain in the
ass when I was on my hands. Still, whatever Hester wanted was worth it.
I stopped and watched her, all titties and hips and pumping thighs, coming across the sand in her shiny black bikini. I couldn't get enough of
her legs. Sometimes I could spend the whole afternoon licking her
around the knees. Jesus, in the sun she was a single leaping muscle.

When she got to me, she caught me around the hips and hugged me
and I pressed my head between her thighs, nuzzling up toward that lap.
She lifted me off my hands, turned me right side up and kissed me, her
mouth still hot and juicy with the taste of beer. She would go 140
pounds, and she had enough enthusiasm for six people. Sometimes you
had to be careful or she would hurt you.

"You're looking great," she said. "Those arms are really pumped."

She walked about ten feet away from me so I could see her mouth. I
couldn't talk back to her very well as long as I was on my hands but I

smiled and gave her a wink. She winked back and made a little sucking pout with her mouth. I felt good walking along the sand with her. My arms and back and chest were pumped, like she said, from the workout, and I was wearing a tight T-shirt and my purple shorts with the zipper in the bottom. The sun was warm and heavy on my ass.

"Have you asked him?" she said.

I just looked back at her, and then did a little spin on my hands trying to distract her.

"I can see by your face you didn't ask him."

She looked out at the white waveless Gulf where two motionless sails cut tiny wedges out of the horizon. I had the feeling she was talking. The back of her head made little savage jerks on her neck. She may even have been screaming. When she looked back, the skin on her cheeks was mottled, but her eyes were quiet and steady.

"You didn't even ask him," she said again. "Maybe you don't want me there. Maybe you don't want me at all."

I looked helplessly at her terrific lap and hated her.

"I don't see what it'd matter," she said. "He's already got a goddam grit and a nigger living there."

I dropped onto the sand, brushed off my hands and said: "You don't understand a thing. I do the best I can."

"I'm tired of hearing that," she said. "That's what my parents give me and you give me and everybody gives me. Who cares if something's the best if you can't stand it? I'm not interested in what your best is, I'm interested in something I can stand."

We were nearly to the place where her beer sat on the railing. I flopped onto the sand again. "You couldn't stand it where I live."

"I've got to stand it somewhere," she said. "I've been kicked out of the house."

"I don't believe that," I said.

"You don't believe it?" she said. "You don't believe it? What the fuck's to believe? They say I can't live there anymore. It's done. Finished." She watched the boats on the horizon for a moment. "You've ruined my day. I thought sure you'd ask him."

"Well, I didn't," I said, "because I know the answer already. And you haven't done a hell of a lot for my day either, if you want to know." I got on my hands again.

"Fuck it," she said, "let's get a beer."

She picked up her beer and drained it as we went across the porch. It wasn't even noon yet but a rock and roll band—all flashing teeth and pumping elbows—were working out on a little raised platform in the back and the dance floor in front of the platform was jammed with spinning, hunching dancers. I stood watching the band, watching the boy on the drums and the boy on the electric guitar, and if I concentrated I could hear it all: the spitting of the drummer's wire brushes, the wailing of the guitar, even the dancers' bare feet sliding over the sandy dance floor.

I've never been able to talk—the roof of my mouth has a hole in it—but I didn't lose my hearing until I was ten years old. Al had me at a garden party, balancing for these old skins with flowers pinned to their chests and blue hair floating over their powdered skulls, and Al had me up on these two ladder-backed chairs, one hand on the top of each chair and the chairs tilted onto the back legs. The floor was waxed and right at the top of the handstand, a chair slipped and I went straight down like a diver and drove my forehead into the terrazzo floor. When I got up, all those old skins were clapping and flashing their false teeth, and I sat there on my ass watching them clap—they must have thought it was part of the act because it seemed to please the hell out of them—but I couldn't hear a sound. It was as quiet as if I'd been twenty feet under water. And it's been that quiet ever since. But I know what most things sound like, so if I concentrate I can remember it until it rings in my ears.

The deaf and dumb volleyball team was in the back to the right of the platform where the band was playing and I saw Herby's hands shoot up from the table and he said: "Get your ass over here and have a beer, you stumpy little freak." Herby's smaller than I am and he's got legs. A fucking comedian is what he is, but he's a hell of a volleyball player. Herby can't spike the ball of course, but he can set it up as well as anybody that plays for us. Hester put her hand on my ass, which when I'm standing on my hands only reaches to her waist, and guided me through the tables and dancers to the back. When I'm in a crowd I can't see what's coming and I'm an easy target for a drunk or somebody who's not looking and if I'm not careful I'll get knocked down and stepped on. Particularly in a place like the Ocean Club which is full of defectives anyway.

Herby was in my chair when we got back to where they were all sitting but he got out of it and let me have it. He at least has some sense of decency. There was a pitcher of beer on the table and Hester poured me a glass. She pulled a chair over close to mine and kissed my neck. I'm always dehydrated after a workout and I sucked off a big swallow and watched the dancers. That's one of the things I've always regretted, that I can't dance. Once in a while I'll get out on the floor with Hester and we'll move around a little with her holding tight to my ass. But I've never liked it because it's something I can't be good at. Some jackoff is always stepping on your fingers or knocking you off-balance. Actually, I can tango pretty good. But where do you ever hear a tango? It hurts me to say it but rock and roll is too much for me. I can't boogie.

Herby was trying to talk to me, but I wouldn't look at his hands, pretended I didn't see him by kissing Hester. She was rubbing my back and had pulled one of my hands into her fantastic lap.

"You want to come to my place after the game?" she said.

"I thought you said they kicked you out."

"They didn't say I couldn't fuck there. They said I couldn't live there."

Herby reached over and slapped me on the back of the head. I looked at him.

"She been kicked out?" he said.

That's the trouble with using your hands to talk, any son of a bitch with a pair of eyes can listen in.

"Right," said Hester. "I don't care though."

"Where will you live?" asked Herby.

"Oh, somewhere." She looked at me. "I don't worry about it. I got friends."

I saw what was happening. I saw what was going to happen. Hester knew how I was about her lap, about her, about the fact that she had everything that was coming to her. When I met Hester I was going with a girl who was pretty enough but who had curvature of the back. That's the thing about deaf mutes, they almost always have something else wrong with them, too: cross-eyed, dwarfed, albino, legless, bald, or some damn thing you can't imagine. I once got into bed with a deaf-mute lady and when I pulled her drawers down, she was a hermaphrodite, a little shrunken peter and balls there beside the glory hole. I went ahead on with it though. It's too hard to get laid if you've got my disadvantages without going around turning it down. So like I say, I just hustled her balls out of the way and went ahead on with it.

But Hester was something else. Not only could she see and talk, but her hair was thick and cut like a helmet and her titties made your mouth hurt to look at them and her legs were straight and long and strong as a sprinter's. If I let her go, I'd be back hooking on twisted backs and half-blind wonders. I sighed and rubbed my eyes with the ends of my thumbs. Damned if life didn't get to press in on you at times.

Hester caught my face between her hands and turned me to look at her. "What's the matter with my baby?"

"I didn't eat," I said. "I need me three eggs up and a steak."

Hester's hand shot up to order the steak from Arnie, who owns the Ocean Club and who is deaf, can't talk, and queer besides, but then her hand just stayed up there and I saw her face change and I knew Aristotle had come in. I didn't have to look at the door to know that it was him. All I had to do was look at Hester's face which was not a real pretty face; but it was a strong face, made stronger because she had been around the block. A lot of blocks. And one of the blocks she'd been around was Aristotle Parsus. She used to be his lover. She didn't tell me that, I just knew it. Aristotle lived in a place about twenty miles up the coast called Tarpon Springs, which was a settlement of olive-oil-sucking Greeks who made a living out of sponge fishing, whatever the hell that is. Mostly, I think the whole thing is a tourist trap where they line up these old creaky boats and charge middle-aged ladies from Iowa to come aboard and see these Greeks fucking around with sponges.

I looked back, and over the heads of the dancers, Aristotle was just inside the door, tall and dark and oily, with picket-fence teeth, wearing a red, white and blue polo shirt, and doing little tricks with a white volleyball. His team had come in with him and they were all jacking around with each other, dressed like Aristotle in polo shirts and blue shorts. I told him when he bought his team the uniforms that I thought it was a good idea to give them a little class like that since they didn't have any as players, which was not exactly true. Our teams were pretty evenly matched.

I touched Hester in her fantastic lap. She looked at me. "Go tell Arnie to get me the goddam steak," I said. "I'm dying."

Aristotle was talking to Arnie with one hand and balancing the spinning white volleyball on the society finger of his other hand. When Aristotle was talking to Arnie, God Himself couldn't get Arnie's attention. Hester went across the dance floor on her ballbearing stride and leaned over the bar and spoke right in Arnie's face. Arnie turned and wrote the order on a spindled wheel in the window that opens to the kitchen out back. Aristotle put his hand on Hester's shoulder and gave her his picket-fence smile.

"How have you been?" he asked.

"Well . . . is . . . and . . . enough," she said.

The dancers whirling on the floor kept getting between me and their hands. I took hold of the table and pushed over on the two back legs of the chair trying to see better.

". . . and looking good," Aristotle said.

"Thank you, Ari," said Hester, looking very serious.

"It's a damn shame that I don't ever . . . but on Sunday," he said.

"Yes," she said. "I . . . yes."

"All right" he said. "That's just fine."

"You up for . . . and . . ." she said, ". . . spike hell out of it."

A young garbanzo-bowl spick windmilling back and to across the dance floor kept cutting their hands off. The son of a bitch was wearing a yellow shirt and yellow shoes. Myself, I've never cared for spicks, and it seems like half of Cuba's ended up in Tampa, all of them wearing yellow shirts and yellow shoes, and smelling like garbanzo beans.

"It'll be right up, baby," said Hester, pulling a chair close to mine. "Arnie said he'd put a rush on it."

"You pretty thick with the Greek," I said.

"What?"

"I don't know how you can stand the bastard," I said.

"I've known him a long time," she said. "Besides, what's to stand? We were just talking."

The waiter, a boy named Bill, brought my food. It was on a huge plat-ter with the letters OC on it. For a faggot, Arnie ran a pretty classy place. I cut off a piece of meat and chewed.

"I never thought much of Greeks," I said.

"He's all right," she said.

"I never said he wasn't all right. I said I never thought much of Greeks. What was it you were discussing anyway?"

"He only asked me how I was."

"He may be Greek," said Herby, "but he can dance some."

Herby was sitting across the table from us with a very pretty girl whose forehead was burned and bruised with acne. Her name was Sarah and she could talk but she had lost her hearing when she was fifteen.

"I don't think you ought to be jealous of him just because he's beautiful," said Sarah.

"Nobody's jealous of nobody," Herby said.

"He's beautiful," said Sarah. "I'd suck him off in a minute."

"You'd suck off a statue of Napoleon," said Herby.

"Now just what the fuck's that supposed to mean, Herby?"

She was actually chewing gum and drinking beer. Every once in a while she'd pop another stick in her mouth and take another pull at her beer. She was a low type. They were both very low types. I was eating my eggs and trying not to look at the dance floor which had been taken over by Aristotle and his volleyball team. But there, just beyond the table's edge I couldn't help seeing the blurred flash of red, white and blue polo shirts and I couldn't help feeling how stiff Hester sat beside me, and my nose was suddenly rotten with the smell of olive oil.

I was finished with the steak and eggs so there was nothing to do but look at the dance floor and there was Aristotle, a whirling, jerking figure locked into an obscenely hunching dance with his best spiker, a very tall girl, polo-shirted and blue-shorted, who danced with her head back and her mouth open, her tongue compulsively thrust out onto her chin. Bright drops of spit hung on her lips.

Across the table the girl with the ruined forehead raised her hand and said, "I'd suck him off in a minute."

"You ought to shut up," I said.

"He's right," said Herby. "You ought to quit for a while."

"You should try not to be jealous," she said. "Everybody can't be six feet tall and dance like that."

"Why don't you shut down for a while?" said Herby. "You can't even get your forehead cleared up."

The band was going crazy. They got worked up every time Aristotle danced. And I'm not taking anything away from him; even if he was a Greek, he could dance. But what's so fucking great about dancing? All you need is a pair of legs.

Now balancing, that's something else. Sure you need arms, but only special arms will do. *Everything* has to be special. The hairs in your middle ear have to be special. Discipline has to be special. Nobody ever stood on their hands by accident. And nobody ever did it the first time they tried.

And all that was probably the reason I did what I did right then. I sort of *had* to do it. I mean I could feel Hester sitting stiff beside me and that asshole was out there performing, demonstrating who he was, if you can follow that. I put my hands flat on the top of the table in front of me. The music throbbed in the wood. That was what they were dancing to, the beat in the wood coming through the floor into their feet. There probably wasn't more than half a dozen people in the place—and Hester of course was one of them—who could actually hear the music. But we all felt it, ringing in the glasses, in the beer, and most of all beating in the wood.

I took one last look at the dance floor, entirely taken up now by Aristotle and his volleyball team, and with my hands planted flat on the table, pressed out of my chair beside Hester into a handstand. I no more than had my hips in the air when I felt the music falter in the wood. Slow as you could want it, I rocked over into a one-hander, and under my hand in the table the music missed three beats.

That was a very proud band Arnie had playing in there, but they couldn't hear the music either. They were from the Miffit Exceptional School of Music over in St. Petersburg, a place that teaches deaf mutes—and sometimes ones that are blind too—to play music. But the way I see it, playing an instrument is only a little better than dancing. If there was anything to it, so many people couldn't do it. But you can fuck up whole dancing volleyball teams if you bridge onto four fingers from a one-hander. Nothing much was coming through the table from the band now. Nothing much at all. And when I went from four fingers to three, everything stopped. But I could still sense Aristotle whirling and hunching half-hearted around out there on the floor.

Everyone was looking at me. I knew it. The whole Ocean Club had quit moving, because, goddammit, a fingerstand is a fucking miracle. Every cell in your body has to cooperate. And what is the picket-fence smile of an oil-sucking Greek compared to that? Nothing. Not a fucking thing, which was the point to start with.

I started turning. Slow as breathing, I was going round and round on two fingers—thumb and index—of one hand. Hester's face was bright as a light looking up at me from where she sat. And Herby's face passed too, watching me the way Peter must have watched Jesus. Oh, they were proud to be sitting there, they were. Then Sarah's face came around and her eyes looked through me, focused beyond where I was

turning slowly in the high point of my act. Her bruised unlovely forehead was flushed, swelling, like it might bleed or burst, and I knew she
was watching not me but Aristotle, who had to be somewhere near, just
there behind me on the dance floor.

When I turned her face out of sight, I looked right into the lean and
mean hips of Aristotle Parsus. I stopped turning. He came closer. He
leaned over and put his face in front of mine. His upside-down mouth
was huge over my eyes. Our noses nearly touched.

"That's a monkey's trick," he said. I didn't understand at first. The
words were upside down. Then he turned his hand over.

I reached up with my free hand—looked as though I was going to
speak—but ended up scratching my ass, slowly.

"That's still a monkey's trick," he said. His whole red, white and blue
volleyball team stood ranged behind him glowering at me.

I went—so slow at first they didn't even know I was moving—into a
one-handed press. The table trembled just slightly with the strain. I
heard the blood whistling in my heart. Then I felt my chin touch the
table and before I could start the press back into the stand, spontaneous
wild applause shook the table under me. My eyes had been closed, concentrating, and when I opened them there was the whole upside-down
Ocean Club clapping and banging glasses and stamping their feet. Even
Aristotle's volleyball team—everybody but the tall female spiker—was
clapping and grinning.

"You have to spoil everything, don't you. Freak," he said, his hand so
rigid he could barely talk. "Freak."

I was very calm. I felt good. I said real slow like Al would have said, as
though my fingers were speaking through a yawn: "I never cared for
Greeks. Why don't you go on back where you came from?"

"Why don't you come on out on the sand and play volleyball?" he
said.

"Don't mind if I do," I said. I bent my hips and pushed my ass in his
face and then hopped off the table, landing in a two-hander. More applause shook the floor under my fingers and the band struck up in what
could only be a salute. The entire Ocean Club followed me down the
steps and out onto the sand. I felt good.

Three

WE were lying in Hester's bed on the other side of the wall from where her mother sat embroidering on potholders. She was there when we came in over an hour ago sitting in a square of sunshine by an open window, the same place she had been every time I had come home with Hester. She was a tiny lady with gray skin, who always wore a blue bonnet and steel-rimmed glasses. The embroidering fingers were very slow. The sun sent little sparks of light from her thimble and needle. I looked the other way in case they wanted to say anything. I respect privacy. But I don't think they ever spoke to each other.

"You were pretty damn wonderful today," Hester said.

"You weren't bad yourself," I said.

All the blinds were pulled and there was barely enough light in the room to talk. Hester was on her hands and knees, hunkered over me as I lay on my back on her bed. We were both naked and her skin was burned almost black except for the triangle of white skin she wore across her ass, big as a baby's diaper, and the two ice-cream titties hanging over my face.

"Listen," I said, "you know I've got to balance for those boy scouts."

"We've got time," she said.

"We haven't got much," I said.

"I'll get you there," she said; "we've got plenty of time."

We had not left the beach until almost five. Aristotle and I had bet two hundred dollars on the best two out of three games. We split wins on the first two, and the final game had lasted nearly two hours. Hester drove her dented Volvo through the streets of Clearwater like she'd gone crazy, her share of the winnings curling out of her bikini top.

"We won't get there in time," I said.

"Don't you like that?"

I groaned.

"You do," she said. "You like that."

We were both greased down good from the beach. She was sitting now. On me. I tried to think about other things. The way the beach had been. The sky. The game.

"And we didn't cheat," she said. "Goddammit we didn't cheat." Her breath whistled in her throat.

And I don't. I play it straight down the line. When we were set to play—when Aristotle had his team in position on one side of the net and Herby and Hester and the rest of them were ready on the other, I climbed up the lifeguard tower, which is where I referee from, raised my hand and called for the game to start. Both teams, surrounded by old people now, were watching me steadily from their places in the hot sand. Hester, who had won the toss and was serving first, hit the ball and it arched over the net, and Aristotle caught it in the back line and set it up for his tall chief spiker and the game was on.

Above me, Hester had started turning in slow revolutions where she sat on my hips. The wall was only inches from the bed and she stared at it dreamily, her eyes glazed in a thousand-yard stare that never focused on the wall. She had been a marvel in the game, playing all over the sand, setting up the ball, spiking, driving it down the throat of Aristotle on the other side of the net, playing nose to nose with him, never giving an inch. In the sand, the old people ate their sandwiches and drank Coke from paper cups and cheered for Hester.

"I don't think I can stand that," I finally had to say.

"Sure you can," she said. Her slow fingers spelled the words slower and slower. "Remember when you started to rotate?"

"Rotate," I said.

"In the Oh Cee," she said. "On the table."

"You're not on a table. In the Oh Cee," I said. "And I don't think I can stand that."

She kept on turning where she sat on me. She was turning good and awful.

"You fucked up his head," she said. "You messed up his head bad."

"Messed up his head," I said, "messed up his head."

She'd ground me down sharp. I kept losing her, kept missing what it was she was saying or trying to say.

"That was the only reason we beat him," she said. "He was messed up from seeing you turn like that in a two-finger stand. When the music stopped and everybody clapped and shouted, I knew we had him. We couldn't lose."

Hester drove on Aristotle Parsus for game point and spiked the ball right off his Greek head. I sat up there on the lifeguard tower with my Timex on the rail and when the ball nailed Aristotle between the eyes and Hester had the second of the two points anybody has to have to take a win, I threw the lifeguard's buoy down between the two teams. Aristotle Parsus just stood there looking at it where it landed between him and Hester. A spot the size and color of a tangerine was growing on his forehead over the bridge of his nose. He looked up at me.

"Take the money," he said.

"We all thank you," I said.

"Don't be a wiseass," he said. "Nobody likes a wiseass."

"Nobody likes to lose," I said.

"You lost when you were born," he said. He looked at me in a long silence. "*Freak*. You're a freak who can only do freakish things."

Hester had been watching us talk. Everybody had. She smiled at Aristotle Parsus.

"Marvin Molar can do some pretty freaky things," she said.

Hester's greased rump had stopped revolving on my hips. She was staring at the wall. Her eyes no longer held the thousand-yard stare. A little tight spot of anger settled on the bridge of her nose.

"What is it?" I said. But I already knew.

"Jesus," she said. "This goddam house."

I reached out and put the palm of my hand against the wall at the side of the bed. I knew I would find it full of knuckles rapping from the other side. It was her mother. They rapped to each other—she and her mother and her father—through the walls, through the floors of the house. They had arguments with each of them in different rooms all the way across the house. Morse code. Hester said she had grown up with it. She said her father didn't like to have arguments with any of his family he was looking at. Sometimes I think I was lucky I was left on the steps of the Fireman's Gym. Even something like that can be a goddam blessing.

"Jesus," she said again. "This house."

She reached out and rapped hard and quick on the wall. I don't know Morse, but I know what she said was a mean thing to say to your mother.

"What does she want?" I said.

Hester bent forward licking my neck. Her hot ice-cream titties brushed my chest.

"She wants to know what we're doing," Hester said.

"What did you tell her?"

"I told her we'd be done in a minute," she said.

"Done what?" I asked.

"Just done."

I've always known there were worse things than being left on the steps. Hester was hunkered down licking my neck but I still had my hand on the wall.

"Your daddy's home," I said.

She drew her head back so I could see her mouth. "I can hear," she said. Her lips were tight, angry.

Her daddy had joined her mother on the other side of the wall. They were tapping steadily, urgently.

"For God's sake," I said. What she was doing to me kept the rhythm of what they were doing to the wall.

"Daddy wants to know if we'd like a cup of tea," she said.

"For God's sake," I said.

"Don't worry," she said. "I stopped them."

"What did you say?"

"I told them I didn't like to talk with my mouth full."

That was Hester. Down the line. I told you she tends to be bitter. But it didn't matter, because it didn't stop them. They kept right on tapping. And she kept tapping back. Telling them—she admitted—what we were doing. Describing her tongue. Her fine teeth. Going into all kinds of things about locked legs and arched backs. Talking about how we were both beginning to sweat.

Finally, I was rapping on the wall, too. Not to say anything to anybody—I don't know Morse—but just because I couldn't help it. Hester had me jammed in a corner and I began banging on the wall with my fist, butting it with the back of my head.

"They want to know what you're saying," Hester said.

I could only glower at her and love her and beg her with my eyes not to stop.

"They say they can't understand you, that you'll have to talk slower."

I was banging with both fists now and jamming at the plaster wall with the top of my head. She had worked me into the farthest corner of the bed. And that's where it ended, with all four of us blindly beating on the wall.

When we quit tapping, her mother and father quit too. I lay in silence listening to my blood whistle. She sat on the edge of the bed, her
eyes gone again, lost in the middle distance. We were both shiny with
sweat. It was getting darker in the room. I reached out and touched her
on the hip. When she looked my way, I motioned toward my Timex
where I had taken it off and left it on the table beside the bed.

"What time is it?" I asked.

She looked at the watch and then looked back at me, but she didn't
say anything.

"Time," I said. "I've still got those boy scouts. They're waiting in the
basement of the church. You promised to get me there."

She didn't look as if she had seen what I said to her. She blinked a
couple of times quickly and her eyes stayed shut. She put her hand over
her heart and then spoke with it pressed into the white flesh of her
breast.

"I lied to you," she said.

"What?"

"Back at the Oh Cee," she said. "I told you a lie."

Now see, you got to understand, I didn't want to go on with the conversation. I wanted to end it right there. I'd just been laid, had my eyes
sucked out, was feeling good, and I didn't want to talk about it now, because I knew that talking about it could only end up by making me pay
for it. If a woman fucks you and then—still lying there on the bed—
starts talking to you about serious things, you can just goddammit figure
you're about to be asked to pay for it. And I didn't want to pay for anything. The way I figure was that with no legs and no ears and a hole in
the roof of my mouth, by God I'd paid enough. That's what I figured.

She kept looking at me. I had to say something.

"Oh?" I said finally, hoping she'd leave it alone, knowing she would
not.

"I said Ari . . . Aristotle and I were just talking."

I didn't say anything. I was hoping her old man would start knocking
on the walls again, anything.

"We weren't just talking," she said. "We used to be lovers."

I rocked up on my ass and started binding my legs.

"I knew that," I said. "Don't worry about it."

"I'm not worried about it," she said. "I just wanted you to know how
it is."

"All right," I said.

"We used to be lovers and he said if I'm kicked out of the house I can live with him. On his sponge boat."

"You wouldn't like living on a sponge boat," I said. "A goddam Greek is only slightly worse than nothing."

"I've got to live somewhere," she said.

"Right," I said, "and I've got to get to the basement of the First Baptist Church. Al'll be pissed. It's sponsored by the League of Women Voters and it's four hundred dollars."

"You don't care, do you?"

"Of course I care," I said. "Four hundred dollars is—"

She said: "I don't mean that."

I knew she didn't mean that. And suddenly I didn't feel up to trying to get around paying anymore. I knew what was being asked and I knew I'd pay it if I had to.

"Look," I said, "you won't have to live on any fucking sponge boat."

Her face brightened. She looked very young. "I won't?" she said.

"Not if you don't want to," I said.

"I don't want to," she said.

When we went out of the room, her mother and father were sitting by the window, waiting. Her mother was working over the potholders. The sun was gone. Her father wore blue bibbed overalls and boots. I never knew where he worked, but whatever it was it must have been hard. His face was seamed and warped from the weather, and his heavy hands stayed half-curled all the time. He had the same gray skin as his wife, and, like her, he looked as though something deep inside him hurt bad, like maybe he had a small intestine with a knot in it. They just depressed the shit out of me. I had always managed not to get to know them by just getting the hell out of the house as soon as I got through thrashing Hester. Too, it's easy not to look at anybody if you're walking on your hands, and since they can't talk, if I don't look at them I don't hear them. Today it was different though. I glanced in their direction and saw that the old man was holding a kind of knobby limb off a tree that had been carved into a walking stick. I smiled, nodded and made for the door. I felt the stick rap on the floor twice—hard. I stopped and looked at him.

"Would you care for a little tea?" he asked.

"I already told you no," Hester said.

The old man was still looking at me. The stick looked mean, but I knew they all had a stick like that for rapping out messages for one another in the house. I'd never seen the old man's before, but I'd seen Hester's and Hester had explained it all to me. Anyway, he just kept looking at me and I felt sorry as hell for him. I sat on the rug so I could talk.

"It's good of you to ask," I said, "but I don't have time. I got to balance."

"Balance?" he said.

"For boy scouts," I said, "in the basement of the First Baptist Church."

"Have a little act do you?" he asked.

"Jesus, Daddy," said Hester, "why don't you get personal?"

"Didn't you ever tell him about my act?" I asked.

Hester didn't answer. She rolled her eyes to the ceiling and puffed out her cheeks.

"I think that's wonderful that you got a act," he said.

"Thank you," I said.

Hester's mother said, very slowly, like she didn't talk very well: "I think it's wonderful too."

"Thank you," I said.

I saw she had arthritis and that that was why she never talked very much. I felt bad. All this time I'd been thrashing Hester and I deliberately never said much to them because they looked so bad they depressed me. They looked like a couple of deaths sitting there. The world is a very shitty place, and at times it is hard not to be bitter.

"I'd like to hear about it sometime," he said.

"He doesn't want to talk about it," Hester said.

"I don't mind," I said, "but right now I'm late. Really." I held up my Timex. "The boy scouts are waiting."

I got on my hands and at the door he rapped his stick again and I looked back to see him say "Good luck there tonight." I had to rock into a one-hander to thank him.

In the Volvo, I said: "Jesus, Hester, he didn't sound like he was kicking you out of the house to me."

"It's a complicated thing," she said.

"He seemed like a good old man."

"I never said he wasn't a good old man."

"Why didn't you ever tell him about my act?"

"Christ, why should I tell him something like that? It never came up, that's all. We don't talk much."

"Bringing somebody home like me must cause talk. Hell, I know what I look like."

"We're not a close family. The old man likes to rap it out with sticks, and the old lady's got fingers that hurt her."

"All right," I said, "but it just seemed like to me they loved you."

"Marvin Molar, the famous mind reader." She was talking with her mouth and it was bitter. "How would you know if they loved me?"

"I was thinking about the way they looked at you," I said. "I could tell by the way they looked."

"Things are not always the way they look." She slammed the Volvo to a stop at a red light. "Are you trying to renege? You thinking of taking back what you said about me not having to live on the sponge boat?"

That was exactly what I was thinking but I knew it wouldn't do to say so.

"Never crossed my mind," I said. "But what you got to understand is Al Molarski runs things at the Fireman's Gym."

"Did he ever tell you you couldn't have a woman?"

"I never thought to ask him. I guess I always just knew I couldn't take a woman to live at the gym. For God's sake, Hester, you can't have a woman living at a man's gym—and with three other men at that!"

"You said two of them are punch-drunk."

"Hell, all three of them are punch-drunk, but they still have cocks."

"I've seen cocks before," she said. "Cocks don't scare me." She slid to a stop at the curb. "Which side of the church do we go in?"

"This'll be good enough right here," I said. "And that was a shitty re-mark about the cocks you've seen."

"I've had more balls in my hands than Willie Mays," she said, making a great show of being casual.

"Hester," I said. "You're awful."

"Awful good," she said, "and you better believe it."

The church was one of those Baptist strongholds, a huge pile of gran-ite with about ten steeples and a block square and stained glass and a black billboard out front with cute sayings and the week's menu. The cute saying for this week was: WALK IN AND HAVE YOUR FAITH LIFTED; which I thought was pretty horrible and comes, I think, from bad reading habits, from reading the Wallaces of this world: Wallace Irving and Irving Wallace and Wallace Wallace. Under the Faith Lift job it said what the preacher would do on Sunday, which was called "A Lesson in Love," and under that, what attendance had been like lately. It was enough to make God throw up.

I one-handed it and said: "I've been here once before when it was paid for by the Ford Agency. You'll like it. They're like us."

"Like us?" she said.

"A special troop of deaf and dumb Cub Scouts."

"Speak for yourself," she said.

"That's right," I said. "I keep forgetting, you've got all that's coming to you."

"You forget a lot of things," she said.

"What's that supposed to mean?"

"Nothing," she said.

The basement was behind an enormous hedge trimmed to look like a cross. Yellow light was pouring up the granite steps and in the yellow light were two fat ladies and five little boys who were hitting each other and talking with their hands. They came up the steps and onto the grass to meet us.

The fattest lady held up her hand like a phony Hollywood Indian and started slowly and idiotically to spell out: "We are so . . ."

"I can talk," Hester said.

"Oh, you can?" said the other lady.

She looked disappointed. Both of the ladies were looking at me now.

"And this must be him," one of them said, "the famous Mr. Molar."

I went onto one hand and said, "Tell her to call me Marvin Molar. Tell her it's my stage name."

Hester told them.

"Why look," the lady said, "he can even do it on one hand."

"Lady," said Hester, "Marvin Molar can do it more ways than you can think of."

Both ladies stared blankly at Hester. The five little Cub Scouts had quit hitting each other and were standing quietly behind the women's broad backs spelling out things to me like: "How do you take a shit?" and, "Do you ever fart in anybody's face?" I thought they seemed like pretty normal kids, which meant they scared the hell out of me. Kids will stone you, lynch you, set the dogs on you. That's been my experience with children which I'll tell you about in a minute.

I just looked up at them and said: "Your mothers were all fucked by goats. That's why you can't talk and hear like regular people."

That quieted them down some. They fell back a step in a tight little group and watched me.

". . . and this is Mrs. Alice Chalmers." The fattest lady, who seemed to be more or less in charge, was introducing herself and her friend. Hester said her name was Hester.

"I guess we better . . ." one of the ladies was saying, but I missed most of it because it was darker now and I couldn't see her mouth.

We went inside and found a thin scoutmaster, trying to interest fifteen small boys in tying knots in pieces of rope. They were trying to tie each other up, instead, and the scoutmaster, who couldn't keep their attention because they wouldn't look at him, was standing in front of them, his pale face damp with sweat, pretending he was in control and that everything was the way it was supposed to be. I remembered him from the last time I balanced here. His face was smooth as a girl's and his hands were nervous and full of panic. The last time he insisted I let him measure me with a tape for the scouts. *"Just to get the numbers of you,"* he said. And I let him do it. The kids of course didn't give a shit one way or the other, but he seemed to get a kick out of it. The only way you could have interested the Cub Scouts is if you'd let them hang me with the tape measure. No, don't ever tell me a thing about kids. I know about kids.

The scoutmaster saw us—or rather saw me—and threw down his rope. He rushed over and bent down to look into my face. I was afraid he might knock me off-balance.

". . . so pleased," he was saying. "We are so very pleased and honored."

The Cub Scouts were all sitting on metal folding chairs. There was a podium in front of the chairs and behind the podium a low stage, probably no more than two feet high, with curtains at either side. Hester and I sat on chairs in the front row while the ladies and Mr. Robert, the scoutmaster whose name I'd forgot until I saw one of the ladies say it, introduced me. Or rather, they didn't introduce me as much as they did their own notion of what hard work would do for you, if you only would let it. The kids, as always, didn't seem to give a rat's ass and spent most of the time trying to tie each other to the chairs with the pieces of rope. Because the kids were too young to be much at reading lips, or because they weren't paying attention, or some other reason I didn't know, the fattest lady introduced me first—moving her lips in slow motion and in an exaggerated way like she was speaking to idiots—and then Mr. Robert repeated what she said with his hands.

"Some of us are not as fortunate as others of us, but those of us who are not so fortunate must remember that fortunate is as fortunate does and realize that the only difference between fortunate and unfortunate is *un* and that we must never be unduly undone by *un*."

She stopped, her hands clasped between her massive titties, and waited for Mr. Robert's panic-stricken hands to try to say what she had said to the children who weren't watching anyway. After he had done the best he could with it, she told the children that all of us have something wrong with us and that hard work, perseverance and a belief in God Almighty would make something wrong into something right.

Now, you might think that I was sitting there surprised or angry with this fat lady's bullshit, but you'd be wrong. I was used to people doing just what she was doing. I've learned that I'm a living excuse for assholes to talk about how wonderful it is to be born with a hole in the roof of your mouth, no legs, and on top of that how wonderful it is to lose your hearing by accidentally driving your head into the goddam floor.

Beside me, Hester lifted her hand and said: "That's a strange lady. Those are two strange ladies."

I said: "They are only your everyday, normal United States American Christian ladies out doing your good works on your Sunday night."

Finally the two ladies and Mr. Robert were looking at me and smiling wildly and clapping for all they were worth. The children were still amusing themselves on the seats with their ropes. Not one of them clapped, even though the ladies tried to encourage them to, but as soon as I went off the chair onto my hands, they settled into a sullen quiet and put their ropes under the seats. I knew what it was. The word had passed through every one of them that I said their mothers fucked goats. They would respect me for that if nothing else. But that's children for you.

I went right into my hard stuff instead of working up to it. You don't fuck around with children. They'll throw things. I went down on my back, arched, and bridged back into a headstand without using any hands. It's a sensational, gimmicky bit. All it takes is perfect balance. The Cub Scouts didn't clap, but they did sit up straighter and move to the edge of their seats. Their faces were bright and upside down and savage out there leaning toward me from the metal chairs. I cut my eyes over to Hester. She looked bored. (Of course, she had seen me do all of this dozens of times before.) Mr. Robert, who had picked up the piece of rope and given it to his hands to twist and turn in his lap, watched the children and you could tell how pleased he was because at last he had something (me) to entertain these cute little things.

I had a childless childhood. Al got me a deaf and dumb teacher who was also an iron freak and worked out in the Fireman's Gym, and I'd go whole months without even seeing another child. The teacher worked with me three hours a day and in return Al gave him all the Hoffman's hi-protein food supplements and vitamins he wanted and let him use the gym for nothing, plus Al would have the nigger give the teacher a free rubdown on Wednesdays and Saturdays.

Then eleven years ago, when I was either five or six or seven, Al got a ruptured nut, and had to go to the hospital. He didn't want to leave me with Pete, who was just as punchy then as he is now, so when one of the freaks in the gym—not the teacher because he was single and bitter and hated children anyway—offered to take me home for four days because he had a large family, six huge children, two of them girls, Al thanked him and sent me to four days that almost ruined me and which I never got over. I could feel those four days on the back of my skull as I looked out at those goddam upside-down Cub Scouts who could only have been satisfied by letting them take me in the back room and torture me. But they would not have called it torture, they would have called it play.

When Al dropped a nut, the iron freak who took me home was, as they say, normal, with, as they say, normal children. I mean they had everything that was coming to them, tongues, eardrums, legs and so on. It was the so on that almost killed me.

See, they could talk and I couldn't. And their daddy couldn't read my lips or my hands or anything else. You can see what happened. You know what happened. I don't even have to go into it, right? They played with me.

"What's that little thing trying to say?" asked their daddy, after I'd managed to belly down the hall to the living room. "Little thing, what you trying to say?"

"It wants to play some more," said one of his thick-wristed, bullet-headed daughters coming up behind me.

Remember, I could hear in those days. I couldn't talk because I've always had the hole in the roof of my mouth. But at that time I had not yet taken the dive between the chairs and lost my hearing. So, I did what anybody would do. I looked up at the girl's daddy and shook my head and very slowly tried to tell him with my hands that his children were killing me.

"That little thing's shaking its head," he said. He called his wife in from the other room. "Look at that little thing shaking its head."

"What's it want?" asked his wife.

"I don't know," said the man.

"It wants to play in the back room," his awful daughter said.

"That's right. That's what it wants," said the oldest and most vicious boy, who had just come out of the torture chamber to join his sister.

They took me by the legs which in those days were like two ropes and dragged me into the back bedroom. The other four children were waiting for me back there. My upper arms were already fourteen inches around but there were six of them and one of me and all I could do was lie there on my back and see what they'd do to me next.

"Don't let it get away again," said one of the girls.

"It can pull itself along on this shag rug quicker'n you'd think," said her brother.

"The thing I can't get over," said the youngest and smallest of the boys, "is you can stick pins in it and it can't even holler."

"We're going to have some fun with this little thing," said one of the girls. "Take its clothes off."

And they did. And all I could do was try to tell their father his children were killing me. At the dinner table or when he'd come in to kiss us goodnight (the nights were worse for me than the days) I'd shake my head and do the best I could to spell out something with my fingers that he could understand. And he would say to his children: "Tonight when you turn out the light, just thank God, get down on your knees and thank God you're a regular human being."

When they turned out the light, they tried to kill me.

The scouts were finally beginning to clap and bang their fists on the metal folding chairs. I give dollar value for dollar paid. There's two things about me: I'm not bitter and I don't cheat. If I'm paid to entertain an audience, I goddam well entertain it if I have to bust a gut. I'm always prepared to risk something if I have to. I mean run a real risk that the audience knows is not a regular part of the act.

I was in a one-hander on top of the flagpole. That was what had got the scouts clapping and kicking the chairs. The flagpole was one of those portable deals about eight feet tall with a little round base so you could set it wherever you wanted it. The base was uneven though and the pole itself was too flimsy for ninety pounds. After all, it had never been expected to hold up anything heavier than the flag. Now the pole had me and the flag riding on it and it swayed and rocked on the wobbling base while I held fast to the metal eagle's head that formed a kind of cap above the flag.

I was still on one hand when I noticed the ladies talking about me. I can't read an upside-down mouth but I can get a word now and then, especially if the word is my name. I saw the words *Marvin Molar* form in the fat chin of the lady from the voters' league and then I saw her short spit-pink tongue come out and lick where the words had been and just like magic—as if the words had flown across the little space between their faces and stuck there—*Marvin Molar* formed in the chin of her friend. I let myself down from the one-hander and held my body parallel to the ground—hip on elbow—so I could see what they were saying. I found the weak place in the flagpole and was deliberately bending it to the point of breaking. The Cub Scouts were going wild, but Mr. Robert looked worried. I don't think he felt it was patriotic to balance on the flagpole.

"Well, he went up it like a monkey," she said.

Ah, yes, lady, didn't I. I'd like to get you up here upside down with your fat ass looking at an eight-foot dive into cement.

"He *is* a monkey," the other lady said. "He's a good part monkey."

My ass is purple like a baboon's. I sit on two points on my rump about the size of half-dollars. All it takes is perfect balance.

"Do you suppose he can do it?" one lady asked.

Her friend looked at me and said: "God! God!"

"He must can do it."

"You mean the girl?"

"Of course I mean the girl."

"She's not his sister, that's for sure."

"Oh, he can do it. There's no question. I had a brother-in-law that got in a car wreck and paralyzed his legs, and he could do it."

"I always wondered about that."

They were quiet for a moment and then both of them as if on signal turned to look at Hester. Hester turned her bored eyes toward them. They smiled. One of them winked. Hester didn't smile. The two ladies looked back at me and said: "God, what a freak!"

"Wonder what a normal girl like her's doing with a thing like that?"

I tipped the flagpole over. I'd been rocking it back and to, back and to, and finally I let it get away from me and it went farther and farther over—all in slow, slow motion—until I couldn't get it up again, so I had to go with it. The only reason I didn't mean to tip it over was the fucking flag hanging on it and I knew the scouts and everybody would get tight if Old Glory dragged on the floor. I've gone off poles higher than that before, making it look like an accident to scare the shit out of the audience and then catching myself in a handstand at the last moment. But this time it was an accident because I wasn't paying attention. It wasn't as though I was doing anything hard, and the lady's question: "Wonder what a normal girl like her's doing with a thing like that?" had stuck in my head like a tack.

I dived from the pole when it was only halfway over, hit the floor in a double roll, came up into a handstand and caught the pole in the groove between the cheeks of my ass. I saved Old Glory and brought everybody to their feet. Everybody but Hester. While everybody else pounded their hands, Hester stifled a yawn.

It was the lady's question about Hester that caused me to lose the pole. I didn't know what Hester was doing with me. Not exactly. It was true that I'm special. I mean if you're with me, nobody can upstage you. You're what everybody's looking at. If you're with me, you're special too. But that was not enough for most women. If it was it wouldn't be so hard for me to score on some skin. So like I said, I didn't know exactly what Hester was doing with me, and I'd never tried to find out, because my experience is that it's better not to talk about those things, or else you get in too deep and end up paying the price.

But up there on the pole I suddenly knew what I was doing with Hester. Not what she was doing with me—what I was doing with her. It was as though it had been there in the back of my head trying to break through for weeks. In her room, two hours before, I just didn't feel like trying to get around paying anymore and realized that whatever was asked, I'd pay it if I had to. Now I knew I would have to. I would have to

because I had the Gypsy's Curse ¡*Que encuentres un coño a tu medida!* I
can still spell it out although I'm not a spick and never have been one.
May you find a cunt that fits you, Fernando would say when we arm
wrestled and I slammed his wrist flat on the table. *May you find a cunt
that fits you!*

Jesus, I had. I had.

I cut my act short and lay in a little puddle of sweat at the foot of the
podium. I could feel the screams of delight from the Cub Scouts and
the banging chairs in the cement under my head.

Four

WE were sitting under a streetlight in the deserted street by the side of the Fireman's Gym. Hester bent lower in the seat to look at the dark door leading to the stairway.

"So that's it, huh?" she said.

She knew goddam well that was it. We'd sat under this same streetlight dozens of times, kissing and fingering until she was juicy and I was chewing at the upholstery. She'd always sit there racing the engine of the Volvo until I got inside the door. But I knew what was coming. I knew better than I wanted to what was coming.

"I'm not going back," she said, leaning into the light pouring through the windshield so we could talk.

I put my hands in the light and watched the shadows they made when I said: "I know."

That was the first thing she had told me when we came out of the basement of the church.

"Where will you go?" I had asked.

She looked at me for a long time. "You know where," she said.

See, you get caught in these things and you can't get out. I didn't want to talk about it, but I didn't see any other alternative.

"To the sponge boat?" I said.

"If that's what you want," she said.

"That's not what I want," I said.

"Then you know where," she said, and she'd cranked up the Volvo and we'd raced across town only to end up sitting there under the streetlight for almost an hour looking at the dark doorway leading to the stairs of the Fireman's Gym.

I put my hand in the light and said: *"Que encuentres un coño a tu medida."*

"What?" she said.

I told her again.

"That doesn't make sense," she said.

"It's called the Gypsy's Curse."

"Say it again."

I said it and then told her, "It's Spanish."

"I didn't know you spoke Spanish," she said.

"I don't," I said, "but I know that because I've got it. I've got the Gypsy's Curse. That's why I can say it."

"Jesus, you've got it? Is it a disease?"

"Sort of. But it's not catching. You can't catch it."

"Christ Almighty," she said. "Those Spanish guys can give you the worse shit in the world. I used to fuck one from Ybor City."

"I wish you wouldn't talk about things like that," I said. "Besides, I didn't get it from a spick."

"Listen, do you feel all right? You don't look good at all."

I felt like hell, and I told her so.

"It was that lady," she said. "I don't know what got into her. Maybe it was you catching the flag in your ass. Or maybe it was me. I wasn't very friendly."

"Maybe," I said.

Hester had walked up just in time to hear the lady say: *Freak! You vile little freak!*

After we got the Cub Scouts settled down and after my breathing was right again, the two ladies came over to talk to me. Hester was on the other side of the podium talking to Mr. Robert.

"That was extraordinary," the fattest lady said. "Just extraordinary."

I was sitting on my rocklike ass behind the podium and they were on either side of it looking down at me. I nodded my head.

"Enthralled," said the other one, "truly enthralled."

I nodded my head. I wasn't going to do it if they would just shut up and leave me alone. I had nothing to gain by doing it. And I am not a bitter person by nature.

"You're an artist, a real artist."

That did it. I *am* an artist. But I wouldn't have had to be very smart to figure out that she sure as hell didn't think so. And I'm no dummy.

I raised my hand and spelled very slowly: "T . . . h . . . a . . . n . . . k y . . . o . . . u."

"Look!" cried one of the ladies. "He's talking to us. He's—"

"Spell it!" shouted the other one. "Spell it!"

They spelled the letters together as they came off my hand. I had to repeat the *h* twice and the *y* four times. It made them feel so good they blushed.

"Oh, you're welcome," said the fat lady. "You're welcome."

Now you've got to understand, she was stretching her mouth over the words one by one like she was spitting out rocks. They'd been talking to me like that ever since my act was over. They didn't think I was an artist. They didn't even think I was bright. They thought I was an idiot.

The slender one, the one that went about two hundred and ten pounds, leaned down almost in my face where I was sitting behind the podium and said: "As soon as we knew you were going to be here we went out and got a little book to learn how to talk with the hands. We've been practicing hard, haven't we, Mildred? I can do it the fastest." She pushed her lips out and her forehead drew together in a worried knot. "Watch this."

She raised her soft hand and her fat ringed fingers said: "He lurp sump ott fure, ikkto the front and."

I smiled at her and nodded. Then I raised one finger and wagged it.

"He's going to talk again," said the fat lady. "He's going to!"

Before I could start, though, the other lady leaned down and said: "I knew it would help if we got the book and learned your language . . . *Laan guu agge*. When Frank, Frank's my husband, when Frank and I travel we find that the natives like us more if we try to learn their *laan guu agge*."

Jesus, I thought, I may have to kill them. Anything less may not be enough. But I lifted my hand anyway. They hunkered their huge corseted bodies in a half crouch in front of my fingers. I said the words very very slowly and only had to repeat seven letters.

"I a . . . m q . . . u . . . i . . . t . . . e c . . . a . . . p . . . a . . . b . . . l . . . e o . . . f f . . . u . . . c . . . k . . . i . . . n . . . g y . . . o . . . u . . . r f . . . a . . . t a . . . s . . . s . . . e . . . s."

They stayed crouched there in front of my fingers, their faces blank. They were white around the noses and I could almost hear them thinking. They had spelled the whole sentence through, word by word, right to the end, and never stopped smiling until about three beats behind the last letter. Then the smile fell and they stayed crouched wondering: Did we? Did he? I loved it. It was better than killing them.

Just about then, Hester walked up and heard the fattest one, still in her hunker there in front of my hand, which was still raised like a blank page, say: *"Freak! You vile little freak!"*

"We could sit here all night," said Hester.

She stretched to look at the dark door leading up to the gym again.

"Maybe you could," I said. "I'm tired. I want to go to bed."

She reached over and took hold of my cock.

"I want to go to bed, too," she said.

"If you'd just be reasonable," I said.

She took her hand away. "Sure," she said. "I'll be reasonable. If that's what you want, that's what you want."

"Goddam," I said. "You can understand, can't you?"

"I understand fine," she said. She had pushed her hand into the light to speak and refused to look at me.

"O.K.," I said.

"Goodnight," she said. "Sleep good." She still didn't look at me.

I opened the door and went down on the sidewalk. I hurried toward the gym, trying not to think about it. But behind me, I knew she was racing the engine of the Volvo. I looked back once and saw the little blue spurts of vapor from the tailpipe. I couldn't tell if she was looking at me or not. By the time I got to the door leading up the stairs to the Fireman's Gym, my nose was rotten with the smell of olive oil. I could feel the boat shifting under me, and feel her hand, that same hand that had held me, holding him, Aristotle Parsus.

Jesus, the world does get heavy at times. It does.

Hester must have seen me coming back down the sidewalk toward the car because when I got to it, the door swung open. I sat down on the curb under the streetlamp and looked up at her.

"It won't work," I said.

She smiled at me, showed me her tongue. "You sweet thing," she said. "You darling."

"I don't know any other way to do it but to do it," I said.

"What?"

"They sleep like dead men," I said. "If you want to go up there with me, let's go."

There was no way to get ready for it. I didn't know what Al would do. I thought I knew what he would say. I wished I had tried to talk to him about it, but I hadn't. And that was that. You've got to take it like it comes.

"You're sure this is what you want," she said, already out of the car.

"I'm sure," I said. If it was a choice between this and the sponge boat, I was sure.

She locked the car and we went down the sidewalk together. All the lights were off in the gym. Al goes to sleep right after the gym closes, which is ten o'clock every night but Sunday. The gym's not open at all on Sunday, so he can go to bed as early as he wants to. That's usually about six-thirty. Al says sleep is strength. He likes to get about ten hours a night. And like everything else, Leroy and the nigger are right behind him. He lies down, they lie down. And they all sleep like dogs. Brain damage makes you sleep like a dog. I've always wondered just how much that Hudson Hornet hurt Al when it ran over his head. I think it hurt him more than he knew. It might even by why he talks like he does. But it may not.

When we got onto the stairs, Hester put her hand on my ass because it was impossible to see anything much. I guided her across the landing and into the gym. Light pouring in from the lamp in the street made the benches and weights and pulleys dark against the windows. She could see now but she held on to my ass anyway. Her hand felt afraid. She stopped and looked at the framed pictures of Al that showed dull against the wall, and at the Roman rings coming down out of the black ceiling like nooses, and finally at the back of the gym where the door was only a blacker square on a dark wall. She had never been up there before, and I was sure no other woman had ever been there either.

Her hand tightened on my ass when we started for the door in the back. I took her to my bed against the wall on the other side of the kitchen. She bumped the table when we went by it and I felt her stiffen. But she didn't have anything to worry about, not tonight anyway, because you would have had to hit Al in the head with a shovel to wake him up. Tomorrow was something else.

I zipped out of my suit and climbed up on the bed. I could hear her getting out of her clothes. She came under the covers and wrapped me up with her body. Her good mouth pressed mine. Her hands found me and she worked at me like she was chopping wood. But then she pulled back and she took one of my hands and put it on her mouth. I felt her lips move, words forming. But I couldn't get any of them. Nothing. She kept my fingers there though and wouldn't let them away, and the words kept coming. I reached up into the first shelf of books and found my flashlight. I snapped it on and put it on her mouth. Her tongue sent shivers through me in the yellow light.

"Don't you have a steam room here?" she said.

I turned the flashlight on my hand. "Yes," I said.

"And massage tables?" she said.

"We give rubdowns," I said.

I swung the beam of light between her mouth and my hand.

"Who gives 'm?"

"We take turns. We all do whatever needs doing."

"Just one happy family," she said.

You may think when you read lips that you don't hear sarcasm. But you do. You hear it better than you'd think.

"No," I said. "I wouldn't say it was a happy family."

"Where are they?" she said.

"There's a door back there," I said. "You can't see it, but it's right there. It's a room in there and that's where they sleep."

She had seemed afraid before, but not anymore. Maybe it wasn't fear to start with, only excitement. She'd had the covers up around her head when she first lay down, but with the flashlight I could see her stretching her neck, turning her head, squinting into the darkness. It felt like what she was really going to do was get up, turn on a light, and begin examining everything, touching stuff, turning it over to see if anything was written on the bottom.

She moved on the bed. I hit her in the mouth with the light. "I'd like to get up right now and catch a little steam bath."

"Christ, you can't do that," I said.

"Why not?" Her face drew in on itself, like a hand closing.

"Because we're liable to wake Al up."

"You said he slept like a dead man."

"I know what I said. We're still liable to wake him up."

"You afraid of Al?"

I didn't know what the hell we were talking about. Except I did. I had brought her into a place where she had no business, and things were going to become instantly and automatically shitty. What I should have done was ease back the covers, bind up my legs, and take her downstairs to the car. But I didn't. Instead, I touched her lap.

"I don't see why you can't be reasonable," I said. "For Al, this is the middle of the goddam night and—"

"Oh, I can be reasonable," she said. "I can be as reasonable as anybody else."

She took her hand away and rolled onto her side. I lay there on my back with my hands locked behind my head looking up into the ceiling.

Just before she went to sleep, she reached up to the shelf where she'd seen me put the flashlight. She snapped the light on her mouth and said: "There's no reason to be afraid of Al, you know. He may need you. But you don't need him at all. Not at all."

Then before I could answer, she turned off the light. And she didn't put it back on the shelf where I could get it either. She kept it beside her where she lay and went right to sleep. If she'd let me have the light I'd have snapped it on and told her what happened to me the time when I thought I didn't need Al.

I ended up as a dummy. I mean really a dummy. Sitting in a guy's lap. It hurt. It hurt me bad. He was a ventriloquist, a huge man, maybe six six, and he'd come walking out on stage with me under his arm, sit down, and plop me in his lap. I'd let my head roll around for a minute, my arms loose and out of control. Then he would stick his hand under the back of my coat and my head would pop up and I'd start blinking. Jesus, it was awful. But there was nothing else to do. When I couldn't stand that anymore I ended up on a little cart with rollerskate wheels on the bottom of it, pushing myself along with rags wrapped around my hands. I sat on a corner all day selling things, apples at first, then pencils.

See, I lost my arms. Without Al to train me and without the gym I grew up in, my arms went down. They went from twenty inches to a little over fifteen. I could still stand on my hands, but I couldn't do the tricks anymore. The food I was eating was bad. I couldn't talk to booking agents. And worse, the worst thing of all, is nobody loved me.

Do you understand that? Nobody loved me. It's easy to think I didn't love Al. But I did. I knew he was a strange old man and smelled like a goat. But like my legs, he was all I had. And just like I couldn't cut off my legs, because after all, no matter how fucked up they are they're still my legs, I couldn't leave Al because he was all I ever had.

I didn't always know that. It came to me the hard way. I thought I'd leave the gym and go out and conquer the world. Well, I left the gym, but I didn't conquer the world or anything else. I starved. I'm one of the best hand balancers in the world. I know it, and every booking agent who has ever seen me work knows it. But I starved anyway.

I'm too grotesque is the way it was explained to me. Ed Sullivan's Sunday night variety show was still cooking in those days. I auditioned for it but didn't make it. Ed said I'd do better in a smaller room. He said I was great but that television magnified the wrong things.

"What wrong things?" I asked the booking agent who had got me the audition.

"Instead of seeing you stand on one finger, they only see a guy with his legs strapped to his ass," he said. "They see a man with the wrong size head."

My head is overly large, and tends to be squarish. That's one of the reasons I can bridge into a headstand using no hands, my head being like a box on top. You can't tell it with the hair but it's flat as your hand. So this booking agent took me to New York and I auditioned for Ed and Johnny Carson and two or three low-rent shows, but none of them wanted me because I'm too grotesque for the big time. Actually, the booking agent was the one who told me in just those words.

"You're too grotesque for the big time," he screamed at me. He was out the price of two tickets to New York and meals and the rest of it, so I could see why he was tight.

I lay on the bed and thought about it. I put my hand on Hester's good rump. I was who I was and nothing was going to change that. And yet I felt like by bringing Hester here to the gym I was trying to change something that couldn't be changed. But what it was I was trying to change I couldn't figure out.

Well, Fernando always said the Gypsy's Curse would make you do strange things.

"Find a cunt that fits you and you'll never be the same," he would say. "Never find any peace. See, it won't matter if she dishonors you. It won't matter if she lies to you, hurts you, spits in your face, fucks other men. All you'll want to know is: are you coming back to me? are you going to let me have that fantastic cunt one more time? One more time with that cunt that fits you is all you'll care about. Ruin your family, ruin yourself, nothing will matter."

I would slam his wrist to the table and Fernando would cry out, sweat flying from his lips: "*¡Que encuentres un coño a tu medida!*"

That night I had a dream I never had before. And I dreamed it over and over again. I was looking out on an empty street. It was late in the evening. A man and a woman came around a corner into the street. They were well dressed and you could tell they were good people. Decent people. The kind who, if they hit a dog with their car, would stop and take it to a vet. The man had me in his arms. A nice blanket, soft and warm, was wrapped around me. As they walked, the lady at least twice reached over and tucked the blanket tighter under my chin. The top of my squarish head was quite plain against the man's shoulder, and I was asleep. They walked slowly and without any sign of uneasiness to the door leading to the stairs of the Fireman's Gym.

"How about here?" the lady said.

I was asleep but I could hear them.

"As good as any," the man said.

Their voices were gentle and intelligent. They were not dummies. I opened my eyes and looked at them. They smiled kindly and the woman pinned the note to my blanket. I saw for the first time that I was in a kind of plastic carrying case.

"Shall we just put him on the steps?" said the man.

"I think that'll be fine," said the lady. "That will do nicely."

They put me down on the first step. I opened my mouth to tell them that this was no way to treat a baby. When nothing came out, I took my hands from under the blanket, but they were baby's hands, soft, illiterate, speechless. They turned without another word and walked back down the street. Before they were halfway to the corner, I kicked out of the cover of the blanket and stood up in the plastic carrying case. I was clearly at least three years old and my legs were fat and dimpled and strong. I ran down the street after them. They turned and saw me coming. Both of them smiled and the man kneeled down and opened his arms as I ran toward them.

"He can walk," cried the lady.

"His legs are as good as any you could ask for on a boy," the man said.

"He'll have to come then," said the lady, "he just will."

We turned the corner together and the street was empty. Immediately a man and woman came around the corner, the man carrying me in the plastic case with a blanket wrapped around me, and the whole sorry dream was repeated again.

I woke up exhausted, feeling the feeling that had been in my legs all night but was not there now. Pete was standing at the foot of my bed in the sweat suit that he used for pajamas. He was looking at Hester, where her dark hair spilled over the pillow, her mouth slightly open, probably snoring. Pete's face showed nothing, not the slightest expression, and I could tell he thought he must be dreaming.

"Sometime you see sompin," he said. "Howsomever, it's other times you see sompin else."

He turned his back to us and stood there for about two minutes. Then he turned around and looked at Hester again.

"He said, "Marvin Molar, one of us is in big trouble."

Hester opened her eyes and looked up at him. "My name's Hester," she said.

"It you," Pete said, and turned around and went through the door where he sleeps with Al and Leroy.

"What was that?" asked Hester

"Pete," I said.

"What did he mean when he said, It you?"

"He thinks I'm in trouble."

"Oh," she said. "Don't worry about it. You know you don't have to worry, don't you?"

"I'd be very happy to know that."

"Well, we'll see what we see," she said.

What we saw was Leroy coming through the door with Pete behind him. His corn-colored hair twisted up on top of his head like the comb of a rooster. The edges of his eyes were matted with sleep. He stood at the foot of the bed staring at Hester, then he turned and walked on his heels through the door with Pete still following him. He was wearing an old bathrobe that Al had given him. He had sewn the words BATTLING KID LEROY on the back of it, and because he knew less about sewing than he did about boxing, the words dribbled down his back at a forty-five-degree angle.

"Don't tell me," said Hester. "That was Battling Kid Leroy." She had a smirk on her face, and I was surprised at the little rush of anger I got by her making fun of Leroy.

"His name's Leroy," I said. "He's from Georgia and his brain is bruised. He's not worth making fun of."

"I wasn't making fun of him," she said.

"All right," I said.

"Who's next?" she said. "Will Al be next?"

Al appeared in the door. Pete and Leroy were behind him, looking over his shoulders.

"Is this her?" said Al.

"This is Hester," I said. "Hester, that's Al Molarski."

I didn't know what was going to happen. I felt a little sick to my stomach.

Al reached up and fingered his cauliflower ear. Hester and I had the blanket pulled up to our necks. Under the cover I had my hand on her lap, trying to convince myself that there was no other way to do this.

"Al don't allow women to work out in the Fireman's Gym."

"That's all right, Al," said Hester as easy as if she had been talking to a child. "I didn't come to work out."

Al's cheeks darkened. The lines got deeper in his face. He said: "Al . . . Al . . ." But he didn't know what he wanted to say.

"It was bound to happen sooner or later," I said.

"Al don't allow nothing like that around here," he said.

I knew he didn't know what he meant by that, and I sure as hell didn't.

"My name's Leroy," Leroy said.

"I know," said Hester.

"And the nigger's name's Pete," he said.

"Marvin told me," she said.

"You understand fingers, I guess," said Leroy.

"Yes," she said.

"The nigger ain't got good sense," Leroy said.

"Well, none of us is perfect," Hester said.

"Leroy," said Al.

"What?" Leroy said.

"Shut up," said Al.

"Don't take it out on him," said Hester.

"Al takes it out on anybody he wants to," he said.

I felt Hester stiffen a little under the covers.

"Well," she said, "how about taking it out of this room while I get dressed."

"What did you say?" said Al, looking into the shelves of books above our heads.

"I'd like for the three of you to get out of here. I'm a lady and I want to get dressed."

"Al's not a gentleman," he said.

Hester gave him a real ball-freezing look. "That's all right by me," she said. "I was only kidding about being a lady."

Al turned and stomped out of the room with Leroy and Pete right behind him. Then a funny thing happened. Leroy stopped in the door, looked over his shoulder and winked at Hester. Hester, who was already half out of the bed winked back at him. While she pulled on her clothes she was looking around at everything, reading some of the titles on the shelves, staring at the pictures of Al posed in bathing suits and wrestling tights on battleships. Finally, she looked at me where I still lay in the bed my eyes locked on her incredible lap that was just now disappearing behind the zipper of a pair of tight jeans.

"You sleep in the kitchen?" she said.

She was looking at the four-burner gas stove in the far corner.

"Well, that's the stove we cook on."

"If that's the stove you cook on," she said, "then you sleep in the kitchen."

"We don't have a lot of room up here," I said. "This is not the Ritz."

"It'll be all right after we make a few changes," she said.

"You can't make changes up here," I said.

She just glanced at me and went on pulling herself into a jersey. Then she went over to the room Al slept in and called through the door: "O.K., you can come in now."

When Pete and Leroy and Al came in, she had the door of the ice box open and was bent looking into it. Al stood in the door watching her. I had my legs bound and my purple suit on that I ordinarily never wore except for performances. She straightened from the ice box and looked at us.

"What do you guys usually have for breakfast?"

Al's cheeks got darker. He didn't say anything and by now he was looking at the ceiling.

"I get my workout before the gym opens," I said.

"Well, I'll start it," she said.

"Al cooks breakfast," I said.

"That's all right," she said. "I'll take care of it. What does he make?"

Leroy's eyes were bright and he was grinning, showing his broken teeth. There was something in him that liked all of this. He winked again. Al saw him this time and I thought he was going to pound the kid's head. But he didn't, and Leroy said: "It's some juice in there. And Al'll cook us some eggs, maybe a stack of cakes, some wheat germ and cream. Them little boxes over the sink's vitamins."

"What time's the gym open?" she asked.

"Ten," I said.

She looked at the alarm clock on the first shelf above my bed. "You'd better get started," she said. "Don't worry about this in here. I'll take care of it."

Pete reached out and put his hand on Leroy's shoulder and moved him out of the way. He came to stand in front of Hester.

"Who you be?" he said, and did a little shuffle with his feet.

"My name's Hester," she said.

"At ain't it. At ain't it at all," he said. "I axe who you *be*."

She walked over and leaned her face toward him until she almost touched his flat broken nose and said: "I be the lady who's gone cook your breakfast."

He smiled her three yellow teeth and said: "At be good. Now at be good!"

I slid off the bed and started toward the steam room because Al was looking bad. Not just angry, he didn't look angry. He looked . . . well, baffled, and worse than that, hurt. He had laced his old, long-fingered hands in front of his belt buckle, and they were wrestling each other. Purple veins stood knotted in his bone-white wrists. But I started down the hall toward the steam room, and Pete followed me, then Leroy, and when I got there Pete opened the door for me, and I saw that Al had come too. We closed the door to the hallway, which we had never done before, so that Hester wouldn't see us. Pete peeled out of his sweatsuit, Leroy took off his bathrobe, and Al got out of his striped pants he wore with wide dirty suspenders. Nobody said a word. I wore my purple performance suit into the steam room and pulled myself up on one of the wooden benches. The three of them filed in naked behind me. Pete came over to where I lay and started working on my arms, talking to himself as he always did.

"Wake to his body," he said. "Wake to his body. Hands come down, wake to his head. Stick and move."

Al's hands were still wrestling each other there where he sat in front of me. Finally, he said: "Christ's sake, set down and shut up."

I'd never heard him talk to Pete like that.

Pete stopped. "Whut you say?" he asked.

"Al said set down. Set down and shut up."

"Pete do that," Pete said.

He hooked the air a couple of times and went to sit beside Leroy, who gave that same crazy wink again, this time at me.

"Leroy," Al said.

But Leroy already knew what he wanted, so he looked the other way and pretended he didn't hear. Al wasn't having any of that either. "Al wants you to stop that goddam winking."

"I think I got something in that 'ere eye," Leroy said.

Al's hands struggled in his lap while he glared at Leroy. "Al thinks you ought to bite your tongue. Al thinks lies are the worse . . . the worse . . . the worse . . ."

Al sat there struggling with himself and with the words that had stuck in his mouth because the door to the steam room had opened and Hester came in naked and stood under the light.

"I've got the bacon on slow," she said.

Pete had turned to face the wall when he first caught sight of her in the door. He sat with his nose touching the tiles. Leroy didn't turn his head, he just pinched his eyes shut and blushed, the wave of blood flooding up out of his chest into his neck and not stopping until it ran under the sandy roots of his hair. Al was staring directly at her, his eyes running down her fantastic legs. I don't think he had realized until then what kind of body she was walking around in. Al would forgive a lot for the right kind of body. And God she did look tough standing there with the yellow light pouring down over her, the shadows marking her high easy breasts and the six clean ridges of muscle that started in her solar plexus and ended finally in her shining pubes.

Al said: "You . . . you . . ." He was looking at her, but when it was obvious that he was not going to be able to think of anything to say, he swung his eyes to me. ". . . you better get on in the gym and work out."

As I got up, she took my place, lying on her back, letting her legs lie wide. "I'll just catch a little more of this steam," she said.

Leroy and Pete ran into each other trying to get through the door without looking at her.

When we got into the gym, Al said: "You didn't tell Al she worked out."

"As far as I know, she doesn't," I said.

He looked back toward the steam room. "A natural athlete's the best kind."

"She's pretty good," I said. "She's not bad."

Al cut his eyes to me. "Al don't see how she can stay."

Leroy had been shuffling, bobbing and weaving, behind Al. He pointed to the steam room. "She . . . she . . ." He reached out and spun old Pete and hooked him in the shoulder. Pete immediately started talking to himself, coaching himself, and slipping everything the kid threw.

Al watched Leroy, who really seemed to have gone over the edge of something. "Al cain't have women taking off their clothes in front of his fighters."

"Al, for Christ's sake, there's no fighters here," I said.

"It's two," he said. He pointed to Pete and Leroy still dancing through a make-believe bout. "It's two. One, two."

"Shit, Al," I said.

"What?" he demanded, even though he had been looking right at my hand when I said it.

There didn't seem to be any point in going on, so I rocked up off my ass and walked over to the brick pile. I walked back with one brick in each hand and put them in front of Al.

"All right," Al said.

He had his stool out of the wire cage and was sitting on it. Pete and Leroy were on either side of him. I could smell the bacon on the stove. I wondered if Hester was still in the steam room, and while I stacked the bricks and prone-pressed and ran the stairs, I thought of her lap, damp and spread on the wet bench under the yellow light. I was still thinking of it at the end of my workout, hanging in a rigid iron cross between the Roman rings with Al standing below me shouting: "Marvin, I love you. I love you, son!"

It was a tight, controlled workout, and I came down the hemp rope feeling good, but as soon as I touched the floor I knew something was wrong. I looked to the back of the gym. Hester was standing in the door, a towel wrapped around her at the armpits, her thighs spraddling and flexed. And I'm a son of a bitch if she didn't have that picture of Al, the one with the Hudson Hornet running over his head. All I could see was that she had a square of stiff paper in her hands, but I knew it was the picture. Al and Pete and Leroy were as still as if they'd been looking at a snake. Hester came walking slowly toward us, holding the picture pressed face down against the towel, talking as she came.

"The workout's all right, but you shouldn't be shouting at him like that." She was talking to Al. "When he's trying to concentrate in the cross, all that shit about love is distracting." She suddenly held up the picture of Al getting his head run over. "You don't see anybody there talking about love when Al got his head caught, do you?"

Al leaned forward and stared at the picture the way a man might look at his own coffin. Then I saw his old mouth twist in a way that must have been just like he screamed when his head got run over to start with. Then he whirled and struck Leroy solid between the eyes. Leroy went down like a dead man. Al would have hit Pete too, but the nigger just slipped the right hand Al threw and calmly started coaching him: "Wake to the body, wake to the body."

II

Five

SEE, I told her about that goddam picture. On a Sunday about three weeks ago, drinking beer down at the Oh Cee, I told her Al had it in the little leather trunk under his bed. I guess I was making fun of Al, laughing at him when I told her. But I didn't mean it that way. It's just that there's little enough to laugh about if you've got my disadvantages in the world, and I figure you take the laugh where you can get it. So, anyway, that's how she knew about the picture to start with. Naturally when I told her, I never thought someday she would be living in the Fireman's Gym. But that's the world for you: give it a little leverage and one day it'll tear your ass.

Al threw a couple more clumsy shots at Pete, who turned them with his elbows and kept on coaching him. Then Al seemed to see Leroy, still stretched cold on the floor, for the first time. He stopped, shook his head, and got on his knees beside Leroy. He shouted something into Leroy's face. I couldn't tell what because from where I was standing I couldn't see his mouth. But I knew he was shouting from the way his head was making little jerks the way a dog'll do when he's trying to swallow a piece of meat that's too big and from the way the back of his neck was red and swollen. I went over to where Hester was still standing in the towel with the picture of Al pressed between her great titties.

"That was an awful thing to do," I said. "And besides that, stupid."

"I don't think so," she said, watching Al's broad jerking back where he still bent over Leroy.

"If I were you," I said, "I'd get dressed and get out of here."

"Don't be so weak," she said. "Don't be such a candyass."

If I had been tall enough to slap her, I probably would have. But since I wasn't tall enough, what I really wanted to do was press my head into the fantastic lap that rode the air in front of me just above nose level and tell her that I was no candyass and beg her to believe it. It was a little humiliating to feel like that, but I've been humiliated before. One or two times.

Leroy had come to and was sitting up now. Al suddenly stood and turned to Hester. His old face was dark as leather. But he didn't really look angry, he looked like he wanted to cry.

"Al wants his picture," he said.

Hester didn't say anything. She stood facing him, relaxed and easy as you could ask for.

"Al wants it now!" He was screaming. And he still didn't look angry. He seemed way past that. It was scary as looking down the barrel of a gun. He didn't look like he really knew where he was. A little path of spit slipped from the corner of his mouth and swung from his chin.

I turned to look at Hester just in time to catch the last part of whatever she was saying: ". . . your picture."

Al went toward her, not fast, his fists balled, the knuckles showing sharp enough to cut the skin. His back was to me but I could tell he was talking. Hester stayed where she was, sweat running on her from the steam bath. Al reached for her. He may have been reaching for the picture, which she was still holding between her breasts, but it scared me because it looked like he might be reaching for her throat. I was getting ready to take a steel barbell plate and beat him on the foot with it if he grabbed her. She was facing me and just as he got to her, she held her hand out with the picture in it. When she lifted her arm, the towel slipped to the floor, and her sweat-shining titties were looking Al right in the eye. He stopped and she raised her other hand and touched his cauliflower ear.

"No man I've ever known could have done it," she said. She was stroking his ruined ear. "Where is the man that could have done it?" She turned the picture she was still holding and looked at it. "It's the most beautiful thing in the world. To stand a thing like that." She had his ear caught in her fingers now and she was actually pulling at it tenderly. "Al Molarski, I won't ever meet another man who could take a car on his head like that." His fists were relaxed, and she pressed the picture in his open hand. "I want you to know," she said, "I want you to know I honor you." Then she turned and walked across the gym, her hard, sweet rump pumping over the rhythm of her legs.

I went over to where Al was, sat down and said, "Listen Al . . ." But he only brushed me aside and got Leroy to his feet, taking the damp towel Hester had left to wipe his face.

"You all right, son?" he asked.

"I'm sure . . . sure," said Leroy, looking around. "What . . . I . . ."

"You got caught wif a lef hand," said Pete. "Right when you weren't paying good attention, you got caught wif a lef hand."

"O.K.," Al said to Leroy. "Come on, it don't matter."

We went into the kitchen, and I don't know how she did it, but there on the table was the bacon, a plate of it, scrambled eggs, wheat germ with cream, a stack of vitamins beside each plate—a multi, a reinforced B-1 complex, two E's and two dolomites—and in the middle of the table a big pot of steaming tea laced hard with honey. She came in before we'd had time to sit down—dressed in her jeans and a bleached work shirt, her hair damp and pulled to the nape of her neck where it was held with a copper clip.

There were four plates made up at the table and she sat down when we did. Nobody said anything. I thought she would ruin it all by trying to talk about what had happened, but she only poured the tea and passed the cups to Al who was sitting next to her. Al sent the tea around to me and to Pete and to Leroy and then kept a cup for himself. He went to work on the bacon, his head bent, his enormous jaw working.

Leroy was not eating. He sat looking straight ahead at nothing. He was only then just coming out of the lick Al gave him. You could see his eyes, flat, pinched, and a little milky, starting to clear. He had his hands in his lap and when he finally saw the food on the table in front of him, he looked as though he had no idea how he got there. He turned his eyes on Hester and blinked a few times. His mouth opened and closed, opened again and hung unhinged.

"Al," he said.

Al looked up from his wheat germ.

"Did you really get your head run over, Al?"

My heart jumped, and I thought, Christ, we're going to start all over again.

"Pictures don't lie," said Hester, matter-of-factly. She included us all at the table. "It's in the record." She reached over and touched Al's arm. "You probably won't find another strongman in the world who's ever done that and lived." Now she was looking right into Al's eyes. "Leroy, you're sitting at the table with one of the great ones." She paused but held Al's eyes with her own. "A world beater."

Al finally looked over at Leroy. "That's right, son. Al got his head run over with a car. A Hudson Hornet. How come Al's got this ear up here." He touched where the cauliflower was growing in the side of his head. Then he smiled at Hester. Smiled. I can't be for sure, but I think it was the first time I ever saw Al Molarski smile in my life.

"Ain't nobody can stan a car on he haid," said Pete without looking up from his plate.

Al put his fork down. "Pete's not paying attention," he said. "Pay attention is one thing Pete won't do."

"I knows what I know," Pete said. "It ain't no haid hold up no car."

Al picked up the picture he had put face down beside his plate. He held it up for Pete to look at. Pete kept eating. Finally, he carefully put his knife down and took the picture from Al. He brought it only inches from his face and stared at it a long time. He looked at Al, then back at the picture.

"Al Molarski," said Pete, "can do anything. Didn't say Al Molarski couldn't hold no car on he haid. Said ain't anybody else haid hold no car."

Leroy took the picture out of Pete's hand. He put it down beside his plate and stuffed his mouth with eggs while he looked at it. "God-amightydamn! Look at it. Right in the ear!"

Al looked away from the table shyly, embarrassed by this wonderful thing he had done—letting somebody run over his fucking head with a car.

"How come you didn't show it to us before?" said Leroy.

"Al don't show everything," said Al.

"There's a lot of things that are personal," said Hester, touching Al lightly on the arm. "You do something like that, it's a personal thing. Right, Al?"

"Right, Hester," Al said.

"Can we keep it out now?" said Leroy. "Put it in a picture frame with the othern?"

"I guess," Al said. He made a big thing out of pretending it didn't really matter one way or the other, but I could tell he was pleased. He was glad the goddam picture was finally out from under the bed. "You want to frame it up, Al don't mind."

"It ought to go in the most important place in the gym," Hester said.

Al stood up. "Time to open, Pete."

Usually nobody came in until the afternoon, but Al was careful that the gym opened exactly when it was supposed to and closed the same way. He was careful like that about everything. If he told you something was going to happen at nine o'clock on Tuesday, you could put it in the bank. I was glad it was time to open, time to get away from the table, before somebody asked Hester how she happened to find that picture when nobody else had. I was afraid she would tell Al that I told her about it, that I had known for years the picture was under the bed. That would've hurt the old fucker. I know it would have. He didn't need that on top of everything else. Because if you think about it, Al doesn't have the sweetest life in the world, shacked up like he is with two punch-drunk fighters and a legless hand-balancer who can't talk or hear. And now he's got Hester, who God knows he doesn't need but I do.

Pete went to open the front doors, while Leroy got fresh towels for the steam room and the massage tables. Al took a little spiral notebook out of his pocket and looked in it. He keeps everything we have to do written in there and when we have to do it. He studied the page a long time, then without raising his eyes he said: "How did you find Al's picture?"

Hester had taken the dishes to the sink. She came and sat at the table again with another cup of tea. She blew on it before she answered. "I was cleaning," she said.

"You cleaned Al's room?" he said.

"Swept," she said. "Swept it out good. Trunk under the bed." She was sipping the tea. "Nice trunk. Lot of dust under there too." She blew over the cup again. "Shouldn't have looked in the trunk. But it was such a nice trunk." She put the tea down and leaned close to look into Al's eyes, but couldn't because he was still staring down into the little spiral notebook. "I am sorry I looked in your trunk, Al."

He looked up and I'm a son of a bitch if he didn't smile again. Then he put the notebook down on the table in front of him and ran his thick finger along the line while he read: "Marvin at Sunshine Shop-

ping Center. Balance for charity but we get kickback of thirty-five dollars." We do a lot of charity work for part of the profits. "Pete knows to
pick up Russell Muscle at ten-thirty. Act goes on eleven-fifteen." Al
flipped the notebook shut. "Be on time," he said, and left the table.

When he was out of the room, Hester said: "Russell Muscle?"

"Name's really Russell Morgan, called Russell Muscle, sometimes balance with him. Did you really sweep Al's room?"

She watched me over the lip of her teacup, then moved the cup so I
could see her mouth. "Are you crazy?"

"Did you?" I said.

"Fuck no." She sipped the tea. "I just went in and got the goddam
picture."

"That's asking for trouble," I said.

"I'm not asking for anything."

"He'll see the room. He'll know."

"He'll see what he needs to see. And what he needs to see is what I
happen to want him to see. Simple as that."

"Are you coming with me this morning?"

She looked up, distracted. She was only half looking at my hand.
"What?" she said.

"What were you thinking about?" I asked her.

"Nothing," she said. "What did you say?"

"You sure as hell were too thinking about something."

"Don't be a prick," she said.

I said: "I'm not."

"Do you want me to leave?" she said.

"Al's not going to let you live here," I said.

She said: "That's not what I asked. Do you want me to leave?"

"No," I said. "I don't want you to leave."

"All right," she said. "Now what did you say to me?"

"I said are you coming with me this morning to the Sunshine Shopping Center?"

"To see you balance?"

"Yes."

"Christ, no! I've done that."

"What'll you do?"

"Stay around here with Al."

"You're crazy," I said.

"I know," she said.

I left her back in the room beside the steam bath where the massage tables are kept. Al was explaining the procedure. He had already inspected her hands and announced that she could give a terrific massage if she wanted to. She told him she would probably want to.

Pete brought the Dodge around and I got in the back seat. We started across town to Russell Muscle's. I was thinking about Hester left back there with Al, when I felt a tap on the seat beside me. It was Pete reaching behind him to get me to look in the rearview mirror. He had turned it so I could see his mouth.

"You ain't the first man been pussy-whipped," he said.

I didn't answer him because it wouldn't have done any good. He's never been able to learn to read sign language with his old bruised brain. I looked away from the mirror, but he reached back and touched me.

"Don't be shamed a pussy-whipped," he said.

I pointed a finger at my chest and shook my head.

"Why you gone lie to ole Pete?" he asked. "I know. You know. She know. She know good." He looked away for a moment and then back into the mirror. "Ain't me knowing or you knowing that gone kill you. It the gul knowing. A gul know she got you pussy-whipped and you daid. Yesssss sir, it ain't a thing but the truth."

I raised my hand and quickly told him he was a son of a bitch. He watched my fingers and then said: "Ain't no use you going on lak at to ole Pete. Ole Pete don give a shit bout at."

"Drive the goddam car," I said.

"Ain no use to do at," he said, not understanding a word.

"You goddam nigger dumb asshole sucking slave son of a bitch," I said.

"You just beside yourself," he said. "Hell, ole Pete knows."

He was right of course, and that's what had me pissed off. I was pussy-whipped, and knew it. But what made it bad was Hester knew it, too. I sighed and fell back against the seat. There were worse things than being pussy-whipped. It didn't seem fair though. But then *fair* was not a word I'd ever had a lot of use for. It never seemed to apply.

Russell Muscle lived three blocks off Tampa Bay on a street filled with narrow shotgun houses that all had grassless yards and Cubans sitting on the steps and more Cubans standing about on the sidewalks and dirty Cuban children playing on the broken curbstones, chasing each other into the streets with sticks.

"Run over a few of those goddam spick children," I said. Pete wasn't watching me, and it wouldn't have mattered if he had been. But just saying it made me feel better.

Pete stopped the car in front of Russell Muscle's house. The whole street stopped. The men who were lounging at the sagging yard gates slowly turned their heads to look at the car. The children quit chasing about in the street and watched. They had all seen that car before, and they always reacted the same way. I could feel the silence run in the street when I came down to the sidewalk on my hands. I don't think they knew what to make of Russell Muscle to start with, and I know they didn't know what to think of me. Once when I was going across the sidewalk to Russell's house, a little boy threw an empty Carnation milk can and hit me on the ass with it. I was just about to sit down and see if I could find a rock to wing at the little bastard when another spick— maybe the kid's daddy, I don't know—another spick, dressed in tight black pants and black shirt with a narrow-brimmed black hat and gold teeth clamped around a gold cigar, without even seeming to look, reached out and hit the little son of a bitch who had thrown the milk can in the back of the head with his fist and turned him heels up in the air. Then he took his cigar out of his mouth, and bowed just like I'd been a goddam king. The kid he'd hit in the back of the head with his fist hadn't moved from where he'd pitched face first in the dirt. A week later when Russell was in the gym, I called Al out and told him what had happened and then told him to ask Russell about it. I have to have Al translate because Russell doesn't read sign language. Or anything else. He's a first-class twenty-four-carat dummy. A dummy with a body that'll stop your heart.

Al told him what had happened and Muscle just stood there flexing for a minute and then he looked at me and said: "They think he drinks chicken blood, the Cubans do."

That even turned Al's head. His old pinched eyes disappeared, folded right back in his head, and then came out again, him blinking. "Chicken goddam blood?" Al said.

"A Cuban's funnier than you think he is," Muscle said. He breathed and his whole body seemed to expand. Even his fucking head got bigger. "They think Marvin Molar might could lay a curse if he was a mind to." He looked down at his own magnificent legs, admired his swollen calves and said: "It's because he's so goddam ugly, with them legs strapped up on his ass like that."

That's Russell Muscle for you. He is not a kind man. He is not a smart man. He is not a subtle man. Instead, he is a muscle, a Russell Muscle, if you can understand that.

"He's waiting for you," said Muscle's wife. She had opened the door just enough to stick her face through. Her face was long and narrow and yellow, and she always looked like she had been crying. She couldn't have weighed more than ninety pounds and I watched her hips as I followed her down the hall. She had a crippled ass, sort of a cigar box with a hole in it. Her ankles were slightly blue above the fake ballerina slippers she was wearing that could only have been bought out of the Woolworth's. Real cheapies.

At the kitchen, she stopped and leaned on the table with one hand and held her hip with the other.

"Could I fix you a nice cup of coffee, Mr. Molar?" she said, "Or maybe some tea with honey. Russell had me go get some clover honey just yesterday."

I shook my head and smiled up at her. I'd never been in her house that she didn't offer me something to drink or a slice of organic nut bread that Muscle made her bake. Always something. She had seemed like a real class lady ever since I met her, even if she did buy ballerina slippers out of the Woolworth's.

"I'd be pleased to do it," she said.

I just shook my head again and tried to show her I was pleased that she'd asked by the way I smiled. But I don't know if she understood. I wished I could talk to her. There aren't many people I ever want to talk to, but I wished I could talk to that lady.

Two children, a little boy and a little girl, both of them under four and both wearing soiled white pants, came into the kitchen and sat on the floor beside a rat-colored hot water heater. They were both licking red suckers. The little boy had several black teeth. I knew their names but I'd never seen either one of them say anything.

"If you want to git him," she said, and made a vague little wave toward the back of the house.

I went down the hall to the last room in the house. I sat down and reached up and opened the door. A wave of cold air rushed over me.

Muscle lay naked on the bed. All the shades were drawn and an air conditioner roared in one window. The walls and the ceiling were painted black. I closed the door and pulled myself up into a stuffed chair.

He was lying on his back with his hands folded over his fifty-two-inch chest. He turned his head, then he opened his eyes. A little sour spot settled on each side of his nose. He got off the bed and took five deep breaths. Except for his head, he was hairless, even his pubes. He used Nair liquid hair remover, about a bottle a day. The slightest bit of hair on his chest or legs drove him crazy. All the body builders stayed hairless, claiming as they did that hair blurred the line of the muscle, their definition, and Muscle was one of the great ones. He had more than forty titles to his credit, things like Mr. Muscle Beach, Mr. Southeastern United States, Mr. Florida, and Mr. Dairy Products. In the dark room, he glowed like a light. But it wasn't just because it was dark. He glowed wherever he was. It was like his skin had been hand-polished all the way from his wide intelligent-looking forehead down to his beautiful feet where blue veins ran in perfect symmetry up into thin, almost delicate ankles and on finally into nineteen-inch calves that were honed and toned into razor-cut definition. He was so fine that Al didn't charge him to work out in the gym—it was good advertising to have an iron freak like him around—and Al also went out of his way to get Muscle a little work, like this gig at the mall where we were going now.

Muscle didn't look at me while he got dressed. I could have been the cat that had come in and crawled up in the chair for all the attention he paid me. But Muscle was like that and I was used to it.

"When'll you be back, Russell?" his wife asked when we went through the kitchen. She hadn't moved from where she leaned on the table. The children still sat beside the water heater.

Russell stopped and looked at her as though he had not noticed her until that moment. "I'll be back when I get back," he said.

But then he didn't move, just stood there in the kitchen looking around him, like he couldn't imagine how in the hell he had ever come to be in such a place. He was six feet, two inches tall, two hundred and ten pounds of finely trained muscle, with blond shining hair falling down his neck, and standing there in the kitchen between those damp plaster walls and that skinny wife and those ruined children, it was like his body had somehow managed to suck all that had ever been handsome or strong or alive right out of his wife and out of the children and out of the house itself. The little boy smiled his bad teeth at his daddy, and Muscle only shook his head slowly and then went down the hallway on his machine-smooth stride.

I left a ten-dollar bill on the chair beside the kitchen table. I always did that when I came to pick up Muscle. The lady had never mentioned it and I was glad she hadn't. Because I wouldn't have known what to say to her. You probably think I was leaving the money there for her and those ugly kids. But I wasn't. I left it there for myself. See, Muscle doesn't work—except for a little balancing gig with me now and then— doesn't do anything but train at the gym and lie back there in that air-conditioned black room (he told Al he found black walls restful) eating protein foot supplements and sleeping, while that starving beast of a wife and those rotting children creep around the house like mice trying not to disturb him. I know she must have a job somewhere to feed the kids and pay the rent on that shotgun house, so I just dropped a ten on the kitchen chair when I went by so I could get through the rest of the day without going into a funky depression thinking about it. Shit, I'm not ashamed to say I've got feelings.

The Cubans watched us come down across the yard and sidewalk and get into the car. Pete twisted in the seat to look at us.

"How you today, Mistah Muscle?" said Pete.

Russell stared back at him. "My name is Russell Morgan," he said.

"I know at be what you mammy named you," Pete said. "But you done made it sompin else. You done put youself together another way."

"Leave my mother out of it," said Russell. "And how I put myself to-gether is my business. Get this fucking car over to the mall so I can get back to the A/C."

"I do that Mistah Muscle," said Pete, jerking the old Dodge into gear. "An I see how you be today."

Russell looked out the window at the grassless yards filled with Cubans and the dirty children chasing each other with sticks. Then he looked back at a spot between his knees and said: "Goddam world."

I wanted to tell him it may be a goddam world but it wouldn't make it any better by living off a lady with a crippled ass and letting your chil-dren's teeth rot out while you laid up in the A/C drinking protein milk-shakes. But of course I couldn't tell him anything, so I deliberately looked away because I didn't want to see anything else his mouth had to say.

I wondered what Hester was doing back at the Fireman's Gym. Al was liable to have run her off or thrown her out of a window by now. But I knew in my heart that he hadn't. She'd handled the whole thing like a champ and they were probably thick as thieves by now. Buddies. And I wondered why that pissed me off, because it did, it really did. I tried to think about it like an intelligent man, because I'm no dummy, and finally after about ten blocks I had to admit to myself that I didn't trust Hester, that there was something in her that scared me. As mad as I was for her fantastic lap, as much as her great pointing titties made my liver turn over, I had to admit that there was something about her that terrified me. And I knew what that something was. Just as Pete was pulling the Dodge into the mall, I knew that the reason I was scared of her was that I realized suddenly there was nothing in the world I would not do for her, nothing I would not risk for her. Now, hell, I'm a realist, I try to look things in the eye, and not blink. If you look like me, if you get dealt the kind of hand I was dealt, then you better be damn careful what you risk. I know that. You better try to cover your ass at every turn of the road. A man can't deny his nature though. And I knew the day I saw her for the first time—I couldn't have said it, but I knew it in my blood—that I would follow her right on through the front door of hell. As we were pulling to a stop beside the temporary bandshell that had been set up in the parking lot of the mall, it occurred to me that Hester would probably ask me to do just that.

Pete stopped the car and then turned to look at us. "Seem lak you gone have a nice crowd today," he said.

Russell got out of the car without answering or even looking at him. He went straight across the macadam that was already sending up little risers of heat and up the five steps to the temporary band shell. Immediately, he began taking off his clothes. He stripped out of his shirt, peeled out of his trousers and stood there in a pair of posing briefs, glowing against the green painted background of the band shell. There were probably three hundred people walking around on the parking lot where a Pepsi-Cola truck had set up a drink stand and somebody else had put up a place to sell hotdogs and cotton candy. But when Russell locked his two hands together and threw his entire body into a solid quivering knot of muscle, people were drawn from all over the lot. They pressed in upon each other in front of the band shell looking up at him. Pete and I were still in the car, watching over the heads of the crowd, as

Russell fell from one pose to the next in a rhythmic solitary kind of dance. From all that showed on his face he might have been alone, still lying back in the bed in his black room.

"Ain't he something?" said Pete.

I could only nod.

"He ain't nothing but a muscle," Pete said, "but he be something else. Indeed he do."

A little man in a green suit came up on the band shell and put his mouth to Russell's ear. Russell didn't look at him, never dropped a stitch in his posing routine. The man was Mr. Royce Tutin, who owned a ladies' shoe store inside the mall. He was the one who set this whole thing up and had hired me and Russell to perform. Deaf mutes were his favorite charity because he had three children himself, all of them deaf mutes. Russell wasn't paying any attention to him up on the platform and Mr. Royce Tutin kept shifting from one ear to the other while Russell posed.

Pete tapped me on the shoulder. I looked at him. "That Muscle ain't got but one mind, do he?" he said. Pete smiled and showed me the whole purple inside of his mouth.

I got out of the car and went across the parking lot. The people standing in front of the band shell were not cheering or clapping. I could tell they were standing in what must be a stunned silence. Mr. Royce Tutin was still up on the platform with Russell, but he was no longer trying to say anything into his ear. He was standing off to one side with his arms folded over his round little chest. He looked distressed.

I knew what it was. He'd been up there trying to get Russell out of the band shell so the choir from the school could go on. Russell wasn't even supposed to be posing anyway. He was here to balance with me, but you show Russell a platform and an audience and he'll flex for you.

I felt rather than saw the eyes swing from Russell in the band shell to me handing along in front of the hotdog and cotton candy stands and then through the little aisle of people that opened up for me as I went to the steps leading up to where Russell was swooning through another pose with his eyes closed. That was good, his eyes being closed, I liked that. It would serve the bastard right.

I'd already seen the Pepsi bottle that somebody had left on the edge of the platform and I figured it was the right thing to do, the only thing to do if we were going to get Russell down from there. I went up the steps to the band shell, feeling all the eyes fastened on my legless rump pumping along across the stage. I stopped in front of the empty Pepsi bottle. Behind me, Russell danced on with himself, shifting from poses that emphasized chest to poses that best showed stomach to thighs to back and on and on, his eyes still closed. It was like he was jerking off up there in the band shell in front of those people.

I took the neck of the Pepsi bottle in my right hand and went into a standing one-arm press. I arched my back and looked out over the audience. Some of them had started to clap. I eased the Pepsi bottle onto the outside edge of its bottom and slowly began to revolve. Every time I passed the audience, I could see that more and more of them were clapping. Russell opened his eyes to see what the applause was about. He saw me and his mouth went thin. A spot appeared on each wing of his flared nose. He went immediately into his famous stomach pose. He had won Best Abdominals in the Mr. Universe contest six months earlier. I didn't do a thing but put the society finger of my left hand into the neck of the Pepsi bottle and went into a one finger revolution. The shouts and screams of delight and disbelief came up out of the band shell and through the Pepsi bottle into my superfinger.

Then Russell's face appeared in front of my slow turning eyes. The white spots on his nose had spread to his cheeks. He said the words slowly, giving me little bursts of words on each revolution. "At least I . . . still got legs . . . and I am . . . not deformed . . . like you are."

When I made the next turn and came by where his face was, he was gone. I saw him with his shirt and trousers in his hand going down the steps to the parking lot. I got down off the Pepsi bottle and walked over to where Royce Tutin was grinning. He squatted down and looked into my face.

"Thanks," he said.

I rocked over into a one-hander and said: "O.K."

"You don't think he'll leave, do you?"

"No."

"Just sulk for a while I guess."

I said: "I guess."

"That'll be fine," he said. "Give us time to run the choir in here. When that's over, you two can balance and we'll wrap this up and be done."

"O.K."

"Look," he said, "if they're generous when we pass the pledge cards for the Speak Again, Hear Again School Charity, I'm going to give you and Al everything over five hundred dollars. That's what I set the goal for, five hundred, and you can have everything over that."

"Al'll like that," I said.

"How is Al?" he said.

"Al's all right," I said. "Look, I had a bad night last night, didn't sleep well. Could we get this started so I can go?"

"We sure can," he said. "Be glad to."

I went down the steps and over to the stands where Russell was glowering at the people who were drinking Pepsi-Colas and eating hotdogs. There was a really fat lady who had three hotdogs in one hand and a drink in the other. Russell kept glaring at her and then every once in a while he would pull up his shirt and stare at his beautiful ridged stomach. He was mumbling something and at first I couldn't make it out. But when I got closer I could see that he was saying over and over again: "Goddam world. Goddam world."

Royce Tutin had brought the choir from the Speak Again, Hear Again School. They were young boys and girls, no more than fifteen or sixteen years old, wearing white robes, and taken together very handsome, with scrubbed skins and bright eyes and shining hair. They were deaf mutes. There was a teacher from the school with a black robe with red trim on who had come to direct the choir. He was a deaf mute, too. I knew him from the Ocean Club. A very bad volleyball player. His name was Purvis, Lintin Purvis.

Royce Tutin held his arms up for attention. But as far as I could tell everybody was paying attention already, except for eating hotdogs and drinking Pepsis. I watched Russell and saw that calmly and without passion, like he might have been saying the days of the week, he was still repeating over and over: "Goddam world."

"Ladies and gentlemen," called Royce Tutin, his arms still raised above his head, "I've brought the choir, a really great singing group of boys and girls, here today from the Greater Tampa Speak Again, Hear Again School for Exceptional Children."

I didn't get all of it, because I'd heard it all before, and most of the time I wasn't watching. But Royce Tutin went on to tell the audience that this entertainment in the shopping mall today was being held for the benefit of his favorite charity, and to demonstrate that exceptional children—those who for a variety of reasons could not talk—could, in fact, do just about anything anybody else could do, he had brought a choir of deaf mute children here to sing for them.

"Now," he said, "everybody sit back"—Royce had lost his head and forgot that there was no place to sit—"sit back and enjoy the work of this fine group." Royce was already going offstage when Lintin Purvis flashed him a sign and frowned. Royce ran fatly back onstage and said that the first number would be "America, the Beautiful."

Purvis stepped smartly to the front of the choir and raised his hands. When he brought them down, the hands of all the children flew up and their fingers—synchronized as pistons of a motor—began to pump out the rhythms and words: *America, America, God shed His grace on thee*.

All the shoppers stopped eating. I looked around and there was not one of them still chewing. Even the fat lady with the three dogs caught in her chubby fist stood without moving. When the choir finished, the audience threw down their hotdogs and dropped their Pepsis and stamped, shouted, whistled, clapped and up on the stage the boys and girls spelled out *Thank you* over and over in careful, practiced harmony. After "America, the Beautiful," they sang a medley of old Christian favorites beginning with "Give Me That Old Time Religion" and ending with "That Old Rugged Cross."

The choir had hardly finished fingering the last word when Russell Muscle reached over and grabbed me where I was sitting under the shade of the tin awning of the Pepsi-Cola stand. He held me under one arm like a sack of flour and headed for the stage. It was time for our act, and he was in a hurry to get through and get back to his A/C like he usually is, but I didn't mind him chucking me under his arm like that because it made a more dramatic entrance. I always tried to give a good show.

We were just going up the steps to the band shell when I saw Hester's daddy over by the cotton candy machine. He was wearing the same faded overalls, and waving the knotted wooden stick he used to beat out messages with. When he saw that I saw him, he dropped the stick, clasped his hands over his head and shook them. Then with his thumb and forefinger he gave me a big O, and winked, all the time showing his teeth in a mechanical smile that made him look sad enough to cry.

Russell Muscle and I did our act. It didn't take long. He threw me around like I was a ball or a trained monkey, tossing me high in the air and then catching me hand to hand when I came down. The balancing wasn't really the point of the act anyway. I knew that, and it didn't bother me. The point was the contrast between me and Muscle. That was what the crowd was applauding and shouting for. Royce Tutin didn't understand, but I did. Royce thought they were cheering because I was a deaf mute who could do something besides sell pencils or apples on a streetcorner. But that wasn't it. They were cheering for Muscle's legs, and their own, for his ears and tongue and their own. But you had to live through a little shit in the world to understand something like that, and Royce Tutin owned a ladies' shoe store in the Greater Tampa area. What could he know?

When we were done, Muscle set me down on the stage and without waiting for the clapping and shouting to end or even acknowledging it, he stalked off the stage and over to where his clothes were beside the Pepsi-Cola stand. By the time I followed him over there he had already put on his pants and shirt. Hester's daddy was waiting for me there, too. He held his long stick like a staff and beat it against the macadam in rapid little bursts of tapping. He still had the awful mechanical smile fastened to his face. It looked like somebody had told him to smile, and he was doing it but he didn't know why.

"You looked good," he said, "just sensational."

"Thank you," I said. "Good to see you."

"I read in the paper," he said.

He didn't look at me when he talked. Sometimes when he was talking he would actually have his neck twisted all the way around, looking behind him. He was very shy, and it was several minutes before I realized that he was blushing, the blood pumping up out of his neck and fanning across his cheeks. All the while, he was tapping the stick with one hand, talking with the other, and looking behind him or else up at the single gray cloud that covered the sun.

"What?" I said.

"I read about your act in the paper," he said. "It said you had a nice little act and you were going to be here in the mall."

I was sitting on a turned-down Pepsi-Cola case in the shade of the metal awning, and Muscle reached down and pinched the hell out of my shoulder. I looked up at him.

"Let's get out of here," he said. "Come on."

Hester's daddy said: "I don't believe I know you. My name's George Maile."

Muscle watched George's hand until it stopped and then said: "Goddam world."

George said: *"What? What?"* his fingers frantic.

I said: "He can talk and hear, Mr. Maile. He doesn't understand us. Don't pay any attention. Don't think about him. He's not a kind man."

"Oh," said George Maile, the smile for the first time slipping on his face. But in a gesture like a man might use to reach down and pull up his pants, George pulled the smile back up into his cheeks.

"Are we going?" demanded Muscle.

"Could you ask him if I could have just a minute of your time?" said George Maile. "Why don't we step over there to the Walgreen's and let me buy the two of you a cup of coffee?"

"That's good of you," I said. "But he doesn't drink coffee and I couldn't tell him anything anyway because there's no way to talk to him, because he doesn't understand hands or lips."

"You mean you're out here with him and you can't talk to him at all?" he said.

"We only came to do a job," I said. "Our act. We wouldn't have a lot to talk about anyway."

"I thought I might buy you a cup of coffee and . . . well, talk to you a minute about Hester."

"Hester?" I said.

"Right."

"Let's go find Royce Tutin," I said. "I can tell him and he can tell Russell Muscle."

"Russell Muscle," said George Maile.

"He doesn't like it," I said. "It's just a name that stuck to him."

"Well, everybody has his cross," said George Maile, rapping an intricate code on the side of an empty trash can as we went by.

Russell Muscle followed us, mumbling all the way, to find Royce Tutin. We found him talking to Lintin Purvis and the choir. I told him what to tell Russell Muscle. Russell snorted through his nose and said he'd had about enough of this. I told Royce Tutin to tell him it was air-conditioned in the Walgreen's store. Muscle said it was air-conditioned in his room and that he had to have a piece of bread and yogurt. I told him it was no use talking about it, and he told me I was a legless son of a bitch, which shocked Lintin Purvis and George Maile.

But Russell followed us across the parking lot to the Walgreen's store and inside, where George Maile and I sat in a booth together and Russell sat on a stool at the counter right in front of us. He spun himself wildly on the stool top while we talked.

"See, we love her," he said.

"Yes," I said.

"But it hasn't been easy."

"Well, I can understand," I said, not knowing what we were trying to talk about. Across from us, Russell Muscle grabbed the edge of the counter, lifted his feet off the floor, and sent himself spinning like a top.

"Her talking and hearing but living there with us not talking and hearing," he said. "It's not been easy for her. It hasn't been easy for anybody."

I didn't think Russell was going to last much longer so I figured I'd better try to find out what he wanted. "Mr. Maile, what was it you wanted to tell me?"

He looked the other way and picked up the salt shaker. At the counter, Russell was a blur on the stool. George Maile tapped rapidly with the salt shaker. I saw him doing it, but I also felt taps in the table. It was a moment before I realized what he was doing.

I reached across the table and touched his wrist. He stopped and slowly swung his head to look at me.

"I don't know Morse," I said.

"Oh," he said.

"No, I never learned that."

"I wish you had," he said.

"I never did though."

"Well," he said, "I don't want you to think I'm speaking against her. I want you to know that I'm not speaking against her."

"I know that," I said. But I didn't really know any such thing and I was beginning to think I should have left like Russell wanted me to. "But I am in a kind of a hurry." I pointed to Russell. The waitress had come over and asked him to stop playing on the stool.

"Hester is a good girl," he said, "but in some ways she is strange, if you know what I mean."

"No sir," I said. "I don't believe I do."

"She gets bored easy," he said.

"I'll do the best I can to keep her from getting bored."

"I mean with everything," he said. "She gets bored with everything and everybody. It makes her do funny things." He looked at the ceiling and said: "She told me is how I know. She told me she gets so bored with everything, it about drives her crazy, and that's how come she does strange things."

"What kind of strange things?" I said.

"You haven't known her as long as I have," said George Maile.

"What kind of strange things?" I said.

Russell came over and stuck his face in front of mine. "Goddammit, are we going or not?"

I put my palm on Russell's face and raised his head and looked under it at George Maile.

George Maile said: "She locked me and her mother in a room one time for nearly a week."

Russell Muscle reached down and picked me up and put me under his arm. He started down the aisle with me. George Maile sat in the booth with his wooden staff beside him, watching Russell carry me off. I raised my free hand and asked George Maile, "What? Repeat! Repeat!"

"Hester locked me and her mother in a room," he said, "for a long time. Don't you let Hester ruin you." He was talking as fast as he could now as Russell got close to the door. "I love her and I'm not speaking against her. But don't let her ruin you."

Russell opened the glass door and the last thing I saw was George Maile sitting at the Formica table giving me a big O with his thumb and forefinger.

Six

MUSCLE carried me across the parking lot and threw me in the back seat of the Dodge. Pete was asleep behind the steering wheel, right where we'd left him, his old cap pulled down nearly to his nose. I said some really bad things to Muscle as soon as I was where I could and he knew they were bad things but he didn't care, wouldn't even look at me mostly.

"Take me home," he said to Pete.

Pete smiled slow but didn't move to start the car.

"Yassuh, Mr. Muscle," he said.

"And you quit that with my name," said Russell, screwing up his face like he meant to cry.

"Ain't no use to fight it," said Pete. "Ain't no use to fight the truth." He started the car and then looked back one last time. "You ain't nothing but a muscle and you done it to youself."

"The shit I have to put up with," said Russell Muscle. I said a few more terrible things to Muscle and a few to the back of Pete's head, trying to make myself feel better, but nothing took my mind off Hester for very long. Locked her folks in a room! For a goddam week? I could understand bored. All the shit that's come down in my life, I could understand practically anything, but that didn't sound like bored. That sounded like your ordinary lunatic behavior. Could that be why Hester's daddy learned to rap out messages with a stick? Being locked in a room when you couldn't scream or even talk through the door to whoever had you locked up could make a man do some pretty funny things. All of them having sticks and tapping through the floor to each other didn't seem nearly so strange now that I knew about them being shut up in a room. If they really were, that is. He may have been lying. I've learned not to trust very much what anybody says in this world.

After we dropped Muscle off, and drove back across town, it was nearly three o'clock. The gym was full of iron freaks and boxers. Al was sitting inside the wire cage.

"Where's Hester?" I said.

"You want something to eat now?" Al said.

"Hester can cook me something," I said.

"Get Leroy or Pete to do it," he said.

"Where is she?"

"Busy," he said. "Taking care of a guy."

"Taking care of a guy?" I said.

"Massaging," he said. "Al thinks that girl's got great hands."

"No question about it," I said.

I went through the kitchen and there on the wall beside the note that was pinned to me when I was abandoned was the picture of Al with his head under the wheel of a Hudson Hornet. It was in the same kind of cheapy gold-gilt frame my note was in. Leroy was washing dishes in the sink. He saw me looking at the picture.

Leroy said: "Al didn't want to at first. Now he loves it." He put the dishcloth down and came over to where I was sitting on the floor. "You feel all right?" he said. "You don't look real good."

He was still talking when I flipped up on my hands and went down the hall to the massage room. There were three tables in front of a rack full of liniment and sponges and different kinds of oils. Hester was standing at the middle table wearing one of Al's old white smocks he used when he gave massages. There was a guy on the table where she stood. All I could see was his naked feet sticking off the edge.

I knew she was using an oil called Baby Rose Bud, because the room smelled like a garden.

She looked to be rubbing the guy's thighs and she didn't stop when she saw me in the door. She smiled in what I thought was real pleasure at seeing me. It made me feel good. "How was the mall?" she said. "I've just been having a hell of a fine morning."

"I'm glad," I said. "I see you got Al's picture on the wall out there."

"He put it up," she said. "I didn't."

"Leroy told me," I said. "I guess I was wrong about you coming to the gym. You're working right in."

"I've just been having a hell of a morning."

The feet on the end of the table moved. They were shining under the light from the rose oil. I wondered if she had a towel over the guy's balls. But I didn't want to ask. It seemed small-time and low-rent to care about a thing like that.

She looked down at the table and said: "Sit up and say hello to Marvin Molar."

Like a jack-in-the-box the guy popped up between his feet. "Hello," he said.

It was Aristotle Parsus, and he was smiling like he had just been told the funniest joke in the world. With him sitting up I could see there was no towel. I cut my eyes away. I was afraid he had a hard-on. I felt dizzy and a little sick to my stomach. But I wasn't going to let him know it.

"Getting a little rubdown, are you, Ari?" I said. "Jesus, you could stand to get toned up some." I winked at Hester. "Give him a good one, sweetheart. I've got to eat a little protein."

I left them smiling and went out into the hall, but as soon as I was around the corner, I sat down and leaned against the wall. My eyes felt hot and I wondered if I was going to cry.

I went out to the table and let Leroy make me a steak. He sliced some tomatoes and put a mound of cottage cheese beside the meat on the plate. I cut the meat up and ate it. I didn't taste it very much. It was like swallowing rocks. I kept thinking about her fantastic lap and that goddam Greek lying in there.

Al came in and stood by the table. "Al wants to thank you for bringing Hester to the Fireman's Gym," he said.

"I didn't bring her," I said.

"She came with you," he said, "and Al wants to thank you."

"All right," I said. "I don't want to talk about it now."

"She's a smart girl," he said. "Not a dummy."

"No, she's not a dummy."

Al went back out into the gym, and Leroy sat down at the table across from me. He took a piece of meat off my plate with his fingers and sat chewing it slow and steady like it was something he'd memorized.

"What ails that 'ere girl?" he said. He looked toward the hall leading to the steam room. "I never seen a neked girl before. When she come up on us in the steam room like that, it felt like my whole heart was gone splode." He took one of my tomatoes and chewed it slow as meat. "She's you girl friend, is she? What I want to know is how you feel about her walking around neked like thatear? And rubbing guys laying neked besides?"

The mistake he made was not saying it, but smiling when he said it. I felt something kind of tilt and slide out of place in my chest. He reached for another piece of steak on my plate and I reached at the same time and closed my hand on his wrist. Everything seemed to be moving in slow motion. I saw his hand coming and I saw my hand going out and it was like they were never going to meet but then they did and my hand closed over his wrist and in the same instant his mouth stretched in what must have been a howling scream. I've told you about Al's hands— how big they are. Mine are something else. There's nothing like them. Using them for feet'll do that.

I watched my hand. It seemed unreal. I knew I was maybe fracturing the bones in his wrist and that this was Leroy and he was nothing but a kid who meant nothing more than a joke probably, but it was all like something I was seeing in the movies, and I didn't feel anything as I watched the bright tears fly from his eyes and his mouth stretch and him stiffen on the chair so rigid that he couldn't move, couldn't do anything but sit there and howl like a dog.

I felt the heavy feet running in the floor and then saw Al come through the door and he seemed to be running and not running, to be moving in the same kind of half-speed everything had been played in. He came plunging through the air toward me his thick knees pumping, his enormous fist swelling toward my eyes until finally it blocked out Leroy and the table and the whole room. Then I was off the chair and on the floor looking up at him. The door had filled with iron freaks and boxers who must have heard Leroy scream and were pushing against each other trying to see what had happened. And it was like I'd been unconscious and was coming to, wondering myself what had happened. Al's face was white and rigid as stone except for his lips which looked almost yellow and were trembling. He stood looking down at me.

"My God," he said, "my God, Al . . . Al didn't . . ."

Then he must have heard the iron freaks at the door and he turned and I saw the back of his neck redden and I knew he was yelling at them and they were suddenly gone. Leroy lay holding his wrist, crying at the table. Al came back to where I was.

"It's all right," I said.

"Marvin . . . What?" He pointed toward Leroy. "Why?"

"I don't know," I said.

Al had never hit me in his life. Not once. He stood over me and now his whole body was shaking. I could see Leroy's wrist. It was almost black and swelling. I could see the marks of all my fingers on it.

"Tell him I'm sorry," I said.

"Al wants to know why you did it!" He wasn't talking with his hands but screaming the words, his old nail-bending mouth dark with snagging teeth.

Leroy looked up from the table. His eyes were red and tears were running on his face. "The girl," he said. "The girl."

And as if by magic, Hester appeared in the door. She was smiling. She looked us over slowly, letting her eyes linger on the boy's ruined wrist. Then she stopped smiling. But she was still smiling, if you can understand that. It was like the smile was buried there in her face, the way her eyes shined, the way her mouth stayed tight, like she was just enjoying the shit out of herself.

"What happened?" she said.

"He broke my arm," Leroy said.

"Who?" she said.

"Him," Leroy said.

"Did you do that?" she said.

"Yes," I said.

"Well," she said, "well."

Aristotle Parsus stood in the door behind her. He was buckling his belt.

"What happened?" he said.

"Marvin broke the kid's arm," said Hester.

Aristotle Parsus looked at me. "You ought to get yourself one of those massages, Marvin, it'll calm you down."

Al had squatted down beside me. He hadn't touched me but he was looking at the place on my neck where his fist caught me. I could barely swallow. It felt like my throat was swelling shut.

He kept looking at me, but he raised his hand behind him and said to Hester and Aristotle: "You'll have to go. This is family."

"Sure," said Hester. "A family needs to settle things together."

When they were gone, Al said: "Al's sorry he hit you."

"You couldn't do anything else," I said.

"It's bad," he said. "This is still bad."

He looked like he wanted to touch me, but he didn't. He raised his hand once as though to put it on my neck, then he rubbed his eyes instead.

"You better go put a cold poultice on that neck," he said.

He stood up and went over to Leroy, who was sitting with the tears
dried on his face, holding his right forearm tenderly in his left hand. Al
took the arm in his fingers. Leroy's whole body shook, and I could tell
by his mouth that he made some sort of whimpering sound.

"How is it?" I said.

"Broke maybe," said Al. "Maybe not. He better get it x-rayed. Tell
Pete to bring the car around."

When I went by the table, I stopped. Leroy was looking at me in a
way I have never seen him look before, like a man might look at a favorite dog that had just bit him for no reason.

"I'm sorry," I said.

"What's he saying?" Leroy asked Al.

"I'm sorry," said Al.

"I didn't mean to do it," I said.

Al said that.

"You didn't mean to?" Leroy said. "Jesus, you didn't mean to? How
could you do that to my arm . . ." He held his arm up toward me.
". . . 'thout meaning to?"

"I . . . I . . ." I didn't know what to say to him. "It was something
else," I said. "It wasn't you. It was something else."

Al said that.

Leroy leaned across the table and looked down at me. His blond eyebrows bunched over his nose and his chin went almost blue with concentration. "You let me tell you what I think, you goddam . . . goddam
. . . I think you gone crazy. I think you lost you fucking mind. Reach
for a goddam old bite of meat offen you plate and you break a feller's
fucking arm. That ain't nothing but crazy." Spit flew from his mouth
with the words. He started crying and rocking with his arm hugged
against his chest.

I said: "Tell Leroy that . . ."

"Al's telling you to get the car. You've said enough. None of it
amounts to anything. Nothing. Find Pete and tell him to bring that car
around. Now."

Finally, because there was nothing to say that made any sense, I went
out into the gym, where all the boxers and guys pumping steel stopped
and stared at me, and down the stairs to the place on the sidewalk
where I found Pete sitting on the empty crate he kept there. He had his
cap pulled forward, taking the sun. I made the signal that meant to

bring the car around but as soon as I touched him he pushed his cap up and turned his yellow eyes on me.

"To the horsepital?" he said.

I nodded my head.

"Did you do what Miss Hester say?"

I only stared back at him.

"Say you hurt Leroy. Say you squeezed him bad on his ahm."

I nodded my head and looked down the street at the place under the lamppost where the Volvo should have been parked.

"She went on off," said Pete. He stared at me and I could feel the blood rushing to my face, and I was humiliated. "Thas right," he said. "She lef with him. Say she gone drop him by his boat, then she going to see her momma and daddy. An for me to tell you, say you be sure and tell that Marvin Molar that I be back. Ain't no way I ain't coming back, she say. Tell'm late this afternoon."

I pointed for him to get the car and bring it around, but he just sat there looking at me. Then a slow soft smile touched his old nigger mouth, and I could have killed him. Anger, sharp as a knife, made my nerves sing like wires. I turned and raced up the stairs. I sat in a chair by the window on the street side of the gym and watched Al lead Leroy down to the curb where Pete had the car waiting. I just sat there for a long time, but I could feel the guys who were working out watching me out of the corners of their eyes, and finally I couldn't stand that anymore, so I went back to the steam room, but it had about ten lifters in it sitting cheek to jowl sweating their enormous naked asses. Their huge heads swung in the steamy layers of air under the yellow light, water beading on their lashes as they squinted. I backed out the door and closed it.

The thought that she had gone off with Aristotle Parsus had stuck in my head. Every once in a while it seemed like I could actually see the words glowing across the back of my skull: *Say she gone drop him by his boat.*

I went down the hall to the kitchen and climbed up in my bed. I took down an *Atlantic Monthly*. But I couldn't read it. Actually, I didn't want to read it. I still wanted to do what I had done at the table with Leroy: hurt somebody or something. My jaw was aching from clenching my teeth. I stared at the blurred page of the magazine. She said she was taking him by his boat and then she said she was going to see her parents.

Well, why not believe it? I thought: Why not take her at her word and believe what she said and not sit here eating your liver making something else out of it? Going home for a visit to the dear ole momma and daddy she locked in a room for a week, right?

But that's only what her daddy said. He said she locked them in a room. That doesn't mean it happened. Why would a man say that about his own daughter if it wasn't true? Who the hell can answer that? Why does anybody say anything they say?

I lay in the bed for a long time thumbing through one magazine after another. I even took down my favorite book in all the world, one I've read more times than I know, Graham Greene's *The Power and the Glory*, and tried to read in it. But it wasn't any good. I didn't want to read. I felt utterly violent and utterly helpless at the same time. The violence was aimed as much at myself as anything else because I could feel self-pity beginning to drain behind my eyes. And, goddam, is there anything I hate more than an asshole who goes sucking around, whimpering about how the world isn't being fair? I told you before, fair is not a word I've ever been able to get much use out of.

So I lay in my bed and chewed my teeth until finally I got up and zipped into a thick terry-cloth workout suit and went out into the gym. Most of the guys who had been there when I hurt Leroy were gone by then. Others had come in, but the gym wasn't crowded. One of the body-builders who had come in was Muscle. He worked out six days a week. Monday, Wednesday, Friday: upper body. Tuesday, Thursday, Saturday: lower body. He was a freak, but he was one of the great freaks. I'd never liked who he was and never got along with him, but I liked what he was and had always admired him—if you can understand that.

I had put on my suit and gone out there to work out to get outside myself. One of the things I've found in my life is that in a tortured muscle there's a kind of peace you can't find anywhere else. Exhaustion drives out the world. I sat by my pile of bricks watching Muscle. When he works out, he wears two huge baggy sweatshirts and a pair of slouching sweatpants. He'll isolate and work one muscle for an hour, then he'll isolate and work another. He peeps at whatever muscle he's working. He calls it spying on it. I watched him get off the prone-press bench, where he was doing flat-backed presses with four hundred pounds, and go over and spy at his throbbing swollen chest. One whole wall of the gym is nothing but mirrors because an iron freak can't work out without a mirror. He was in front of the mirror looking down the neck of his sweatshirt. He was flexing and concentrating on his chest, looking down his sweatshirt which he was holding open at the neck with his rough, square-fingered hands. Then suddenly he stretched the neck of the sweatshirt all the way down and exposed one lobe of his chest to the mirror, where he stared at it, flexed, pumped, swelling with concentration. Abruptly he sacked the pectoral muscle down the neck of his shirt and went to the bench and dropped onto his back. He did a fast set of twelve repetitions, leapt up and stared at himself down the neck of his shirt, after which he went to the mirror and exposed the left lobe of his chest so he could concentrate on it.

I wasn't the only one in the gym watching him. The other body-builders and even some of the boxers had paused and were quietly watching one of the great bodies in the country flex and stare at itself in the mirror.

I don't know what it did for anybody else, but it helped me. It got me up for the workout, put a little fire in my blood, made me want to compete with myself, to get up on the rope and meet some pain and see if I could handle it. Because, finally, the thing about a real workout is that you know you're going to meet pain, and the only question is how you're going to be able to handle it.

Fuck it, I said to myself, I don't care if she dropped him by the boat. I don't care how the son of a Aristotle bitch got here to start with. Didn't she tell Pete to say she was coming back? That's enough for me. That's more than enough.

I was stacking bricks like a goddam madman, racing up to seven bricks high, tearing them down, then stacking them all over. I knew that on the other side of the gym Russell Muscle was watching me. Without looking, I knew he'd stopped, the neck of his sweatshirt pulled open, but his head turned staring at my twenty-inch arms stacking and pumping.

See, it worked both ways with Muscle and me. It was like a sound and its echo. I bounced off him and he bounced off me. He got so goddam worked up sometimes when he saw me going through my routine that he just about killed himself pumping steel. And when I watched him working, it fired me up. And there we were on that hot Monday afternoon going one-on-one across the steamy gym.

As my mean swelling arms pumped bricks, the words shouted in my head: *Hester, you fucking cunt, what are you compared to this?*

I kept stacking, did one-arm stands, the finger routine, went up the rope, went up it upside down, swung into the rings, held iron crosses, ran the stairs, started over on the bricks. A high whistle started in my head. I didn't listen to it.

Whistle, son of a bitch, whistle yourself blind!

The terry-cloth suit was soaked and it dripped a huge ragged stain of sweat on the floor under where I hung in the Roman rings. On the other side of the gym, Muscle was slamming himself through a workout: upright rowing, bent-over rowing, flying laterals, pull-overs, military presses, back to the prone. Finally he went to his lower body even though that was not his day for it, and ended up under a weight that bowed the olympic bar when he took it off the squat rack.

I don't know how long it went on. Gradually, I was aware that there were fewer and fewer other people in the gym as the lifters and boxers left. But Russell Muscle and I kept at it, working counterpoint to each other at opposite ends of the gym, lost in a sweaty, mindless world where only the next exercise was important.

At some point I remember Leroy and Pete and Al coming back, climbing the stairs, two gray faces and a black one, standing for a moment watching Muscle and me. They weren't much more than a blur to me at the head of the stairs (I was doing two-finger stands) but I could see that Leroy carried his right arm against his chest wrapped in a white bandage. Leroy standing like that sent me into one last blind series of exercises that ended only when I looked up from a final press-out on the bricks to see Muscle, with his hand out. I sat down on the floor and reached up. We shook hands.

"That was a workout," he said. His beautiful mouth gulped air like water. "There can't ever be but one like you." His hair hung in dark sweat-damp coils over his neck and trembled with his breathing.

I looked up at him. There was nothing I could say to him. There was no way I could say anything to him. I thought about going back to get Al to translate. But what would be the use? What would I say? I let my head drop forward on my chest, and when I raised it, he was already heading for the dressing room.

I lay there on the floor wishing I could go on with the workout, wishing I never had to stop. But I had to. I was pumped tight as a tick, and I could barely get my hands up high enough to touch my head.

The gym emptied out about five-thirty in the afternoon and stayed that way until after supper, around seven or seven-thirty, when the body-builders and boxers who could only train in the evening began to drift in. That's when we always ate our supper, because Al didn't like to eat after the gym closed at ten. Too late then, he said.

There were only two young kids and an old guy with a clubfoot in the gym, all three of them looking at themselves in the mirror. The smell of cooking food came from the kitchen. I didn't want to eat, but I didn't want to break the routine of things either. I didn't want to think about the fact that she had been gone three hours, that she'd left with Aristotle and was not back yet, and I didn't want to think about hurting that poor dummy because of her.

Jesus, the shit a man does have to go through to get to the end of it. I went back to the steam room and stripped. After I'd steamed down, I got under a shower as hot as I could stand it. I went down the hall to the kitchen and climbed up on my bed. The kid was sitting at the table, at the same place where I'd ruined his arm. He had his bandaged wrist hugged to his chest, and Al stood at the stove cooking. Pete came in and sat down at the table across from Leroy. I could tell by the way Al's elbows were jerking on each side of his stiff back that he was slamming the pots around over the stove, making a big racket, probably mumbling and growling to himself. I got a magazine down and pretended to be reading it. After a while, Al came over and took the magazine out of my hand. Behind him, Pete and Leroy sat on opposite sides of the table staring at me. Bowls steamed between them.

"It's ready," Al said, concentrating on the spot just above my head where the first shelf of books started.

"I'm not very hungry," I said.

"Hungry or not," he said, "a balancer's got to eat. You got to feed them arms."

"Maybe later," I said.

"Look," he said.

I looked up and his eyes dropped directly into mine, and it was like he was touching me, like we were balancing each other over something thin and dangerous. I saw that his eyes had little chips of gold in them, and that the gold made them look almost like the eyes of a boy. He didn't say anything for a long time and I felt very close to him. I wanted to tell him something good, something that would make him happy, but I didn't know anything to say.

"Whatever it was, it was," Al said. "You cain't say what it was, Leroy cain't say what it was. But it happened. Al don't have to understand. Al can go on and not understand." He touched my shoulder. "Come eat," he said.

At the table, we all looked at our plates. Al had cooked fresh vegetables, broiled some mackerel and put a wedge of sharp cheese out, along with wild honey and cracked-wheat bread. But I didn't taste it much. If I let myself think about it, the chair under me seemed to rock gently and inside my head the water lapped against the dock and I could hear a girl laughing.

Three rapid taps came through the wood of the table into my plate. I felt the taps run in the tines of the fork. I looked up, and across from me Leroy tapped with his knife again. He glanced at his arm and then back at me.

"It don't matter, Marvin," he said.

I looked at Al and said: "I'm sorry."

Al said it to Leroy.

Leroy smiled. "Hell, it ain't even broke," he said. "X-rayed it and it ain't even broke. Bruised bad. Something a little pulled. It's what you call your fracture." He touched the bandage with his good hand. "But this'll be off before you can say Jack the rabbit been here and gone."

"I'm glad for that," I said.

Leroy said: "I used to have a dog that'd bite if you took something off his plate. It's a natural—"

"It wasn't the meat, Leroy," I said, "for Christ's sake . . ."

Al slapped the table, not hard, just letting his thick palm drop flat beside his plate, but it was hard enough to make the bowls jump. "We cain't get to the end of that," said Al, "so we won't talk about it anymore. Al don't want to hear it."

"Yes sir," Leroy said, and dropped his eyes.

Al slapped the table again, this time harder, and Leroy's eyes snapped up. "Now goddammit," he said, "things are gonna be normal! Be like they were! Stop acting like this. Be happy!"

It was one of the few times I ever heard him curse and Leroy dropped his eyes to his plate again, but not before I saw that he looked like he was about to cry because Al had shouted at him. He mumbled, "Yes sir," again and hugged his bandaged arm.

Al looked disgusted, like he wanted to spit. He got up from the table and walked stiffly back to his room. Pete and Leroy and I finished eating, or at least we sat there for a while before we got up. But I don't think anybody ate very much. I went to my bed and lay down. This time I didn't pretend to read. I just lay there with my hands behind my head and watched the window by the sink that looked out onto the building next door. Leroy had left the table and Pete was washing the dishes. I could feel the weights slamming to the floor out in the gym. The lifters were coming in. Somebody was doing heavy clean and jerks with the olympic bar.

I took a note pad down from my bookshelf and a pencil. With the spine of the notebook, I banged on the floor. Pete looked over his shoulder from the sink. I motioned for him to come to the bed. I started to write on the pad. He reached down and touched my arm.

"Say this evening," he said. "She say for me to say she gone drop by the boat, then she gone see her momma and daddy, then she be back this evening." He saw me looking at the window by the sink. The building outside was fading in dusk dark. "It do look lak she late," he said. Then he went back to the sink.

Al came through the kitchen without looking at me and went out to the gym. I watched the window until I could not see the building next door at all. I got off the bed and went out to the wire cage where Al was sitting on his stool.

"I want to go off for a while," I said.

"Go," he said.

"I mean in the car," I said.

"Where?"

"I want to go to Hester's house," I said. "Then maybe to Tarpon Springs."

"Tarpon Springs?" he said. "It's late."

"I know what time it is," I said.

"Be careful how you talk to Al," he said.

"All right," I said. "I'm sorry."

"Al don't care if you sorry," he said. "But be careful."

"I'll be careful," I said. "Tell Pete Hester's house first. It's at the corner of Third and Fifty-third Boulevard. Then tell'm if I say so, to take me to the sponge-fishing docks at Tarpon Springs."

"What you doing at sponge docks?" he said.

"I don't know," I said.

He watched me through the wire cage for a minute, then he said: "Al's tired of looking at you today. You might as well go."

Al told Pete what I'd said and Pete brought the car around and I was waiting at the curb. Pete never looked back at me once on the drive across town. He sat with his cap dropped almost to the bridge of his flattened nose, the yellow dash lights making his old pitted face bumpy with shadow. When we got to Third and Fifty-third Boulevard, the house was dark.

"Don't look lak no Volvo aroun," he said.

I wanted to tell him that I could goddammit see. He looked over his shoulder. We sat staring at each other. I had to wait for him to speak, and he was punishing me for Leroy. Without thinking about it I raised one of my hands toward his arm where it rested on the back of the front seat.

"You ain't thinking bout squeezing up on old Pete's ahm too, is you?" He smiled and there was no fear at all in his face.

I shook my head and smiled back at him.

"You gone be all right," he said. "You want to go to that Tarpon Springs now?"

I nodded yes and he ground the old Dodge into gear and we drove up the coast twenty miles to Tarpon Springs. There are several sponge docks where more than fifty boats are tied into slips. A full moon had come up out of the Atlantic on the other side of Florida and there wouldn't have been much more light if it had been day. I didn't know where the Greek's boat was moored or what it looked like. But I knew its name. It was called the *Parthenon*. Hester had told me the name. I didn't remember when, but I remembered that she had told me, and that I thought it was an impoverished imagination that would call a boat the *Parthenon*.

Pete parked the car and pulled his cap down and was immediately dozing. I got out of the car and went down the first dock. It took me a long time to find the boat. Some goddam Greeks were sitting on the decks of the boats and each time I went by one, I could see them stand up and stare at me. I could see them pointing. I thought one of them threw something at me, maybe a bottle cap. A young boy came up off one of the boats and tried to talk to me. He wanted to know what I was.

"What are you?" he said.

I just went on to the end of the dock. I didn't know what the hell I was doing. I wondered why I had come. But I knew. In my heart I knew. I wanted to see. Fool the ear, maybe. And everybody fools everybody with the mouth. But nobody fools the eye. The sovereign sense, the eye. I read that somewhere. I kept thinking about it while I searched for the boat.

The *Parthenon* was at the very end of the third dock I went down. I saw the Volvo before I saw the boat. It was parked out on the end of the dock. When I got closer I saw the name on the side of the boat. I went past it at first, out to the very end of the dock and sat down. After a while, I went back and walked across a ridged board that joined the boat and the dock. There were lights on in the boat. Every porthole was blazing. I just took them as they came. At each one, I sat down on the deck, reached up and pulled myself to the metal rim of the porthole and looked in. The first one had nothing but a lot of hemp rope lying on the floor and some nets. The next one had what looked like a metal coffee urn and some metal sinks. I went right on around the boat looking in one after the other at nothing but a lot of junky shit, just the kind of thing I would expect a goddam Greek or a spick to have.

Then I found them. A little room, but really kind of nice. A couch, a bed, a lamp with a little yellow tassel hanging all around the shade, even a rug on the floor. They were on the couch. Naked. All I could think of watching her was how beautiful she was. She lay long and brown as baked bread, wearing the bikini of white skin at her breast and across the bottom of her stomach. Aristotle was at the end of the couch, a hand on each of her knees, and I hung from the metal rim of the port-hole and watched him chew the bottom out of the skin-white bikini. There was an open bottle of wine on the floor and two glasses. Water was running on her body. A silver puddle of sweat stood in her navel. I watched the line of her legs tremble, her back arch and strain, her teeth white in her open mouth.

I let myself down from the porthole and went back out onto the dock.

At the car Pete was not asleep but he was acting like he was. I sat down, reached up and opened the back door and climbed up into the back seat.

"You ready to go?"

He was looking over the back of the front seat at me. I didn't nod or anything. The image of her on the couch and him chewing at her burned on my eyes. I just sat there and watched. I don't know if Pete said anything else or not but the next time I heard him, we were at the curb in front of the Fireman's Gym and Pete had come around and opened the door for me. He stood on the sidewalk looking at me.

"Marvin Molar," he said, "listen to me, listen to an ole man that seen all the ways a day can do. It be a lot of ways to die in the world, and the worse way of all is for a woman. It ain't been a man walked God's earth couldn't die for a woman. All of us could. Some of us did. But it be a cheap way to go. You understand?"

I went down the sidewalk with him still holding the door and then up the stairs to the gym. Everything was dark, the lifters gone, the moon coming through the windows showing the racks and the ropes and the bags and the sparring ring.

I found my bed and climbed to it. I didn't undress, but lay on my back, watching her on the backs of my eyelids, her bright skin shining with sweat, and the Greek straining to get her into his mouth and thought: the nigger ain't wrong. All the ways a day can do, and she's gone and I'm here, where I was to start with, where I belong. And that's not much, but it's something. It's enough. It has to be.

After a while Pete came through the kitchen, and I saw him stop for a long time, purple in the half light from the moon, watching me before he finally went on in the back. I lay there with my teeth gripped until my jaw hurt and concentrated—the way I concentrate to do a final press when everything in my arms says I can't, that it's impossible—concentrated on burning her off the backs of my eyes.

Maybe it was because I was tired, maybe it was because I hadn't been able to eat, whatever it was, I dozed, dreaming that Al and Pete and Leroy and I were on a beach, talking and watching the ocean, laughing and loving each other in a way we had never done since I had known them. I could talk and I was saying all the things I want to say to Leroy and Pete, and they were laughing and Al, who didn't have to translate anything, sat on the sand and smiled at us.

Then suddenly I was awake. I was straining in the clothes I hadn't taken off and straining to hear because I was still half in the dream where I could hear and then I knew I was awake and that there was nothing to hear and nothing to say. I rolled against the wall and then back again, trying to understand where I was and what was happening. Then I smelled her. Smelled her. It was sweat first, and then the oil she used to rub herself in the sun, and her hair, and the half-sweet tainted smell of her when she loved me in her tight little room with her mother rapping messages on the wall by the bed.

She was standing beside me. I felt her hands touch me. She took one of my hands and pressed it against her lips. I got the flashlight and put it on her mouth.

"I'm sorry I was gone so long," she said. Then: "Why are you lying here in your clothes?"

I snapped the flashlight off. I watched the dark silhouette of her drop her clothes by the bed. Then I felt her hands on my legs, unbinding me, then on my clothes. When I was naked she came into the bed with me. But the image of her and the Greek locked on the couch flared in my eyes as she embraced me and an awful shout, a kind of scream started in my throat, and it never stopped as I lay in the dark listening.

Seven

THE next few days are not very clear, but they are very clear, if you can understand that. I mean Hester was always around the gym, and I remember that part as clear as I ever remembered anything. She started to work out herself, and showed a real talent for balancing. It was her back where the talent came from. She had a great strong flexible back. Of course, that's where her stroke came from, too. I couldn't get enough of watching her walk around the gym, that tremendous lap, that back that gave it stroke—God, she was fine.

So I remember that part clear, but there was another part of the next few days that was like a dream. Aristotle Parsus. He was like a dream. The two of them together was like a dream, like something I'd dreamed. I guess that's the way I wanted it to be. Anyway, Aristotle didn't come around, not at all. Hester didn't go off at night. She went right to bed. With me. Took that tremendous lap and put me in it every night. So the whole thing got to be like a dream—Aristotle trying to get her into his mouth, chewing at that strip of untanned skin, Hester spread and sweating, me chinned and looking through the porthole—all of it got to be like a dream.

Except I knew it was real. I'm no goddamned dummy, and I knew back there where it felt like a dream that it was real as breathing. But it made it easier to let the days go by, to let everything go by. After all, she was there in the gym with me. No matter what she had done, no matter who she had done it with, it was me who was getting her lap every night.

After we got under the covers at night sometimes, I'd switch on the flashlight and show her my hand. "Goddam, you're here."

She'd take the flashlight and put it on her mouth, and I'd put both hands on her ass while she said: "Where else would I be? I like it here. This gym is interesting, just as interesting as I could ask for."

No doubt about it, she had taken an interest in the gym. The room back where Al and Pete and Leroy slept, for instance. She put a big bullfight poster up on the wall, and curtains over the windows. It did something to Al and them. They were never what you would call pig sloppy, but they were never very neat either. The room usually smelled too. Not terrible, just locker-roomish. All that changed. Little Lemon Pledge wax polish. Little Lysol. Little breeze blowing through those new curtains. Old Al quit trying to get too much mileage out of one pair of drawers. Pete and Leroy actually started hanging up their clothes instead of piling them at the foot of the bed or in a corner.

The meals at the gym had always been good, but they got better. Hester didn't cook all the time, although she did it now and then. But she planned what we were going to eat, made a list, and sent Leroy out in the Dodge with Pete driving to get it. Al had always had to do that before, take care of it, but now she did it. They all loved her. Leroy followed her around like a dog, and when Pete wasn't dozing in a corner he followed her with his old yellow nigger eyes, and I could tell in spite of him being the one who drove me down to the sponge docks that night that he liked her, really liked her a lot. I'd see him in a corner, see his old caving mouth saying: "Some kinda woman. Enough rope in that woman to tie anything up good and tight. Got to be the righteous truth, one fine-walking, high-stepping woman."

And just like she reorganized the meals, she reorganized everything else. She got an appointment book for the massage room. Always before, if somebody wanted a massage, he'd walk in and say so. If Pete and Leroy were there and they weren't busy with something else, they might do it. If Al felt like it, he'd come out of his cage and he would do it. Sometimes, I'd swing up on the table and I'd pound the shit out of some slob. We just did it however it felt good and didn't worry about appointments or who was on duty.

Hester changed all that. We took turns, including her, and it was all set up ahead of time. I have to say it worked better and pulled in about twice as much money for Al. Al loved her. He was just so goddamned glad to have her in the gym, he didn't know what to do.

She had him order two towel-dispensing machines, so that he didn't have to sell them for a dime out of his little cage to the iron freaks or the boxers. Just drop a dime in the machine and out popped a towel wrapped in cellophane. She did the same thing with the food supplements, put'm in machines you could drop coins in.

Al had all kinds of free time. Instead of sitting in his cage all day looking like a ghost, he began walking around the gym, his thumbs hooked in his back pockets, his chest out—smiling.

Hester'd been in the gym probably ten days—that is, it was ten days since I'd found her on the *Parthenon* with Aristotle—when I came in from doing a little gig at a shoe store that was having a going-out-of-business sale. I'd been doing it every year for the last five at the same shoe store and we always had a good crowd, an enthusiastic crowd. So I was feeling good coming up the stairs of the gym with Pete, who had taken me over in the Dodge. I knew something was wrong though before I was halfway up the steps.

There was no sound in the wood. The worn wooden steps were quiet as death. There should have been the fast rattle of a speed bag trembling into my palms, or the teeth-shaking vibration of an olympic bar slamming to the floor. But there wasn't a sound in the wood. Nothing.

When I got to the top step, I saw that all the iron freaks and boxers were gathered around Al's wire cage. Their faces were as solemn as masks. Pete came up beside me and stopped. He touched my ass. I looked up.

"What you spose it be?"

A chill ran over me. The first thought I had was that Al'd had a heart attack, that he was lying in there on his back, gray and dead. I ran across the floor and—rocking from hand to hand—shoved my way through the sweating legs to the door of the cage. Al was sitting on his stool. He had a twenty-penny bridge spike with a cloth wrapped around the middle of it caught between his teeth and a hand on each end of the spike pressing down on his jaw. His old arms were ridged and trembling slightly. Veins swelled in his wrists and snaked through his forearms. The artery in his neck was big as a pencil. His nose was flared and pumping over the wrapped spike. There was no light on in the cage—there never was—and Al sat in the shadows trembling, his face still gray as ever but now with an awful purplish cast under the skin. Hester stood behind the stool, bent close, her mouth at his ear moving, but I couldn't tell what she was whispering in the bad light. Her hand was making slow rubbing circles on the back of Al's swollen neck. Al's got most of his teeth. A few of the back ones have rotted out, but he's got pretty much a full mouth of teeth. He's so old though that they're dark, about the color of shit when you've been constipated three or four days.

Not only that, but they're chipped and cracked with little crooked seams running through them like veins in quartz rock. I stood there watching him caught in the strain over that spike and it seemed to me every tooth in his head was going to shatter and fly out of his mouth like bits of glass.

Then just as slow and nice as you could ask for the spike started to bend. It was then I realized I'd been holding my breath. Everybody else was, too. Except Hester. Her face was unconcerned and relaxed as if she'd been watching a monkey pick fleas in a zoo. Once Al got the spike started, he never stopped with it until it was wrapped in an upside-down U around his jaw. His eyes had been pinched shut but when he slid the spike through his lips his lids snapped open and he rolled his old yellow eyes up at the iron freaks and boxers. The floor shook under my hands as everybody jumped up and down and clapped and shouted. Everybody but Hester. She slowly reached out and took the spike out of Al's hand. She unwrapped it, just slow as hell. Everybody else was still clapping and stamping. A couple of the lifters forearmed the wall. But nothing showed in Hester's face. Nor Al's. He was watching her. Watching her watching the unwrapped bridge spike. She was going over it like it was a disease and she was examining it. After about a half a minute she looked down at Al and smiled. He sat absolutely still while she bent forward and pressed her wet lips against his old rusty forehead.

Leroy, who was standing right behind Hester, turned and ran blindly into the side of the wire cage which caught him like a sheet of rubber and flung him back through the door. The cross-hatched imprint of the wire was on his face and he was laughing, blubbering through his broken lips: "Did you see him? Did you see Al? Did you see . . . ?"

I felt Pete touch me. I looked up. He smiled his old blue-gummed smile, but it was sad enough to make you cry. "Thas it," he said. "Thas it right there." Then he walked off.

I was already tired from the gig at the shoe store, and watching Al with the spike in his mouth had exhausted me. I went back to the kitchen and climbed up on my bed. I locked my hands behind my head and tried to relax. But even with my eyes closed, I kept seeing Al with his teeth caught on that nail as though he was hanging on it for his life. About ten years ago Al had quit doing any of his stuff—tearing tennis balls, or bending dimes, or quartering decks of playing cards—said he was getting too old. He talked sometimes about it to one of the iron freaks in the gym, and he had his pictures to prove who he was and what he'd done. I didn't know why it bothered me so to see him bending a spike. Hell, if he wanted to bust a blood vessel doing that stuff again, what business was it of mine?

To try to take my mind off thinking about it, and to try to relax, I sat up in bed to get a book from the shelf. But I didn't get the book. I stopped with my arm in the air. I don't know how I missed it when I came in but directly across from me on the same shelf where the picture of Al posing on the deck of a battleship used to be there were three new pictures of Al, pictures I'd never seen before. They were all disasters of one kind or another, pictures like the Hudson Hornet running over his head.

In one picture, a bear had Al in a cage and was sitting on his back with his teeth buried in the cheeks of Al's ass. Al was screaming.

In another, Al was squatting under a wooden beam with four fat men sitting on each end of it. But Al's right knee had twisted in and under him. Al was screaming.

In the third one, I could figure out what happened. Al used to hang himself. He could take a rope and tie it around his neck and stand up on a chair and then kick the chair out from under him and swing by his neck. He always had somebody tie his hands behind him to make it look more dangerous, which it did and which it was. The thing was, somebody had to put the chair back under his feet. But the thing was, in the third picture, somebody hadn't. Al's eyes were closed and his face was black and his tongue was out. Left carved in his cheeks and pinched eyes was a look of utter and humiliating terror. He wasn't screaming.

I flopped back on the bed and just stared. In a little while Hester came in. I waved my hand at the pictures.

"Jesus," I said. "Jesus."

Hester smiled. "Into every life a little rain must fall."

"You don't have to tell that to me," I said.

"I know," she said.

"Where did you get those things?" I said. "I didn't even know he had them."

"I knew he must have more than just that car on his head," she said. "So I asked him."

"You asked him and he went and got'm, just like that?"

"Well, practically," she said. She pointed at the pictures. "That first one there, see, Al was supposed to wrestle this bear and—"

"I know, I know, goddammit!"

"I thought you said you didn't know he had them."

"I didn't, but a fucking disaster is a fucking disaster," I said. "I'm not a dummy."

"Now, Marvin, relax. I think they're interesting."

"Maybe," I said. "But I don't see why the old man would want to put his failures on the wall."

"I've got a theory," she said. "You train off your failures. They're better than your triumphs any day."

"Train off your failures," I said. "Train? Train, for God's sake?"

"Right."

"Since when is Al in training?"

"Since this morning," she said.

"Training for what?"

"The Fourth of July."

I lay there on my back feeling like I'd made a wrong turn somewhere, missed a transition, and ended up in the middle of some kind of crazy conversation that would any minute now shut itself off and everything would be all right again.

"There's still two more days in June," she said, "so we have plenty of time."

It wasn't going to shut itself off. I thought hopelessly: this madness is going to go on and on and I'm going to have to go with it.

"Time," I said. It wasn't even a question. I just said it.

"To train," she said.

"For the Fourth of July," I said.

"Right," she said, "at Clearwater Beach. There's a beauty contest. And fireworks. The usual thing. Except this year, Al's going to put on a demonstration."

"Christ," I said, "how did you talk him into that?"

"I didn't talk him into a goddam thing," she said.

Her lips were cold when she spoke; they hardly moved. I thought of how warm she could make them. How I'd miss them if they were ever gone. Things would never be the same. Her lap was terrific. But her mouth was inspirational.

"O.K.," I said. "You didn't talk him into it. I didn't mean anything by it anyway. You're taking it wrong."

"I don't talk people into things. People do what they want to do."

"Right," I said. "O.K." There was an awkward moment while we watched each other. I didn't know if I ought to try to talk to her anymore about it or not. Finally I said, trying to make my fingers as offhand as possible: "Listen, what's he going to demonstrate? Bend a spike, is he?"

"No," she said. "That's just training."

"Well, what then?"

"We don't know yet," she said.

"The Fourth's not far away," I said.

"There are lots of things he can do. It's his decision anyway. But we'll think of something."

"Hester, he's seventy-two years old, Al is."

"Yes?"

"That's all. He's seventy-two."

"I didn't talk him into a goddam thing," she said, her lips thin and icy again.

Al came into the kitchen from the gym. His face was still darkened with the purplish cast he'd had in the cage. And on each side of his chin a red trough slipped from his mouth where the spike had finally formed the upside-down U. It was enough to break the old bastard's neck. Seventy-two and giving demonstrations at beauty contests. Maybe he was losing his mind.

"Did you see Al do it?" he asked.

"I saw Al do it," I said.

If I'd thought it would've done any good, I would've told him he was a fool, but I'd been around Al long enough to know that anything I said wouldn't have made any difference one way or the other. Besides, he looked so pleased, so happy. He never smiled, but he was smiling now. He never talked but he was talking. And he was looking right into my eyes, not just meeting them briefly but staring right dead back at me.

"First spike Al's bent in a long time," he said.

"I know," I said.

"Al's training again," he said.

"Hester told me."

He was carrying the bent spike in his hand and while I watched him, he slowly reached up and took it in his teeth like a horse takes a bit. He just stood there looking down at me with that thing in his mouth.

"You looked goddam great out there, Al," I said.

He said something with his mouth but I couldn't tell what it was because he still had the nail in it.

"Right," I said.

He took the nail out of his mouth and said: "Al knew you would."

"What you doing for a demonstration at the beauty contest?" I asked.

"Something great," Al said. He had taken the nail out and handed it to Hester. He was smiling, his face like a light.

"Bend a spike?" I said.

"Hell no."

"I already told him that," said Hester.

"Al's doing something great."

"What?"

"It's got to be a surprise," he said. "You'll see."

"But you already know what it is?" I said.

He was about to say something when Hester touched his arm. "We have to figure it out," she said. "We'll think of something."

Al looked from her to me. "We'll think of something," he said, and winked.

I rolled my face to the wall and groaned. I lay there a long time thinking that it was all getting pretty shitty and that it was probably going to get worse. But I was not going to do anything to change it. If anything was changed—meaning if Hester was going to be thrown out, or controlled in some other way—then somebody else was going to have to do it.

A hand touched my back. I turned to look. It was Hester. She was smiling. She looked so pleasant and pretty I was ashamed of what I'd been thinking.

"Your appointment is here."

"My appointment?"

"For a massage," she said.

"I'm tired, Hester," I said, and that was true. The gig that morning and then watching Al drained me.

"The appointment was made," she said, "and it's your turn."

"Give it to Leroy," I said.

"I sent Leroy to the grocery store. Pete drove him."

"Jesus, can't you do it or . . ."

"Al and I are working out," she said. Then over her shoulder as she walked out of the room: "The guy's already on the table, waiting."

I started to say I wasn't going to do it and would stay where I was but Al was funny about appointments. He was funny about anything we said we would do and then didn't do. I guess because that's the way he was himself. He never told guys he'd take three inches of fat off their waist in three months, or that they would get a lot of muscle and fuck a lot of girls if they worked out with weights, like those phony bastards at those phony gyms do. He never promised anything that he couldn't do. And he never promised anything that he didn't do.

Nothing would have happened to me if I hadn't gone to give the massage. Al wasn't like that. But it would have hurt him. Really, Al was like that. He would have been hurt. That's the kind of man he was. So I rolled off the bed and went down the hall to the massage table.

There was somebody on the table all right. The feet hung off the end of the table, toes down. A little *zing* of feeling went through me like somebody had me from asshole to mouth on an electric wire and had just plugged me in. I knew those feet. But I didn't believe it. I handed over to the chair where the appointment book lay open. I reached up and pulled it down. There it was, third line down: *Parsus, A.* When I turned, he was sitting up on the table. He wasn't smiling. He was very calm and serious, like this was just the most natural thing in the world. But I knew the smile was there. His whole body was smiling. A contemptuous, patronizing greasygreek smile.

"I'll have the Baby Rose Bud," he said.

I was so stunned that I answered without thinking, without understanding: "What?"

"I want the Baby Rose Bud Oil," he said. "Hester says it makes the skin softer."

And he had me. He had me but he didn't have me, if you can understand that. I could have told him to go fuck himself. Or I could have not said anything and walked out. But if I had done either of those things then he'd know it was not because of what happened at the Oh Cee and not because of the volleyball game, but because of Hester, because after I let her in to live with me, he took her back to the sponge boat and fucked her eyes out. I would be admitting that I knew and I was letting her stay anyway. Of course he did know. And he knew I knew. Which made giving him the massage just as bad. I mean I was going to rub down the guy who had put the horns on me. He had me either way.

But it was actually worse than that. I glanced down at the appointment book again. There was the name, *Parsus, A.*, in Hester's cramped, square little writing. She had set the whole thing up herself.

"You want Baby Rose Bud?" I said. "You got Baby Rose Bud."

That was when he smiled. Which was his second mistake. The first was in ever letting Hester talk him into it to start with. There was no doubt in my mind that Hester had thought of it, suggested it to him— probably giving him some kind of super fuck to make him agree. I went over to the rack built only a couple of feet off the floor and got the Baby Rose Bud. I caught the cap in my teeth—a plastic bottle with a plastic cap—and went back over to the table. The table had once been used in a hospital operating room and Al had got it secondhand from God knows where, but it was steel, sturdy, and very high.

I banged on the leg of the table with the plastic bottle of Baby Rose Bud. Aristotle Parsus looked over the edge, down where I'd got off my hands and was sitting on my ass. "You'll have to help me," I said.

"Help you?" he said.

"Up on the table," I said.

Apparently he hadn't thought it through very well.

He raised his head and looked around the room. "Don't you have some kind of bench you put beside the table?"

Now I knew he hadn't thought about it at all. It was Hester's idea all right.

"A bench wouldn't do me any good," I said.

I held up my thick callused hands and watched the idea slowly work its way into his thick Greek head. If I walked on my hands and massaged with my hands, I couldn't walk along the bench and massage him.

"Jesus," he said, "do you have to get up here on the table with me?"

"That's right," I said.

I saw him turn his head, gauging the width of the table.

"Oh, it's tight," I said. "But it works all right after you get used to it."

He swung his legs over the side of the table. They were great legs, the son of a bitch. He was naked and he stood looking down at me as though he had turned a corner and found a Martian sitting in the middle of the sidewalk. He clearly didn't know how to go about taking hold of me.

"Under the arms," I said.

"What?"

"Take me under the arms," I said. "I only go ninety pounds. You can manage."

He reached down and lifted me. I was heavy enough so that he had to pull me in against his body to raise me to the table. He blushed and I felt him tremble. There's a lot of people who think Aristotle will hit from either side of the plate. But he won't. Aristotle will not suck a dick. And he is not a dirt-track specialist either. Pussy's his game, and hugging me was a little more than he'd bargained for. Hell, it didn't bother me though. I was used to it. I had wallowed around up there on that operating table with half of the perverts in Clearwater. He set me on the table and stood watching me. I motioned for him to lie down.

"Let's get on with it," I said. I gave him the meanest smile I had. "One Baby Rose Bud Special, coming up."

He lay down on his stomach. I sat in the small of his back, which I didn't have to do. There was room on the table for me to pull myself along beside whoever was getting rubbed. But I bounded into his back as hard as I could. He twisted his neck and cut his eyes back at me. I knew by now he wasn't sure what he'd got himself into. I splashed about half a cup of Baby Rose Bud across his shoulders. I put the bottle down and told him to relax. He was still straining to watch me over his shoulder. His face was red from me sitting in his back.

"Listen," he said, "listen, I—"

I waved him off and said: "Relax, this won't take but a minute."

He turned his head and let his cheek down against the sheet. I took careful measure and hit him as hard as I could at the base of the skull. It was a miracle I didn't kill him, and for a second after the punch I was sure I had. I didn't mean to hit him that hard except I did mean to, if you can understand that.

He was still breathing, but knocked colder than a cod. I drew my hand up and slapped him in the middle of the back. Baby Rose splattered the wall all the way across the room with oily little dots. The red imprint of my hand was left on his back in great and perfect detail. Then I slapped him on the shoulder. And left another hand. I slapped him in the ribs. After a while I turned him over to give him a few shots there. I left probably twenty prints of my hand on old Aristotle Parsus. Then I pushed him off the table.

I watched him lying on the floor for about a minute, my hands tingling, feeling damn fine. Then I reached under the table and got a broom we kept there and started beating on the wall. I hadn't hit it more than five or six times when Hester came running in. She stopped in the door and looked from Aristotle, who hadn't moved and didn't seem to be breathing, to me where I sat.

"He fell off the table," I said. Which, of course, was true.

III

Eight

SHE knew damn well Aristotle hadn't fallen off the table, or rather he *had* fallen off the table—after all he was lying under it—but he had been helped to do it. I loved that look on her face. She couldn't believe me. But then nobody ever has. Whoever, for instance, has seen a man do a one-finger stand? And then revolve? Except maybe one or two Chinks from Mao's China. But they don't count, because we all know what Mao is liable to do to a Chink if he doesn't stand on one finger. And then revolve. But a goddam American, who can eat TV dinners and drink Cokes and lie split-level in his house waiting for retirement, doesn't need discipline or difficulty because the President and his B-52's have all the discipline the country or anybody in it needs and he and they will take care of whatever is difficult.

All right. All right. I didn't mean to get political. For the record, I didn't mean it at all. I'm not political. I don't give a shit about it one way or another, and I know practically nobody else does either, but I'm just trying to explain how what happened happened. Not that it'll make any difference. I know that.

"What did you do to him, you little bastard?" she finally asked me.

"He fell off the table," I said.

"You said that."

"It's crowded up here," I said. "I was giving him the Baby Rose Bud—that's what he said he wanted—and he fell off."

She stepped back through the door and I saw her yell something down the hall. Aristotle was beginning to thrash around under the table. She went to him and knelt on the floor. Al—I guess that's who she screamed for—came in.

"What happened?" he said.

"A Baby Rose Bud Special," I said, "and he fell off the table." I lay on my stomach on the table and watched them working over Aristotle Parsus. His legs were jerking in little spasms which reminded me of the way Ingemar Johansson's legs looked when Floyd Patterson caught him with a hand.

Aristotle had opened his eyes. His pupils were dilated big as pencil erasers. His mouth moved like a fish's. He gulped and gulped. Al discreetly covered his little Greek cock with a towel. Aristotle was lying on his back and he pulled his right hand on top of his chest. It moved feebly, the fingers kind of fluttering. He was trying to say something. Hester kept trying to read it. Then we all read it.

"What happened?" he asked. "What happened to me?"

I dropped my hand off the edge of the table, let it dangle over Aristotle's face. "That was the Rose Bud Special," I said.

Al looked up at me. "Al don't like you treating it funny. Boy's hurt."

"Jesus, he's had the shit beat out of him," Hester said. She said it to Al and she said it with her mouth, but I saw the awe in her face and it must have been in her voice too. She looked up at me. "You've beat the shit out of him."

The hands I'd left on Aristotle were still on him. They were so clean and well-made in his white skin they looked painted on. I'd hit him harder, I guess, than I meant to. I'd done everything harder than I meant to. The skin was blistered.

Hester had found the lump at the base of his skull. Her fingers traced around it. Her mouth hung slightly open while she touched it tenderly. She took Al's enormous hand and brought it under the Greek's head so he could feel the lump, too. Al turned Aristotle's chin and hunkered lower so he could look at what his fingers felt. Then he stood up.

"Why?" he asked me.

I didn't say anything. You can see that there was no way for me to explain. Where would I have started? Besides, everything I knew, I knew because I knew it, not because I could prove it. But Al looked mean. He was mad, genuinely and really mad. I'm not ashamed to say I was scared.

"Al wants to know," he said.

I could smell the anger in his old sour skin. He was sweating it right out into the air and it scared me. I was in the right, but I was in the wrong, if you could understand that. Aristotle deserved the shot he got, but all Al could see was that a customer had come into his gym expecting a rub and ended up with a knot the size of a lemon growing on his skull and about twenty-five handprints in his blistered skin.

I didn't say anything. I shrugged in what I hoped was a helpless and baffled kind of way. I didn't for a minute think Al was going to hit me or anything like that. But I didn't know for sure. I knew what was going through his head. He thought I had maliciously and stupidly betrayed the Fireman's Gym, which was the same as betraying him.

"Al says . . ."

Hester touched him on the arm. "Let's put'm on the table." I swung down to the floor. See, before when I told Aristotle that he would have to lift me, I was lying. I could have been up there in a flash. I just wanted to make the bastard lift me up and position me and then take it in the back of the head. It only seemed justice.

Al took his shoulders and Hester his feet and they picked him up. He hung like a bag of shit in their hands. She went to a basin beside the door and wet a towel and brought it back. She slapped Aristotle in the face with it, I thought much rougher than she had to.

Al started to say something else to me, but Hester stopped him. "He could have fallen off the table," she said. Al still wasn't pleased. "It's a high table," she said.

She slapped Aristotle with the towel again. He came spluttering up off the table, gagging, and swung his feet off the side. He sat there swinging his head from side to side.

"What happened?" Al asked. "Tell Al what happened, Mr. Parsus."

I was sitting behind Al on the floor watching. When Aristotle saw me, the blood drained out of his face. He looked like he was going to faint. He pointed to me, his gagging mouth gulping air, then he let his hand fall back on the table.

"I don't remember," he said. "I remember . . . I remember . . ."

"What?" Al asked.

"On the table," he said, "on my stomach. I was . . . and then it all went . . ." He pointed at me. "He . . ."

Hester slapped him twice across the face with the wet towel, hard enough to snap his head around.

"He's still addled," she said. "He doesn't even know where he is."

I scooted on my ass across the floor to a place between Al and Hester. "A fall from a table'll do that to you," I said.

Al looked down at me. "Al don't want to hear that anymore," he said. "Al don't even want to see you for a while. You get out of here. Go work out."

I winked at Aristotle where he still sat. He was stunned more I think from Hester's tremendous shots with the wet towel than from my fist to the skull. Anyway, I couldn't keep from giving him the wink. I don't think he saw it, but that didn't keep me from feeling good about it. I went to my bed and lay down. I had missed my workout that morning because of the early shoe store gig, but I was too relaxed to work out, felt too good. There has to be a little tension, a little dissatisfaction, for me to get a good workout. But everything felt too *right* in me then. I felt too much on top of things. I'd been fucked over, but I'd turned it around. I'd been set up, but I'd set down the mother who had been part of it.

I folded my pillow high behind my head, and took down Greene's novel, *The Power and the Glory*, and turned to the part where the drunken priest meets his Judas. I settled down to read and had been steaming around in the Mexican jungle about thirty minutes with the priest on his little mule and the Judas following along behind, smiling, as ugly as sin and sure as death, when Leroy came in with his arms filled with two sacks of groceries and Pete shuffling behind him, talking to himself, slipping a punch now and then.

Pete had just put the groceries on the table when Al and Hester appeared on the other side of the room with Aristotle between them. Aristotle had himself together, his eyes clear, the color back in his face, but there was something strange about him still, because he stared straight ahead as though the bones in his neck had fused and his eyes, though clear, had a kind of cast to them. Pete stopped slipping punches. He watched them standing in the door with Aristotle, who had his pants and shoes on but carried his shirt in his right hand, the tail of it dragging on the floor. Red handprints glowed beautifully in his chest and shoulders and back.

"What ail him?" said Pete.

"Get the car," Al said. "Al wants you to drive Mr. Parsus home."

"I'll bring it rat round," Pete said. "Mr. Parsus don't look lak he feel real good."

I kept the book up to my face, but I saw it all. You learn to see good when you can't hear, learn to pick it up out of the corner of your eyes, and learn to take what you can get and fill in the rest. You make mistakes now and then, sometimes pretty bad ones, but taken in the long haul, you'd be surprised how many times you come out right. I was looking at Pete from the side when he spoke, but I got it all. He was facing Al but he was saying it to me. And he said a lot more than he said. He had seen Hester leave with Aristotle that afternoon. He had driven me to Tarpon Springs. He had seen me go on that sponge boat. He had seen me come back and get in the car. Now he saw Aristotle standing there with hands all over him and that stove-up look in his face. Pete didn't know what had happened, but he did know what had happened, if you can understand that. Pete doesn't miss much for a punch-drunk nigger.

Neither Al nor Hester looked at me when they led Aristotle out of the room. And I was back in the jungle with the priest before they were hardly through the door. Without even thinking about it, I just took for granted that she'd go with Aristotle. And I didn't even care. Well, I did care, but I didn't care, if you can understand that. If she had to go and fuck Aristotle, that was something I could live with. I wouldn't like it but I could live with it, if she would just come on back to me when she was through, and—more important than anything else—if she would do it with a little style, a little class, or said another way, a little decency. That's what I was doing back there in the massage room, trying to teach Aristotle a little style, a little decency. He's got to learn to keep his ass out of my way. They—he and Hester—have got to learn not to fuck over me too bad. Fuck me over some, sure. A guy that's been around the blocks I been around expects to be fucked over some. But not too bad.

She didn't go with him though. Ten minutes later she came back through the kitchen. She stopped and looked at me. I kept the book to my face, but I felt her stop, felt her steps stop in the wood. Then she was gone. After a while, Pete came back and sat on the side of my bed. I can't talk to him so I just kept my book up. But I was reading half-heartedly now. I'd skipped some in *The Power and the Glory*—I've read it so much, I just start anywhere—and where I'd skipped was to the end, where the lieutenant was closing in on the priest, and I knew where that was going to lead: to a bullet in the head of the priest. I'd never liked that part, even though it had to be that way. The lieutenant always gets the priest. But I didn't have to like it. So I was reading half-heartedly and when Pete's old blue-nailed fingers touched the top of the book, I let him push it down.

"You coulda killed him," Pete said.

I shrugged.

"Yeah, at's what them folks do when they lock'm up, lif up they shoulders lak that. You know why? Ain't nothing else. You coulda killed that boy. Put my own fingers on where he got caught in the back of the haid. I didn't spend twenty years in the ring not to know what you can git killed wif. And for what? For what, Marvin Molar?"

I rolled my eyes up to try to show him I didn't want to listen to this.

"Aw right," he said. "Just this. You straighten at boy out. At be good. That fine. But, son, you cain't win at war. I done tol you. You cain't win at war." He stood up. "I'm gone go on out in the gym and watch Al. You know what he doing out there? She got'm bridging with a hunnert pounds on he chest. On he chest! Now how come, you think? I tell you, I rather face Bo Jack blind in both my eyes and one leg broke than I would face that Hesta. I ain't telling you nothing but the truth."

He shuffled out and I threw my book up on the shelf. I lay there for the rest of the afternoon, at first feeling nothing much at all, not good nor bad, just drifting through, watching the sun get long against the brick of the building across the alley and listening to the sound in the wood, my hand on the wall, hearing the sharp flutter-step of the speed bag and the bone-jarring crashes of the olympic bar when one of the iron freaks missed a lift. Then toward dark I began to feel better. I don't really know when it started but I know why it started. It was Hester. At some point when the lifters and boxers began to drift out of the gym and the wood beside my bed began to get quieter, I started knowing that Hester was lurking. Lurking. That's the best way I can say it. Once she was in the door, almost totally in shadow, when I first saw her there. Later I looked up and she was at the kitchen table dicing carrots, only she wasn't moving. She had a carrot in one hand, pink in a mote-filled ray of last sun at the window, and the knife in the other hand, watching me still. And she had a strange little tilt to her mouth, a funny little cast to her face that I had never—I mean *never*—seen before. She looked so helpless, so whipped, done in, and it was as though she was asking me to do something, say something, be something to make it right. Mind you, this is just the way it seemed. And I've always known that seeming is not to be trusted. Seem in one hand and shit in the other—see which hand fills up first, is what I've always said. But still, she had that look on her face, and she kept buzzing around my bed, through the kitchen, watching me.

By the time supper came around, I figured I had her pretty well dick-whipped. I was going to wait, though, to see if she left the gym after we got through eating.

She didn't. She sat through the meal with her eyes on her plate, passing something if somebody asked for it, answering something if somebody spoke to her, all the while glancing shyly up at me from her plate.

It gave me a tremendous hard-on. Her being beat down like that gave me a dick like a brick. I caught Al looking the other way and I raised my hand and said: "I got a dick like a brick."

I swear to God I think she blushed. Maybe not, maybe it was the light, but that's the way it looked. She pressed her lips together and got very pink around the eyes and when Al bent to scoop another enormous bite into his mouth, she said: "What did you say?"

"You've made my dick like a brick," I said. "I can't stand it."

She threw back her head, her fine throat arched in the light, her heavy mouth opened, and I could feel the vibration of her laughter in the table. When she looked at me again, her mouth was damp and heavier than ever, and her eyes were shiny and black as wet olives.

"I can't stand it," I said.

"Don't worry," she said. "I can stand it." Then she did a little thing with her pointy tongue. "I can stand it all, all of it."

I just about couldn't keep from slamming my head against the table. Pete was the only one who had been watching the movement of our hands as we talked. He couldn't understand it, but I knew he had been watching. He pursed his lips, and chewed the inside of his mouth in a slow tentative way, like a man'll suck on a match sometimes. Then he got up and left the table.

"What ails him?" said Leroy.

Al looked up. "What?"

"Pete. What's the matter with him?"

"How should Al know? Why wouldn't it be something the matter with'm? It's something the matter with everybody else around here."

He was looking at me. I rolled some peas around on my plate and pretended not to notice. Hester reached over and put her hand on Al's arm, and I swear to God what she said was: "Poor baby, you worked out too hard today."

Al showed every one of his old cracked teeth. A seventy-two-year-old baby that'd worked out too hard. You had to give it to Hester. She had him in her hand and he loved it.

"You take it easier tomorrow," she said.

"All right," Al said.

"You're rounding into shape O.K.," she said.

"You really think Al is?" he said.

"Sure," she said.

Now there it was right there. Al's never done anything in his life but work out. He's trained more guys than Hester's got hairs on her pussy. But there's the rub. That pussy. Old as he was, Al was still sniffing it even when he didn't know he was sniffing it. I hated to see him making such a fool of himself, but it seemed to make him happy and I told myself it was only because he was in his second childhood.

"Don't bridge any tomorrow," she said.

"It's . . ." Al counted on his hand. "It's not long to the Fourth of July."

"Don't think about it," she said. "You're coming along fine."

"But don't bridge?" Al said.

"No," she said. "No bridges."

Now you understand what I mean when I say *bridge*, right? A wrestler's bridge? Where you lie flat on your back, pull your heels up against your ass and then arch your body in the air so that finally only the top of your head and your two feet are on the floor? Wrestlers do it obviously to keep from being pinned, to get their shoulders off the mat. Well, Al had probably only done several million bridges in his life. Even at his age he had a neck that went nineteen or twenty inches. There were seams in it, it hung in places, but it was still an awesome thing to carry a head around on. There was about as much chance of him being able to use more bridges as there was for me to use a new pair of shoes. That night in bed, I asked her about it.

"Why have you got him doing all those bridges?"

She turned the flashlight from my hand to her mouth. "I haven't got him doing anything."

I said: "He's doing what you tell him to do. Give me credit for some sense. I'm not a goddam dummy."

Her mouth went soft under the light. "He wants to do *something*," she said. "He's done bridges before. It's good for'm, he can't get hurt. I'll stop if you say to."

It had been that kind of night. Her giving in to me, pressing against me in a kind of sucking, helpless way that made me keep getting wall-breaking hard-ons. I thought of Aristotle lying out there on his goddam sponge boat nursing the shape of my hands in his blistered skin, an ice pack maybe on the back of his skull where I'd given him the shot.

Hester and Aristotle had deliberately taken me down to the wire to see who had the balls, and I'd shown them. He was lying in a bed of stinking sponges and I was lying up next to Hester's sweet-smelling lap. Or not lying next to it, really, but controlling it, putting it through its paces. Since we'd come to bed, I'd brutalized her pretty good, in a way I never had before, and she had made little singing sounds of pleasure the whole time. I kept my hand on her throat so I could feel the flesh vibrate with her pleasure of me. You've got to understand that when I say I brutalized her, I only mean I loved her right. I made it mean and low-down and good, but I never would have done it if I hadn't felt the pleasure vibrating in her throat under my hand.

"I don't think he ought to bridge anymore," I said.

"If that's what you want," she said.

"That's what I want."

In the dark the flashlight beam switched from my hand to her mouth and back again.

"I don't know what he'll do on the beach for a demonstration," she said.

"Maybe he'll quit thinking about that," I said.

"I don't think he will," she said.

"He can only look like a fool. He's too old."

I put the light on her mouth but she didn't say anything. Her lips looked swollen and slightly discolored. I bruised them pretty good that night.

"Anyway," I said, "stop with the workouts for Al."

"All right," she said. "But if he keeps on with it, I swear it's not my idea."

"I believe you," I said.

"It might be better for somebody to decide what he's going to do at the beauty contest—I mean if he does anything—because if I don't decide for him, or you don't, he's liable to do something to hurt himself."

"No he won't. Al's pretty old but he knows what he can do and what he can't do."

She said: "Whatever you say."

I kept the flashlight on her mouth and it didn't move again. We lay that way for a long time. After a while a thought came to me that I had never had before. I put the light on my hand.

"Are you talking?" I asked.

"What?"

"When you talk to me like this in bed in the dark, are you making the sounds?"

I knew the answer before she said it. I realized in the asking that I had never felt the words.

"No," she said. "They're just on my lips, the words are. There's no reason to make the sound. Even whispering might wake up Al, if we did it long enough."

"It wouldn't," I said.

"It might."

"From now on when you talk to me, make the sounds."

"All right," she said. Then after a little pause while her tongue touched her lips: "You hurt Aristotle."

"Yes."

"You could have killed him," she said.

I said: "I guess I lost my head."

"It can happen to anybody," she said. "I feel like that all the time."

"Like what?"

"Like I've *got* to lose my head. You know what I mean?"

"No."

"Things get so . . . so . . ."—she moved on the bed, seemed almost to struggle— ". . . so dead. Everything just dies and then I have to do something."

"I don't think we're talking about the same thing."

"I guess not," she said. She pressed against me, her hands in the small of my back. A tremor shook her. Her fingers pressed into my skin hard enough to hurt. "I just want you to understand this. All I'm trying to do is stay alive. When everything starts to die, I get this dreadful loneliness. No, not lonely. Alone. Like I was the only one in the world. Like everything else is a desert. People dry up and die. Food's got no taste.

Color goes out of the trees, out of everything. Tomorrow won't ever come. Yesterday isn't worth remembering. Or if you can remember it you wonder how you lived through it." Her lips stopped moving, but I held the light on her mouth. My hand was shaking. More than the words, it was the look on her face. In her eyes. It was the look of someone who's having a nightmare and can't get out of it. "That's when I . . . well, when I have to change things. I just have to. What I *want* to do has nothing to do with it. I have to turn things around, and then it's all interesting again."

"Christ," I said.

"So I know why that happened with Aristotle Parsus," she said.

"That's not exactly it," I said. "I don't think that's the way it was."

"You were defending yourself," she said. Her eyes seemed to grow more solid and opaque, to recede in the light. "I expect you to defend yourself," she said. "That's something I always expect."

I kissed her. Then: "Lady, I've been defending myself all my life."

She smiled that slow soft heavy smile. "You do it good. It's what makes you interesting," she said. "Marvin Molar, you're a very interesting person."

We went to sleep exhausted, but I woke in the middle of the night. I opened my eyes onto the blank moonwashed face of the brick building across the alley. I stared at it a long time before I realized Hester had never made the sound of the words, never once had done what I asked her to do. I made love to her again before I went back to sleep and I was able to make her throat rattle and shake with the pleasure of me, felt it come into my hand and race right down my blood. But I never felt a word. Maybe she didn't know I could feel the noise in things. She wasn't a deaf mute, only her parents. Maybe she didn't know how it was with me. I watched her face, helmeted with the dark hair on the pillow beside me, and went back to sleep thinking that there was probably a lot she did not know about me.

Nine

Al kept working out. Worse than ever. But he didn't do any more bridges. For the most part what he did was old stuff: tearing tennis balls (he had to start with worn-out slick ones that he sent Leroy down to the public courts to beg off the players) and tearing decks of cards—he couldn't quarter them anymore but he could snap a single deck in two smooth and clear as a knife. In the late afternoon he went to the heavy stuff: half squats with two hundred pounds taken off the rack, and stiff-legged dead lifts with two-fifty, and military presses using the wide lifters' belt to support his back. He went around the gym with a heavy soured expression. I saw him tell Leroy it was his competition face. Except when Hester was near. Then he walked with a hip-stiff strut and smiled a lot. He was eating salt tablets like M & M candies and taking about two hours of steam a day. His old gray skin was pink as a baby's when he finished his final workout late in the afternoon. But it only made him look like he was about to have a heart attack.

"Al, you going too fast," I said.

He stopped with his hands positioned on the olympic bar, about to take it off the squat rack. "You telling Al how he's going?"

"What's wrong with you?" I said.

"What's wrong with you?" he said. "Al's got a big demonstration at Clearwater Beach. Fireworks. Pretty girls. The mayor. And Al. Al's not through yet. Step out of the way."

"I told you he wouldn't quit," said Hester, who was leaning against a wall, watching us.

"I know what you told me," I said.

Hester had been good as her word. I hadn't seen her talking to Al about working out or about the Fourth of July celebration at Clearwater Beach. Not that it made any difference to Al. He kept right on. If anything, it seemed to make him crazier. But I was trying not to let it bother me. Things seemed to be all right, or as all right as they ever were with us at the Fireman's Gym.

Hester stayed home at night. I hadn't seen or heard anything about Aristotle Parsus and I figured he was over on his boat with the rest of the Greeks cheating middle-aged lady tourists from Kansas, or whatever they do in Tarpon Springs now that Dupont has made Greeks and natural sponges obsolete.

Al let the weight slip from his shoulders in a half squat when it started to get away from him, and the plates slammed onto the lifting platform. Waves of sound ran in my hands from the floor and all the way up to the bones in my hips. Al stood there glowering down at the weight. Russell Muscle came across the gym from the place where he'd been doing dips on the parallel bars. He stepped between Al and the weight, snorted through his nose once, did a flat-backed squat, and cleaned the bar to his shoulders like it weighed two pounds instead of two hundred. He dropped it onto the squat rack and started toward the parallel bars again. Al grabbed Muscle by his flapping sweatshirt and spun him around.

"What you doing?" demanded Al, the vein stiffening and leaping in his neck.

Muscle didn't move. His mouth came slightly open.

"Al wants to know what the hell you trying to do?"

Muscle looked at me. He looked back at Al. Still he didn't say anything. Of course, the truth is, the only guy I ever met who was quieter than Al was Russell Muscle. His idea of a big conversation was: Hello.

"Work out," he said finally, and you couldn't tell by the way he said it if he meant that's what he was trying to do or if that's what Al ought to do.

I got between them anyway. Russell admired Al because he was an old-time strongman, but I wasn't sure he couldn't be provoked into killing him. I also might as well admit that I wasn't sure Al might not kill him. The old man was still dangerous.

"Come on, Al," I said.

"Al don't come on," he said, just like a kid ten years old standing on a playground.

"You slipped the weight doing squats," I said. "Russell only put it back on the rack, for Christ's sake. What are you doing?"

I don't know what you know about weights but the issue was this: a man can squat with much more weight than he can clean to his shoulders, so he normally takes a weight he's going to squat with from a rack.

But, Jesus, he was only using two hundred and fifty pounds and even Al could clean that, so the whole thing was silly. Muscle saw that, and so did I, but what we didn't see, and I think we both understood it at about the same time, was that the reason Al had his back up was not the weight on the rack but Hester standing six or seven feet away watching it. Russell looked at me.

"You're kidding," Russell Muscle said.

I shook my head.

"Disgusting," Russell said. He turned and went toward the dressing room, his workout apparently ruined, leaving Al still bowed-up and red-faced.

"What did he mean?" said Al.

"I don't know," I said.

"He cain't talk to Al like that."

He started toward the dressing room but before he could get off the lifting platform, Hester stepped in front of him. "It's all right," she said.

"Al don't know that," he said.

"I don't think he meant anything," she said.

"Said 'disgusting.' "

"Well, said Hester, "you know how that is."

"Right," said Al. He went back to the rack. I'd been watching what they said to each other and it didn't make a bit of sense. But Al calmed right down. He went back to the bar and started doing half squats again.

"I didn't mean to get into it," Hester said.

"O.K.," I said.

"The last thing I wanted to do was put my two cents' worth in," she said.

What could I say? Her two cents' worth in? The thought, the words, came out of the ends of my fingers: she's making fun of you. Worse: she knows you know it. We stood there watching Al strain under the bar, looking like he was going to die any second, gray-faced, eyes walled, his old legs varicosed to the point of rupture. I was sitting beside her on the edge of the lifting platform. I touched her leg. She looked down at me.

"I know what you're doing," I said.

She held my eyes for a long time. Nothing showed in her face. Then she said: "Good, it won't be a surprise, will it?"

And just like on a signal the surprise walked in: Aristotle Parsus. He had his volleyball team with him. They were dressed out in their uniforms and sneakers. For a moment when I first saw them, a sort of panic started in me. There was no reason—just something that came over me—but I was scared. No, it was more than that, terrified. Then it passed as quick as it came.

Aristotle and his troops stood at the top of the stairs watching Al at the squat rack. The players were joking and talking, their hands flying. But Aristotle did not move at all and nothing showed in his face. Maybe that was it, what scared me. Maybe it was because Hester seemed totally indifferent to Aristotle suddenly appearing. She watched him across the gym like she might have watched a dog pissing on a fire hydrant. And he watched us the same way. Al still trembled and strained under the weight. When, finally, Al stepped forward and dropped the bar back onto the rack, Aristotle came rushing across the gym toward us. He was smiling wildly now. The second Al dropped the weight, the smile had popped into Aristotle's face like magic. Coming across the gym, he had his arm out, his hand extended in my direction. He looked like a fool.

He stopped in front of me. "Shake," he said.

I sat watching him.

"Now, listen," Aristotle said, "I've forgotten all about what happened. You don't have to worry."

"Shake," he said.

Al had turned around. He watched us, gray-faced. Each of his cheeks had a single spot of purple in it, artificial and phony-looking, like something somebody had pasted on.

Aristotle stood with his hand extended down toward me where I sat. He glanced over at Al, held up his other hand, and said: "You looking good, Al. Jesus, you're shaping yourself up."

I don't know if Al even saw what Aristotle said. He was watching me. "Shake," Al said.

"Sure," I said, and shook Aristotle's hand.

"I forgive it," said Aristotle. "Everything. Hell, I know how those things happen."

I said: "I know you do."

It was late enough in the afternoon that most of the lifters and boxers had left. Ordinarily, we would have been sitting down to eat soon, but since Al started training we had been eating later and later.

Aristotle's players were moving around in the gym through the uncertain light filtering from the high windows, lifting tiny dumbbells, punching the heavy bag, two of them lifting a bar together. Dressed in their striped shirts and winged shoes they reminded me of fish swimming in a tank. I wondered what they were doing here. Had Aristotle come all the way over here to make this obviously fake gesture of shaking my hand? Whatever was about to come down, I thought I ought to be ready, so I flipped up on my hands and went to lean against the wall by the squat rack.

Three of the volleyball players were down at the other end of the gym now. They had climbed up in the boxing ring. One of them reached up and pulled the string that turned on the single bulb hanging from the ceiling. The aluminum reflector above the bulb cast the ring in sudden bright light. The other players went down to the ring and sat on the apron. Al and Hester and Aristotle drew closer together beside the squat rack. They were talking but I didn't try to see what they were saying.

Muscle came out of the dressing room, his blond hair plastered over his forehead and dark from the shower. He had a towel around his neck. He stopped just inside the gym and looked back toward the dressing room. He stood absolutely still, his wide beautiful hands raised and holding each end of the towel around his neck. Leroy and Pete came through the door and I felt the hair on the back of my neck move. They were both in shorts and wearing boxing gloves. They were eight-ounce gloves. You might as well get hit with a bare fist as with eight-ounce gloves. Leroy had on a headgear. Pete didn't. Leroy, when he came by Muscle, went into a flurry of fakes and feints, shadowboxing all around Muscle's head and belly, while Muscle looked at him as though he thought the kid might have gone crazy. Leroy smiled up at Muscle and I saw he was wearing a mouthpiece. Pete had gone to the ring and climbed up through the ropes. His old legs had knots of dark varicose veins behind the knees and trailing down into his calves. Standing in the ring, he was moving to some rhythm—not moving much, just barely, but keeping the rhythm with his head, his feet, his hands. From the hips up, he bobbed and weaved counterpoint to the rhythm. I went onto one hand and asked Al what was going on. But he pretended not to see me. He and Hester were already walking toward the ring. Leroy climbed through the ropes and stood under the bright light with Pete.

Muscle followed him over and leaned on the apron of the ring, watching. Aristotle and his players were leaping about the ring like children, somersaulting over the ropes, skipping into and out of the resin box, and sparring with each other. Pete and Leroy stood facing each other, looking very serious.

"What the hell?" I said, hitting Al in the leg and pointing up at the ring. "What the hell?"

He had taken a chair beside the bell. He had a stopwatch in his hand. "Hester said Leroy ought to be in training."

"Al, for God's sake, that kid is . . ."

Al started ringing the bell and he never stopped until Aristotle and his players cleared the ropes and got off the apron. Hester climbed up into one corner and Leroy came over to stand beside her. They stood with their heads almost touching. Hester's back was to me, but I knew she was talking because Leroy kept nodding and glancing across the ring where Pete was still in his shuffling dance. Leroy kept showing his rubber mouthpiece and snorting through his nose. Muscle had dried his hair and taken a chair on the far side of the ring.

"Leroy's no boxer," I said to Al.

"Pete is," he said.

"Pete's a seventy-year-old punch-drunk nigger," I said.

He stared at me a long time. "Why do you hate us?" he said.

"What?"

"Why do you hate us? Al never gave you reason. Pete and Leroy didn't. Al didn't."

"That's stupid," I said. "Where did you get the idea . . ."

"Al is not stupid," he said, and smashed the bell with the little iron hammer hard enough to dent it.

When the bell rang, Leroy spun away from Hester and went flat-footed to the center of the ring where he stood facing Pete under the light. But then I saw that they weren't going to box. They weren't even going to spar. Leroy started hooking and jabbing the air, and Pete kept up a steady little song of coaching, every now and then stopping Leroy and showing him how to cross with a right over a left jab or how to use his shoulder to cover his chin. I felt a little better. I didn't give a shit if they killed each other, except I did, if you can understand that.

I hate to see anybody make an asshole of himself trying to do something that's not in him to do. You can do what you can do, you have the talents you have, and to try anything beyond that is assholeland. Besides, as people go in the world, Leroy and Pete weren't bad guys. Dummies? Sure, but not bad dummies, if you can see what I mean.

They worked for what I guess was three minutes and Al rang the bell. Leroy went to stand head to head with Hester in the corner. Pete went to the other corner, dancing all the way, looking like a wrinkled, varicosed, shrunken child. I couldn't help but feel sorry for him in those shorts he was wearing. You forgot how tiny and shriveled he was when he had his clothes on. Even in the steam room, he didn't look that bad. But up there in the ring under the light he was just as sorry-looking as you could ask for.

"Al," I said, "I shouldn't have butted in. If they want to work out that's their business."

Al stared in rage at his stopwatch and wouldn't look at me. The two purple spots in his cheeks were flushed. His gray neck had a ligament standing in it. He hit the bell again.

Pete and Leroy went out and did another round. Aristotle and his players stood in a line on the far side of the ring, not moving or talking, looking now a little disappointed, or maybe angry. Muscle was already heading for the stairs as Pete and Leroy were coming out for the third round. Leroy came right to the center of the ring and caught Pete with a right hook that dropped him like an empty sack. Muscle ran back and jumped up on the apron and started shouting to Pete, who hadn't moved. Leroy had gone to a neutral corner. He flashed his white mouthpiece at Hester. Al was counting. Every time he counted he slapped the ring with his hand. Pete had got to his hands and knees. Aristotle and his players were jumping up and down and clapping. Without thinking about it, I had been counting every time Al's hand slammed onto the canvas, and even though Muscle was screaming for Pete to take nine, he was up at seven, wobbly, shaking his head. Leroy came running across the ring and threw an off-balance, looping left hand that missed by about a foot and almost took him through the ropes. Pete had got his old hands and feet working, bobbing and weaving. He was smiling. He was actually smiling. Leroy came back and missed five or six more times before he managed to catch Pete with a low blow that dropped him again. This time the bell saved him on the floor.

Muscle threw a stool into the corner, leapt over the ropes, and dragged Pete over to it. He poured everything in the water bottle over

Pete's head. Muscle lifted Pete's old skinny chest so he could breathe. He
slapped him gently, kneeling in front of him.

It went five more rounds and Leroy never was able to take him out,
which I kept hoping he'd do. Instead, he just beat the living Jesus out of
Pete, Pete smiling all the time, even after he began to bleed from the
mouth, and Muscle shouting to him from the corner and working on
him between rounds. Aristotle and his players enjoyed the shit out of
themselves, like dogs on a gut wagon. For Al's part, he rang the bell and
counted at the knockdowns—four of them. Bless his old heart, the nigger's head was like a rock, solid bone from ear to ear. Still, it was a sorry
enough show.

That night, Hester went home with Aristotle. After Pete and Leroy
went to take showers, she said: "I need to see Daddy and Momma. Ari
can drop me by."

"I sure can," said Aristotle.

And then they left, straight for that goddam sponge boat and a
fuckathon.

"Mr. Muscle ain't a bad corner man," said Pete, his mouth swollen so
that I could hardly tell what he was saying.

We were sitting at the table. Al had cooked steak and potatoes. He'd
made a bowl of soup for Pete. But nobody was eating very much, except
Leroy, who was slashing at the bloody steak with his knife and spooning
great gobs of mashed potatoes into his mouth.

"I figure a month of that and I'll be ready," said Leroy, gasping around
a mouthful of steak, "to go a ten-rounder."

"Mr. Muscle ain't a bad corner man," said Pete.

Pete's eyes looked like they had been painted on, dulled and stunned.
I don't think he knew where he was. Russell Muscle had hugged him after the fight and told him goddammit he'd given it everything. That was
all Muscle was interested in, giving it everything. A psychopath who'll
end up cutting some woman's titties off someday.

Leroy said: "Yes sir. Boy oh boy! One month of that and—"

I slammed the table with one hand and with the other one said: "A
month of that and Pete'll be dead."

Leroy looked at Al. "What'd he say?"

"It don't matter," said Al.

I said: "Right! It doesn't matter. Your stupid asses mean nothing to
me one way or another."

Al sat there with his elbows on the table and finally said: "Why do you hate us?"

Sometimes I wish I could scream. Sometimes I really do wish I could scream. But all I could do was drop off my chair and go climb up in my bed. I snatched up a novel and opened it and couldn't read a word. It all ran together, I was so mad. It might as well've been written in Russian.

I thought Hester would come back early but she didn't. I lay in the bed while the lifters who work out in the evening came and went, listening to the olympic bars crashing into the platform on the other side of the wall from where I lay. Then I watched the moon stretch shadows across the brick wall on the other side of the alley.

Sometime during the night—I don't know what time it was—I took the flashlight down and went into the room where Al slept. Pete and Leroy were lumps in twin beds on opposite sides of the big bed where Al lay, the sheet pulled away from his chest, his skin damp and the color of granite in the bad light coming from the window. I rapped him on the hip and then turned the light on my hand.

"I don't hate you," I said, and then put the light on his mouth. He blinked against the light and waved it away. I kept it on his mouth anyway.

"Hester explained it all to Al," he said.

"What?" I said. "Tell me what she said."

"We can do things," he said. "All of us can do things."

"Is that what she said?"

"Al's not finished yet," he said.

"I know you're not finished," I said.

"Take the light out of Al's eyes," he said.

I took it out of his eyes. I put it on my hand. "I don't hate you," I said; "you've got everything wrong."

I went back and lay on the bed and waited. I heard her—felt her—on the stairs. I felt her all the way through the gym. I felt her come across the kitchen and saw the dark shape of her stand beside the bed. She took the flashlight down. She turned it on.

"Do you want me in your bed?"

"I told Al a while ago that he had everything wrong," I said. "I think you've got everything wrong too."

"I had to see Daddy and Momma."

"Yes," I said.

She was getting out of her clothes. Then she was beside me in the bed. Her long terrific body. Her legs. God, her legs, ending there in her lap.

"How long you going to have Leroy beat up the nigger?" I said.

"I didn't tell him to beat him up."

"He's an old man," I said. "Pete's an old man and you'll kill him."

"I won't kill him," she said.

She'd started. She'd started and I couldn't stop her, didn't want to stop her. Everything went out of my head. Nothing mattered at all except where she was losing me. And I was being lost, I really was, if you can understand that. Maybe you can't. It's a hard thing. Some men will never know. But those who know know, and know that I can't explain it.

The next day was the Fourth of July and the gym was closed, but Leroy beat up the nigger anyway. Pete went down about four times in six rounds. Aristotle was in the nigger's corner because Muscle didn't show up, it being the Fourth. Aristotle and his players got to the gym so early that Leroy had to get out of bed and go down and let them in. We were all going together to Clearwater Beach Celebration.

"I'm sorry I got here so early," said Aristotle, "but I'm nervous."

We were waiting by the ring for Hester to come out with the kid. Pete was already up in the ring shuffling around.

"Aren't you nervous?" Aristotle said.

"No," I said.

"Don't you want to know what Al's going to do?"

"No." I was lying. I'd stayed up part of the night thinking about the old bastard.

"He's got something up his sleeve," said Aristotle.

"He's a silly old man," I said.

"Well," he said, "men lose their heads sometimes." He gave me his picket-fence smile.

I looked up at him. "They sometimes lose their ass, too," I said. The smile never wavered.

Hester came out with Leroy and we all watched him slam the shit out of Pete, who coached the whole time. Sometimes he coached himself. Sometimes he coached Leroy.

When it was over, while Aristotle and his players worked over Pete's leathery face with an ice bag, I went over to where Hester was talking to the kid. She had her arm across his shoulders. Their heads were almost touching. She took her arm away when she saw me.

"Ask him why he's doing this," I said.

"What did he say?" said Leroy.

"Leave the kid alone," she said to me.

"Will you ask him or not?" I said.

She looked at me blankly for a moment and then shrugged. "Sure," she said. "I'll ask him anything you want me to." She looked at Leroy. "He wants to know why you're doing this."

"Doing what?" asked Leroy.

She looked at me. "Well?"

"Beating up the nigger," I said.

"Beating up the nigger," she said to Leroy.

The kid lifted his hands. He looked from her to me and back again. "Jesus, Marvin, I'm in training."

"You're not a boxer," I said.

"You're not a boxer," Hester said.

"Of course I'm a boxer!" he said. His face was flushed. "What's wrong with him, Hester?"

"I honestly don't know," she said.

There was no use going on with it. Aristotle and his enormous spiker came by with Pete between them. He turned his painted eyes on Leroy and said: "The lef got to come over the right. Over the right!"

The kid went over to Pete. He put his arms around Pete and hugged him. They looked at each other and smiled, Pete's lips puffing over his blue gums.

"Thank you." said Leroy.

"You gone be awright," said Pete. "Awright!" They went off to the showers together, Leroy not holding Pete up but kind of guiding him. They kept talking as they went but I doubt Pete knew where he was. It was all instinct. He'd just been whipped again for the second time in two days. Even if he did have solid bone from ear to ear, he was still an old man.

I was about to say something to Hester when Al appeared in the doorway. He was in a tight, fake-leopardskin bathing suit that had a strap over the left shoulder. You couldn't have bought such a thing. Hester probably made it. He stood spraddle-legged, his fists balled on his hips. I felt a vibration in the floor and looked back to see the entire volleyball team, including Aristotle, ranged in a line, clapping, and grinning, and jumping up and down.

Al stood still for a long time, and then, very slowly, he actually bowed.

"It's time," cried Hester, and raced for the stairs.

We all drove over to Clearwater Beach together. Pete sat in the back with Leroy and Al—Al in the middle—because nobody trusted Pete to drive. Pete was fighting a bout with a boy by the name of Sugarstick Johnson. You could tell by the way he bobbed and weaved on the seat and the way he kept psyching himself up to hang in with Sugarstick that this was a fight he'd really had somewhere back there in the long-gone days when he was a ranked welterweight. Ever since he and Leroy had come out of the showers, Pete had been fighting the bouts over that had finally made him number two in his division. He was having a hell of a time with Sugarstick. I turned on the front seat to watch Pete. Through the window in back I could see Aristotle's minibus filled with his team right behind us. Players were hanging out the windows and waving. They were having great fun. Hester drove the old Dodge flat-out on the causeway to the beach, whipping in and out of traffic. But Aristotle hung right on our bumper.

"You better do something about Pete," I said.

I didn't know if Al had seen me when I spoke to him. Tiny drops of sweat stood on his gray face. Without turning his head, he raised one arm and put his hand on Pete's shoulder, shook him gently, and pulled Pete against him, hugged him.

"Pete," Al said. "Pete."

Pete went quiet as a rabbit, dropped his fists, stopped weaving. But the fight went on. He never stopped talking.

"Sugarstick he cut. Wake to the cut. Wake to the cut. Don't hurry nothing. Lef. Cross. Hook."

Behind Pete, Aristotle was trying to put his bumper on the Dodge as Hester swung into the left lane to pass a truck. By the time we got off the causeway, traffic was solid in the streets. It couldn't have been more than eleven o'clock, but the sidewalks were filled with children carrying balloons and eating cotton candy and popcorn and hotdogs, while their parents sweated and waved tiny American flags at each other. Hester seemed to know right where she was going. About two blocks from the Ocean Club, a platform, high and wide as a stage, had been built out on the beach. Hester pulled onto the sand. The minibus slid in beside her. Cars were parked every which way, some of them on the sidewalks.

Hester turned on the seat and looked at Al. "That's where the beauty contest'll be held at one o'clock."

We sat looking at the platform.

"What we gone do till one o'clock?" asked Leroy.

"Demonstrations," she said. Aristotle and his players had come to hang in the windows of the Dodge. "There's a karate expert who is going to break a block with his head."

"Hot damn," said Leroy.

"And a sword swallower and a fire eater," Hester said.

"Better'n a circus," Leroy said.

"What's Al going to do?" I said.

"What did Marvin say?" said Leroy.

"He wants to know what Al is going to do."

"What is he going to do?" asked Leroy.

"That's a secret. I guess we'll have to wait and see," she said. "Right, Al?" She winked at him. Al didn't look at her. I don't think he heard her. He sat hugging Pete, who was still talking steadily. Al stared straight ahead.

We drew a crowd as soon as we got out of the Dodge. But I was used to it, except I never got used to it, if you can understand that. We went over to the platform, where, just as Hester had promised, a guy was sticking a sword down his throat and another guy was spraying his mouth with gasoline and spitting fire. Pete began bobbing and weaving—sparring—this time with somebody named Battling Kid Felix, and Al had to put his hand on him again to quiet him down. There was a man dressed like Uncle Sam talking to the crowd from a microphone on a little platform built just to the right of where Hester said the beauty contest would be. I sat down in the sand while Hester went over to talk to the guy dressed like Uncle Sam. She pointed back at us. Uncle Sam pointed, too. Then he was shouting into the microphone. We were too far away and he was shouting and I couldn't tell what he was saying but I knew it was about Al and I felt a little sick sitting there in the sand beside Al's huge varicosed legs, white and ridged as granite, while Aristotle's volleyball players raced around us like children. The crowd pressed in tighter.

What happened next happened quick as an execution. That's the way I remember it. Like an execution. Al stepped out into the center of the crowd and lay down in the sand. Two young boys came running from the back of the platform with thick boards in their hands. They put them on Al's chest. Like they had spent all morning practicing it, the crowd parted and a bright red Ford Maverick with racing slicks came barreling across the beach toward us. When it was about twenty yards from Al, the slicks grabbed in the sand, and the car slowed until it was barely moving. The driver had on mirror sunglasses. He looked very young. He never hesitated. He drove his Ford right up on Al's chest. I couldn't move. I was looking at Al's face. He had his eyes closed and he never opened them. But his mouth flew open and his tongue pushed out three inches.

Ten

IT took Al three days to die. I never went to see him. Leroy'll tell you that. Pete—for what it's worth—will probably tell you the same thing. I couldn't stand to go and look at him. I closed the gym and lay up in my bed.

Leroy stayed at the hospital except for once when he came home to change clothes—some nurse sent him because he was beginning to stink—and twice to get something to eat. He was always just starting to cry, or just getting through. He tried to talk to me but couldn't. His mouth would break up into trembling and spit. Pete didn't cry though. He smiled a lot and talked to himself and followed the kid to and from the hospital.

Hester came back that first day but didn't stay.

"You don't think I meant for that to happen," she said.

"No." I lay staring at the ceiling. She put her hand over my face.

"Cars are heavier today than when he used to do that," she said.

"He used to do that a long time ago," I said.

"It wasn't my idea."

"I don't want to talk about it."

"I don't either," she said. "The doctors say he doesn't have a chance."

"I don't suppose so."

"Are you coming to the hospital?"

"No."

"Do you want me to come back here to the gym tonight?"

"Do whatever you want to."

"All right," she said.

I felt her cross the gym and go down the stairs. I lay around the gym the next two days trying to think. But I couldn't. I didn't work out and I didn't shower and I don't think I remember eating twice in three days.

Sometime in there the phone rang. I watched it across the room, feeling it in the wood. It kept ringing. There was nobody else in the gym. After it had been ringing a long time, I slid off the bed and went over and knocked it off the stand. I picked it up and put it to my ear. I could feel the voice in my skin. I jerked it out of the wall and put it back on the table. It could have been Muscle calling. It could have been anybody. That was the first time I cried. It shamed me.

I wished I could scream. I wished I could do *something*. But there was nothing to do but lie around and wait for Al's mashed chest to kill him. And when it finally did, Hester came to the gym and offered to take us on the *Parthenon*. She insisted that Pete and Leroy and I go out in the Gulf on Aristotle's boat. She said it was morbid to lie around the gym. Death, she said, was inevitable. She said the sun and the salt air would remind us we were alive. It was a tonic, she said.

"We all loved him," Hester said.

I didn't say anything.

"I loved him," said Leroy.

"The heart be a knockout punch," said Pete. "Wake low, come high. Cross wif a right to the heart."

"Anyway, Aristotle here says we can go out for a day's fishing in the *Parthenon*. He says it'll relax us all," Hester said.

Aristotle, who had come with her, looked serious, which made him look silly. I was numb and didn't know what I was going to do. One thing seemed as good as another.

"Then it's settled," said Hester.

"I loved him," said Leroy.

"Stick and move," Pete said. "Stick and move."

Aristotle and Hester came for us in the minibus at daylight the next morning. Hester had a lunch. She showed me the basket. Aristotle had bought several bottles of white wine and a half a case of beer. He showed me the cooler.

Al had died at a little before noon the day before. Leroy and Pete had been there. I didn't even go to see him before they got rid of him. It was all done and there was nothing I wanted to see.

Al left instructions in writing to be burned and scattered. Burned and scattered. No funeral. No service. No viewing the corpse. Nothing. That's the way I felt then. Nothing left.

The sponge boat was about thirty-five feet long. I'd never been out on a boat before. It stunk of Greeks and the musky smell of sponges. There was a little closed closetlike house raised about the deck where you drove the thing from. Aristotle insisted I see it after we got away from the dock and out into the Gulf. We were going south toward Clearwater Beach. The boat was old and very slow. It groaned a lot.

"Great view up here, right?" said Aristotle.

I was sitting in the chair beside the wheel. He slapped me on the shoulder in a good-natured way. I turned to look through the window behind the wheel. Hester was at the rail at the back of the boat. Leroy and Pete were sitting in camp chairs with rods and reels. Hester had opened some white wine and was sipping from the bottle.

"You guide by compass, see?" said Aristotle, after touching my shoulder to turn me around. He pointed: "This is our heading here, and if you just keep this lined up with that, there's nothing else to it."

I couldn't think of anything to say to Aristotle, and I couldn't stand to watch him explain things on his Greek boat anymore, so I slid out of the chair and went down the iron ladder to the deck. Hester was finishing the bottle when I got to the back of the boat. She reached in the cooler for another bottle. Out here on the flat, windless Gulf, the sun was scalding hot. Her upper lip carried a beautiful little shining line of sweat.

She drew the cork and said: "You want some of this?"

"I don't drink wine," I said.

"You ought to," she said.

"I know."

She reached out and touched my cheek. "Poor baby," she said. "You're sad."

I pushed my cheek against her hand. I couldn't help it.

Pete turned his puffy face to me and said: "Whyn't you git yourself a fishing pole?"

"Tell'm not now," I said to Hester. "Tell'm I don't want to fish."

Hester told him and then said to me: "I'm going to take some of this wine up to Ari."

"Sure," I said, and watched her fantastic legs tick across the deck smooth and steady as a clock. Climbing the ladder, her rump flexed round over her thighs. She was showing about a dented inch of ass above the back of her yellow bikini. I lay on the deck and watched three silver birds glide in looping half circles after the boat. The sun was a white hole in the sky. Pete and Leroy worked over their tangled reels and helped each other with the slippery fish they were using for bait. They had the concentration of children, their tongues caught between their teeth, their faces knotted. I wondered what in God's name they would do now that Al was dead.

We'd gone down the coast about ten miles and weren't far from the Ocean Club at Clearwater Beach. Hester came back. I think she was a little drunk. Her eyes were bright and she was smiling.

"You want to take the wheel?" she said.

"What?"

"Ari says for you to come and take the wheel."

"No," I said.

"Oh, come on. I've done it myself. It's fun. You'll get a hell of a kick out of it."

She swayed a little. I don't know if it was from the roll of the boat or from the wine. I think I knew then what was going to happen. There was no use to fight against it. There was nothing left to fight for, so I went with her up to the little house where the wheel was. Aristotle showed me his teeth and explained again where to keep the wheel so the heading on the compass was true. There was a chair bolted to the floor in front of the wheel. I climbed up in it.

"We're going back to try our luck with the fish," said Hester.

"Sure," I said.

She watched me from the door. "You look great sitting up there," she said, "just great."

I waved at the wheel and the instruments. "It's all very interesting," I said.

"I think so too," she said. "It's interesting as hell."

They went down the ladder. It was cooler up there in the little house and I didn't pay any attention to the compass. Some porpoises rolled in the flat blue water off to the right. Finally I saw the Ocean Club coming up on the left and I turned in closer to shore until finally I could see the posts where we put the volleyball net up and the lifeguard tower where I refereed. I looked through the little window behind me. Pete and Leroy were sitting quietly, watching where their lines cut the water. Aristotle and Hester weren't at the back of the boat. I hadn't expected them to be.

I had been feeling them in the wood. The noise came right up through the boat to the wheel and into my hands. Never mind that I *couldn't* have felt them in the wood. I *did* feel them in the wood. I *couldn't* but I *did*. Hester sometimes beat her heels against the wall when she was coming. I felt her heels as clearly as if I'd been on top of her.

There was a piece of rope on a bench beside the chair where I was sitting. I reached for it and tied the wheel. I had to try several times before I got the wheel tied so that the boat went in a long slow circle about fifty yards offshore directly in front of the Ocean Club. Then I slid off the chair and went down the ladder.

I'd seen the hatchet when we first came aboard. It was fastened in a little leather holder on the wall. I suppose it was used for cutting rope or fish or something.

I took down the hatchet. I didn't even check the porthole to see if what I knew was true was true.

I opened a door and went into a little hallway. When I opened the next door they were naked.

Hester was kicking the wall with her heels. That's probably why they never heard me until I tapped Aristotle on the shoulder with my finger. His head jerked up and his mouth opened to scream but I don't think he could and he fell off her and off the bed onto the floor where he scrambled on his hands and knees to a corner. I swung up on the bed.

Hester looked steadily at me and smiled.

I hit her in the smile with the hatchet. I felt breaking bone run in the wood of the handle. I don't remember anything else until I was going toward the door. I was covered with blood. The whole room was splattered with it. Aristotle was as bloody as I was even though I never touched him with the hatchet.

I went up on deck. Pete and Leroy sat watching their lines trailing in the water. There was a ladder that went to the top of the house where the wheel was. I climbed up it. On the very top of the boat I went into a one-hand stand. The boat kept its slow circle. When it passed closest to shore, I went to two fingers. A crowd was gathering on the sand. I could see the people pointing. The next time around, I went into my impossible one-finger stand and saw out of the corner of my eye the entire crowd burst into applause.

A swimmer saw that I was covered with blood. The boat was still circling. Pete and Leroy were still fishing, and I was still on one finger when the Coast Guard got there.

The guy from the public defender's office brought me a message from her father. The lawyer thought we might be able to use it somehow in defense.

Her father said he held no grudge. That he didn't understand but he held no grudge. He said he'd looked through her things. There was a diary full of the usual stuff. But one thing it said, he thought I ought to know. She had written—and this is a quote: "Someday I'll find somebody who loves me enough to kill me. And someday I'll find somebody I admire enough to make him do it."

The lawyer thought we could use it in defense. I told him to go fuck himself. Defense for what? Still, it's something for me to take with me when I go. Since those nine old men said you can't electrocute anybody anymore, I guess I'm looking at life.

I hear they've got a good gym at Raiford Prison. I'll tell you one thing: I bet there's not a swinging dick in the place with twenty-inch arms.

The Car

THE other day, there arrived in the mail a clipping sent by a friend of mine. It had been cut from a Long Beach, California, newspaper and dealt with a young man who had eluded police for fifty-five minutes while he raced over freeways and through city streets at speeds up to 130 miles per hour. During the entire time, he ripped his clothes off and threw them out the window bit by bit. It finally took twenty-five patrol cars and a helicopter to catch him. When they did, he said that God had given him the car, and that he had "found God."

I don't want to hit too hard on a young man who obviously has his own troubles, maybe even is a little sick with it all, but when I read that he had found God in the car, my response was: *So say we all*. We have found God in cars, or if not the true God, one so satisfying, so powerful and awe-inspiring that the distinction is too fine to matter. Except perhaps ultimately, but pray we must not think too much on that.

The operative word in all this is *we*. It will not do for me to maintain that I have been above it all, that somehow I've managed to remain aloof from the national love affair with cars. It is true that I got a late start. I did not learn to drive until I was twenty-one; my brother was twenty-five before he learned. The reason is simple enough. In Bacon County, Georgia, where I grew up, many families had nothing with a motor in it. Ours was one such family. But starting as late as I did, I still had my share, and I've remembered them all, the cars I've owned. I remember them in just the concrete specific way you remember anything that changed your life. Especially I remember the early ones.

The first car I ever owned was a 1938 Ford coupe. It had no low gear and the door on the passenger side wouldn't open. I eventually put a low gear in it, but I never did get the door to work. One hot summer night on a clay road a young lady whom I'll never forget had herself braced and ready with one foot on the rearview mirror and the other foot on the wing vent. In the first few lovely frantic moments, she pushed out the wing vent, broke off the rearview mirror and left her little footprints all over the ceiling. The memory of it was so affecting that I could never bring myself to repair the vent or replace the headliner she had walked all over upside down.

Eight months later I lost the car on a rain-slick road between Folk-ston, Georgia, and Waycross. I'd just stopped to buy a stalk of bananas (to a boy raised in the hookworm and rickets belt of the South, ba-nanas will always remain an incredibly exotic fruit, causing him to buy whole stalks at a time), and back on the road again I was only going about fifty in a misting rain when I looked over to say something to my buddy, whose nickname was Bonehead and who was half drunk in the seat beside me. For some reason I'll never understand, I felt the back end of the car get loose and start to come up on us in the other lane. Not having driven very long, I overcorrected and stepped on the brake. We turned over four times. Bonehead flew out of the car and shot down a muddy ditch about forty yards before he stopped, sober and unhurt. I ended up under the front seat, thinking I was covered with gouts of blood. As it turned out, I didn't have much wrong with me and what I was covered with was gouts of mashed banana.

The second car I had was a 1940 Buick, square, impossibly heavy, built like a Sherman tank, but it had a '52 engine in it. Even though it took about ten miles to get her open full bore, she'd do over a hundred miles an hour on flat ground. It was so big inside that in an emergency it could sleep six. I tended to live in that Buick for almost a year and no telling how long I would have kept it if a boy who was not a friend of mine and who owned an International Harvester pickup truck hadn't said in mixed company that he could make the run from New Lacy in Coffee County, Georgia, to Jacksonville, Florida, quicker than I could. He lost the bet, but I wrung the speedometer off the Buick, and also—since the run was made on a blistering day in July—melted four inner tubes, causing them to fuse with the tires, which were already slick when the run started. Four new tires and tubes cost more money than I had or expected to have anytime soon, so I sadly put that old honey up on blocks until I could sell it to a boy who lived up toward Macon.

After the Buick, I owned a 1953 Mercury with three-inch lowering blocks, fender skirts, twin aerials, and custom upholstering made of rolled Naugahyde. Staring into the bathroom mirror for long periods of time I practiced expressions to drive it with. It was that kind of car. It looked mean, and it was mean. Consequently, it had to be handled with a certain style. One-handing it through a ninety-degree turn on city streets in a power slide where you were in danger of losing your ass as well as the car, you were obligated to have your left arm hanging half out the window and a very *bored* expression on your face. That kind of thing.

Those were the sweetest cars I was ever to know because they were my first. I remember them like people—like long-ago lovers—their idiosyncrasies, what they liked and what they didn't. With my hands deep in crankcases, I was initiated into their warm greasy mysteries. Nothing in the world was more satisfying than winching the front end up under the shade of a chinaberry tree and sliding under the chassis on a burlap sack with a few tools to see if the car would not yield to me and my expert ways.

The only thing that approached working on a car was talking about one. We'd stand about for hours, hustling our balls and spitting, telling stories about how it had been somewhere, sometime, with the car we were driving. It gave our lives a little focus and our talk a little credibility, if only because we could point to the evidence.

"But, hell, don't it rain in with that wing vent broke out like that?"

"Don't mean nothing to me. Soon's Shirley kicked it out, I known I was in love. I ain't about to put it back."

Usually we met to talk at night behind the A&W Root Beer stand, with the air heavy with the smell of grease and just a hint of burned French fries and burned hamburgers and burned hot dogs. It remains one of the most sensuous, erotic smells in my memory because through it, their tight little asses ticking like clocks, walked the sweetest softest short-skirted carhops in the world. I knew what it was to stand for hours with my buddies, leaning nonchalant as hell on a fender, pretending not to look at the carhops, and saying things like: "This little baby don't look like much, but she'll git rubber in three gears." And when I said it, it was somehow my own body I was talking about. It was *my* speed and *my* strength that got rubber in three gears. In the mystery of that love affair, the car and I merged.

But, like many another love affair, it has soured considerably. Maybe it would have been different if I had known cars sooner. I was already out of the Marine Corps and twenty-two years old before I could stand behind the A&W Root Beer and lean on the fender of a 1938 coupe. That seems pretty old to me to be talking about getting rubber in three gears, and I'm certain it is *very* old to feel your own muscle tingle and flush with blood when you say it. As is obvious, I was what used to be charitably called a late bloomer. But at some point I did become just perceptive enough to recognize bullshit when I was neck deep in it.

The 1953 Mercury was responsible for my ultimate disenchantment with cars. I had already bored and stroked the engine and contrived to place a six-speaker sound system in it when I finally started to paint it. I spent the better half of a year painting that car. A friend of mine owned a body shop and he let me use the shop on weekends. I sanded the Mercury down to raw metal, primed it, and painted it. Then I painted it again. And again. And then again. I went a little nuts, as I am prone to do, because I'm the kind of guy who if he can't have too much of a thing doesn't want any at all. So one day I came out of the house (I was in college then) and saw it, the '53 Mercury, the car upon which I had heaped more attention and time and love than I had ever given a human being. It sat at the curb, its black surface a shimmering of the air, like hundreds of mirrors turned to catch the sun. It had twenty-seven coats of paint, each coat laboriously hand-rubbed. It seemed to glow, not with reflected light, but with some internal light of its own.

I stood staring, and it turned into one of three great scary rare moments when you are privileged to see into your own predicament. Clearly, there were two ways I could go. I could sell the car, or I could keep on painting it for the rest of my life. If twenty-seven coats of paint, why not a hundred and twenty-seven? The moment was brief and I understand it better now than I did then, but I did realize, if imperfectly, that something was dreadfully wrong, that the car owned me much more than I would ever own the car, no matter how long I kept it. The next day I drove to Jacksonville and left the Mercury on a used-car lot. It was an easy thing to do.

Since that day, I've never confused myself with a car, a confusion common everywhere about us—or so it seems to me. I have a car now, but I use it like a beast, the way I've used all cars since the Mercury, like a beast unlovely and unlikable but necessary. True as all that is, though, God knows I'm in the car's debt for that blistering winning July run to Jacksonville, and the pushed-out wing vent, and finally for that greasy air heavy with the odor of burned meat and potatoes there behind the A&W Root Beer. I'll never smell anything that good again.

CAR

A Novel

One

MISTER sat at the top of the car-crusher as close to joy as he'd been in a long time. The afternoon had come up Cadillacs. It seemed a good sign, a great sign. He needed one. They all needed one. The enormous machine that he used to smash cars into suitcases throbbed and pulsed under him. In the small yellow cab thirty feet off the ground, Mister took the controls in his hands and revved the engine. The leather seat that held him rocked and swayed. He waited patiently for the next car to slide into the cradle below.

No pattern had developed during the morning, and that was all right because he did not expect it to. He never expected a pattern, but he was ready if one came. For a while, the middle of the day—just before lunch—had been interesting when two Hudson Hornets had appeared like magic one after another in quick succession. But it was a fluke. Nothing you could really take hold of. So Mister just quickly crushed them, smashed the Hudson Hornets into solid metal suitcases, and sent them sliding down the chute where the barge would pick them up.

Then in late afternoon, the Cadillacs had started. The first one had been a forty-seven two-door hardtop. It sat in the cradle, finless, but full of chrome. Pow! He smashed it shut. A fifty-seven slid into the cradle. It sat creaking gently in its own momentum, full of fantastic fins. A drunk's dreamfish. Pow! With great untender satisfaction, Mister returned it to an earlier time, back to raw unmolded metal. Then a third Cadillac appeared. And a fourth. Mister's heart pounded. A small wave of heat washed through him. A fifth! He'd had five in a row now. He sat hunched and waiting over the rubber controls.

A brand-new 1970 Cadillac slid into the cradle. Mister whipped a red bandana out of the bib of his overalls and signaled Paul, who was working the crane, that this was the last one for today. Mister sat gazing fondly down upon the Cadillac. The sixth in succession. A record.

Cadillac: the poor man's car (Once you git yourself one of them babies, you got youself something. Your regular Cadillac is a pree-cisionmade machine. Low upkeep. No depreciation to speak of hardly).

Cadillac: the rich man's car (I didn't work eighteen hours a day and get three ulcers at the age of thirty-six to drive a Volkswagen. You show me a man who can trade in for a new Cadillac in October of every year and I'll show you a man in the mainstream of America).

The voices pumped quietly in Mister's head. Quietly he participated in the car's evolution. He saw the first Cadillacs—solid and square as Sherman tanks. But gradually they were attenuated by the wind, stretched and smoothed like teardrops. Then the first evidence of a fin began to appear. A small bump at the small end of the teardrop. And from that small bump there grew a giant fin of such proportions as to take the breath away. It swam through all the garages from ocean to ocean, from Canada to Mexico. It went upstream, savage and unrelenting, to the headwaters of the American heart. And there it remained. There it would *always* remain. Who could doubt it?

Mister took out his bandana again and wiped his face. There below him in the cradle was what the Cadillac had become. The fins were still there, but no longer fluid or functional. They were massive, straight and unmoving. Mister revved the engine of the car-crusher. Its noise was the only noise anywhere.

He was sitting on the edge of forty-three acres of wrecked cars. Below him to his left was the roiling excremental flow of the Saint John's River. Ten feet of gasoline on top of fifty feet of shit was the way his daddy described it. But his daddy didn't seem to like anything much anymore. And across the river in a pulpmill haze cast red by the setting sun was Jacksonville, Florida. It was time to quit for the day, time to crush the last car suitcase size and let it slide down the chute where it would eventually be loaded onto one of several barges anchored at the concrete dock. Twenty-five tons of machinery waited, poised on rails at either end of the car-crusher, to shorten the Cadillac, to reduce it to a manageable unlovely square lump.

The Cadillac had already been shortened by about a third when they got it. It was a pale-green four-door sedan with a paisley vinyl roof. But now it wore its chromeshining breast-bumper around its doors. The entire hood had been shoved back into the stomach of the car where the front seats once had been.

Ten miles north on U.S. 1, between Jacksonville and Saint Augustine, the driver had apparently fallen asleep and run the Cadillac head-on into a concrete bridge abutment. The state troopers had taken the driver out with an acetylene torch and a putty knife. And put him in a rubber sheet. That's what Junell said when she towed the Cadillac into Auto-Town.

She had brought the Cadillac in on the back of Big Mama, her red ten-wheeled tow truck. Then she had the boys strip it. The Cadillac had a wooden hand-carved walnut steering wheel, and strangely, because the steering column had been driven all the way through the left side of the back seat, the walnut wheel was undamaged. It was hanging in Salvage House right now. She had removed it, along with the hubcaps off the back. Then she had taken the rear window glass out, the door handles off, the glass taillights out, robbed the trunk of jack and spare tire. Finally, there was nothing left but the stripped-bare skeleton of metal that lay in the cradle below him now.

Mister touched the red-rubber lever in front of him and a colossal vise clammed shut on the Cadillac. A solid piece of metal the size of a suitcase slid down the chute. Mister sighed and turned off the engine of the car-crusher. He climbed down the iron steps and walked toward the concrete dock. On three sides his horizon was mountains of wrecked cars. Every possible kind of car in every possible kind of attitude: upside-down, sideways, on end, pitching, yawing, tilted. The ground under his feet was not ground at all but an unknowably thick layer of glass shards, glass of all colors, rose, yellow, clear, tinted blue and pink, and even black. Mixed with the glass were ragged slivers of aluminum, scarred lumps of cast iron, and other pieces of metal worn down fine as sand. From long practice he walked evenly over the uneven pieces of metal and glass.

He stood on the dock and regarded the day's work with satisfaction. Hudson Hornets vanished, Oldsmobile's Youngmobile gone, Pontiac reduced, Chevrolet canceled, Buick Believers undone. Just suitcases now. Enormously heavy suitcases. Tomorrow they would go up the river. Mister squinted and looked in the direction they would go. His eyes burned and his vision blurred from the palpable breath rising out of the water of the river. Being this close to the Saint John's River was like being too close to the open door of a furnace. An airy blast of gas and chemicals and stopped-up toilets rushed about his head. Mister turned up the collar of his denim shirt, hunched his shoulders against the hot blast of the river and walked back into Auto-Town.

It was nearly a half-mile to Salvage House, half a mile on a trail that led through a valley that wound between abrupt cliffs of automobiles.

A hundred and fifty yards before he got to Salvage House, he broke out onto a plain of wrecked and mangled cars laid out neatly in rows, one after the other, more than ten acres of them spreading out to his left and ending where the expressway arched over Auto-Town toward Jacksonville.

Mister refused to look at the rows of cars but walked doggedly on. Now that he had the mountain of cars between himself and the river, there was no wind. It was very late. They'd probably have to pay Paul an hour or more overtime.

Salvage House gate was shut and locked. Through the wire-mesh front, hubcaps and rearview mirrors and steering wheels glowed dully where they hung on display from the walls. Big Mama stood out by the high yellow fence that hid Auto-Town from the superhighway. Or at least the fence hid Salvage House and the three-foot-high sign that said that this was Auto-Town, but it did not hide the mountains of wrecked cars.

There was a taxi parked at the iron-grilled gate, closed and padlocked now. It was near enough dark that the taxi had its headlights on. A woman in a wide black hat and a black veil stood at the grilled gate with her hands on the bars. Mister sighed. God knows who she was. He was prepared to have anybody arrive at their gates. If it had been a woman come to take him away and butcher him and sell him as meat in the local supermarket, it would not have surprised him. But of course it was nothing so interesting and unusual as that, and he had known it wouldn't be.

"Where is Fred's car?" she asked through the gate.

Mister was close enough that he could see right through her veil even through the light was bad. He saw that her eyes were black and hollow and her nose was blunt and spoon-shaped. Without answering, he turned from her and looked back toward forty-three acres of wrecked cars, dark and jagged and indistinguishable one from the other now. He looked back at her. Why couldn't any of them see it was impossible?

"I don't know," said Mister.

She weaved gently on her black-shod, delicate feet. Then she turned loose the iron gate and opened a black purse, took out a piece of paper, and squinted at it in the bad light.

"Is this Auto-Town?" she asked.

"Yes," Mister said.

"Is this your place of business? Do you own it?" Her voice was light and, in its grief, lilting.

"My daddy owns it."

"His car was brought here," she said.

"Whose?"

"Fred's. My husband. The one he was …The one he had the accident in. They told me it was brought here. Please. If I could just see it? For a minute. Please help me."

"When was it brought here, lady?"

"Six days ago." Through the veil, he could see the little place between her eyes tighten. "In the afternoon."

"Make?"

"A Cadillac. A vinyl top. A paisley vinyl top."

"A new one?"

"This year's, yes, a new one."

It would have been that one naturally. Which other one could it have possibly been? And now it was a very solid suitcase, lumped in with two hundred and sixteen other suitcases on the dock waiting for the barge. Mister took a key ring out of his pocket. The ring was fastened to a leather strap attached to his belt. He unlocked the gate.

"This way, lady."

She looked at the taxi. "I'll be a little while. You can turn off your lights."

It was getting dark now, but she followed him all right, making only a little sound like rats scurrying over dried grain. Mister knew exactly where to take her. Less than fifty yards from Salvage House, laid out in one of the first rows, they came upon it, a foreshortened Cadillac car in perfect condition except that the front seat was filled with the engine and the windshield on the driver's side had a star-shaped shatter where, unmistakably, a head had stopped.

They stood in the darkness watching it. It was a sixty-nine and not a seventy, but Mister knew that even if the light had been good she probably would not have known. Women were emotional and full of gestures.

She walked closer to the Cadillac. She stopped by the back door. She looked at him. He knew exactly what to do. He took the handle of the door and pulled. The hinge was jammed. He pulled harder. It groaned and scraped, but it opened. She wedged into the back seat. He closed the door.

"I'll just sit here a while," she said.

"Right," he said. He left her there and went back to Salvage House and climbed the outside stairs to the second floor where he lived with his father, his sister Junell, and his twin brother Herman.

Herman was not there. But Mister had not expected him to be. The light was dim in the single vast room they used for kitchen, dining place, and living room. The wall was a solid bank of windows on the side next to the wrecked mountains and the river. His father, Easton Mack, whom everyone called Easy, stood at the windows looking down. Junell stood beside him. She was dressed in black motorcycle racing leathers. The long hair spilling down her back was red and burned like a light against the black jacket. Mister's father turned his head and glanced at him as he came through the door. His eyes were thin as knifeblades. Mister went over to where they were standing. They were looking down at the sixty-nine Cadillac where Fred's new widow sat. The three of them stood there a long time. The windows were open to the wind from the river. From this distance the wind was pleasantly warm and thick with an odor like ripe cheese.

A sound came to them from below. Metal on metal, a groaning. Easy Mack turned and walked quickly across the room and came back. He stared down into the gathering darkness where the sound had become more urgent, insistent. Fred's widow was trying to get out of what she thought was Fred's Cadillac.

"She won't be able to get out of there," Junell said.

"She'll get out," said Mister.

"Who died in it?" asked Easy.

"Husband," said Mister. "Name of Fred."

"Fred?" Easy said.

"Fred."

They could hear her voice now, faint, lilting, full of grief.

"Go down and get her out," said Easy Mack.

"She'll make it," Mister said.

"Go on down," Junell said. "Daddy caint stand it."

"I guess it's about time he stood *something*," said Mister.

Easy Mack's knife-thin eyes touched Mister briefly about the face, but Easy said nothing. Mister was sorry for what he'd said. He knew that his father felt bad enough about what had happened without being made to feel worse. It had been Easy Mack who had finally made Mister's twin brother Herman give up his last venture, which had been called CAR DISPLAY: YOUR HISTORY ON PARADE. Fred's widow was sitting in part of the parade right now. And because Easy Mack hadn't been able to stand it, hadn't been able to stand the crowds, the arc lights at night, the laughter, the tears and angry accusations, his brother Herman was lost now for good.

The thing about Herman was that he couldn't take hold. He never had been able to. The others took hold and found their places, but not Herman. Junell drove Big Mama and ran Salvage House. Mister ran the disposal end of the business, operating the car-crusher, directing the hired man Paul on the crane, and overseeing the loading at the dock. Their father, who had founded Auto-Town, kept the books and tried to see into the future. But Herman was a dreamer. That was what his daddy, who loved him, said. But Herman's dreams never seemed to amount to much, or when they did amount to something, there was always somebody to stop him, somebody to say no.

Take CAR DISPLAY: YOUR HISTORY ON PARADE. They were turning money with both hands when their father said they had to stop.

"You got to stop," he said one morning. "I caint stand it anymore."

It had all started one day when a well-dressed man had come into Auto-Town and asked if they had a 1949 De Soto. Of course they had one. Could he see it? Mister and Herman took him back to look at it. The man climbed up the slope of wrecked cars to the place where the 1949 De Soto stuck out. Mister and Herman climbed up with him and sat on the crushed fender of a Plymouth, watching. The De Soto was in bad shape, not wrecked or mangled, but covered with a heavy skin of rust. The man looked in through the back window. He stared for a long time. When he finally straightened, he had tears in his eyes.

"I just lost my son in Vietnam," he said.

They got off the Plymouth fender. They didn't know what to say. Mister thought he might be crazy.

"In 1950, I had one of these," said the man, gently touching the rusty car. "A year old and ran like a dream. Had twenty-three coats of paint on her. Put them on myself. And every coat buffed—hand-buffed—before the next coat was put on." He looked at them, but not at them either, through them rather, on into something else. "You could comb your hair in the lid of the trunk." He looked toward the back seat again. His face was now away from them, his voice distant, muted. "And that's the only reason she ever married me. I've always known that. Right in the back seat of this *very* car on the first date. And she caught." He looked suddenly at Mister. "She caught. You believe that? She caught. You believe that?"

Mister didn't know what to say.

"The *first* time on the *first* date, she caught. Pregnant. And now the boy's dead." He looked back at the car. "Thanks. I wanted to see it again."

Walking back to Salvage House after the man was gone, Mister was about to cry. It was the saddest goddam thing he'd ever heard. But not Herman. That Herman was a dreamer.

"How many of the American people do you think fucked for their children in the back seat of a car?" asked Herman. "What percent?"

"Goddam, Herman," Mister said.

"I'd say ten percent," Herman said. Herman smiled at his brother. "Hell, the old man may have got *us* in a back seat."

That was his brother Herman, a dreamer of mad dreams. But Herman was never willing to let mad dreams remain just dreams. He insisted upon acting on them. And so when he thought about YOUR HISTORY ON PARADE, he mined the mountains for individual cars.

"Everything that's happened in this goddam country in the last fifty years," said Herman, "has happened in, on, around, with, or near a car." He smiled his dreamy smile. "And everybody wants to return to the scene of the crime."

And so he mined the mountains for cars, individual cars for each of the last fifty years, cleared off ten of his father's acres, and laid the cars in rows. From 1920 to 1970, the cars sat there rusted, broken, and mutilated with parts missing, but all still recognizable. And they *did* want to return to the scene of the crime. Thousands of people.

Herman put up a billboard: SEE THE CAR IT HAPPENED IN—THE EVENT THAT CHANGED YOUR LIFE. And they came: to relive the love affair, the accident, that first car, that last car, the time the tire went flat, the time he ran out of gas, the time he *said* he ran out of gas, the place where Junior was conceived ("You had your foot braced against the dash light and the other foot against the door handle, honey. Remember?").

But finally, his daddy couldn't stand it. Easy Mack was losing his balance over what was happening. A man stabbed his brother-in-law over the hood of a forty-seven Ford coupe. A woman lost her sanity when her husband opened the door of a forty Studebaker and said: "See!" So Easy Mack had told Herman that there was no alternative but to take the billboard down and close up the ten acres, close up YOUR HISTORY ON PARADE.

"But why?" his son had asked.

"There is no joy. No love," said Easy Mack.

Mister remembered it and was suddenly angry again. Insisting on love and joy had lost them Herman. Herman was gone, and they'd not get him back again. Whether he lived or died, he was gone.

There was an abrupt squeal of metal on metal, followed by the dry rush of feet over the glassy yard below.

"Thank God," said Easy Mack. "She got out."

"She's all right now," Junell said.

They heard the taxi fire up and roar away from the gate.

"Some people will do anything," said Easy Mack. "Come in here to set in a wrecked Cadillac. Goddam people are crazy. It's a puzzle to me."

Mister clenched his fists. "I wouldn't say a word if I was you," said Mister. "I just wouldn't say one word if I'd raised a son who was advertising in public that he was going to eat a car."

I will eat a car. I will eat a car from bumper to bumper, Herman was saying over the radio. On the television. In the Florida *Times-Union* newspaper.

Junell and the old man had jerked their heads to stare at Mister as though he had said some unimaginable obscenity. They had not spoken of it directly before this. They'd said things like, "Herman's a fool if he thinks he can do that." Or, "It's a unnatural thing and cannot be done." But they had avoided the actual words *eat a car.*

"You might as well say it, daddy," said Mister bitterly. "You might as well say it right out. You have raised a boy who is going to eat a car."

Soft and flat, as though it were some ritual thing memorized and only half understood, Easy Mack said: "I have raised a son who is going to eat a car."

Junell's face was red, and a pendulous drop of sweat swung at the end of her nose. "Happy now, you shithead?" she spat at Mister.

"No," Mister said, "I'm not."

Two

EASY Mack stopped on his way to the Sherman Hotel to consider the fence. Lady Bird Johnson had put it there. It was part of her beautification plan for America. At least that was what Easy had been told. Lady Bird wanted a fence around all the junkyards in the country. Well, she didn't really want a fence *around* the junkyards, but she did think there ought to be a fence between the junkyards and the public roads. It was more seemly, she thought.

That was what Easy was told when the man had come by to enforce the city ordinance. So Easy put up the fence, a high wooden fence painted yellow, four hundred yards of it, between his place of business and the limited-access superhighway the state had jammed through five years ago. Lady Bird could have the fence if she wanted it. She was the President's wife and he was only the owner of forty-three acres of junked cars. But that didn't mean Easy thought the fence was a good idea.

He thought it was a lousy idea and a lousy fence. It offended him. Easy *loved* cars. He had always loved them. Always in all ways. He had started working on Fords almost as early as Ford started working on them. With the gentleness of a lover he had stuck his hands into their dark greasy mysteries, and in time he had become the best shade-tree mechanic in Lebeau County, Georgia. Then later he had owned a little garage and sold used cars on the side. After that he got a job as shop foreman for a new-car dealership in Waycross, Georgia. Finally, he had seen his chance, bought forty-three acres of land on the bank of the Saint John's River in 1939 just before the beginning of World War II, and opened Auto-Town. It was a junkyard. But he called it Auto-Town. It gave a little class. It honored. He was determined always to honor the thing he loved. You didn't get to own forty-three acres of anything without love. That's what he believed and that's what he had always tried to teach his children, all of whom were in the business with him.

"Your bread floats back off the water," he had told them, "because of love."

What had floated back off the water was a son who said he was going to eat a car. On a high platform in front of the Sherman Hotel in downtown Jacksonville, Florida. Herman was sitting on that platform right now—Easy glanced at his watch—yes, right now on Forsyth Street, two blocks west of Main, up on a platform lighted with a white arch of fluorescent light, Herman was sitting up there with a brand-new Ford Maverick. A Ford Maverick that Herman intended to eat.

Easy had never actually seen it. But he had read about it in the newspapers. He'd heard Mister describe it down to the last horrifying detail. Now it was time to go see it for himself. It was time to talk to Herman. Mister had been in to see his twin brother Herman several times already, and even Junell, who was probably the hardest working member of the family at Auto-Town, had visited Herman at the Hotel Sherman.

Right after the widow had escaped from the Cadillac about an hour ago, a call had come in on the police radio that had sent Junell roaring off in Big Mama. The call was an emergency asking for ambulance and police support from neighboring Saint John's County, because twenty miles north of Saint Augustine there had been one head-on, followed by seventeen bumper-to-bumpers. The police radio asked for as many metal-cutting torches and crowbars as possible. The news of nineteen crushed and mangled cars had sent Junell flying out of Auto-Town in a great shower of crushed glass and gravel. She hadn't even stopped to close and lock the iron-grilled gate.

Easy left his International-Harvester pickup truck idling while he made sure the lock was secure on the gate. Then he climbed back into the cab and sat waiting for a chance to enter the road. It was black-surfaced macadam that ran about two hundred yards along the high yellow board fence before it finally entered the limited-access highway which arched over Auto-Town toward Jacksonville across the river. The road was a solid river of light that roared and blinked from bright to dim, dim to bright, flashed and swerved.

Easy sat relaxed and waiting in the cab of his International-Harvester, his hands loosely firm on the steering wheel. He trusted the truck. He knew what it could do. He had literally built it with his own hands for reasons of love. He had incorporated into the vehicle parts of cars not because they were the highest performance parts that could be found but because they were parts that held special memories and associations for him.

The truck was a 1937 and it had grown as he had grown. It had fenders on it from a 1940 Ford sedan, and a 1965 Lincoln Continental engine dropped into it by expanding the chassis to support it, and a
Continental transmission, and load-leveler shocks, and a crash bar
made of rolled and tempered steel, and countless other small modifica-
tions: a tachometer suspended from the headliner, pushbutton doors,
chrome airhorns mounted on the roof, Glaspak mufflers, tinted windshields, tape deck, air-conditioning, power steering, zebra-striped Naugahyde upholstering, and more. The truck throbbed and rocked where
he gunned it at the side of the road.

Then Easy saw not a break in the river of headlights pouring by but
the smallest hitch—a blink and a swerve, a little rapid in the flow of
light—and he hit the highway and wound it out to nearly fifty in first
gear, dropped to second and felt the racing slicks on the back of the
truck grab, and he was on his way to Jacksonville.

It was only about five miles to the Sherman Hotel from Auto-Town,
but it was more than twice that—better than ten miles—if he went on
the limited-access highway, which was the only possible way to go on a
Friday night because the traffic made the short way the long way. So he
drove the long way, locked into the streaming headlights, over the Saint
John's River into Southside and then over the Main Street bridge into
downtown Jacksonville. Because it was the start of the weekend, a lot of
young people were out in Cougars and Furys and Sting Rays and other
low, sleek, powerful cars. And Easy Mack drove defensively because he
was convinced they were dangerous.

The young people refused to lock into traffic and stay put. Instead,
they jockeyed for position, their oversized engines whining and snarling,
challenging for the right to break out and leave the pack. But cars were
bumper to bumper for twenty miles in any direction. There *was* no way
to leave the pack. Which made the night dangerous. But Easy Mack sat
contained and ready in his International-Harvester, glancing now and
again into the enormous chromed side mirrors, on the lookout for
young men and madmen.

When he got to the Sherman Hotel, he couldn't find a place to park.
He circled the block several times, each time trying not to look at Herman but looking anyway. Herman was on a high, specially built platform in front of the Sherman Hotel behind a sheet of clear bulletproof
plastic. There had been more than one threat on his life. They said

they'd kill him—shoot him dead—if he ate that car. But it hadn't stopped Herman. There he was, sitting up there beside a fire-engined Maverick ("A Ford six with a straight stick shift and no options" was the way it had been advertised in the Florida *Times-Union* newspaper).

Finally he swung into a Park 'N Lock building that covered the entire block next to the Sherman Hotel. It was completely automated and nobody was in attendance. A little machine spat a yellow time card at him when he swung onto the elevated ramp. He snatched the card on the way by and roared toward the second floor because a blinking light said the first floor was full. But so was the second floor, and Easy ended up parking on the twelfth floor and taking the elevator down.

The sidewalk in front of the Sherman Hotel was jammed with people looking up at Herman. A section of the walk was roped off and four special guards kept people back behind the rope barriers. Easy Mack did not know how to go about seeing his son. Herman was up above the marquee and there was no apparent way to get to him. Easy didn't want to talk to Mr. Edge, who owned the Sherman Hotel. He was anxious to avoid that. He went through the double glass doors into the instantly cold, red-carpeted lobby where the bell captain stood talking to a very young, very pretty girl in a blue miniskirt. She had red beads about her neck. Easy walked over to where they were. The girl smiled. The bell captain made a little bow and looked as though he wanted to click his heels.

"May I be of service, sir?" said the bell captain.

"Well, yeah," said Easy. Then he stopped. How to say it? He cursed the world that had given him a son sitting with a car on the top of the marquee of a hotel. "Could you help me see my son?" asked Easy. "I want to talk to him."

The girl, still smiling, told the bell captain good-bye and walked away toward the bank of elevators at the back of the lobby. The bell captain begged Easy's pardon, and Easy repeated it all again.

"And who is your son, sir?"

Somehow Easy thought the bell captain would know immediately that he was the father of Herman Mack. At the same time that he knew it was impossible, he thought everybody must be able to look at him and tell he had raised a son who was going to eat a car. It weighed heavily on his conscience.

"His name is Herman Mack," he said. Easy pointed toward the ceiling of the lobby. "And he's up…"

"But of course," said the bell captain. "Right this way, sir."

But the bell captain did not take him to see his son. Instead, he took him precisely where he did not want to go. He took him to see Mr. Edge, which—because he had never been in the hotel before—he did not understand until the bell captain opened a door and said: "It's him, Mr. Edge. Easy Mack," and left Easy standing in the door to a small plain office where a short man sat behind a desk, the top of which was completely bare except for a black telephone.

The short man stood up and smiled pleasantly, "Ah, Mr. Mack, so good of you to come," as though he had known all along that he was coming and had been sitting there waiting for the door to open.

But Easy knew that to be a lie no matter what Mr. Edge pretended. Mr. Edge had been out to Auto-Town twice to get them to come in to the Sherman Hotel for a family portrait. He wanted them to all stand behind Herman in front of the Ford Maverick and have their picture taken for the advertisements. Easy had thanked him very much, but said he didn't think so. He actually liked Mr. Edge. It was disturbing, but it was true. Mr. Edge was a hard man not to like. He was quiet and courteous and told Easy Mack that he knew how Easy felt, but that he, Homer Edge, was just trying to run a business—the hotel and entertainment business—and that the public expected a certain *something*, a little of the old pizazz, from a man in the hotel and entertainment business. Mr. Edge was dressed as usual in a plain black suit with a plain black tie over a white shirt. He had on black wing-tipped shoes with short black socks that showed four inches of very white, hairless shin when he sat down. He reminded Easy of an undertaker, and he wanted to get away from him as soon as he could and with as little talk as possible. It embarrassed him to talk with a stranger about his son Herman sitting on top of the marquee with a Ford Maverick.

"I'm not here for the family portrait," said Easy.

"Oh," said Mr. Edge. His smile got smaller and he sat down again at his desk. "How is Mister and Junell?"

"They all right," Easy said. "Junell's out on a run."

"I heard about that wreck," said Mr. Edge. "Out by Green Cove Springs. It's been on the news every thirty minutes. Sounds like a bad one."

"Well, they ain't no good ones," Easy said.

"That's the truth," said Mr. Edge. Mr. Edge had offered a chair with the motion of his hand, but Easy had remained standing. Easy liked him. It was remarkable how he liked him and how the two of them always got talking just as though the awful knowledge of Herman was not between them, just as though it wasn't Mr. Edge's power and organization that built the platform over the marquee and got the Ford agency to donate the Maverick for promotional consideration, just as though Mr. Edge was not going to pay Herman, a harmless dreamer, three hundred dollars a week to eat a car.

"I was just going to have a drink," Mr. Edge said. He brought a bottle out of a drawer in his desk. "Would you join me in a whiskey?"

There were few things he could think of that he'd have liked more just then, but it was clearly impossible. "No, I don't think so," Easy said.

A pained look came on Mr. Edge's face. "Easy, I wish you'd try to understand."

It annoyed Easy that Mr. Edge had used his first name. He knew well enough that Mr. Edge's first name was Homer, but he would never have thought to use it. He just chalked it up as another symptom of the general sickness of Mr. Edge's business.

"I saw him when I came up out front," said Easy, making a vague motion toward the ceiling with his hand.

"Yes, it's part of the preparation to let'm see him for a while."

"It didn't seem any way to get up there to see him."

"Oh, there's a way." Mr. Edge laughed. "You don't think we put him up there every night with a hook and ladder, do you?"

Easy did not laugh. "No sir, I don't."

The two men watched each other over the empty desk.

"You get onto the platform from the second floor," said Mr. Edge. "We'll move him into the ballroom when it comes time."

"Into the ballroom?"

"Well, I'm not going to have him..." Mr. Edge paused. "...well, *perform* out there free for the public."

Easy Mack was pleased to see that Mr. Edge apparently had trouble saying *eat a car*, too. He tried to remember if he'd ever heard him say it. He thought, and he couldn't remember.

"I've got to make my money back," said Mr. Edge. "You can see that."

"Listen," said Easy Mack, reaching behind him and snatching the door open. "I'm parked on the twelfth floor of the building next door and I can't stay long." That was as close as he could get to saying why he had come.

"And you wanted to see him?"

"Yes. See him."

Mr. Edge picked up the phone and asked for Number One, then put it down and said, "My bell captain will show you the way. Make yourself at home, stay as long as you like." Easy was already going through the door when Mr. Edge said: "Oh, and one other thing."

Easy stopped. "Yes?"

"Have the bell captain stamp your parking ticket." Mr. Edge smiled as though he were in pain and shrugged. "It's the least I can do. We have an arrangement with the Park 'N Lock."

Three

THEY had converted a window into a door on the second floor of the hotel. The bell captain led Easy down the freezing red-carpeted corridor to the door which obviously had been a window until very recently. Through the glass top of the door, Easy could see his son.

Herman was sitting on a stool. He was sitting very still. The top of the stool was red. The same shade of red as the Maverick, which was standing with its wheels blocked on a ramp beside the stool where Herman sat. The fluorescent light made little suns in the bulletproof plastic in front of Herman.

Beyond the plastic whole families stood together on the other side of the street looking up at Herman. Many of them seemed to be eating one thing or another: cotton candy on brown-cardboard cones, peanuts out of paper sacks, and at least one family sat on the curbstone eating out of a box of Colonel Sanders' Kentucky Fried Chicken. Easy could see Colonel Sanders' white hair and white beard even at this distance. From time to time several children waved. Herman did not wave back. Easy wondered how they got the car onto the marquee.

"There he is," said the bell captain with satisfaction.

Easy went through the door and closed it behind him. The noise of traffic and shouts and stamping feet roared below. He went over and leaned against the fender of the Maverick. Herman looked at him and smiled shyly in a way that broke Easy's heart. Such a gentle boy. He was always such a gentle boy.

"I'm glad you could come, daddy," Herman said.

"Well," said Easy Mack. "Well." He ran his hand over the shining hood of the Maverick. He backed off and inspected the wheel. Then he kicked the tire. "They tell me these are good little cars."

"That's what they say," Herman said.

"Your ordinary Ford was always a good little car," said Easy.

"Best in its price range, they say," said Herman.

"I always thought so," said Easy.

A silence fell between them which seemed louder in Easy's ears than the noise below. He hung his skinny shank over the fender of the Maverick and he and Herman sat watching the family finish up the fried chicken in the Colonel Sanders box. The mother carefully put all the bones and napkins and empty gravy cups back into the box and set it on the sidewalk where her small son turned the box on its side, backed off, aimed carefully, and kicked it. Chicken bones and napkins and gravy cups flew across Forsyth Street.

"What do you think of the hotel?" asked Herman. Herman had not been home in two weeks. He had a room on the fifteenth floor, given him as part of the agreement by Mr. Edge.

"I'd seen this place before," Easy said.

"I meant inside. Had you ever been inside?"

"Not before tonight."

"What do you think of it?"

"Cold enough in there to keep hamburger," Easy said.

"That air-conditioning's something," Herman said.

They sat looking down at the street. The crowd had grown. More people had stopped since Easy had joined his son over the marquee. Easy shifted nervously on the fender of the Maverick. He didn't know how long he'd be able to stand them looking up here at him this way.

"I don't know how you can stand them looking up here at you like this," said Easy.

"Oh, it's all right," said Herman. "I don't mind a bit. Besides, they're looking at the Maverick as much as they're looking at me."

Easy blushed and popped down off the fender of the car. It had suddenly occurred to him what he was sitting on. He looked back at the red car as if seeing it for the first time. Herman, a shy boy always, was blushing too and seemed to know what Easy was thinking.

"It's all right to set on it, daddy," Herman said. "That won't hurt a bit."

Easy turned angrily on his son. "Boy, when the hell you coming home?"

"Sir?"

"You know what I said, and you know why I'm here." Easy had meant above all else not to lose his temper. But fuck it, he wasn't getting anywhere and the crowd was getting bigger every minute.

"And you know why *I'm* here," said Herman, softly, calmly. "It's on the television and the radio and every newspaper in the state."

As calmly and softly as he spoke, the boy's voice still rang with pride, and Easy Mack simply could not make himself believe that this was *his* Herman.

"Boy, are you proud of this?"

"I don't guess I'm setting out here because I'm ashamed of it," Herman said, his voice now taking an unfamiliar edge.

"Have you lost your mind, Herman? Has something slipped in there and made you crazy? Just tell me if it did and I'll do everything I can to help you. I've got a right to know."

"I don't know what you've got a right to, daddy. But I know I'm thirty years old, never had anything, nothing. We been squatting out there on those mountains of rusting cars, and it ain't coming to nothing. But now, at last, I've got something."

"That's what I've come to find out, son. What've you got?"

"I've got something to *do*. At last I've got something I *can* do."

"But for God's sake, why? Why would you want to...to..."

"Why would I want . . . to . . . eat . . . a . . . car?" Herman said the words very slowly as though he might be tasting them. "I can tell you. The car is where we are in America." He paused again and said slowly, "I'm going to eat a car because it's there."

But Easy had already heard that on the television advertisements and read it in the *Times-Union* newspaper. And he had recognized it immediately as a lie. Or if not a lie, at least something that evaded the truth.

"Are you going to eat a tree after you get through with a car?"

"Sir?"

"A tree? Eat one because it's there? It'd make as much sense."

Herman smiled fondly up at him where he stood next to the Maverick. "Now, daddy, don't say something like that. You know better. How can you talk about trees and cars in the same breath?" He waved his hand toward the street below. "Look at that," he said, "just look at that."

Forsyth Street was one way going west; and there below them, four lanes of traffic had gradually come to a honking, roaring halt. It was partly due to the weekend rush and partly due to the crowd overflowing the sidewalks looking up at Herman. But whatever it was, the traffic was there, stalled and solid and roaring in a gaseous mist of combustion.

"You don't see a tree down there," Herman said matter-of-factly. "Not a one. Your car is where it's at." He put a hand on each knee, lifted his chest, and breathed deeply. "Smell it? Smell that?"

The air was blue. The day had been overcast and now a thermal lid enclosed the life of the city, pressing their breathing and the breathing of the racing gasoline engines back upon the streets. In a slow horror Easy realized that Herman liked it, liked the bumper-to-bumper cars there below, liked the noseburning, eyewatering emissions from hundreds of smoky tailpipes.

It was like finding out that your son liked to hang around public restrooms smelling the toilets, or that he was secretly eating shit.

Who would have thought it would come to this? Who would have thought it *could* have come to this? Easy remembered the first car he had ever seen. High and square and shining and open. Sure it had been noisy. But everything else had been so quiet that the noise had been beautiful and singular for the very reason it was manmade. It had been smoky too, but the smoke had only been lovely on the pristine, almost brittly pure air of the world.

Easy saw the flash. And then saw it again before he saw Mr. Edge standing beside and directing a man with a camera on a tripod, a camera wearing the long expanding snout of a zoom lens. The son-of-a-bitch had his picture. His Family Portrait. Or as much of the family as he wanted. Mr. Edge had made it plain that all he *really* wanted was the father. Well, he had the father, and in that helpless and hopeless moment, Easy knew that they were going to do it, do it all. It didn't matter whether he, Easy Mack, understood it or not. It didn't matter whether he loved and grieved for his son or not. And it was utterly of no consequence whether he wanted it to happen or not. They were going to arrange everything so his son could eat a car.

In a flat dispirited voice, Easy Mack asked: "How are you going to do it?"

"Do what?"

"Eat it. How are you going to eat it?"

"If you don't know that, you don't know anything," Herman said. "We've explained it on every TeeVee show and in every newspaper ad."

"I guess I always turned off the television or stopped reading before I got to that part."

"Swallow it piece by piece. Half-ounce cubes. Burn the edges so they won't be jagged. Encapsulate the oil and gas and things like glass and seat covers and things."

Easy felt his own stomach lurch, then squeeze. "Encapsulate?"

Herman smiled. "Learned that from Mr. Edge. It just means put that stuff in a capsule, a capsule that won't digest, so I can pass it. You'd be surprised the stuff I've learned from Mr. Edge. If you didn't encapsulate it, you could never swallow stuff like seat covers and windshields and oil out of the crankcase."

Easy turned his back on the street and the crowd below. "I guess I'll go," he said.

"Daddy?"

"Yes."

"You always knew I wanted to be somebody. I never come right out and told you. But you always knew it, didn't you?"

"Yes, I think maybe I did."

"A man has to take the chances that come to him. You can just set out there on the mountain of wrecked cars so long before you have to make your move. You can see that."

Easy took another long look at the Maverick. A horrible wave of nausea swept up from his stomach, and he had to swallow against the thick warm smell of vomit.

"Junell and Mister," said Herman: "say hi to them for me."

Easy snatched the door open and rushed down the freezing corridor. He passed the elevator and took the stairs down. Mr. Edge was standing in the lobby with the photographer. He went directly to Mr. Edge, who saw him coming and flashed a smile and threw up his pudgy hand.

"I saw your man with that camera," said Easy Mack.

"Got some good shots," said Mr. Edge, "some great shots."

"You use that picture of me and that goddam Maverick and I'll sue you." Easy tried not to strangle but did in spite of himself, gagging a little behind his closed fist.

"Easy, I wish you'd try to remember that he came to me," said Mr. Edge, making a soft fat little shrug with his shoulders. "The boy came to me, I didn't come to him." The fat between his eyes got firmer but he still smiled. "I'm trying to run a business here. Why don't you go run yours?"

Easy turned in a blind rush and half ran over the bell captain, who was talking again to the girl in the blue mini-skirt and red-bead choker.

"And one other thing, Easy," called Mr. Edge.

Easy stopped and looked back.

"I got you and him and the Maverick all in the picture. He's a public personality, Herman is. I can put the picture anywhere I want to, any-time I want to. And if you sue, it'll just help the sales when the show re-ally starts." Homer Edge did not smile at all while he spoke.

But neither did Easy when he said, "There's other things besides su-ing, things that won't help the sales a goddam bit."

Easy went out of the lobby into the street. The hot wet blue air clung to his face and neck, the backs of his hands. He twisted his neck to look up at Herman smiling wildly on the red stool beside the Ford Maverick.

My son! My son! You always wanted to be somebody. God help you, now you are.

Easy put his head down and walked away from the crowd toward the Park 'N Lock where his International-Harvester waited on the twelfth floor.

He had forgot to have the bell captain stamp his yellow time ticket.

Four

BIG Mama had a supercharged eight in her and she could do a hundred and fifteen miles an hour on the straight, a fantastic speed for an eight-ton tow truck with ten wheels on the ground. But it was only by having such fantastic speed that Junell was able to compete. It was the only way, so she had taken it. Junell felt how basically unnatural it was to have a racing ratio in the rear-end of a tow truck used for hauling ruined cars, but without such a transmission, she'd never get to tow anything back to Auto-Town.

When the call went out on the police radio that there had been an accident on the state highways involving more than one car, wreckers (which word she never used. Hers was a tow truck, thank you) from a half-dozen cities roared out onto the roads, all aimed at getting to the accident first and getting away with a mashed car. They sometimes had awful accidents in their efforts to arrive first on the scene of the accident. But it was the only way if you wanted to come back a winner with something hanging on the back of your tow truck.

So Junell had Big Mama's red lights and blue lights popping on and off, and her airhorns singing and her throttle three-quarters open even though it was a Friday night and the double lanes on Highway U.S. 1 were filled with cars. Once already she had to take to the grassy median with Big Mama, and once she had to force a Volkswagen to back down, but she knew what she was doing.

There was a little private hospital four miles south of Jacksonville that did a pretty good business off collisions and roll-overs and wounded hitchhikers from the highway, and Junell always tried to tie in with one of their ambulances when she was able to. You had a better chance at making a claim on one of the mashed cars if you could tie in with an ambulance. The ambulances all had sirens, which the wreckers were not allowed to have, so if you could just cut in behind one of those wailing ambulances, traffic parted in front of you and you were sure to return with something hanging on the back of your truck.

The ambulances didn't exactly belong to the hospital, they belonged to an ambulance service that had sprung up next door to the hospital and Junell knew that they would have every one of their ambulances out on this one. If she was lucky she would catch one. She rounded a long slow curve north of the hospital and saw the low gray silhouette of an ambulance slip into traffic headed south, and at the same time she saw it, she heard the pulsing moan of the siren that rose to a scream as the ambulance picked up speed.

Junell hunched over the wheel and eased Big Mama's throttle open. It was as though the scream of the ambulance's siren was a winch that reeled Big Mama in. Junell put the tow truck right on the gray limousine's bumper and hung there like magic.

The ambulance driver waved out the window. His name was Bubba, and Junell was fond of him. He had hair as yellow and silky as a baby's and Junell thought he was awfully young for an ambulance driver. But God, could he handle that rig! It was a joy to watch him work. His yellow hair lifted now in the whipping wind as he one-handed the ambulance through a tight series of maneuvers involving a Greyhound bus, a panel truck, and—strangely, because you rarely saw more than one at a time—two Saabs.

The other attendant, Bubba's partner, who was named George, was lying in the back of the ambulance on the white-sheeted roll bed taking oxygen, which he frequently did when he came on the late shift with an intolerable hangover. He was a sullen, middle-aged man, with dark yellowish skin and a head as slick and hairless as an egg. He could only use the oxygen when they were out on a run and away from his supervisor, so if the hangover was really a bad one, he often stayed on the green cylinder of oxygen for the entire trip. As Bubba swung and weaved through the heavy traffic, George rolled and pitched on the bed, but he kept the black oxygen mask to his face. Junell knew it was a terrible hangover.

You could see the accident long before you ever got to it on U.S. 1. Flares lit up a stretch of highway almost two miles long. Most of the wrecked cars were off the highway, either in the ditch or on the grassy median. The highway patrol had been able to keep one lane open to keep the traffic from stacking up too badly. When they got close enough that they could see the popping flares and whirling lights of patrol cars and the still burning lights of wrecked cars, at least three of them upside-down, and the multicolored lights of what looked like dozens of wreckers—when they got close enough to see it, Bubba swung out of the line of cars and went roaring off down the median strip with Junell right behind him. Bubba stopped where four patrol cars formed a barrier. He cut his lights and siren, got out, leaned on the door, and lit a cigarette. He smoked and waited for Junell to get out of Big Mama and come up and join him. George never moved from his bed in the back of the ambulance.

Junell left Big Mama's lights on and her motor running. She touched a lever and let the winch chain down. She wanted to be ready. Jesus, it was a bad one, you couldn't even get in to claim a car. But she knew she'd be taken care of. Joe, who was not her fiancé but said he was, would be here. Besides, they all knew her. And most of the wreckers (she didn't mind the word for other people's trucks) were from body shops anyway. They were interested only if the car could be repaired. But Junell wanted just those that had been totaled. There weren't many wreckers that were out for totals, so she was always willing to be civilized about it because she knew she'd get her fair share.

As she walked up to Bubba, four men with welders' masks on and acetylene torches in their hands rushed by. Another man followed with a gas cylinder on a two-wheeled dolly.

"How're they hanging, girl?" asked Bubba, his smiling child's face wreathed in smoke.

Junell refused to wear a bra under her leathers and Bubba always made a big thing out of it. But it was all in good fun, buddy to buddy, one driver to another.

"They're all right" said Junell. "Yours?"

"Mine ain't hanging," he said. "They squeezed right up next to me after that ride."

"You can drive that dam rig," she said in honest admiration.

"Some got five talents, some only one," he said. "Mine's in a short clutch and a straight shift."

"That thing's not got a stick in it," she said, pointing to the ambulance. She was talking wildly, saying the first thing that came to her, afraid as she was that Bubba was going to start talking about Herman. Everybody wanted to talk about her brother. And she did not know what to say.

"I wouldn't drive it, if it didn't" he said.

As they talked, the night was ripped by blaring horns, the shouts of angry drivers, and cries for help. An enormous highway patrolman walked up. His belly, mobile and round as a ball, swung under his khaki shirt.

"Joe's right over there," said the patrolman to Junell. "He's got you one staked."

"Right," Junell said.

She was hurrying away when the patrolman said: "Herman started on that car yet?"

It was such a direct, simple question, there was no way to evade it. "No, not yet," she said, looking back.

"I want you to tell him something for me," the patrolman said.

"Yeah?"

"Tell him I admire him."

She didn't say anything, just stood there watching the patrolman.

"Tell him he's got my admiration. I'm in his corner."

"That goes for me too," Bubba said.

They stood leaning on the door of the ambulance. Junell thought she might cry. "Sure," she said. "I'll tell him that."

When Junell had first heard about Herman's latest caper—eating a car—she had dismissed it as some kind of harmless publicity stunt. Herman *was* a dreamer, and if he said he was going to swallow a car, it only meant that he had something else up his sleeve, and the business of eating a car was just a way to call attention to it. But she had gone to see him at the Hotel Sherman and found out that he really meant to do it. And while she was there she had found out that opinion was divided on the spectacle.

Herman had been threatened. Contempt had been heaped upon his head. His own father said that he might cut Herman out of his Last Will and Testament. But most of the people most of the time seemed to love Herman for what he was about to do. They saw it as an act of great courage. They felt the pride that a man would have to have to attempt such a thing.

When Junell met anybody these days, she never knew which way they would jump. And she was so emotionally involved with Herman and his determination to eat a car that when people were contemptuous and angry like her brother Mister she was ready to fight, but when, like Bubba and the patrolman back there, people said they were behind

Herman all the way, said they knew he'd swallow every goddam ounce of that Maverick car, then she just choked up and felt her eyes go hot with tears and love.

Joe was directing a welder who was cutting the trunk out of a Barracuda. There were three tow-truck drivers standing around smoking and talking. They nodded and spoke to her and then stepped back in a tight little knot to watch. And again, she felt Herman's presence, as the drivers backed away, watching her secretively as though to find in her the reason for Herman's obsession. Ordinarily the three tow-truck drivers watching her now would have been joshing her, mock complaining about Joe staking a claim for her on a total. But tonight, they grunted briefly in her direction and watched.

Joe saw her and stood up from where he'd been squatting with the welder. The Barracuda was on its back. The doors were pleated like curtains. The car had obviously been hit from the back and in turn had run head-on into something. Joe had his flat-brimmed highway patrol hat pushed onto the back of his head. His young sharp face shone in the light of the welder's torch.

"Anybody alive in there?" asked Junell.

"Well, somebody is alive in there," Joe said, "or some *thing*. Maybe it's a dog. Sounds a little like one. Jesus, what a fucking night. Nineteen goddam cars. I got in here first and the wreckers started coming and I didn't have time to check anything." He pointed to the Barracuda. "A goddam wrecker tied onto this one and was hauling it out when I heard somebody scream in it. The driver would have hauled it back to the yard with a whole family in it."

"A family?" Junell said.

"I got down and felt in through one of the windows and shined my light around in there," Joe said. "I think it's a family. Everything I could touch or see seemed dead though."

"This one mine?" she asked.

"Right," he said. "A total."

Something inside the Barracuda screamed.

"That's not a dog," said Junell.

"Didn't sound like it that time," admitted Joe. "But a while ago it sounded just like a dog."

They listened for it to scream again, but it didn't.

"You want to step over here to the cruiser?" Joe asked. "He'll be a while with that torch. He's got to cut through part of the chassis too to get in there."

"Sure," she said. "I don't mind."

They walked over to the cruiser. It was a four-door Chrysler with a special bored and stroked engine that could produce five hundred horsepower. Joe opened the door and they got in the back seat. A foreshortened double-barreled riot gun stood in a cradle on the back of the front seat.

Joe's cruiser was part of a special force patrolling the highways of the state. A special force full of special men. Not only did you have to be of a certain height and weight to be on the special force, but you also had to be a high school graduate and, finally, a great handler of cars—a natural driver.

Joe had perfect vision and the reflexes of a ping-pong champion. He was a mechanic whose expertise was so great that they let him build and modify his own car. Before joining the highway patrol he had been known and feared on dirt-tracks and back streets all over the Southeast. And he was in love with Junell.

"Junell," he said, raising his voice to get over the sound of a siren passing just to their left, "I love you."

Outside, the night flashed and popped with blinking spinning lights. Motors revved and backfired. Something screamed inside the crushed Barracuda. But in the Chrysler, in the midst of the terrific odor of combustion, Joe had begun as he always did, with a confession of love. He told her he loved her and caught the zipper of her jacket and zipped it down and groaned like a dying man at the sight of her breasts white and full of sweat, popping free and pendulous. Junell sighed and leaned back against the seat. Joe carefully removed his wide-brimmed highway patrol hat and put it on the front seat. She watched him go down on her breasts, his mouth sucking like a baby's before he ever got there. The top of his incredibly flat crewcut head was just level with her eyes.

"How was it out there today?" she asked softly.

He chewed desperately at her nipple and did not answer. But she knew he would. He always did. They had never had a date, never been out together. They only met at wrecks. But that meant they saw each other four, maybe five times a week. Sometimes more. They necked in the back seat of his cruiser. Joe never tried to go all the way. Joe had been the youngest Eagle Scout in the history of the state, and he respected Junell. That was the second thing he always told her. First he told her he loved her and then he said he respected her.

"I respect you for this," he said, his mouth full of her breast.

Then, after having said what he always said, with the amenities out of the way, he was content to lie between her breasts—now and then taking a long pull at one of them as though drinking from a stream—and tell her about his car.

Junell loved to hear about that car, that Chrysler Cruiser. He'd talk about how it had run that morning, how he'd stopped and made a minute adjustment on one of the two four-barrel carburetors. His voice would get high and urgent as he put together the story of a chase: laying a hundred-yard streak of rubber, a curve taken in a power slide, maybe—once in a while—a few bullets would come flying back at him from the car he was chasing, then he'd whip out his special tire-shooting gun, a thirty-ought-six, and blast the tires off the car he was chasing (his ping-pong champion reflexes never failed him) and watch the car swerve, roll over, vault into the air and, if he was lucky, explode. And while he talked he would from time to time give Junell a great probing grope up between her beleathered thighs, and without exception, when he gave her the grope, he always stopped whatever he was telling her about and said:

"I respect you for this."

And she would take the profession of his respect without saying anything so as not to interrupt the story of the car, anxious as she was for him to get back to tune-ups, adjustments, new speed equipment he'd found for his supercar to make it even more super, faster, and more powerful.

"*Joe!*" It was the welder calling from the Barracuda.

Joe gave a quick suck to each of her breasts, a quick kiss on her mouth, a darting probe to her thighs, told Junell he loved her, grabbed his wide-brimmed patrol hat off the front seat, and bounded out of the Chrysler. Junell sighed. He'd been right in the middle of telling her about a new fuel mixture he'd been fooling around with. She palmed her breasts back into her jacket, zipped up, and followed him out to the wrecked car.

The scream belonged to a six-year-old girl. Or what had once been a six-year-old girl. Or what they *thought* had once been a six-year-old girl. She was wedged onto the floor in front of the back seat with the stick

shift from the Barracuda stuck through her pelvis. Her legs were doubled back under her. One of her arms was torn off at the elbow. She was
a lump of blood that screamed.

"Jesus," said Joe. "Jesus Christ."

"Godamighty," Junell said.

"She's a mess," said one of the tow-truck drivers.

An enormous piece of the chassis driven up through the body of the
car had been cut out of the way by the welder and they could plainly see
the rest of the family now. There was a body wearing a bloody business
suit, but no head. A woman had been ripped open from breastbone
downward. Her guts lay in her lap. A small boy hung dead from the
windshield, hanging half in and half out of the shattered glass.

George, his eyes webbed in veins and his skin yellower than ever,
came in with Bubba and made a tourniquet for the girl's arm and put
her on a roll bed, where her blood instantly soaked through and dripped
in slow thick drops onto the grass. Other ambulance drivers rushed in
and claimed the other bodies. Joe and Junell watched Bubba, with
George sitting in the back beside the dying girl giving himself oxygen,
roar off down the highway back toward Jacksonville.

"Well, I guess I better tie on and head out," Junell said.

"Yeah, I guess," Joe said. He took his patrolman hat off and turned it
slowly in his hands. He shifted from foot to foot. "Listen," he said.

She knew instantly that he wanted to say something about Herman.
Something that he was finding difficult.

"What?" she said.

"You know last time I was joking about your brother, that Herman?"

"Yes?"

"I believe he means to do it," he said.

"It looks like it," she said. "It looks like he does."

"Does it make you feel . . . feel funny?"

"Not funny," she said.

"You know what I mean."

"I guess I do."

"Listen, I love you," he blurted out. "And I respect you."

"I know that," she said.

Five

HERMAN couldn't sleep. He kept thinking about *it*, the car. He couldn't stop thinking about it being right down the hall, blocked up on that ramp, waiting. Four days ago he'd had Mr. Edge give him another suite, bring him down off the fifteenth floor of the Hotel Sherman so he could sleep on the same floor with the Ford Maverick.

"You what?" said Mr. Edge.

"I want to sleep on the same floor with it."

Mr. Edge, sitting behind the bare desk in his empty grubby little office, examined the floor under his feet, and said, "You want to sleep on the same floor with it?"

"Right."

Mr. Edge looked at him with tired dark-rimmed eyes. "You're not getting freaky on me, are you, son?"

"No, sir," Herman said.

As the day got closer when Herman would actually begin to eat the car, Mr. Edge's face got tireder and darker. There was a rumor that some Society For The Prevention Of Something was going to try to stop Herman. Mr. Edge had begun saying ten or twelve times a day to anybody who would listen and sometimes to nobody at all: "I've got a lot of money invested here. I *have* got a lot of money invested here."

"Our agreement was that you would not get freaky on me," said Mr. Edge.

"Yes, sir. That was the agreement."

"I mean we've got a business deal," Mr. Edge said, "nothing more. So don't get freaky on me."

"Right. No, sir," said Herman. "But still . . ."

"But what?"

"But still I *have* to eat it. Finally, *I* am the one who's got to eat the car."

Mr. Edge seemed to grow darker and sag in himself. "Yes, eat the car," he said. "And you're concentrating, is that it? You're beginning to concentrate and you want to be on the same floor so you can concentrate."

"That's it," said Herman.

So Herman's quarters had been moved down from the fifteenth floor where he had the Bimini Suite to the second floor where he had a single room and a bath which was called the Honeymoon Special and was right down the hall from the brilliant red Maverick.

But it was not to concentrate. Herman could concentrate easily enough on the car from the fifteenth floor. He could have concentrated on it from the dark side of the moon. The Maverick was stamped on the back of both eyelids so that it was what he immediately saw the moment he closed his eyes. He listened to the rhythm of his heart and it beat to the cadence of six perfectly tuned and firing cylinders.

Herman swung his feet over the side of the bed. This was the second night he'd gone without sleep. He looked at the clock on the nightstand beside the bed. Seven minutes after four A.M. He got up and put on his shirt and trousers and, barefoot, went out of his room and down the hall to the new door over the marquee. He looked through the glass and there it was. Ramped and blocked, glowing dully, the fluorescent light off now, but two special show lights on, rigged by Mr. Edge himself to make the Maverick look like it floated there on the front of the hotel. Herman went quietly through the door, his heart racing. The street below was empty. The moon was pale and diffused through the thermal haze that pressed upon the city.

Herman had always felt himself special, felt himself being saved by a force bigger than himself and outside himself, saved to do some fantastic and special thing that would set him apart from other men. He had felt it as a youngster when his father got Mister, Junell, and him a job washing the cars on Flint's Honest Deal Used Lot every morning before school, and he had felt it later when he worked in the parts department of the Downtown Ford Agency, and he still felt it the day he was taken into the business at Easy Mack's Auto-Town.

Herman had never had any luck talking about this feeling. The first time he had mentioned it was to his brother Mister. It was right after the state had jammed through the expressway, a six-lane, limited-access road that soared seventy feet over Auto-Town where it joined Turner Memorial Bridge that went over the Saint John's River to Jacksonville.

Ten minutes after they opened the expressway, a truck coming over the bridge lost its airbrakes and was abandoned by the driver who died instantly when he jumped from the speeding truck and was run over by a tailgating Toyota. The truck smashed through the concrete divider and met the officials from the ribbon-cutting ceremonies—a whole autocade of them complete with motorcycle escorts and the state beauty Queen riding in an open convertible.

The truck destroyed the autocade. And it took the entire night to free the expressway. They ended by taking down the guardrails and pushing the wrecked cars right over the side where they fell some seven stories down from the expressway into Easy Mack's Auto-Town.

"Hot damn," said Mister, dancing a little jig, "that's making money."

Herman and Mister were standing down in the yard watching cars fall from the sky. The full cheesy breath of the river was everywhere about them, drifting in and among the mountains of wrecked automobiles. It was already after dark and the three lanes that were open on the expressway above them roared with light. And on the west side— the side jammed full of the wreck—huge unrecognizable lumps of metal fell with the sound of cannon into the yard in front of where they stood.

"God," said Herman, "it's scary."

"Nothing scary about making money," Mister said.

But that wasn't what Herman meant and he told him so.

"Then what the hell *do* you mean?"

Herman didn't know exactly but he tried to tell Mister, because Mister was closer to him than anyone else and because if he could say it to Mister then he would know himself.

"Did you ever think you wanted more than this?" Herman asked.

"Damn right," said Mister. "And Junell does too, and I *know* daddy does." He burst into laughter as something that had once been an Oldsmobile came vaulting off the expressway. "Someday I want these forty-three acres to be forty-three miles deep in wrecked cars. Wow! Pow! Right up to the fucking sky!"

"I don't mean more *of* this," Herman said. "More *than* this."

"Oh Jesus," said Mister. He stopped laughing. "You're not going to do something, are you?"

Herman, even then, was known as a dreamer and he knew his family was uneasy for him, or maybe only uneasy for themselves, afraid as they were that he was going to do something that would cause fingers to be pointed at all of them.

"I only know there must be more than this," said Herman.

"What *are* you talking about?" Mister asked. "Do you even know?"

A highway patrolman had come and asked them to step a little far-ther back. He was afraid they would be hit by a falling car.

"I only know that I refuse to have my life measured out in cars," cried Herman, choking on the knowledge of some awful truth that he could not say. "Goddam cars are measuring *me! Me!* Don't you see we're on the wrong end?"

"Maybe *you* are," said Mister slowly. "I don't know what end *I'm* on. Don't know. Don't care. But I know that I own a quarter interest in the largest car-wrecking business in the state. That's good enough for me."

"Well, it's not for me," said Herman, trembling where he stood on the glassy earth. He was looking into the crushed mouth of an Edsel that had just landed in front of them. "If there's any measuring to be done I'll do it." His wailing voice lifted over the Edsel and the other cars and over the expressway itself: "I'll take the fucking measure."

Mister, alarm and grief clearly showing in his face, put his arm around his brother's shoulders and said, soft as a lover: "There, there, there, maybe your chance will come."

And his chance had come. He was standing on the marquee of the largest hotel in Jacksonville, Florida, looking at his chance. He reached out his hand and with the end of his finger touched the flaring nostrils of the maverick. A lifting swell of excitement, so great that he could hardly bear it, ran in his chest. He traced the curved powerful horns with his finger. Finally, he closed his hand over the maverick and, gazing up into the weakened diffused moonlight, sighed.

He looked down from the moon, went closer, and lay his long thick body over the hood. The metal was cool as some wide slab of stone be-side a stream. And he imagined it so—a stone beside a stream—and he remembered the voices as they had been there in the street below this afternoon, the babbling broken voices coming up to him as sound from a stream breaks over stone. And he was utterly at peace stretched out there on the hood with his cheek pressed tightly against the thing he loved.

He solemnly opened his mouth as though about to take upon his tongue a sacrament, but instead his pink lolling tongue lapped out of his mouth and touched metal, touched the hood of the Maverick car. It was clean and cold and he felt himself tighten around his stomach. He longed to have it in his mouth. To feel it in his throat. To hold it in his stomach. It would amaze the world.

"It's a nice night, Herman."

It was the girl. He knew without looking that it was the girl. He slowly pulled in his tongue and deliberately closed his mouth. He rolled over on the hood of the car. She was standing where he knew she would be, over by the door, wearing her blue miniskirt and choker of red beads. She was a hotel whore and her name was Margaret. But she liked to be called Margo. She said she had no last name.

"Nice enough," Herman said, "nice enough." He looked up where the moon was trying to show itself. "I couldn't sleep, so I got up and come out here to catch a breath of air."

"I guess you're nervous," said Margo.

"Oh, I'm nervous all right," Herman said.

"You've got every right to be," she said.

She walked over and put her saddle on the maverick. He watched it. He had his eye right on it. The miniskirt was made of some fine material that lay against the lines of her body. And he saw the pie-shaped wedge of her pussy press directly against the emblem on the front of the car.

"I thought to keep you company," she said.

But he knew it was the Maverick she had come to keep company as much as it was him. She had had the bell captain introduce her to him two days ago.

"Herman," the bell captain said, "this young lady'd like to meet you."

Herman thought she had come for his autograph. Mr. Edge let people in for a free autograph between the hours of two and four every day, and since Herman could never keep up with what time it was, he started scribbling his name onto a sticker—suitable for framing and donated by the same agency that donated the Maverick. The sticker said: FORD GIVES YOU BETTER IDEAS.

"No, no," said the bell captain. "She didn't come for that. She's not one of them, she's one of us. Her name is Margaret. Margaret, this is Herman Mack."

"I like to be called Margo," she said. "I'm a hotel whore. I work for Mr. Edge too." She went over to the car and touched the emblem of the maverick. "Is this the one you're going to eat?"

"From bumper to bumper," said Herman Mack.

And he had liked Margo from that moment on, from the moment she had touched the Maverick. He could tell—or thought he could—that she was glad he was going to eat it. She loved that Ford. Her young face absolutely glowed when she looked at it. And the touch of her hand was the touch of a lover. But loving it as she did, she was still glad he was going to eat it.

Margo walked past him where he sat now on the fender of the car and leaned against the bulletproof shield and looked down into the empty street.

"Tomorrow's the day," she said, not looking at him.

"It's not really *the* day," he said. "We just move into the ballroom tomorrow."

"At least after that there won't be anybody else looking at you free," she said. "At least after you get to the ballroom, the son-of-a-bitches'll have to pay."

"Yes," he said, "today ends the freebees."

"That always bothered me," she said, "them looking at you free. It's not right."

"Well, Mr. Edge's been paying me right along. Three hundred a week since it started."

"Sure he's paying *you*," she said. "But *they're* not paying. That's what burns my ass. *They're* getting it free."

Herman wished she wouldn't talk about her ass. He didn't want to think about her ass. He wanted to think about car. Car, he thought, car car car car car car car. But out of the corner of his eye he saw the scooped indentation of her perfect ass. Ass, he thought, ass ass ass ass ass ass ass ass. And it broke his heart, because it was against his will, against everything he wanted to do.

She came over and climbed up on the hood of the car. She stretched her legs out and leaned back against the windshield. Herman got off the fender, went around and got in the front seat. Her ass, pressed into neat rolls and divided, was just there in front of him on the glass.

"You know where I was a year ago this time?" she asked.

"Where?" he asked in a strangled voice.

"High school," she said. "I was a cheerleader for the football team."

"Right," he said, not listening. He had leaned forward and taken the top of the steering wheel between his teeth.

"But the fullback had a Vette," she said.

He took his teeth off the steering wheel.

"And I ended up in an orange grove."

"A goddam orange grove?" he said.

"On my back," she said. She laughed. Her voice was conversational, offhand. "There was no way he could have missed. It was a snow-white Vette with Goodyear racing slicks. It was the night of the championship game and he scored four touchdowns, a school record. He came out of the locker room like a bull, threw me in that Vette, roared away from the stadium and whipped in the first orange grove we passed just south of Tampa. He dragged me right up on top of that Vette and drove me like a truck." She slid down on the hood of the Maverick, turned, and smiled at him through the windshield.

Herman had always been shy with women, intimidated by them. Junell had a man who said he was her fiancé (she had taken the family with her in Big Mama one Sunday and introduced them to the young man at a wreck) and Mister had been divorced twice, but Herman had not had a girlfriend since childhood. They scared him. So now caught in her smile, he said the only thing he could say.

"Day after tomorrow at six o'clock sharp, I've got to swallow the first bite of the bumper."

She stopped smiling. "Do you think you can do it?"

"No problem," he said. "A half-ounce of metal, burned with a torch so there's no jagged edges."

"I mean the whole car. Do you think you can swallow the whole car?"

"I honestly don't know." It was the first time he had admitted that to anyone. "I'll have to take it as it comes."

"How much will you swallow a day?"

"I'll start with a half-pound a day. Doc thinks I can handle that."

"Doc's all right," she said. "He won't steer you wrong."

Mr. Edge's doctor, the same one that examined Margo every week to make sure she didn't have the clap or something worse, had examined Herman.

"He's helped me a lot. He had me swallow some different weight ball bearings to see how they'd pass."

"And the half-ounce worked the best?"

"Right," Herman said. "We settled on the half-ounce."

"That's great," she said, "really great."

She got off the hood and came round to the door and got in. She reached up and touched the overhead with her hand. She stretched her arms and seemed to measure the width of the car from window to window. They sat a long time, their eyes running over the lines of the car, while down in the street an enormous sweeper roared up one curb and down the other. Motes of dust rose and hung in the light outside the bulletproof plastic. Finally the sweeper roared to the corner and turned. They listened to the sound of the sweep diminish and fall to silence between the high buildings of Hogan Street. When it was quiet, she measured the car again with her eyes: the rubber mats, the compressed plastic steering wheel, even the metal door handles. He saw what she was doing.

"It won't be easy," he said. "I never said it was going to be easy."

"No, it won't be easy," she smiled at him, "but then nothing is." She put her hand on his hand. It was the first time she had ever touched him. "Listen," she said. "I'm with you all the way."

"You are?"

"One hundred percent," said Margo. "Anything I can do for you, say the word, *anything*."

Herman blushed. Her eyes had caught the blue of her skirt and were as translucent as glass. There was an urgency in her voice and a nakedness that Herman had never heard in a voice before. He didn't know what it meant and he didn't know what to do with it.

"You've never come to me," she said. She looked away from him toward the blank face of the building across the street. "I thought you might, but you never have." She looked back at him. "You know it's free to you, don't you?"

"What's free?" he asked, his voice tight because he knew.

"Me," she said.

"Oh," he said, trying to keep his voice offhand, his expression neutral.

"I'm always free to you, and I'll never be so busy that I can't slip you in."

"But why? You don't even know me."

"I don't know anybody that fucks me," she said. "I don't and never have."

"But the fullback," said Herman, trying to help her, "he . . ."

"Don't you see," she hissed, pushing her burning face inches from his.

"He didn't get me, the Vette did. Can you understand that? He drove a Vette, and my goddam pimp here at the hotel drives a Jaguar. But *you*," she cried, her voice triumphant. "You're going to eat the fucking thing!" She trembled in a fury where she sat. "Jesus God, I wish I could eat it, too, swallow it all." Her eyes burned his. "Can you understand that?"

"Yes," he said quietly. "I can understand that."

Six

MR. Edge had to lower the Maverick from the marquee with a crane, and then remove the double glass doors, two concrete pillars, and four plate-glass windows, before he could get the car through the lobby of the hotel into the enormous ballroom where Herman was going to eat it.

"At tremendous goddam expense," shouted Mr. Edge, "*tremendous* goddam expense."

"That's bullshit and you know it's bullshit," said Mister.

They were in Mr. Edge's tiny office, and Mister had raised the issue of money. When Mister first brought it up, Herman said it didn't matter. Mister had replied that in an enterprise in which he could understand nothing else, he could at least understand money—finances, he called it—and that finances mattered. And now, with Herman in the ballroom with the Maverick, Mister had taken Mr. Edge to task about the money.

"You're going to get rich, you cheerful bastard," said Mister, who could see through Mr. Edge's insistence that he was doing whatever he was doing just for the love of a job well done.

"Maybe I will and maybe I won't," said Mr. Edge, in a kindly voice, in a father's voice. "That's the point. Don't you see? This is all on speculation. I'm liable to lose my shirt."

"Does *that*," asked Mister, pointing toward the great roar of voices coming from the ballroom where Herman was about to be examined in public in preparation for the first eating, "does that sound like you may lose your shirt?"

"One cannot depend upon the public," said Mr. Edge.

"You can't depend on anybody and that's why I'm here to tell you that if Herman doesn't get more money the deal is off."

"You can't do that," said Mr. Edge, choking a little but smiling anyway. "I've got a contract. I'll sue."

"Sue then," said Mister. "But you'll still be stuck with a Maverick car and nobody to eat it."

"You son-of-a-bitch."

"Right," Mister said.

"How much do you want?"

"Not how much. Not a lump sum. We want a royalty, a percentage."

"How much of a percentage?"

"After you make expenses back—you're entitled to that—we want twenty-five percent of everything: the admission to the ballroom, and twenty-five percent on the Maverick replicas, and anything else that comes in off the deal or that you dream up." He raised his hands to quiet Mr. Edge who looked as though he were about to scream. "And you can stop the three-hundred-a-week salary as of right now. It's fair. If you think about it, it's fair. If Herman can't eat it, if the public tires of it, we don't make a cent. But I have faith in Herman; and I have faith in the American people."

"Herman came to me when nobody else wanted to talk to him. I listened to him and started him on three hundred a week that very day. We had an agreement. This is robbery."

But Mister knew just in the defeated way he said it that he had Mr. Edge. Mister shrugged. "You recognized a good deal and a boy you could take advantage of." He smiled. "Now we're just settling accounts."

Mr. Edge got heavily to his feet. "I can tell you I'd fight this to the last step, but it looks as though there'll be plenty for everybody. I had television feelers this morning."

"You had television feelers?" It sounded to Mister like some kind of recurrent illness, like malaria.

"From NBC. From CBS. From ABC."

"Jesus Christ, what for?"

"If you are going to be partners with me, don't be so goddam dumb," Mr. Edge said. "What do you think for, to ask about his health? They're talking about coast-to-coast coverage for that brother of yours. One of the networks has already even explored some of its overseas affiliates." He slowly examined his fat yellow palms. "We're liable to send Herman to Japan via satellite."

Mister's mouth was so dry he could hardly talk. "I want everything written out. A contract—a new one—written, inspected, signed, sealed, and delivered by tomorrow morning or Herman's not taking the first bite of that car."

"You're the greediest son-of-a-bitch I've ever met," said Mr. Edge pleasantly, "but your utter stupidity gives you a certain charm."

"Someday, if you're not careful, you'll write a check with your mouth that your ass can't cash."

"Ah," said Mr. Edge, "but I'm always careful. Let's go out and get this show on the road."

"I think it's time we did," Mister said.

The ballroom in the Sherman Hotel in Jacksonville, Florida, was the largest ballroom in the Southeast and it had been specially prepared for Herman and the Maverick. HERMAN AND THE MAVERICK was the way they were billing the show now. Bumper stickers had been made up which read HERMAN AND THE MAVERICK. When the advertisement came on local TeeVee, the four words simply appeared on an otherwise empty screen. Mr. Edge had taken a full page in the Florida *Times-Union* and in the Miami *Herald* and in the Saint Petersburg *Times* and in the Atlanta *Journal-Constitution* and a half-dozen other southern newspapers.

The entire page in each of the papers was filled with the simple and enormous words HERMAN AND THE MAVERICK. For those who already knew what was going on, the phrase struck a note of horrific anticipation in their hearts. For those who did not, it ran crazy with curiosity until they found out. It was an Ad Man's dream.

The special preparations in the ballroom had taken the form of a small square stage raised in the center of the floor with rising bleacher seats on four sides. There were to be two shows a day. Herman would eat at six in the evening, and Herman would pass at nine-thirty in the morning—give or take an hour for the passing.

Everything was to be done live and on stage. There would be no taint of hoax. There was a rod suspended from the ceiling that encircled the stage. From the rod hung a white draw curtain that would be pulled to completely close off Herman and the Maverick from the audience in the bleachers. The curtain was closed now as Mr. Edge and Mister made their way across the crowded floor where small boys were selling programs and small autographed photographs of Herman and the Maverick to the overflow crowd who had got in for half-price, which was a dollar fifty each, to watch the doctor examine Herman, to see the Maverick at close range, and to hear what had been billed as a special and interesting announcement from the management.

Mr. Edge was a good organizer, but you couldn't tell it from the confusion behind the curtain. When Mr. Edge and Mister got back there, it was two or three minutes before they found Herman. But they finally did find him sitting in the back seat of the car. Margo was with him.

"What are *you* doing in here?" asked Mr. Edge.

"She's with me," said Herman. "Leave her alone."

Margo put a hand on Herman's arm. "Honey, I work for Mr. Edge too," she said. "If he doesn't want me back here, I better leave."

Mr. Edge raised his fat palms, smiling. "If Herman wants you back here, I want you back here."

"I want her where she is," Herman said.

Mr. Edge had been leaning in the window of the Maverick talking to them. He straightened up and said under his breath, "Evergoddambody else seems to be here, no reason the hotel whore shouldn't be here too."

A welder squatted beside an acetylene tank beside the front bumper of the Maverick, lighting and relighting a torch that he could not seem to get adjusted just like he wanted. A fire marshal, in uniform, with a gold badge on his hat squatted beside him. A doctor, famous in Jacksonville for internal medicine, sat on a stool holding his black bag on his lap. Junell and Easy Mack stood by the curtains. Easy, dressed in a black suit and black tie, every few seconds turned to peep through the curtains at the audience. Junell was wearing a white dress with a black bow on the back. Mr. Edge had insisted that she either buy a dress or not come to the party.

"Those leathers are bad for the image," Mr. Edge had explained. "We'll have the press people here in force."

And they were there in force, more than Mr. Edge could really accommodate. But as he had proudly pointed out, they would never have to buy any more publicity. From here on in, it was a free ride. But the free ride meant putting up with eleven reporters behind the curtain, admitted by special arrangement with Mr. Edge, and three still photographers, plus three radio newsmen. And in addition to those men, there was a movie cameraman, whom Mr. Edge had hired to make his own personal record of the proceedings, against the day when some unforeseen opportunity might present itself.

Then there were the guards. There were three plainclothes detectives from the Pinkerton Agency behind the curtain. Fifteen more Pinkerton people had watched the crowd closely as it filed into the ballroom, inspecting parcels and suspicious bulges. They'd had more threats on Herman's life and several on Mr. Edge's since the Ford Motor Company had gone to court several days ago to try to get an injunction to stop Her-

man from eating their Maverick. They claimed it would ruin the image
of the car in the minds of the American people. The court had had little sympathy and Ford Motor Company had been dismissed, but the
new threats made it necessary to come to a quick decision about the
bulletproof plastic, whether or not to place Herman and the Maverick
in a bulletproof bubble on the stage in the ballroom. Mr. Edge felt there
was a loss of intimacy with the plastic. So he decided to ignore it, hire
the Pinkerton people, and take his chances. It meant a lot of extra people—people who were being paid instead of paying—milling around,
taking up valuable space, but it seemed necessary.

One of the reporters was sitting on the throne where Herman was
going to pass every morning at nine-thirty. It was an elaborate struc-
ture, designed and fabricated by Mr. Edge's own interior decorators.

"Do you think the public is ready for this?" the reporter asked Mr.
Edge.

"Would you be surprised to know that I'm . . ." He glanced at Mister
standing beside him. ". . . that *we're* negotiating to put it on nationwide
TeeVee?"

"Nationwide TeeVee?" asked the reporter. He whipped out a pad and
wrote on it. The other reporters who had gathered close behind him
wrote too.

"Of course," said Mr. Edge, "the immediate area—a three-hundred-
mile radius or so—will be blacked out."

"Could you tell us about the negotiations?"

"Only to say that we're talking to all the networks." Mr. Edge
shrugged. "What the hell, I guess it's all right to say that the network
we're closest with is ABC. They want it for their 'Wide World of Sports.' "

"And you think you can put this on national TeeVee?" The reporter
howled like a dog, and dissolved in laughter.

"Sponsored by Preparation H," shouted another reporter.

"And brought to you also by—"

"Here!" cried Mr. Edge, stamping his foot. "This is a great moment in
American show business and vulgarity has no place in it."

That seemed to sober them up. Herman had come out of the Maverick to stand beside Mr. Edge. Herman was wearing only tennis shorts.
He had a great sloping belly, and his skin was whiter than the shorts he
wore. A pattern of blue veins showed behind his thick white knees.
Margo stood with him and held his hand.

"I don't know what the big deal is," said Mr. Edge. "Look how we've got this made." The reporter got off the throne and they all stood looking at it, while Mr. Edge talked. "It's ingenious. American knowhow. You can see his head. These drapes will conceal his body. Here is where the Maverick drops. The audience can see it drop. But they can't see him." In exasperation he looked at the reporters, all of whom were scribbling furiously. "For God's sake give us credit for a little class and a little taste. We wouldn't show his rectum to an American audience."

"Mr. Edge?" It was a reporter from an out-of-town newspaper.

"Yes?"

"If he eats a half a pound a day, seven days a week, do you know how long it's going to take him to eat a Maverick automobile?"

"That's a fairly simple-minded question," snapped Mr. Edge. "Of course we know how long it'll take him. We can count."

The reporter who had been figuring on his notepad looked up incredulously. "Ten goddam years. *More than ten years!*"

"Not much more," Mr. Edge said, "which as you probably know is about what an excellent play will run on Broadway."

"There have only been a few plays in the history of American theater that have even approached that kind of run," said the reporter from the Miami *Herald*.

"Well," smiled Mr. Edge, "this little drama will set a record for American theater to shoot at for the next hundred years."

"Mr. Mack, do you think you can take a ten-year run of this?" It was the same reporter who had pointed out how long it would take.

Herman was staring at the Maverick, and his eyes never moved from the place where they were fastened on the right side of the front bumper. He made no sign that he'd heard the question.

Mr. Edge frowned and stared the reporter down. "I asked you not to speak to him. You all had instructions when you came in here. He's concentrating. He knows what he's got to do, and he's concentrating. If you have comments, address them to me."

"But it's not your . . . your . . . your . . ."—the reporter who was trying to speak kept losing his voice in laughter—"not your asshole that's going to be under assault for the next ten years."

It broke the other reporters up. Mr. Edge, his white face stony, waited for the laughter to stop. "I will not repeat this again," he said. "There will be no vulgarity allowed here. We will not allow this effort to be

tainted by common, low remarks. I have guards in attendance and the
next man who—in word or deed—shows himself to be vulgar will be
thrown out of my hotel. Is that clear?"

Nobody said anything. The audience beyond the curtain made a
noise like rushing water. "Very well then," said Mr. Edge, "we're late,
let's start it."

Mr. Edge signaled one of his men. They all took their places. The
man Mr. Edge had signaled pulled a cord that drew the curtain all the
way round the rod until the stage was exposed from all sides. The red
Maverick was on the right side. The enormous ingenious throne was on
the left. And in the middle sat Herman on a special aluminum examination table. The doctor came up and stood beside the table, set his
black bag down, and opened it. Junell, Mister, Easy Mack, and Margo
left the stage. The welder squatted by the Maverick. The fire marshal,
his gold badge flashing, stood by the welder. Two plainclothes Pinkerton
people stood just offstage by the microphone. Mr. Edge approached the
microphone. His man with the movie camera pressed a button and the
camera began to whir.

"Ladies and gentlemen, I . . ."

There was spontaneous applause and loud shouts of encouragement.

". . . thank you. The Hotel Sherman is proud to present an American
first." Applause. Applause. "As most of you know, a car has been eaten
before." The audience moaned. "We're not trying to hide that fact. A
Swede ate a Saab. And an Argentine ate a Fiat. But it has never been
done by an American, and nobody . . . nobody anywhere has ever eaten
a car as heavy as your Ford Maverick."

The crowd went wild with partisan applause. All the while Mr. Edge
talked, the doctor examined Herman in the background. He bound
Herman's arm with a rubber tube and took a quick reading of his blood
pressure. He listened intently with a silver stethoscope pressed against
Herman's chest. The audience listened to Mr. Edge, but its collective
gaze never wavered from Herman. And when the doctor opened Herman's mouth and looked down his throat, a sigh of the most exquisite
agony squeezed out of the men, women, and children in the audience.

"We'll cut a half-pound off at a time," Mr. Edge was saying, "starting
with the right front bumper. From the bumper, we'll go to the grille.
The car . . . the carcass . . . will sit right there, while Herman Mack
feeds off it for as long as it takes."

The doctor had Herman standing now. He was tenderly probing his great sloping stomach. But it was all by prearrangement. He wasn't really doing anything. It was just to accentuate Mr. Edge's announcement. And Mr. Edge made the most of it. He went into great and specific detail. He said it was for those in the audience who might not already know how they were going to proceed. Which was a lie.

Everybody in the Southeast knew exactly how Herman planned to eat the Maverick, just as most of the people in the rest of the country did because, by now, the wire services had picked up the story. Mr. Edge was going through it all again because he knew the audience would never get tired of it, that they wanted the details and wanted them again. And so he told how the metal would be cut into half-ounce lumps, how the lumps would be sterilized, how the doctor had put Herman on a special soft diet to protect the stomach from the metal, how they would put the seat covers and windshield and other unswallowable matter into indigestible capsules, and how Herman would continue week in and week out, two shows a day—the evening to eat, the morning to pass (nervous giggles, irregular applause building into a storm of clapping, followed by shouts of Go, Herman Go!) until finally there would be nothing left of that Maverick car but a memory.

Mr. Edge raised his hands for quiet.

"And now a special announcement. As you know, Herman Mack will eat for the first time this evening at six."

A roar of applause.

"In the morning, the first half-ounce he passes at nine-thirty will be auctioned off to the highest bidder."

Mr. Edge paused. There was utter silence. He could hear the doctor shuffling around behind him. The audience sat stunned. Mr. Edge rushed on.

"We have facilities here at the Hotel Sherman for melting down the half-ounce and casting it into the shape of a miniature Maverick—an absolute replica. And moreover, each subsequent half-ounce will be similarly melted and cast into small cars with a hole through the top suitable for wearing on your key chains. These small cars will be sold at twelve dollars and fifty cents each plus state sales tax on a first come first served basis."

The auditorium roared in a simultaneous burst of approval. Children threw balloons in the air. Men and women stamped their feet and clapped their hands and howled for a chance to buy a miniature Maverick.

When they finally quieted, Mr. Edge said: "We wanted to do this so that each of you might participate in this effort of Herman's in the most intimate way. And what better way than to leave here with a miniature Maverick hanging from your very own key chain?"

The storm of applause burst over the ballroom again, but Mr. Edge cut it short with a wave of his arm. When he waved his arm, the welder struck a flint and his torch popped and a flame, greenish-blue and nine inches long, sputtered and hissed. The fire marshal stood close, his gold badge glittering, his eyes intent. The welder adjusted his torch. The audience neither moved nor breathed. The hiss of the flame, which was now an inch and a half, blue with a little yellow tip, could be heard all over the ballroom.

Mr. Edge, his voice now low and deadly serious, said: "Ladies and gentlemen, a historic moment. We are about to prepare the half-pound Herman will ingest this very evening at six. Those of you here this morning will have first chance at the limited number of tickets available for this evening's performance."

The audience leaned forward. The man with the torch was staring up at Mr. Edge. Mr. Edge nodded his head and said: "Cut it."

The welder lowered his goggles, and bent to the bumper. The extreme end of the bumper on the right side, an area twice as big as a man's hand, had been marked off with a blue line. When the tongue of yellow flame touched the metal a shower of sparks flew about the welder's head. Those in the audience watching Herman where he stood beside the examination table saw a long trembling shudder pass through him the moment the fiery knife began to cut the car. It only took a minute to take off the piece of bumper which fell into a shallow silver pan that Mr. Edge had placed on the floor to catch it.

Easy Mack had taken a seat in the first row, reserved for members of the family, directly in front of the stage. But by the time the torch was halfway through the bumper, he was on his feet. And when the piece of car fell into the silver pan, he threw up.

The vomit sprayed out of his mouth and covered Mr. Edge's legs and shoes where he stood by the microphone.

Seven

AMERICA . . . YOUR 1971 FORDS ARE READY
MAVERICK

170-cu. in 1V 6-cyl. engine (100 hp)   3-speed synchronized manual transmission   Locking steering column   Flashing side marker lamps, four, located on front and rear fender sides (synchronized with turn signals)   Seats w/folding self-locking front seat backs   2 spoke steering wheel   Door-operated courtesy light   Blend-air heater w/3-speed blower, lighted controls   Printed circuits in instrument cluster   Suspended accelerator, clutch and brake pedals   Color-keyed floor mats   Curved ventless side glass   Coat hooks   Cowl top air take ventilation   Flipper-type rear quarter window   Reversible keys   Standard tires 6:45 x 14 black sidewall   Wheelbase 103 inches   Height 52.6 inches   Length 179.4 inches   Width 70.6 inches   Curb weight 2624 pounds   Engine type 170 six   Compression ratio 8.7:1   Horsepower @ rpm 100/4200   Battery 45 amp.   Alternator 42 amp.

The specifications of the 1971 Maverick car filtered through Herman's dulled and dimmed mind like leaves in a slow wind. He had read these specifications again and again, dreamed of them, loved them, conjured with them, until finally they recited themselves whether he was listening or not. He was not listening now. But he was aware of a detailed list of the Maverick car's virtues as he lay in his room on the second floor of the Hotel Sherman.

He was weighted with an unaccustomed fullness. He lay naked on the bed on his back, both of his hands spread over his slightly distended white stomach. He had done it. It was no longer a matter of speculation, of could he or could he not. He had done it!

But he remembered little about it. The day had been a kind of blur with little islands of action that stood out, frozen in time and place, in a blindingly white light. He remembered the little tray of cut sterilized metal being offered to him in the middle of tumultuous applause and cries of encouragement. But he didn't remember how he got to the stage.

He had eaten nothing in the last twenty-four hours. The doctor had gone to a lot of trouble to make Herman a special diet full of things like cottage cheese and heavy cream to protect his stomach from the car, but Herman had been unable to eat anything. Quite literally he could not swallow anything. Several times that day the doctor and Mr. Edge and even his father, Easy Mack, had tried to get him to eat. And he had tried. God knows he had tried. He had—again and again—put a spoon of soft bland food into his mouth, only to find himself unable to swallow. There was some doubt as to whether the first show would go off on schedule. But he had assured them that everything would be O.K.

"Just lead me to it," he had told them confidently, "and everything will be O.K."

And it was. They brought him the silver tray of sterilized half-ounce lumps of metal. Herman looked down, only in that instant realizing where he was, knowing that the moment was finally upon him. He raised his eyes and there the audience sat, rocklike, stunned by what he was about to do, utterly silent. There was his daddy, drained of color, chalky. His brother and sister. Then he saw that it was Margo holding the silver tray. She leaned forward imperceptibly, her quick pink tongue darting over white needle teeth.

"Eat it," she hissed. "Eat it, Herman! Goddam, swallow it all!"

It was as though everything moved at three-quarter time. He saw his hand, agonizingly slow, reach out and plump a lump off the tray and lift it to his mouth. He felt the metal on his lips. He felt his tongue take it, hold it. The taste of metal flooded his throat, his stomach. He felt the taste run, touch his blood, and he almost swooned in the pleasure of it. He swallowed and felt it enormous in his throat, felt it pass, long and unthinkably heavy, down down down and finally stop in his stomach.

The applause shook the ballroom. Mr. Edge gripped his arm and told him he was a champion, a real champ. Margo said it was free any time, day or night. His brother, Mister, said it was a whole new ball game. The doctor, who had watched in disbelief, now would not meet his eyes. The fire marshal was making sure the torch was out and that there was no danger to the Sherman Hotel and the audience of the ballroom. Herman saw it all, saw it in three-quarter time. Unreal and detached, he gulped the remainder of the lumps of metal and was then taken blind and swelling to his room to lie on his back and wonder at the magnificence of what he had done.

The room in which he lay was banked with congratulatory bouquets of flowers sent him by admirers. The doctor had examined him again in the room and announced him fit. A small nightlight burned on the far wall. All the blinds and curtains were drawn. Margo had been in a few minutes ago to try to spoon a little of the special diet into his mouth.

"It'll be easier on you," she whispered, her red mouth wet and swollen.

He could have eaten, but he refused. He didn't want to. He was at one with himself and the world. His eyes were open, but he felt himself dreaming. He heard his blood roar in his ears, and he heard cars in the roar. He saw cars in his blood. They squealed and careened through long curving veinous highways. He took his hands off his stomach and held tightly to the bed. He had not expected this.

Filled with terror and joy, he tried to wake up. But he was not asleep. His eyes filled with cars. They raced and competed in every muscle and fiber. Dune buggies raced over the California sands of his feet; sturdy jeeps with four-wheel drive and snow tires climbed the Montana mountains of his hips; golden convertibles, sleek and topless, purred through the Arizona sun of his left arm; angry taxis, dirty and functional and knowledgeable, fought for survival in the New York City of his head.

And his heart. God, his heart! He felt it separate and distinct in his chest. Isolated and pumping, he knew its outermost limits. And every car that raced and roared in his vision of himself finally ended in his heart. An endless traffic of Saabs and Fords and Plymouths and Volkswagens and modified buggies of every sort and Toyotas and cars from all over the world lined up and entered his pounding heart.

He watched, amazed and stupefied, as he filled up with cars tighter and tighter until finally he was bumper to bumper from head to toe. His skin stretched. His veins and arteries blared with the honking of horns, jammed with a traffic jam that would never be over because it had no place to go. Cars cars everywhere and no place to drive.

But at the last moment, when he was gasping and choking with cars, truly terrified that they would keep multiplying until the seams of his skin split and spilled his life, a solution—dreamlike and appropriate— came to him in his vision. He was a car. A superbly equipped car. He would escape because he was the thing that threatened himself, and he would not commit suicide.

If he needed more air he'd turn on the air-conditioner. If he needed more strength, he'd burn a higher octane gasoline. If he needed more confidence, he'd get another hundred horses under the hood. If the light of the world bothered him, he'd tint his windshield. And his immortality lay in numberless junkyards, all easily accessible from anywhere in America. Go on down and replace his fender, replace his wheel, replace his engine even, replace everything until he was not even what he was when he started. Replace everything with all things until he was nobody because he was everybody.

Herman rolled and pitched on the bed. He stopped stock still. He eased over on his left side. He thought he could hear himself rattle. He tried again. Oh, Lord! A ragged sob caught in his throat.

"Herman?"

It was Margo. He could just see her sitting in the shadows of the far corner of the room. She had changed dresses. She was all in white.

He raised his arms toward her. "Thank God," he said. "Thank God, it's you."

"Herman," she said. "What's the matter?"

"I . . . I'm afraid," he said.

"Of what?" She sat on the bed and automatically put both her hands on his stomach.

"I don't know," he said. "I had a dream . . . a dream or something."

"About what? What was it about?"

"Cars."

"Tell me about it, darling Herman. And then you'll see it's only a dream. I have bad dreams all the time and I just get out of bed and go to the mirror and look at myself and tell myself the dream and it never scares me then."

"Never?"

"Sometimes it scares the hell out of me even then," she said.

"I was full of cars."

"Full of . . ."

"They were in my arms and legs and head, my blood, my heart."

"Well, a dream," she said, trying to soothe him.

"Then *I* was a car."

". . . a dream is always strange," she said.

"But I was awake."

"Awake?"

"My eyes were open. And I was afraid. I'm afraid now."

"Let me hold you," she said. "I'll hold you."

"Yes," he said.

She stood up and he watched her get out of her clothes. The white dress unzipped and all she wore were tangerine briefs. She peeled them down and stood naked. She was a single muscle of dimpled leanness.

"God, you're pretty," he said. He was looking at her stomach which showed layers of banded muscle.

"It was cheering," she said. "There's probably only one thing in the world that's better than cheerleading for your body."

"What's that?"

"Fucking," she said. "If you put your heart into it, fucking keeps you in fantastic shape."

She lay down beside him and pressed her stomach against his. He was surprised how tiny she was without her high-heeled shoes. Her eyes were only inches from his. Her breasts flattened against his chest.

"You shouldn't talk like that," said Herman. "You're too nice a girl to say things like that."

"It's my standard opening," she said.

"What's a standard opening?"

"The way you begin. Every John loves to hear me say fuck. So I say it when I start to get in bed with a John. My pimp taught me that."

"I'm not your ordinary John," he said.

"No," she said, "you're not a ordinary John or a ordinary anything else. God, you were wonderful out there this morning."

"But it turned out bad."

"No, it didn't," she said, trying to coax him out of his vision.

"I thought I was a car."

"You can dream anything."

"I wasn't asleep. I thought I was a car, and it scared me, scared me bad."

"You're not scared now."

"No," he said, "not now. But if it starts again, I might . . . no, I *would* be, I know I would be."

"You're not going to think you're a car with me in the bed with you."

He started to say something. But she licked his chest, licked his chest and it went out of his head.

"Listen," he said, "you don't have . . ."

"But that's what makes it so nice, doesn't it?" she said. She slid down his body until she was licking his stomach. Her tongue was warm and wet and quick. She stopped and looked up at him. "I don't *have* to do anything for you. Now doesn't that make it nice?"

"Yes," he said, "that does make it nice."

Eight

"WELL, I didn't mean to," said Easy Mack irritably.

"Mr. Edge was upset anyway," Mister said. "His wife was in the audience. His daughter had her fiancé out there and everything. And what do you do? You throw up on his shoes. How would you feel?"

"I said I didn't mean to. I couldn't help it."

"I know that, daddy. The doc said it was sympathy."

"Bullshit. Sympathy? What does that mean?"

"Sympathy is what he said," said Mister. "Your stomach for his stomach. It was just like you were going to eat it yourself."

"Godamighty," said Easy Mack. His gorge rose in his throat. He gagged.

"You all right?"

"I'm not all right. No. And I'm not going to ever be all right again."

They were talking in the suite of rooms Mister had made Mr. Edge give them on the same floor with Herman's. The rooms fronted on the street so they could watch the traffic and the crowds below and judge the business they were doing at the box office. The first month's performances were sold out solid. Scalpers were doing a tremendous business on tickets for the nine-thirty passing. Once news raced through Jacksonville that the Mack boy had *actually eaten the Maverick*, orders for tickets had poured in. In two hours, they'd sold out the first month's show, and Mister—from the room where he was talking with his daddy—watched the people lined up, filling the sidewalk as far away as he could see.

"I wish you wouldn't talk like that," said Mister. "Look at that down there." He pointed to the street below.

"I've already looked," said Easy. His voice was the voice of a man who has been told his disease is terminal.

"It's our chance," said Mister. "You always said our chance would come and that the car would bring it. It's here and I'm going to ride it as far as it goes."

HARRY CREWS

Easy Mack wished he had something to say, but he didn't. He *had* said the car would save them all. Back when Junell and Herman and Mister were just little things and their mother was alive, he had said that America was a V-8 country, gas-driven and water-cooled, and that it belonged to men who belonged to cars. He believed it all those years as a shade-tree mechanic, and he believed it when he got the job as shop foreman in the new-car dealership in Waycross, Georgia, and he still believed it when he got his chance and bought the forty-three acres and started Auto-Town, even though nowadays a junked car put through the crusher, packaged and delivered to the barge, only brought fifty cents a hundred pounds.

That Maverick Ford downstairs was worth about two thousand dollars at the dealership; junked (Easy paused and the figures clicked in his head), junked it was worth a little over eleven dollars. He sighed and took what consolation was left him. There were over twelve million cars junked a year in America. A man could still make a living. More cars than people were made in this country every year, and those damn cars had to go *somewhere*.

"I want to go home," said Easy.

"We can't," said Mister. "We've got to help Herman."

"Nobody can help Herman," his daddy said.

"That's where you're wrong," Mister said. "Herman's got a job to do." He paused and looked out the window at the gathering crowd of people around the box office. "Listen, I might as well tell you . . . we're in with Mr. Edge."

"Maybe you're in with him," Easy said. "But I'm not."

"We're all in. He was stealing us blind. There was nothing else to do."

There was a stricken look in Easy's eyes. "Don't say that. It's not true."

"But it is, daddy. It really is. He was stealing us blind."

"I don't mean that. I mean about us being in with him."

"How do you think I got him to give us these rooms?"

"You're not paying him?"

"He's paying *us*. Daddy, we're rich. *Rich*. Home free at last."

"You mean you think I'm going to stay here, live in a goddam hotel?"

"Daddy, there was a television man in the audience this evening. He came to see for himself. He watched Herman swallow that car, and you know what?"

Easy gently put his head back against the cushion of the chair in which he was sitting and groaned.

"Herman's been bought from coast to coast, that's what!" Mister rushed to the window again to watch the crowd on the sidewalk. Then he came back and looked at his daddy, whose eyes were still closed. "And we're getting twenty-five percent of the price of the Maverick replicas, and twenty-five percent of the TeeVee rights, and twenty-five percent of everything, even the tickets to get in."

Easy kept his eyes closed and said: "Get me Junell."

"What?" said Mister, still lost and dazed in his vision of percentages.

"Junell," said Easy. "Tell her I need her."

"Can't."

"Why?"

"She's in her room."

"She got one too?" asked Easy. "A room in the hotel?"

"I told you already, we're all in. She's got the one next to us," said Mister, unable to keep the pride out of his voice. "I made it plain to Mr. Edge we had to have the rooms all together." He spread his arms. "This right here is called the Executive Suite. Junell's is next door."

"Tell her I want her," Easy said.

"Can't," said Mister.

"Goddamit, Mister, quit saying that!"

"Can't."

Easy's seamed face mottled, and a fine spray of spit flew from his lips.

"I mean I can't go get her," Mister said. "She's in there with Joe." He looked out the window. "I think she may be occupied by Joe."

"Joe who?" demanded her father.

"Joe I don't know who. But you remember the guy, the young guy at the wreck. Remember we all went out there that Sunday and met him?"

"He here too?"

"In her room. And I . . ."

"God, is everybody going to end up here?"

"There was another bomb threat this evening right after the show, and Mr. Edge called the capitol for protection because he's a big contributor in the race for governor and—"

"Don't tell me about the goddam governor," cried Easy.

"The governor assigned four troopers to the hotel for the duration."

"And Joe's one of them?"

"He volunteered. Junell was nervous as hell when she found out he was coming. She talked to me about it. It's not like meeting him at a wreck. She asked me if I thought she ought to take him for a ride in Big Mama—she's got Big Mama over there next door in the Park 'N Lock— but I told her, hell no, just act normal. It'll take care of itself. It'll be all right." Mister was looking out the window at the crowd down on the sidewalk. "But she's still nervous, really nervous as hell about it."

Easy Mack sighed. He looked up at Mister. "Well, things are not going to be the same, are they, son?"

"No sir, they're not."

They sat for a long time listening to the sound of the street, the early Friday evening traffic, so loud that it came right through the wall, over the air-conditioning, horns, the growl of engines.

"But I've got a surprise for you," said Mister at last.

"Boy, I'm not in the mood for a surprise."

"You're going to like this one."

"I don't think so. I don't think I'm going to like anything for a good while." Then: "What's the surprise?"

"You'll have to come and see it," said Mister. "It's downtown."

"We are downtown."

"Just around the corner. Come on, you need to get out, anyway. We don't need to stay here, this thing'll run itself."

"I don't want to go."

"But you don't want to stay either."

"No, I don't want to stay either," Easy said.

"Then you might as well come on and keep me company."

So they went, he and his father, downstairs where they were recognized in the lobby and cheered on the sidewalk, shoved about and touched by ticket holders and ticket buyers.

"No," shouted Mister when his father turned toward the Park 'N Lock. "We won't need the truck." The noise of the crowd was deafening. "Easier for us to walk."

Three flashbulbs went off in their faces as they pushed their way out and hurried off down the sidewalk. Across the street from the Hotel Sherman, a man in a white robe carried a placard which read THE LORD SEES ALL BUT BIDES HIS TIME. Several people followed, asking for autographs and for personal introductions to Herman. But Easy wouldn't talk to them, and Mister kept saying that there would be time for such things later. So after a little more than a block, the people turned back and they were left alone.

"How far is it?" Easy asked.

"Not far," said Mister.

"Did you see that guy across the street?"

"The one in the gown?"

"That's the one."

"He's crazy. Harmless and crazy. Mr. Edge had the police check him out."

"I didn't see him before."

"Been right there from the start. Off and on, since Herman started."

"And Mr. Edge had'm checked out?"

"Right. He shows every sign of being crazy, and maybe dangerous too. So rather than chance it, Mr. Edge had him checked out. Your local police are very good about checking out crazies."

They turned onto Main Street and walked north. Easy was just about to ask his son how much farther when Mister put out a hand and stopped him. "Look at that," he said.

A few yards back from the street was an enormous brilliantly lighted showroom. And in the middle of the showroom, up on a revolving platform, was a solid white Sedan De Ville Cadillac car. There was a family—a mother, a father, and two little boys—standing stock still just to the left of the platform gazing intently up at the car.

"There it is," cried Mister. "Come on in here, daddy!"

Easy followed him dumbly into the showroom. As they passed the family, the father was saying softly, "Someday . . . someday," and the little boys' heads were nodding in quiet affirmation. When they got really close to the car, Easy Mack's stomach lurched and squeezed. He tasted metal at the root of his tongue.

"Mine," said Mister.

"What?"

"I bought it."

"But—"

"You know we've always wanted one," said Mister. "The standard of excellence that everything's measured against. They say so, and you've always said so. And we've finally got there. It's ours."

It was true. Easy had always talked of owning a brand-new Sedan De Ville, the most popular of Cadillac cars. But they had never really been able to afford one before. Even owning the largest junkyard in the state, there was always the taxes, and the turnover, and the overhead, and the ever-decreasing value of wrecked cars. And now there it was. It was theirs, and Easy Mack wondered why he was not happy. His stomach rolled and threatened to come up. He was sick to the center of his being.

"Mr. Edge stood good for it," said Mister. "I called them up and said which one I wanted. Said who I was and which one I wanted. They got it ready. All we got to do is drive it away."

They went into a little partitioned office where the salesman leapt up when he found out who they were. He led them down a hall to a flood-lit area behind the dealership. In the midst of an acre of light was a white Cadillac.

"There she is," said the salesman. "Brand-new. Nobody's ever farted on her seat covers."

He laughed long and loud at his joke. He did not seem to mind at all that Mister and his father were not laughing.

"God, it's big as a house," said Easy.

"Your Cadillac is not a small car," the salesman said.

The three men circled the machine. Almost warily. As though they half-expected it to speak or cast a spell. The salesman opened his mouth and in a quiet religious voice said: "Your Cadillac—every last one of them—comes in twenty-one colors. You've chosen white, but it comes in twenty-one different choices . . ."

Circling the Cadillac, Easy was overwhelmed and filled with awe. He couldn't even *think* of twenty-one colors. Were there really that many? Red brown black gold green purple yellow (but yellow was gold, wasn't it?) pink blue turquoise. He was counting on his fingers and that was only ten. He tried to think of more. Couldn't.

". . . and of course this car has power seats and power door locks and power brakes and power steering and power windows and . . ."

Easy was dizzy. Things spun. The word *power* rang in his head like a bell. His stomach had squeezed shut in a merciful cramp that hurt like hell but at least it kept him from doing what he was afraid any minute he would do: vomit.

They circled.

". . . and four cigarette lighters. That's *four*. And then your lights, your Cadillac lights: lights ashtray, lights backup, lights cornering, lights rear compartment, lights reading adjustable, lights courtesy automatic, lights directional, lights front and rear side markers, lights glove box, lights map, lights luggage compartment automatic, lights door panels . . ."

"What is it, daddy?" Mister said.

His eyes swam with light. He was horribly, vomitously ill. But he couldn't say that to his son. Because he did not know why. The longer the Cadillac man talked, the more impossible it became to listen to him.

"We better hurry," said Easy. "We better go."

"Right," his son said. "Listen, we've got to get back."

The salesman made a little swirling gesture with his closed fist and a Cadillac key ring popped between his fingers like magic. "Mr. Edge's agent has taken care of everything. All you have to do is drive it out of here."

"Let's get on the road, daddy," said Mister.

The salesman opened the door on Easy Mack's side and Easy fell into the deep cushions of the front seat. The heavy doors swung shut with the solid deep-throated *click* of a bank vault closing, and they felt themselves hermetically sealed from the world. Mister started the motor and they moved away from the salesman and left him standing in the white pool of light, waving.

"I didn't tell you," Mister said, staring straight ahead, "the evening you went to see Herman at the hotel—that afternoon came up Cadillacs. It was a sign. I knew it, and when the money came I knew the thing to do was come on down and buy one." He glanced at his daddy, who had his head back against the pillowed rest, and his eyes closed. "That's right, just relax and enjoy it." He began telling his daddy about how the Cadillacs had come up one after another into the car-crusher. Mister told him to go ahead and lean back while he listened and enjoy it.

But Easy Mack was not enjoying it. His senses were fastened to lights ashtray lights backup lights cornering lights reading lights courtesy lights glove box. He felt himself surrounded by them, threatened by them. He watched them blink, heard them click, felt their warmth on his dry and sour tongue.

And *power*. Power was everywhere. It was in the windows where levered motors whirred and pumped. It was in the steering wheel that turned effortlessly in his son's hands. He felt it in the four cigarette lighters. Four! He writhed on his seat. Could there ever be a time when four people would want to light a cigarette at the same time and each of them demand a lighter of his very own?

The thought that had been trying to form from the moment he had seen the Cadillac whispered itself over the steady drone of Mister's voice still talking on about the sign that had come up six times in a row on the car-crusher. It was the four cigarette lighters that gave the thought shape and caused it to hiss: *What if you had to eat a Cadillac?* You'd have four cigarette lighters to eat. You'd have all those goddam lights. All that fucking power. The convenience of power windows turned to stomach-churning terror. He thought of every single Cadillac coming in twenty-one different colors. He saw them lined end to end, a metallic rainbow of color.

"Jesus Christ!" cried Easy Mack.

"What? What is it?" shouted his son.

"Stop the car!"

Mister had taken the Cadillac out onto the expressway to try it out, and his daddy—who had been lying back with his eyes closed—screaming like that had scared the hell out of him so that he swerved onto the shoulder of the road. The car pitched and yawed on its powerful suspension system before Mister could finally bring it to a stop. Easy flung the door open and leaned out of the car. Racking noises of vomit ripped up from his stomach.

"Don't puke on the goddam car!" yelled Mister. "Watch the car with that puke!"

But that was not necessary. Nothing but noises of vomit came from Easy Mack's dry throat and empty stomach. He leaned back in the car and pulled the door shut.

"Listen," said Mister. "I'm going to have Mr. Edge's doctor examine you. All this puking may mean something serious. I don't like the looks of it." Then as an afterthought as he was pulling over the rough shoulder back onto the road: "Did you get any on the car?"

The car plunged and rose over a deep gully and was back onto the pavement. Easy's head lifted off the backrest. His eyes popped open.

"It squeaked," said Easy Mack.

"What squeaked?"

"The car," said Easy, his voice triumphant. "The car squeaked."

"Couldn't have."

"It did."

"I didn't hear it."

"I heard it."

In spite of himself, Mister cocked his head and strained to hear. Nothing came to him but the powerful purr of the engine. He smiled. "Your Cadillac does not squeak."

"This one did," insisted Easy. "It's right in there." He pointed.

"In the cockpit instrument panel?" asked Mister, using one of the salesman's phrases.

"Slow down and ease onto the shoulder of the road."

"Daddy, this is an expressway. You have to keep it moving."

"It's got to be fixed," said Easy, his voice going petulant. "Hell, you don't want it to squeak."

"I'll take it tomorrow. I'll have'm come and pick it up and fix it."

"*I'll* fix it," Easy insisted. "Do you think your daddy can't fix a goddam squeak?" He stared his son down. "I was fixing squeaks before you were born, boy!"

"I know but—"

"Then put the wheel on the shoulder, like I say."

Mister found a lane for emergency parking, slowed, eased the wheel onto the dirt shoulder.

"*There!*" cried his father.

And it was true. Mister's 1971 Cadillac car, with only twenty-one miles on the speedometer, on whose seat covers no one had ever farted, squeaked.

Nine

JUNELL and Joe were both nervous as hell. She had been angry when she first learned that he was coming there to the hotel.

"What the hell for?" she had demanded of Mr. Edge, who had brought her the news.

"To guard your brother."

"To guard your hotel, you mean," she said, hot-eyed and dangerous.

"Same thing," said Mr. Edge. "Anyway, if a bomb goes off in here we'll all get it, you, me, your brother, everybody. So I got the governor to send over some of the boys from the special patrol. Joe volunteered. He called and told me to tell you he was on his way."

It seemed to her a breach of manners, a failure in etiquette. This wasn't a wreck. It was a goddam business enterprise. It was a show of determination, a feat of strength. But it was *not* a wreck. They didn't need a guy whose skill was removing broken bodies from broken cars, a guy who knew how to direct traffic through a highway battlefield of broken glass and collapsed piles of smoldering metal.

So it made her angry. At least at first. Then it made her nervous. She quickly got out of the dress she had bought for her brother's first show and into a full set of her racing leathers in case Joe wanted to unzip her and get at her titties. After all, he always did. But she couldn't imagine how he'd do it—how *they'd* do it—in a hotel room. Joe probably wouldn't even bring his Chrysler Cruiser, and Big Mama was a block away on the tenth floor of the Park 'N Lock. Which left her in a hotel room waiting for a man she had never seen when he wasn't attending the desperate screams of automobile victims, or directing tow trucks in to pick up a total, or arranging flashing markers to show the open lane around or through catastrophe.

And when Joe showed up, he was so nervous it only made her more nervous. There came such a timid tap on the door that she couldn't believe it was him. But she opened up and there he stood, stiff as a board, his patrol hat squarely on his head, a smile paralyzing his face.

"Junell," he said.

"Joe," she said.

"Yes," he said.

"Well," she said.

"Moved right in, did you?" He pointed to the room behind her.

"We thought we ought to live here for a while."

"Till you settle old Herman down?" he said.

"He's settled down pretty good," she said, "but we're a close family."

They stood in the door, she still with the knob in her hand and he still at attention, speaking through a paralyzed smile.

"They said he eat it like candy," Joe said.

"It wasn't anymore than if he'd been eating peanuts," she said.

"That goddam Herman," he said.

"He's something," she said. "Even if he is my brother I've got to say he's something."

She finally turned loose the doorknob and backed into the room. He followed her. There was a sofa by the wall at the foot of the bed. They stopped in front of the sofa. They looked at it.

"I couldn't believe it when Mr. Edge said you were coming to the hotel."

"Several freaks have threatened to blow up your brother."

"How long do you think you'll stay?"

"As long as it takes," Joe said.

"Herman won't be through with the car for ten years," she said.

They turned and looked at the sofa again. They moved so their backs were to it. Joe eased a slipping step backward. So did Junell. Their legs touched the sofa. The calves of their legs pressed against it. All they had to do was sit down. But they did not.

"The freaks'll get used to it," said Joe. "If they don't blow him up in the first few weeks, they'll forget about him and go on and let him eat it."

A siren suddenly started down in the street—a loud screaming motorcycle siren—and they both abruptly sat. Joe immediately removed his flat-brimmed patrol hat. He sat holding the hat in his hands. He leaned forward. But there was no front seat to put it on. Junell saw how it was. He had his hat and there was no front seat. He started to put it on the sofa beside him, but stopped. He had always put it in the front seat. It wouldn't be the same anywhere else.

Junell herself missed the riot gun in its cradle hanging on the back of the front seat. She always pressed her knees against it. It was what she liked most to do while he talked about his Chrysler Cruiser. But even more than that, she missed the excitement of the wreck: the sirens, the smell of rubber and cloth burning, the heat, the flashing popping lights, the other tow drivers fighting for position and preference in whatever there was to choose from. And she knew that Joe missed it too. He finally set his hat on his lap and looked at her. There was no chance for *anything* with his hat on his lap.

"How did you get over here?" she asked, trying to find out if he'd brought that Chrysler Cruiser.

"Drove." He turned his hat in his lap.

"Where did you park it?"

"Oh, I didn't park it," he said nervously.

"Who parked it?"

"The man who drove it over."

"Who drove it?"

"Relief man."

"You mean you're not even going to have it here?"

"Chief said I didn't need it. Said you didn't need a Chrysler Cruiser on permanent duty in a hotel."

"That's how much he knows," she said. Then: "Joe, you shouldn't have volunteered."

"I couldn't help it," he said. "The wrecks just weren't the same without you."

"I still think it was too big a sacrifice," she said.

"No other way," he said helplessly. "Even that Chrysler Cruiser wasn't the same without you."

She saw him look long and sadly at her breasts. A man dying of thirst who had just caught sight of a stream that he thinks he'll never reach. It broke her heart.

"I hate to think of it turned over to a relief man," she said.

"He's a good man. Nobody's fool," Joe said. "He's got a tremendous feeling for motors."

"And he just drove you over here, and then drove off with it?"

"Right," he said, putting his hat back on, squaring it on his head absolutely.

"Nobody's ever done anything like this for me, Joe."

"I love you and respect you," he said.

"I know."

But she saw that it was impossible in her room without the car. He couldn't think of her any other way. She saw how it was going to have to be. If she loved him—and now she thought she probably did—she knew what she had to do.

"Have you seen the Maverick?" she asked.

"I came straight to your room. I asked at the desk and came straight up."

"It's down in the ballroom," she said. "And nobody's down there now."

They looked at each other—she at his hat, he at her breasts.

"You mean there's nobody down there at all?" he said.

"That Maverick's right by itself in the ballroom."

"I ought to go down there and check everything out," he said.

"I'll show you," she said.

Mr. Edge met them when they got off the elevator.

"I'm glad you're here," said Mr. Edge. "I'm glad to see you're on the job."

"I'm on the job all right," said Joe, checking his hat.

"I let the Pinkerton people go," Mr. Edge said.

"They're amateurs," Joe said.

"I let'm all go as soon as the governor said he was sending you boys from the special patrol."

"I thought I'd show him around," said Junell.

"I can help you," Mr. Edge said.

"You've got other things to do," she said. "I can handle it."

"Well, I probably ought to look in on Herman." Mr. Edge looked at his watch. "I don't want anything to happen to that boy."

"I'll give you a full report of my analysis on the premises, sir," Joe said.

"Good," Mr. Edge said, stepping into the elevator they had just got out of.

One light had been left on in the ballroom. It was directly over the square stage holding the Maverick. They walked closer. Joe stepped up on the stage. Junell followed him. Joe walked over and drew back his foot to kick the tire.

"This is where he passes," said Junell.

"Passes?" Joe blushed. He stood, his leg drawn back, balanced on one foot.

"Sure," said Junell.

"Godamighty," said Joe. He put his foot down. "You mean he just . . ."

"Squats and drops," she said. "We want no taint of farce." She was be-ginning to pick up Mr. Edge's way of talking. "Seeing is believing."

Joe came over and sat down on the throne. "This is something," he said. "This is really something. He just sits here and . . ."

"Plop," she said, slapping her hands together.

His eyes had fallen on the place where a bite had been taken out of the bumper. He got off the throne and went over to the Maverick. He stared at the bite out of the bumper and then he stared at the rest of the car.

"Ten years?" he said.

"About," she said. "More or less. Maybe less. The doctor thinks his tolerance may increase as time goes on. I don't know, but that's what he thinks." She paused, watching him watch the car. "Herman made it clear in the advertising that he didn't mean to eat the spare tire, or the jack out of the trunk. This is just basic car."

"Still though . . ." His trembling voice trailed off. He spread his arms and seemed to take the measure of the car.

"Oh, even stripped and without the trunk, it's a lot of car," she ad-mitted.

"And a good one, they say." Joe was running his hands slowly over the smooth lines of the hood and the headlights, stopping to trace the mav-erick.

"It's a Ford product," she said.

"They say these little babies've got plenty of room in them."

"The engineers at Ford can stretch the inside of a car," Junell said. "They're known for that."

"Even the back seat," Joe said. "They say even that back seat has plenty of leg room."

"You want to try it?" she said.

Surprise flashed in his face as though the thought had never occurred to him. "You think it'd be all right to try it?"

"Herman wouldn't mind. He'd be pleased to have us try it."

"I *am* on duty," he said.

"You could be on duty as easy *inside* the car as you are outside."

"That's true," he said, carefully removing his patrol hat and tossing it through the window onto the front seat.

She opened the door and pulled the seat up. Joe had his hand between her legs before she ever sat down. He threw her back and tore at her zippers with his teeth. Her breasts popped free and he took several long pulls, first at the left one, then the right one, then the left again.

That seemed to calm him and let him get his breath enough to say, "I love you, Junell, and I respect you for this."

He was very agitated. She could feel the racing of his heart. He embraced her and they sat looking over the front seat and through the windshield past the empty elaborate throne into the empty bleachers.

"Tell me how he did it," said Joe.

"There wasn't much to it. He—"

"Start at the beginning."

"Mr. Edge had a man with a torch and—"

"What about the crowd?"

"Big crowd and—"

"Going wild?"

"Really noisy. Cheering, clapping. But when they got the bumper cut off and cut up, it got quiet. You—"

"Could hear a pin drop?" he said.

"—could hear a pin drop," she said. "You could hear yourself breathe. The . . ."

Joe unbuckled her leather belt and unsnapped the racing leathers.

". . . fire marshal kept his eye on the torch. The doctor kept his eye on Herman. The crowd kept . . ."

Joe unzipped the fly on her racing leathers.

". . . its eye on everything."

He had her down in the seat now. Her booted feet pressed against the headliner. He stripped the black leather from her white rump.

". . . in a silver pan and held under his face . . ."

He was sweating. His eyes squeezed shut. His special patrol uniform was unbuckled, unbuttoned, undone.

". . . and he took it in his fingers and put it in his mouth—"

"—Lord, God," cried Joe. "The car in his mouth."

". . . and we saw it in his throat."

He was jamming blindly at her.

". . . all saw it in his throat and the crowd couldn't stand it."

He found her. And they suddenly quieted there on the seat like two rabbits struck in the dark by the lights of a car. Her voice that had been urgent went soft, intimate.

"... and lump by lump by lump, he ate it all."

"Think of it!" said Joe in a strained whisper now. "He'll eat the bumper. Then the grille."

"Then the fender."

"Then the hood."

"Then the fan."

"The fan belt."

"The radiator."

"The block."

"The pistons."

"Valves."

"Axle."

"Tires."

"Doors."

On the steady stroke of what they had found there in the back seat of the Ford Maverick, they worked their way through the entire car from bumper to bumper, their voices in blind counterpoint to each other.

"Windshield," he said.

"Instruments."

"Ste ... ste ... steering wheel."

Finally they were shouting directly into each other's face as they approached the finish.

"THEN THE REAR AXLE!"

"THEN THE TRUNK LID!"

"THEN THE TAILLIGHTS!"

"THEN THE ..."

"... THE ..."

Together: "BUMPER!"

Ten

IT was the morning of the first passing. Interest was at fever pitch. The people had started lining up at the ballroom door before daylight. By eight o'clock the line was a block long and growing. Nobody really believed Herman could pass the Maverick. But then most people had not believed he could eat it. But he had. And now it was time to pass. If he could pass it, the show could go on indefinitely. Everybody understood that passing the Maverick was a key move. Rumor had spread that Herman might die before their very eyes of anal hemorrhage.

Mister and Easy sat high in the bleachers and watched the crowd file into the ballroom. Mister was full of exhaustion and exultation. He was exhausted because his daddy had kept him up all night looking for the squeak in the brand-new Cadillac car. He had insisted he could find it and fix it. But he had not. Even after he made Mister drive all the way back to the Park 'N Lock and drive up to the tenth floor where he had his tool box in the back of his International-Harvester, he still could not find the squeak.

He had put his tool box in the trunk of the Cadillac and they drove all night through the dark streets of Jacksonville, stopping now and then under a street light for Easy to loosen something or tighten something or put a tiny drop of oil under or into something. At one point, he had the entire instrument panel disassembled and carefully laid out in the back seat; but when he put it all back together, the squeak was still there. Easy had got red in the face. Veins had stood in his neck and forehead. He wouldn't leave it alone. It had frightened Mister terribly. He had never seen his daddy in such a rage.

"I can fix it!" he had screamed, half his body buried under the steering column behind the instrument panel with electrical wiring curling about his arms.

But he had not, and the Cadillac still carried the fine sharp squeak when they pulled into the Park 'N Lock about seven o'clock that morning, Mister exhausted, and his daddy in a stupor of outrage. Then they'd found Mr. Edge in heavy conference with the man from the American Broadcasting Company, a contract full of money already drawn, waiting only for Mister's signature. And Mister, despite his tiredness, had been exultant ever since.

"I wish you'd try to understand what it means, daddy," said Mister.

"I know what it means," said Easy Mack, through clenched teeth.

"Well, all right," Mister said enthusiastically. "That's more like it."

Mister couldn't seem to make his daddy understand what the TeeVee contract meant. They'd sold Herman from coast to coast. He *was* going to Japan by satellite. They had permanent rooms in the hotel and more money than they had ever dreamed of.

But Easy Mack did not give a damn about the money or the rooms in the hotel. At this minute, sitting there on the bleacher seat with his son, watching the crowd file into the ballroom, he didn't feel like he'd ever give a damn about anything again. The thing he had always loved and honored had them all by the throat. And he couldn't get loose. Every time he smelled an exhaust, he wanted to throw up.

If he had just been able to fix that squeak, it would have been different. He felt sure it would have been different. The Cadillac had overwhelmed him. All that power. All those lights. All that everything. But then it had squeaked. The fucking thing had *squeaked!* It may cost ten thousand dollars and have four cigarette lighters to the square inch and more lights than you could count or ever use, *but it squeaked.* And what a squeak in a car required was a *man.* A man who was a mechanic. A man who controlled and understood the car. Understood its weaknesses. Its flaws. But God in heaven! He had opened up that Cadillac car and looked behind the instrument panel, and he had felt his own mortality in a way that he had never felt it before. Such a maze of wiring—blue wires and yellow wires and red wires and green wires—and fuses of every sort! God Himself would have been amazed and confounded before such a thing. Or so Easy had thought. But he told himself that he had to suck it up and go. Either you mastered it or it mastered you. In a blind awful moment of perverse nonreasoning, he knew that if he couldn't fix it, he ought to have to eat it. And after ten hours of effort, they had rolled into the Park 'N Lock with the small squeak still squeaking. Easy would never forget, as long as he lived, how his son had slowed and braked in front of the little machine that gave out the yellow time card at the Park 'N Lock, and simultaneously with the stopping wheels of the Cadillac car, a sound as small and sharp as the sound of a tiny bird had squeaked somewhere in the bowels of the car.

The ballroom was filling up now. Herman would soon be coming in to pass. Mr. Edge had reported that the doctor, by having Margo spoon it into his mouth, had been able to get Herman to eat a special bowl of food this morning at six o'clock. The doctor had assured them that it would make everything come out all right. Herman would be making his entrance pretty soon to take his place on the throne.

The throne had been the center of attention ever since the crowd had started coming in. The television cameras had been trained on it almost constantly. Every once in a while the cameraman panned the audience, but mostly the camera stayed on the throne. Several impartial judges were there to make sure that everything was genuine and above board. ABC owned most of the judges. They had carefully inspected the throne for secret compartments or trap doors, but of course there were none.

A delegation of Japanese judges was there also, flown in especially from New York to represent the company that was sponsoring Herman on television in the Orient. They walked rapidly about in neat blue suits and inscrutable faces, examining with patient thoroughness the Maverick, the cutting torch, the silver pan, the throne, and the stage itself, making sure it was solid and concealed no devices for cheating the public. Now and again they flashed brilliant smiles of approximately one-half second duration, and spoke either in rapid little bursts of Japanese or in similar bursts of impeccable English.

Mr. Edge raced about checking and double-checking everything. He had even come up to the top of the bleachers where Mister sat with his daddy.

"How's everything up here?" he cried in a hearty hysterical voice.

Easy had given him a quick glance of sour hatred and looked away. But Mister was ready to comfort and assure Mr. Edge.

"Homer, everything's just great," said Mister. "Couldn't be better."

"Mister, can you think of anything I've forgotten?" They had got as close as brothers since Mister got power-of-attorney from Herman and they signed the new contracts, especially the TeeVee contract.

"Not a thing, Homer," said Mister. "We've got it covered."

"Shit, we can't go wrong, we can't go wrong," said Mr. Edge. "Nobody can accuse us of anything with all these judges around. Everybody's got to see it's on the up and up. Right?"

"Right," Mister said.

"Right?" cried Mr. Edge, hitting Easy Mack on his knee.

Easy looked at Mr. Edge and belched loudly and tasted the entire Maverick at the root of his tongue.

"What did you think of that Cadillac?" Mr. Edge asked Easy when he didn't answer. "Standard of excellence. Isn't that something? Standard of excellence."

"Great car," Mister said. "Great car."

"It squeaks," said Easy with satisfaction.

"Squeaks!"

"Squeaks," said Easy.

"It's nothing," Mister said.

"They'll stand good for it," Mr. Edge said in a pleading voice. "I know Cadillac'll make it right."

"No matter what you do to it," said Easy, adjusting his skinny shank on the wooden bleacher, "it'll squeak."

"That's a hell of a thing to say," said Mr. Edge. "That's an awful thing to say."

"He's just upset," said Mister, patting Mr. Edge on the shoulder.

"It's still an awful thing to say," Mr. Edge said. "This is a great day and there's no reason to spoil it by saying a thing like that."

"He's just upset," Mister said. "Try to remember that it's his son who is stage center today."

"In the spotlight!" cried Mr. Edge. "In the spotlight!"

"The number one actor!" They beamed upon one another. They had quite forgotten Easy Mack, who was at that moment hiding another gaseous bubble behind his closed fist.

A loud wet word floated up to them from the seats below. Then it came again. It was coming from a Mongolian idiot. A child with slanting eyes, enlarged head, dark skin, and a mouth that had too much tongue in it. The child was in the midst of several rows of seats that swarmed with deformed and afflicted children.

"Look at that," Mr. Edge said proudly. "That little thing knows me." He waved to the child, and the child made the long wet sound again. Its tongue, very pointed, slightly blue and long, licked a wide place over its chin and lips. "That little thing knows me! And it's not seen me in over a month, *more than a month!*"

The children were one of Mr. Edge's charities. He had arranged through the Greater Jacksonville Rotary Club to get the children tickets for the show. They all had miniature plastic Mavericks clutched in their wet little hands and FORD GIVES YOU BETTER IDEAS stickers pinned around their waists, and they were all laughing and crying and singing and trying to get away from their keepers—three enormous matrons in white Supp-hose—and generally having a great time there in the five rows assigned to them.

"You tell me those little things can't learn!" demanded Mr. Edge. "That little thing knows who I am." He was very proud of his work with the afflicted children.

"You oughta take all them goddam things out to the river and drown'm," growled Easy Mack.

Mr. Edge paled and could not speak.

"Daddy, you're just upset," said Mister. "And you're going to upset Homer."

"You oughta gas them goddam crazy children," said Easy. "Give'm gas!"

"He's upset," Mister said to Mr. Edge. He put his arm around Mr. Edge's shoulder and hugged him. "Don't pay any attention. He's just upset."

Mr. Edge got up without a word and went down the bleachers. He stopped and kissed the child that had called to him. The child licked Mr. Edge with its sharp blue little tongue, but Mr. Edge didn't seem to mind. He patted its head, kissed its other cheek, and went on down the bleachers to the stage.

"Daddy, you hurt him," said Mister. "You hurt that man when he didn't do a thing to you."

"Give'm gas," Easy said in his implacable voice.

But Mister was not listening. He was already twisting his neck to see the door where something was happening. The crowd buzzed and whispered, the sound breaking back from the door in waves. It was Herman.

"It's him," said Mister, suddenly beside himself with joy. "It's him, daddy."

"Goddam," said his daddy in the same dead implacable voice. "Goddam every goddam thing to hell."

They led Herman in like a prize. He was dressed only in white tennis shorts and black felt house slippers. His skin was unnaturally pink, his entire body flushed. The crowd rushed forward when they saw him, but they kept a wide open space around him. They fell back when he approached. Joe walked in front of Herman, his flat-brimmed patrol hat squarely set on his head, and the leather flap over his pistol unbuttoned. Margo walked to the right of Herman and Junell to the left. One of Joe's men, identical in flat hat and unbuttoned holster, walked behind. Herman walked in their midst like a man entranced, almost stunned. His mouth was slightly ajar. Breath whistled in his pink wet lips. His eyes were veiled and hooded. His great sloping stomach seemed to vibrate with each step there where it rode before him.

"I should've stayed with that boy last night," said Mister. He turned to his daddy. "Instead of riding around in a Cadillac car, we should've stayed with that boy."

But his daddy paid him no attention. He was not looking at Herman, or at Mister, or even at the crowd—which rose now as one and cheered. Easy had a look on his face shockingly like his son Herman's, who was at that moment being led onto the stage.

"What's the matter, daddy? What is it?"

Easy said nothing.

"Come on, let's get down to the row reserved for the family." He took his daddy's arm and shook him gently. "It's not going to look right if we stay up here. Everybody knows that row down there by the stage is reserved for the family."

But down on the stage, Mr. Edge, by now directing everything, was having Margo slowly turn Herman around and around, and the crowd saw that someone had cleverly modified Herman's tennis shorts. Someone had cut a flap—a trap door—in the bottom of the white shorts, and then sewn on black buttons to hold the flap shut. The crowd knew what that meant, and the screams of delight and anxiety were so great that Mister could no longer make himself heard, so he left his daddy at the top of the bleachers and rushed down to the row by the stage reserved for the family.

At considerable expense—which Mr. Edge let nobody forget—Mr. Edge had installed the machine that was going to melt down the first half-ounce of the car and recast it in the shape of a Maverick. The machine had been set up right beside the throne on the stage. It was about the size of a jukebox with a red-and-green plastic face and a transparent plastic top so that the audience could see the half-ounce lump actually melted and molded.

The Japanese men representing the Oriental television company were clearly suspicious of Herman's trap door. But that didn't bother Mr. Edge. It made him happy. He wanted them to be suspicious and for the audience to see that they were suspicious. That way the audience would believe them when they inspected Herman and found him on the up and up. He invited them to examine Herman, the trap door tennis shorts, the throne, the melter-and-molder, everything.

"It's all right, it's all right," he cried. "Examine him, examine him." He pushed Margo away and herded the Japanese in upon Herman.

Herman stood very still and let them approach him. He still had a distracted bemused look in his face. His head was dropped slightly back so that his hooded gaze looked up into the ceiling of the ballroom. The Japanese had him completely surrounded now. Only Herman's head and shoulders showed above the circle of dark Japanese heads bent in obvious concentration. And gradually, as they pressed closer, a look of outrage replaced the bemused expression on Herman's face. His hooded eyes lifted, stretched. His cheeks turned deep red, the lobes of his ears turned almost purple. And still the Japanese pressed about him, talking in more and more excited voices. Finally, Herman's mouth opened slowly in a great O. But not a sound escaped him.

"Our Japanese brothers are thorough! They're thorough!" cried Mr. Edge to the audience, and the audience that had been watching the spectacle of the examination roared back at him. They had long since been convinced that Herman could not possibly be hiding anything from their Japanese brothers. It was already past ten o'clock and they wanted Herman to pass the car. The ABC cameras were rolling.

"Git them goddam gooks away from him!" yelled a man sitting in the first row.

"Let'm pass!" screamed the man's wife.

But Mr. Edge knew enough to let them have all the time they required. He was getting every bit of this on film. No possible taint of fraud. The Japanese were finally satisfied and, as a group, stepped away from Herman. They left him trembling where he stood. On shaking legs he got to the throne and fell into it. Margo helped him, her arm about his wide flaring hips. Mr. Edge walked to the microphone. He held his arms over his head in a V.

The idiot children sitting in the five rows had been trained by their keepers to say Mr. Edge's name in unison. The two matrons gave the children the sign.

"HO MER! HO MER!" screamed the children.

Homer Edge beamed warmly upon them and threw kisses with his hands. Then he turned serious and faced the "Wide World of Sports." He flashed the signal to a drummer he had hired out of a local nightclub. The drummer rolled his sticks and ended by slamming a cymbal.

"And now!" said Mr. Edge in his best MC's voice.

Another cymbal crash. Another drum roll. The television camera swung to include the drummer, a black boy with dull gold teeth. The silver pan had been placed in the open space under the throne. The collective gaze of the audience fell upon the pan. Mr. Edge spun and pointed to the throne.

"Herman Mack! *This is your moment!*"

The audience quit breathing. The Japanese, as a group, leaned slightly forward. Herman sat pale and perspiring on the throne. Nothing happened. The black, stoned drummer nodded over his sticks. A little tremor shook Herman. Still nothing happened, and the weight of silence pressing upon the ballroom was becoming unbearable. Herman turned his face toward Mr. Edge and his eyes rolled white with effort.

Ping!

The half-ounce of metal fell into the shallow silver pan. The man on the first row who had earlier screamed for the gooks to get away from Herman leapt to his feet and cried, "Five thousand dollars!" whereupon Mr. Edge fell in a faint.

The idiot children had been given the signal again by their keepers and they called in plaintive unison: "HO MER! HO MER!"

But Homer never heard them.

Eleven

HERMAN was a trouper and he knew that the show must go on. Besides that, he believed in what he was doing. But he didn't believe he could do what he believed in much longer. He had not told anybody yet about what was happening to him. The doctor examined him, and generally kept close watch on his physical condition. But he hurt. Herman *hurt* in a long devious line starting at his mouth and running down his throat through several long curling intestines and ending at his anus. And it hurt all the worse because he still loved the car. Since he had started eating it, the Maverick had become like one of the family. He saw clearly that he was defined by the car, that his very reason for living was bound up in the undigested and undigestible parts of the Maverick that still had to be swallowed. But he sometimes felt like every show was going to be his last one.

"How's the crowd, honey?" he asked from where he lay on the bed. He had heard the door close and he knew it was Margo.

"Are you kidding?" she asked, coming to where he was, kissing his cheek as she smiled fondly down upon him. "To the rafters, jammed to the rafters."

It was time to eat again. He had lost track of time, of the days of the week, or even of how long he had been at it. His life was eating and passing, passing and eating. Margo always came in and talked to him, rubbed him down, when it was time to eat or pass. They'd become very close.

She came to where he was and sat on the bed. "How're you feeling?" she asked.

"Fine," he lied.

She had done everything for him. And always without embarrassment or self-consciousness. She had greased him after that first morning when the Japanese had badly damaged him by probing his rectum for secrets. She had at first thought it was the car that made him bleed.

"Fingers, Jap fingers," he'd wept, lying on his stomach on his bed as she greased him afterward.

"Goddam Japs!" she said, soothing him, crooning in his ear. "There, there, darling, I know what it's like to have your asshole split like this. But this ointment I've got here will heal it right up."

And it had. She had never told him wrong. It healed his asshole and his spirit. The next night he passed with hardly any blood at all. That had been a long time ago, and he had finally healed completely. He cut his eyes up at her where she was sitting rubbing his back.

"You do all right today?" he asked.

"It wasn't bad."

He put both his hands under his belly, his fingers spread wide for support, and rolled over. She immediately cut her soft blue eyes to his stomach. It mounded in a soft roll. She touched it and smiled dreamily.

"How many today?" he asked.

"Thirty-seven."

"That's a good day," he said.

"The hotel's full," she said. "That's about average when the hotel is full." She talked in a quiet distracted voice. "But they were all old. The old ones are the only ones who can afford to stay in the rooms since Mr. Edge doubled the rate."

She had her ear against his stomach now listening. Her eyes were closed. Her pink lips parted slightly as she breathed. Her breath flew across his face in little puffy waves. It smelled of Clorets. It was her occupational breath.

"Really old?" he said.

"Ordinarily I would sometimes get a football player or at least somebody under thirty. Not today. Not a one like that today."

"What time is it?"

She looked at a star-shaped watch on her wrist. "You've got about a half hour, darling." She put her ear back to his navel, took his stomach in her hands, and gently shook it.

"Did you notice when you were out there if Mister's got it cut up yet?"

"Yes, cut up," she said. "Cut up, prepared, everything's ready."

Mister had already proved his worth to Mr. Edge. Ever since that first awful passing, Mister had been indispensable to the operation. When Mr. Edge had fainted at the first fantastic bid of five thousand dollars, Mister had leapt over his fallen body into the center of the stage and conducted the auction. He had brought it off like a professional.

"Five thousand dollars is not much of a start," Mister had sneered at the man in the front row. Then he rushed over to the silver pan and picked up the heat-blackened half-ounce lump of Maverick. He held it between his forefinger and thumb. Above his head. He circled the stage. He might have been holding up an enormous diamond for them to examine. "Do you know what this is?" he demanded. "Do you know what this is?"

A woman in the top row of the bleachers screamed, *"Six thousand!"*

Mister didn't even recognize her, did not even pause as he stalked about the stage, his hot flaring eyes raking the audience. "This is an American car. It has passed through an American. It is history. *And you were there.*"

Oh, there was no doubt about it, he was magnificent. He got eight thousand two hundred and thirty-three dollars for it before he was through. But partly that was because the Japanese started bidding, and Mister was able to appeal to patriotism. The fat man in the first row said he would pay whatever it cost to keep the first lump of the Ford in this country and not let it fall into foreign hands. His was an exceptional performance by anybody's standard, and when Mr. Edge woke up and found out what Mister had been able to do, he promptly hired Mister at an extra salary to help with promotion, gimmicks, and operational procedure of the Two-a-Day Shows.

"Tell me," said Margo.

She was curled about Herman's stomach, kissing it, listening now and again with her ear pressed tight against the slightly swelling skin, her tongue darting between needle teeth, at times to touch it. At these times when she came to comfort him before eating or passing, they would talk and talk, telling each other the most intimate things about their lives: what they had hoped, done, believed, loved. He had started out by telling her about CAR DISPLAY: YOUR HISTORY ON PARADE. She had thought it just about the most wonderful idea she had ever heard. Or said she did.

But the pain was on him bad today, killing him, making him wonder if he would have to stop with the car, so there was another story he wanted to tell her.

"I had a girlfriend once," he said.

"Tell me," she said.

"It ended badly," he said.

"Yes, it sometimes does," she said. "It often does."

"And it made me shy with girls. It made me shy ever since."

"Tell me," she said.

"I was only seven years old."

"That's very young," she said.

"And Myrtle was five."

"And it made you shy at seven?"

"Yes," he said.

"You've been shy a long time."

"Yes," he said. He was remembering it. He was starting to remember it all.

"Tell me," she said.

"She lived with her family in a little house on the edge of Auto-Town. She moved into the little house when I was seven and she was five. I remember she always had some kind of ribbon in her hair. Sometimes, it was yellow and sometimes it was red or even blue."

"What happened? Was it awful? Was what happened awful?"

"Yes," he said. "It was awful."

"Tell me," she said.

"We started meeting on the sly."

"Why did you have to meet on the sly?"

"We didn't have to. We just did. It seemed more fun. More grown-up."

"Where did you meet?"

"In a car."

"Where?"

"In the very center of Auto-Town. Under a mountain in the very center of Auto-Town."

"God help us all," Margo said.

"There was no fence around Auto-Town in those days. She would just come across the road from the little house she lived in and take the trail I had marked out for her."

"You marked a trail for her?"

"It went under the cars. A tunnel that went through windshields—coupes, convertibles, four-doors—right on through to the center of the mountain."

"Did you go through the tunnel with her?"

"I had a tunnel of my own. She started into Auto-Town at the place right across the road from her house. I started in at Salvage House through a tunnel of my own. And we'd meet at the car."

"Which car?"

"I spent my childhood tunneling through cars. I explored whole mountain ranges of cars, valleys filled with wonderful cars, made discoveries, staked claims. And one of the claims I staked was right at the heart of the most enormous mountain of all."

"What kind of car was it?"

"A Rolls-Royce. Rotted and old, but wonderful."

"And that's where you met Myrtle?"

"Almost every day. I marked a trail out for her that led into the mountain from the side she lived on. She'd come in from one side of the car and I'd come in from the other."

"And?"

"And we'd play."

"What did you play?"

"Grown-up. I'd get up in the front seat and drive, be her chauffeur. And she would sit in the back and be grand. And then we'd switch it around and she'd drive for me. Then we'd both get in the front seat and she'd read the map and watch the road signs for me, playing mommy and daddy. Then we'd get in the back seat and play mommy and daddy."

Margo groaned and pressed her face against his stomach.

"She'd show me hers and I'd show her mine. I never thought about it then, but I realized later that I loved her very much."

She raised her face and looked at him. "You said it was awful."

"It ended badly," he said.

"What happened?"

"One day she didn't come. I opened the door from my side of the Rolls-Royce and climbed into the back seat and closed the door. I sat there and waited but she didn't come. I waited all afternoon."

Margo didn't say anything but slowly buried her face in his stomach again.

"I did that three afternoons in a row," he said. "Just sitting in the back of that Rolls, waiting. Then I found out she was missing. Her parents were wild. Policemen and firemen and volunteers were looking everywhere for her. They finally found her."

"Under the mountain," she said in a flat voice.

"Under the mountain. She got lost and left the marked tunnel and

went off under some cars that . . . Well, they found her under a Studebaker. It mashed her bad. You couldn't even tell what it was they
brought out of there. Nobody blamed my daddy though. There were
signs everywhere saying dangerous, no trespassing, and no playing allowed."

She sat up and gently massaged his throat and began oiling his lips
with a special oil the doctor had supplied. Her slender fingers began
working the oil onto the inside of his mouth, his tongue, massaging his
throat, encouraging him to swallow to get the oil onto the walls of his
gullet. It was supposed to make the Maverick go down easier.

"I never told anybody that before," he said through oily lips.

She took his hands and pressed them tightly. He felt very close to her.
He was about to say something else to her when there came a loud
knocking at the door. A young usherette in red skirt and red cap—one
of Mister's recent ideas—stuck her head in the room and called brightly:
"Show time."

"We've got to go," said Margo.

As always, Herman was met with deafening applause. The young
pretty usherettes—cheerleaders and called Dragonettes at their local
high schools, here doing part-time summer work for Mr. Edge at the
Two-a-Day Shows—the young usherettes formed two lines and led him
to the stage. Everything was ready. Mister had the half-pound cut and
waiting on the silver pan. Mister was at the microphone. Joe and his
men were at the entrances and exits of the ballroom. Junell was sitting
beside Mr. Edge, with whom she had become good friends, out in the
first row of the section reserved for the family.

Herman looked to see if Easy was there. He was not. Easy had taken
his truck out of the Park 'N Lock and gone back to Auto-Town. Junell
had gone out to see him and had reported back to Herman that she was
afraid he might have a nervous breakdown. He was living in their old
rooms over Salvage House and refused to see anyone. Herman was very
worried about his daddy.

But as soon as he saw the half-pound of cut-up Maverick, he forgot
about Easy and about everything else except the necessity of getting
the metal down his throat one more time. He rubbed his oiled tongue
around his mouth. Swallowed. Felt the awful pain and tightness run the
length of him. But the television cameras were trained on him.

The Maverick was waiting. The bumper was gone now. The grille had been eaten away. He had swallowed both fenders off the front and was partly through the hood. The bowels and workings of the motor shone through the half-chewed-away hood.

"Give him a hand, ladies and gentlemen," cried Mister into the microphone.

The audience was already cheering and clapping but it rose to Mister's urging. The walls shook with vibrating voices. Several people in the audience came again and again, day after day, managing by paying exorbitant prices to buy up tickets to show after show after show. Herman recognized many of them. There was an old lady with carefully groomed white hair who sat in one of the preferred seats and knitted during every performance. She never took her eyes off Herman's stomach. But she never cheered or clapped or let anything show in her face. The man in the long white robe who had picketed the Hotel Sherman had finally thrown away his placard about God and joined the audience. He was an enthusiastic shouter. He must have played baseball at one time because his encouragement was always full of things like: *"Come on now, Babe! Right down the ole line! Watch it over! Come on now, Babe!"*

Mister was dressed in a green silk shirt. His tie had a diamond stickpin. He affected English boots with built-up heels to make himself look taller. And he had become quite professional as a master of ceremonies. As he was fond of saying, he had been quick to catch on to the whole operation. He presented Herman with a grand flourish.

"Ladies and gentlemen, the *star!*"

Herman, as always, was dressed only in white tennis shorts and house slippers. He waved listlessly to the crowd. The doctor, who was always on hand for the eating and passing, made a summary inspection of his body, pausing to listen to his stomach with a silver stethoscope. Herman sat in the special chair at the end of the aluminum examination table. Mister, smiling wildly, gave the silver pan to Margo, who always fed Herman. She brought it to the chair. Herman looked down into the pan and then up at her. The pain swelled in his stomach at the sight of the little lumps of Maverick. A line of fire swung through him. The audience fell silent. The furious click of the gray-haired lady's knitting needles could be heard all over the ballroom.

Mister, the smile now frozen and unfunny on his face, came over and bent toward Herman. "Well?" He breathed the word into Herman's ear.

Herman sat absolutely still. He was alive with pain. The jig was up. He would never be able to swallow another piece of car. Never.

Mister bent even lower, his mouth right against Herman's ear. "For Christ's sake, eat it! Eat the goddam thing!"

But his brother only sat dumbly looking back at him. Mister took the silver pan in one hand, and with his other hand he casually touched Herman's chin. He smoothed the jaw, almost a caress, or so it looked to the audience. But Mister was actually on the verge of dancing in hysterics. It was all he could do to keep from forcing his brother's mouth open and packing the pieces of car down his throat. But instead, he straightened and waved languidly to the four packed bleachers of people. "There is a small difficulty," he said, and surprised himself with his smooth assured voice.

An angry murmur boiled out of the audience. And Junell, dressed in her black leathers, leapt onto the stage and was suddenly standing at Mister's elbow, hot, her body steaming, her face and hands covered as always with a thin lacquer of sweat.

"What the fuck's wrong?" she hissed into Mister's ear.

"I don't know," he said.

She bent to Herman. "*Eat it!*" she demanded. "*Eat it!*"

Herman looked up at her helplessly. "Junell," he said. "Junell."

Mister walked casually back to the microphone. "Ladies and gentlemen, there is a slight problem. Only a very slight problem. The lumps have been improperly cut. They're too rough, too jagged."

The murmur rose again out of the crowd, but now it was no longer angry. The people understood. You had to have everything right. This was nothing to fool around with. They were willing for every precaution to be taken. Mister took the pan of Maverick back to the welder with the torch. He bent and said into his ear:

"Light up your torch. Waste some time. Burn the lumps again if you have to." The welder nodded behind his tinted goggles.

Mister went to his brother and herded him off the stage. Junell followed with Mr. Edge. Back in the room, Mister was beside himself. His face worked with rage.

"Now," he said, as soon as he could speak. "Herman, have you lost your mind?"

"No," said Herman. Margo had come close to him and put her hand on his shoulder.

"Then why are you ruining everything?"

"I can't," said Herman.

"Can't!" said Mister.

"Can't!" said Mr. Edge.

"Can't what?" demanded Junell. But she already knew.

"I can't eat any more," said Herman. "I hurt."

"You can't hurt," said Mister.

"I do," said Herman. "I hurt bad."

"But you love that Maverick," said Mister desperately. "You love it and you're going to eat it."

"It's over," said Herman. "It's poisoning me. It's poisoning me with pain."

"My God," said Mr. Edge. "I tore the whole front of my hotel off."

Mister, stunned, had collapsed onto the chair. He was thinking of his ten-thousand-dollar Cadillac. He was thinking of the clause in the contract with ABC and "Wide World of Sports." They were only filming the highlights—the first batch eaten, the first batch passed, middle sections when famous personalities dropped by to catch the show (it was rumored that when Vice-President Spiro Agnew came to Florida next time, he was coming by to see a batch of the Ford eaten), and of course the final great show when the last bit of the rear bumper went down and the last piece was passed and auctioned off—and the highlights were only important if the entire Maverick was eaten. For that reason the television lawyers had insisted on the return clause if Herman failed to eat the whole car. If he stopped now, they would be bankrupt and broke. All of them—even Herman—knew about the clause.

"The clause," moaned Mister. "The goddam clause." The ten-thousand-dollar Cadillac would have to go back. He'd lose it. He'd be back on the car-crusher pounding junk again, breathing the turgid breath of the turdy Saint John's River.

"I can't help it," said Herman. "I can't eat any more car."

"It's got to be eaten," said Mister, his voice hardening.

"There is no other way," said Mr. Edge.

The sweat was heavy on Junell. She was desperate for a solution. Joe had got her the first time—the first time anybody had *ever* got her—in that Maverick. And they sat every night in the back seat, watching the car slowly disappear in front of them. Very slowly, to be sure, but it *was* disappearing. And they both had come to understand, without either of them ever saying anything about it, that when the Maverick was gone, when the back seat was chewed up and swallowed and they no longer had any place for Joe to get her—when that happened, they'd get married. It would be a long engagement, but at least their relationship now had a direction, a goal. There was no telling what would have happened if they had kept meeting only at wrecks. They might never have been married. But Joe's Chrysler Cruiser had been taken away from him when he came on permanent duty at the Hotel Sherman, and he'd no longer had a car to talk about because he was inside all the time, and the only place they could get together was in the back seat of a car that was disappearing before their very eyes, disappearing down the throat of her brother. Circumstances had forced Joe to find the rest of her sweating but lovely body under those black motorcycle leathers. But now everything was threatened because Herman said he could not eat the rest of the car.

Mr. Edge had been pacing up and down the room. Now he was stopped by the door. Staring at Mister. Junell found that she too was looking at Mister. Mister was looking at nothing. He was holding his head, saying in a low hard voice: *"The car has to be eaten."*

"Of course!" said Junell, "of course!"

Mister glanced at her, saw her looking at Mr. Edge, saw Mr. Edge smiling, knew instantly what they were thinking.

"It's the only way," said Mr. Edge, his voice filled again with happiness and hysteria.

"Oh, no you don't," cried Mister, shooting out of his chair. He landed flat-footed, trembling. "Get back! Get away from me."

"Think about it," said Junell. "Think about the alternative."

But Mister already had. Standing there, he had already thought about the alternative. And before he even answered he felt the awful presence of the car in his stomach. He swelled with it. He felt it smothering him, filling his throat.

"I'd eat it, if I could," said Mr. Edge. "If we could get away with it."

"I would too," said Junell. "I'd gladly eat it myself."

And he knew they would. But they couldn't. He was the only one who could carry it off, because he had had the disastrous luck of being born a twin to Herman.

"Don't, Mister." Herman, his head fallen forward, his chin resting against his slack chest, spoke almost in a whisper.

"If you won't eat it," said Mister, "I've got to."

"Don't," Herman said, in the same small voice. "It'll kill you."

"Somebody's got to eat it," said Mister.

"Right. Somebody's *got* to eat that car," Mr. Edge said.

An angry rush of voices came to them in the room. It was the audience. They all turned toward the door as if they expected the crowd to burst upon them. Mister took a deep breath and without a word starting shucking out of his green silk suit. He took off his English boots. Junell and Mr. Edge stood very still and watched him strip.

Naked, he looked like Herman exactly—the same soft flaring hips, the same sloping stomach, the same dead, white skin. Junell pulled Herman to his feet and unbuttoned his tennis shorts. They dropped about his ankles. He stepped out of them. Mister pulled them on.

"Put on the suit," Junell said. She handed Herman the pants and the shirt. She knotted his tie when he was ready. She put Mister's diamond stickpin in it. All the while the rush of voices in the ballroom had been building until now it roared through the hotel. Margo stood with Herman, her hand resting lightly on his swelling hip. Mr. Edge, who was anxious to get started, took Margo's thin wrist and pulled her toward Mister, who stood by the door in his tennis shorts with the modified seat and the felt house slippers. He couldn't keep his eyes off his elevated English boots which were now on his brother's feet.

"O.K.," said Mr. Edge. "Switch. You're with him now, Margo."

"No," she said.

"What?"

"I said no."

The rushing audience's voice had raised to a kind of scream beyond the room.

"Jesus," said Mr. Edge, raising his eyes to the ceiling. "Now a temperamental whore. Get over there with Mister, goddamit!"

"No."

"But you can't tell them apart," Junell said.

"Yes I can," Margo said.

Mr. Edge put his face right in her face and almost screamed. "You're a whore! Can't you understand? You stupid cunt, you're a whore. When it's time to switch, you switch."

"I think I'm done with that," she said.

"You got to feed him," said Junell. "You've always held the pan." She shrugged helplessly. "The audience . . ."

Mister, whose face was so chalky that his eyes looked burned into his face, said: "You've got to feed me," he said. "Please."

"Do it," said Herman.

"Do you want me to?" she asked.

"It's the least we can do," said Herman.

And so they got in a line and marched out of the room and down the hall into the ballroom. The people in the audience fell silent when they saw them coming. They could tell by Herman's face that he'd been back there worrying about those jagged lumps. The lumps had been too rough today and it must have seemed to him a bad sign because his eyes were terrorized.

Mr. Edge, not trusting Herman with the microphone, went onto the stage himself. "Ladies and gentlemen, for your kind indulgence and patience, the management is most grateful."

Mister saw Margo take up the pan, saw her walking across the stage toward him. He did not believe this was happening to him. Moments ago he had been wearing a three-hundred-dollar suit, talking through a microphone, standing higher in English boots, saying how wonderful it all was. And now he was on the edge of having to swallow a piece of car. Several pieces of car. His throat gripped like a fist. She was in front of him. The people were quiet now, leaning slightly where they sat in their seats in the bleachers. Mr. Edge pointed to the drummer. The drummer, stoned but functioning, rolled his sticks. Margo picked up a lump. Mister saw it coming and thought, "This is it." He closed his eyes and told himself it wasn't anything more than swallowing candy.

But God in heaven! It felt like a boulder in his mouth. Rough. Incomprehensibly hard. As cold as ice. He gathered his tongue, pushed the car to the back of his mouth. It was as though the whole weight of the Maverick hung from the hinge of his jaw. His eyes popped open and he looked wildly at Herman for help.

But Herman's dreamy gaze was lost in the middle distance.

Twelve

THE doctor was dumbfounded and amazed. He had not known that Herman and Mister switched. He had waited on the stage for them to return, generally bored by the whole thing. He would never have consented to hang around for the performances anyway, but he'd been cut in for two percent of the profits. He'd turned his practice over to a junior partner and consented to lend his name and his presence to Mr. Edge and Herman. Nobody had bothered to tell him that they had lost their star and that Mister had taken his place.

Now they were back in the room with the doctor working frantically. Blood was pouring out of Mister's mouth, over his chin, and down his white naked chest.

"It's all right," the doctor was saying, "it's all right. The blood is not originating internally. It's all from the mouth and throat lacerations."

Mr. Edge grabbed his own head and squeezed it. "All right!" he cried. "How the hell is he going to eat the car with his throat cut and bleeding."

They were all standing about watching the doctor swab Mister's throat. Herman and Margo were whispering softly and touching each other in one corner. Mr. Edge and Junell were closer, trying to look down into Mister's mouth.

"Why didn't you tell me?" asked the doctor.

"Tell you what?" said Mr. Edge.

"That you had a new eater."

"We didn't plan it," said Junell. "When we found out, there wasn't time to go around telling everybody."

"His mouth and throat weren't even oiled," the doctor said.

"Exactly what happened?" demanded Mr. Edge. "What exactly happened? I don't understand a goddam thing about this. All I know is I got the front of my hotel torn out, and a TeeVee contract that's no damn good, because I got one performer who *won't* perform and one performer who *can't* perform. Will somebody tell me *exactly* what happened!" He shoved the doctor out of the way and grabbed Mister, who was sitting on a chair, by the head. He pressed one fat palm on each side of his head and pulled Mister half out of the chair until their faces were only inches apart. "Why are you bleeding, goddam you?"

The doctor, who was also Mr. Edge's family doctor, got a vial of white pills out of his black bag. "Homer, you better take a couple of these."

Mr. Edge popped three or four pills into his mouth like peanuts, chewed them furiously, and swallowed them without water. He scowled across the room at Herman. "See what you've done to your brother?"

Herman lifted his shoulders in a gesture of defeat. "I told him," he said. "I told him."

"Goddamit," Mr. Edge said, "you're not bleeding." He pointed a trembling finger at Herman. "You're not even bleeding and you're not hurt."

"I'm hurt."

"You're not bleeding."

"No, I'm not bleeding."

"Well look at him!"

But they had all been looking at Mister anyway. Even while they talked, they had kept their eyes on him where he sat, his face flushed, his throat swollen.

"*He's* bleeding," repeated Mr. Edge. "And what I want to know is why? Why is this man bleeding? Herman didn't bleed, why Mister?"

"I think I can tell you why," said the doctor. "It looks like a common case of his throat expelling what he was trying to eat. That's what I think but we won't know for sure until Mister can talk." The doctor did not look up as he spoke. He kept working on Mister's mouth and throat. He had the bleeding almost stopped.

"A common case of his throat expelling . . . What the hell does that mean?" demanded Mr. Edge. "What are you saying?"

"Mister didn't want to eat it," the doctor said.

Mister's face turned red with effort and he made a grunting noise in his chest.

"Of course he wanted to eat it," said Mr. Edge.

"If he could talk," said Junell, "he'd tell you he wanted to eat it."

"He wanted to eat it," said the doctor, "but he *didn't* want to eat it, if you see what I mean."

"I don't see what you mean because what you say doesn't mean anything," Mr. Edge said.

"His throat kept closing up on him," said the doctor, "trying to expel . . ."

"I can tell'm what you mean, doc," Margo said. "I can explain it."

They all turned to look at her where she stood with Herman by the window. Even Mister, his throat swollen and red, cut his eyes in her direction. He was lying back on the bed. His breath whistled in slightly parted, bruised lips.

"Everybody's got a gag reflex," she said. "If you put something far enough down your throat, you gag, anybody gags, everybody gags. You don't have to think about it, or want to do it, you just do it. That's why it's called a gag *reflex*. Right, doc?"

"Right," he said. "But . . ."

"But listen to this," she said. "There are whores who have no gag reflex." She paused and they stood silently watching her. She saw the look in Junell's face and shrugged. "I'm a whore. It's my business to know such things. Some whores can open their mouths and let a man fuck their throats. It's a beautiful trick, but it's not something you can learn. You've got to want the cock in your throat. You've got to want it so bad that the reflex just doesn't work. Such whores are few and far between because as everybody knows, most whores hate fucking. But once in a while a whore really loves cocks and she's got the best of both possible worlds. A whore like that can make a fortune, an absolute fortune in two or three years. It's a specialty act. And everybody loves a specialty act. But you think a whore like that quits with her fortune? Of course not. Because finally she's not doing it for the money, anyway. She's doing it for the love of cocks. And she keeps that throat of hers in service as long as there's a man who wants to put something in it."

"Jesus," said the doctor, "Jesus Christ!"

Mister's throat was pulsing and heaving while Margo talked.

In a tiny voice, Junell asked, "Can you . . . Do you . . . ?"

"No," said Margo. "I can't. I don't." She looked at Mister. "And he can't either. He's trying to fake it." She walked over to the bed and looked down into Mister's stretched, bloodshot eyes. "You poor son-of-a-bitch, you can't fake it. It can't be faked."

Mister's throat was racked in a convulsive heave, and when he opened his mouth, he was hemorrhaging, his exploding breath spraying blood across Margo's face and across the room. The doctor grabbed his bag and fell to work on Mister's bleeding throat. Mr. Edge took Margo's shoulder and shoved her away from the bed.

"Don't listen to her!" cried Mr. Edge. "Don't listen, Mister. She's a goddam whore." He spun from the bed and faced Margo. "You're a god-dam whore," he said, as if the thought had just occurred to him. "And you're fired. I take you in and give you a place to work and this is the way you thank me. You're fired." He went to the bed, sat down, and took Mister's head onto his lap. "Don't think about it, son. Don't think about a thing she said." He crooned into Mister's ear with the doctor still prob-ing in Mister's stretched mouth with tongue depressors and swabbing sticks. "We can do it. Don't think about it. We can do it together."

"Looks like you lost your job too," said Herman.

Margo, who stood beside him at the window, gave a little smile. "Well, there are jobs and there are jobs. Being a whore is like being a schoolteacher—you can work anywhere in the country. There's always somebody looking for what you do."

Mr. Edge eased Mister's head out of his lap and let it down gently on the pillow. He got off the bed and came to where Herman was beside the window. "Do you still mean to leave your brother like this?" he whispered savagely in Herman's ear.

"I was never with him," Herman said.

"He'll die," said Mr. Edge.

"He will if he eats that car," said Herman. "That's what I tried to tell him. I found out that it can't be done. I thought it could, I wish it could—I love that Maverick—but it can't be done."

"It can be done," insisted Mr. Edge. "It's *got* to be done, and you can do it."

Herman took a deep breath and looked out the window where a thick hazy cloud pressed low over the city. Then he turned back to Mr. Edge. "I can't tell you this so you'll understand it, but I'll try. I'll try one time."

"Try me," said Mr. Edge warmly, in a sudden happy voice. "I knew we could work it out."

Herman looked back at the hazy city. "I love that Maverick car. And I think because I love it so much, I can't stand for it to cause that kind of pain in me. I mean I can stand the *pain*—I think I could stand the pain if it was just pain—but I can't stand that kind of pain from some-thing I love."

Mr. Edge's face hardened. "I am a sensible man. I can understand anything that makes sense. But that does not make sense."

"No," said Herman, "I knew it wouldn't."

Thirteen

"WHAT are we going to do now?" Margo said.

They were out in the hall. The doctor was inside promising Mister that everything would be all right just as soon as he got on the special diet and got his mouth and tongue and throat greased good.

"I don't know," said Herman. He took out his handkerchief and tried to wipe away the flecks of blood that Mister had sprayed across Margo's face. But it was dry by now and wouldn't come off. "You want to come down to my room and get cleaned up?"

"I guess," she said.

In the room Herman watched her wash her face. He sat on the bed and watched her as she started to put back on what she called her professional face: the luminous lipstick, the libidinous skin-colored foundation powder, the red-bead choker.

"Why?" said Herman.

"Why what?" she said, turning from the mirror over the sink and looking back at him through the door of the bath.

"Why are you putting that stuff back on?"

She smiled, dampened a cloth under the tap, and started rubbing at her cheeks, scrubbing away the bit of makeup she had already put back on. "Habit," she said, "just habit."

When she had finished, her cheeks shone with the high color of blood. She came and sat beside him on the bed. They sat a long time without speaking.

"What now?" she said finally.

"We're both out of work," he said.

"Well, we're out of *that* work," said Margo.

They sat another long time.

"Can you think of anything you might do?" he asked. "That you might *want* to do?"

"No," she said.

"I can't either," he said.

They listened to the traffic roaring beyond his window.

"Did the car really hurt you?" she asked.

"Yes."

"You never told me about it."

"I didn't expect it to hurt. It was a surprise. Even when it was killing me and I couldn't stand it anymore, it was a surprise."

"If you'd just told me," she said. "I might could have helped you."

"Maybe so," he said. "But I never thought to say anything because I could never believe I was hurting as bad as I was hurting."

She got up and went to the window and stood looking down into the street. "Why have you never fucked me?" she asked.

"I don't know."

She had often licked him, usually his stomach, sometimes his legs, and crooned to him. It made him feel very close to her. But that was as far as it ever got. He had often wondered what she wanted of him, what she expected.

"Didn't you ever want to?" she asked.

"I don't know."

She looked back from the window. "What kind of answer is that?"

"The truth," he said. "I never thought about it. I was thinking about the car."

"Never? You never thought about fucking me?"

"Sometimes. Yes. Once or twice. But never when it was possible. When it was possible, I was always thinking about the car. You're very beautiful. I told you that. I told you how beautiful you are."

"Well, the job's gone," she said.

"Yes, it's gone."

"And I've still got everything I ever had."

"I've never seen a body like yours," he said. "I never have and you've been good to me."

"Do you want to see my room?"

He had never thought about her room. He just always supposed it was somewhere else, not in the hotel. "You've got a place here, too?"

"Mr. Edge has been good about that. It's the only way it would work anyway. I'm on call twenty-four hours a day. Or at least I was."

"Twenty-four hours a day?"

"Around the clock," she said. "It was the way I wanted it." She took his hand. "Come on, I'll show you."

They took the elevator up four floors. The room was at the end of the corridor at the back of the hotel. Herman stood just inside the door for a long time looking at the room. He'd never seen anything like it, and never thought to imagine that anything like it existed.

She saw him staring. "Just the tools of the trade," she said.

"It's something," he said. "It really is, I never . . ."

His voice trailed off and quit. He was staring at an enormous cock. It was hanging from a peg on the wall, black, thick as a man's wrist, with a swelling mushroom head. It looked to be made of some smooth rubbery substance. She followed his eyes, walked over, and took it off the peg. And while his mouth worked without sound, she strapped the thing on right over her miniskirt, so that finally she was standing there with a rigid upswept cock strapped to her with black belts running across her hips and buckling on her rump.

"A dildoe," she said. "A black dildoe. I've got a white one, a red one, and a yellow one in the drawer." She pointed to a chest by the window.

He couldn't take his eyes off the thing strapped to the bottom of her stomach. "But why would . . . ?"

"Bless your heart," she said. She came over and kissed him lightly on the cheek. She forgot to turn as she leaned toward him and he felt the brutal jab of the cock against his leg. "What do you think whores do?"

"Well, I . . ." He was embarrassed.

"Whores have to sell whatever there's a market for. Sex. However it comes. That's all." She bent and showed him a little valve on the dildoe. "You fill this up with hot water."

"Hot . . ."

"Water," she said. "You poor darling. You don't know anything about this, do you? Nothing about the world you live in? I service women with this. I sometimes service men. I let men go down on it, or women go down on it. I effect rear entries."

Herman went over by the bed and collapsed onto one half of a red loveseat. He sat there while she talked briefly about some of the other things in the room.

"Obviously a whip," she said, taking one of the leather rods out of something that looked like an umbrella holder. She popped it gently against her round perfect calf as she walked. Then used it as a pointer. "Boots. With or without spurs." There were several rolled posters, hanging like window shades from hooks on the walls. She pulled one down.

It was a picture of a nun being mounted by a German shepherd. In a quietly disinterested voice she said, "People want strange things. Red dildoes with me wearing feathers." She pointed to an Indian headdress in the far corner. "Nuns and dogs." She pulled down another poster. It was a picture of her and another girl. The other girl was wearing a dildoe. A yellow one. Margo was on her knees in the picture with the dildoe in her mouth.

Herman stirred uneasily on the loveseat. "Why don't you take that thing off?" he said.

She turned the poster loose and looked down. Apparently she had forgotten that she was even wearing it. She unbuckled it and put it back on the peg in the wall. She came and sat beside him on the loveseat. She put her head on his shoulder. He touched her hair with his hand.

"Did you really want me to?" he asked.

"What?" she said.

"Fuck you."

"It was all I had," she said.

"But was it important?"

"I wanted to do something for you," she said.

"I know it," he said.

"I always wanted to do something for you," Margo said.

"You did," he said.

"I wish I could have," she said.

"You did. Fucking is not important."

"That's not a kind thing to say."

"I guess it isn't," he said. "I don't want to be unkind. But, Jesus Christ, how does anybody ever get caught in something like this?" He waved his hand to include the whole room.

She laughed.

"What's the matter?"

"Nothing," she said.

"No, tell me," said Herman. "What's to laugh at?"

She looked up at him. "What's a nice girl like you doing in a place like this?"

"I never said that."

"A John never says that. Not in those words. But all of them—even the ones that want you to wear Indian feathers and fuck'm in the ass with a red dildoe—all of them end up by saying something that really means, 'What's a nice girl like you doing in a place like this?' "

"All right, goddamit, how *did* a nice girl like you get into a place like this?"

"Oh, Herman," she said, "for God's sake."

"Don't Oh Herman me," he said. "Tell me."

"What a child you are," she said. "Do you think anybody ever *knows* how they got where they are?"

"Yes, I do," he said. "I think they ought to know."

"All right then," she said, "this is the other end of a long line I got into a long time ago."

"What line?"

"It doesn't matter."

"How'd you get into it?"

"It doesn't matter," she said irritably. "You're just full of questions aren't you? You were never like this before. What's got into you?"

"What am I supposed to do?" he demanded. "Look at this fucking room."

She smiled. Then giggled. "That's good. That's pretty good."

"What?"

"Calling this a fucking room," she said.

He looked away from her, at the walls, over the floor. There were any number of things on the wall that he couldn't identify, that he couldn't imagine the uses for. There were two elaborate machines at the back of the room, made of aluminum pipe. At the top of each machine was a little black motor. He really wanted to know about them, but he was afraid to ask. Sitting beside him with her head on his shoulder, she was still laughing. But there was no pleasure in it. It was rasping and light, a sound closer to grief than to joy. He thought he could hear it was on the edge of tears.

"I've got something I want to show you," he said.

"What is it?"

"I can't tell you," he said. "There's no way to tell you. Nobody could ever tell you. You'll have to come out to Auto-Town to see it."

"I can't," she said.

"I saw your room," said Herman. "I came here with you. Now I've got something I want you to see."

"I can't."

"Why?"

"My pimp'll be here in the morning," she said. "By then he'll know I lost my job. He'll be madder than hell about it."

"Come with me anyway," he said.

"I told you, I . . ."

"I mean from now on," he said. "I got something I want you to see at Auto-Town. Then we'll go somewhere else."

"Where?"

"I don't know."

"Why should I?"

"Because I need you more than your pimp does."

"That was the right answer," she said.

Fourteen

THE cab driver thought he recognized them both. They sneaked out the fire exit of the Hotel Sherman the next morning at eleven o'clock right after Mister's first passing, which was a greater disaster than his first eating. And as soon as they got into the cab, the driver thought he recognized them both. They could see him watching them in the rearview mirror as he roared away from the curb.

"Still got that room?" he asked.

"What?" she said, distracted, her thoughts still back there in the ballroom with Mister's desperate morning.

"You still got that room?" His eyes were all they could see in the mirror. They were narrow and blue.

"No," she said.

The cab driver cut his eyes to Herman. "Say," he said, "ain't you the guy . . . ? you're the guy eating the car!"

"No," said Herman.

"But your picture is . . ."

"My brother," said Herman. "My brother's eating the car."

"That boy's got guts," said the cab driver.

Nobody would deny that. They all knew he had guts. Mr. Edge had not tried to hide the fact that Mister (of course he was still billed as Herman. It wouldn't do to let the public know there had been, as Mr. Edge put it, The ole switcheroo) was bleeding, that his throat was cut and hemorrhaging during the night. So Mr. Edge gave out press releases on the car eater's condition. He let the newspaper photographers take pictures, and he let the car eater make written statements. So far, all Mister would write for anybody was, "Don't worry. I can eat the car."

Mr. Edge had pointed out that it didn't make any sense to hide the fact that he was bleeding. Blood would draw customers. If they found out he was bleeding, they'd come in droves. They'd probably be able to double the price of a ticket. Besides that, hiding the blood from the customers would not help Mister eat the Maverick. He could either eat it,

or he could not eat it. So by now the papers, and the television news
and the radio news, were full of stories that gave details about the guy
who was eating the car and about his blood which was there for anybody to see who wanted to come and pay the price.

But of course Herman and Margo didn't find out any of that until
they came down that morning for the passing. Her pimp was not due at
the hotel until just before noon so they had spent the night in her
room. They both wished now that they had gone on to Auto-Town and
missed the passing.

"But maybe I can help him," Herman had said when Margo suggested
they not see the passing.

"That's true," she said.

But she knew that was a lie, and knew also that Herman realized that
Mister was beyond his help, beyond anybody's help. Herman was going
because he loved Mister, and could not do anything else. But even loving him as he did, Herman probably would not have gone if he had
known it was going to come out the way it did.

Mr. Edge had opened the ballroom up to a standing-room audience.
He had been right about the blood bringing customers. They threatened
to tear the doors off his hotel if he didn't allow them in to stand in the
aisles and in every other foot of open space. When the place was finally
packed, when not another single person could be wedged into the ballroom, a door opened up, and Mister was led in by the Dragonettes. They
brought him down an open lane especially reserved for his entrance.

The audience went immediately to its feet, fighting for a look at Mister. He came slowly down toward the stage, his face set in stony nonex-
pression, glancing neither to the left nor the right. His lips were
swollen. His throat was covered with a faintly purple bruise that started
under his chin and faded out between his collarbones. Mister went
straight to the throne and sat upon it. Homer raced to the microphone
to introduce him because it looked as though Mister was going to pass
without being introduced or anything. Mr. Edge was right in the middle
of saying what a courageous American boy this was when Mister
screamed the first time.

Mr. Edge stopped in midsentence, and never did complete the intro-
duction. Mister gripped the arms of the throne and howled like a dog.
Blood flecked his lips as he screamed and enormous drops of blood fell
beneath the throne into the silver pan. There was not another sound in

the ballroom. Even the lady with the constant knitting needles stopped. Junell embraced Joe in the row reserved for the family. Mr. Edge had his hand on the doctor's arm, partially for support, and partially to restrain the doctor, because they had agreed ahead of time that no matter what happened they would not stop the show or go to Mister's aid unless Mister himself signaled that he was ready to call it off.

And Mister made no sign that he was thinking of quitting. He writhed on the throne. His head was thrown back and he screamed and screamed until he was making nothing but hoarse barking groans finally and clawing at the arms of the throne and kicking his feet in uncontrolled spasms of pain.

And then the lump—that first lump that everybody had been waiting for—fell into the puddle of blood in the silver pan and suddenly Mister was passing. Lump after bloody lump. The entire half-pound. When they finally got Mister to his feet and led him out of the ballroom, every man, woman, and child had his gaze fastened to the buttoned seat of Mister's tennis shorts where blood had soaked through in a tongue-shaped stain.

The cab driver was snarling about the traffic on Turner Memorial Bridge. He had been tailgating a garbage truck, but then he saw a sudden opening, swerved and passed it, only to end up tailgating another taxi.

"Goddam stupid hacks," he growled.

In the back seat, Herman tried to forget that the driver was up there or that he knew about Margo's room back at the hotel. He was not going to think about any of that. He took Margo's hand.

"There it is," he said. He pointed off to the west of Turner Memorial Bridge. The mountains of wrecked cars stretched away along the edge of the Saint John's River.

"It's big," she said.

"Biggest one in the state," he said.

"You ever notice how many things are the biggest or the oldest or the cleanest or the holiest?"

"I noticed," he said.

"It depresses the hell out of me," she said.

"Me too," he said. "But it didn't always. Once it didn't bother me a bit."

"Me either," she said.

They pulled up in front of Auto-Town. Easy Mack's International pickup truck was parked in front of the gate. They pretended not to see it.

"That's gonna be nine dollars and a quarter, buddy," said the cab driver.

Herman was still wearing Mister's green silk suit. He reached in to the inside jacket pocket and brought out a new alligator-hide wallet. He opened it. It was full of money. He took out a bill and handed it to the driver.

"For Christ's sake, I caint break this!"

"Keep it," said Herman.

"Fifty bucks!"

"Yes," said Herman, "keep it." It had been the smallest bill in the wallet.

"Listen," said the driver, "it was a privilege hauling you. You tell your brother that, you hear? Tell him I said it was a privilege hauling anybody that was even kin to him."

"Right."

They were out of the car now. The driver looked a long time at Margo, at the hem of her miniskirt and her tight converging thighs. He looked as though he wanted to say something, but finally he just gave a little wave of his hand and roared off. Herman and Margo stood in the layering clouds of blue smoke from the cab's exhaust and stared out over the rolling wrecked landscape. They probably never would have said anything about Easy Mack if he had not suddenly appeared, five hundred yards away on top of the mountain of cars, picking his way across the jagged horizon toward the river.

"Your daddy," she said.

"Yes," he said.

They watched him move slowly across the yellowing sky.

"The poor old son-of-a-bitch," she said.

"Yes," he said.

Easy Mack had been in the hotel room when they brought Mister up from the morning passing. Mr. Edge had Joe send one of his men for Easy because Mr. Edge thought his daddy's presence might help Mister swallow the Maverick better. When the old man got to the hotel Mr. Edge told him about the old switcheroo and told him about the blood that had poured from Mister's throat after the first eating. It had frightened Easy Mack terribly and he had refused to go down to the ballroom for the passing. And when they brought Mister in with blood running down his legs, Easy had started crying. He cried and told his son he'd fixed it.

"I fixed it, son. You don't have to worry about a thing. I fixed it. I fixed it."

The doctor had Mister lying on his stomach on the bed while he worked to stop the bleeding. And Easy Mack kissed Mister on the side of his face and kept crying and saying over and over again that he'd fixed it. It was a long time before they found out he was talking about the Cadillac. And when they did find out, Mr. Edge protested immediately.

"That's a lie," said Mr. Edge. "You never fixed it because nothing was ever wrong with it."

But Joe and Junell and everybody else was worried about whether or not the doctor was going to be able to stop the bleeding. When they finally had time for Easy Mack, he was gone. Mr. Edge sent the bell captain to look for him, but he wasn't in the hotel. And his International pickup was not in the Park 'N Lock.

"Where's he going?" Margo asked.

Herman had taken her up to show her where they lived over Salvage House. They were standing in the living room looking through the glass windows toward the river. Easy Mack was climbing slowly over the broken horizon, descending the mountain of wrecked cars now into the valley.

"I don't know," said Herman.

"What's that?" she said. "What *is* that thing?"

"That's a car-crusher."

"A car-crusher?"

It smashes cars into small pieces so they can be shipped as scrap."

"Shipped where?"

"To car factories."

"What's he doing?"

"He's climbing up on it."

They watched the old man climb up and sit in the cradle of the car-crusher. The cheesy breath of the river floated about them where they stood.

"You want to go for a walk?" he asked.

"If you want to," she said.

"Come on."

He led her down from Salvage House. He took her hand. They walked across the glassy yard, down through the plain of wrecked cars, finally into the valley. Cars pitched in every fantastic attitude rose on both sides of them. They walked on. Finally they stopped in front of the sheer face of a cliff. But directly in front of them, two cars were wedged in such a way as to form an upside-down V, a kind of arch, as high as a man's head.

"That's the tunnel to the Rolls-Royce, isn't it?" she said.

"Yes," he said. "That's one of them. That's the one I used."

"You want me to see it." It was a quiet statement of fact.

"I haven't seen it in a long time myself," he said.

"How long?"

"Since she was killed in there. Since the day they found her in there."

They went under the arch, she leading him, under the mountain. It wasn't really a tunnel at all. It was just a long series of accidental open spaces. It led beside cars, over cars, around cars, through cars. He was leading now, going slowly. The light was not good anymore. The deeper they went, the darker it got. But they could see well enough. And on they went, on down into the heart of the mountain. They both ignored the rust and the grease and the dirt, and slowly picked their way as the light got worse and the tunnel more constricted.

He stopped. She came up beside him, put her face next to his shoulder. Directly in front of him was a Rolls-Royce Silver Cloud, blocking the tunnel, closing it up. A grand ancient ruined enormous touring car. He opened the back door for her. She climbed in. He came in behind her and closed the door. The dust they had raised from the seats settled onto their faces, their arms, their laps, the tops of their shoes. The light was not so bad that they could not see each other.

"I thought I could get rid of fucking by fucking," she said.

"Yes," he said.

"By fucking everybody."

"Yes."

"I don't think the son-of-a-bitch ever knew which cheerleader he fucked that night in the orange grove."

"No," he said. "Probably not."

They sat looking straight ahead. Through the windows of the car the shadows of other cars leaned upon them.

"But I found out that won't work," she said.

"I know," he said. "You cannot fuck everybody. And the only way it would work is if you could fuck everybody."

She took his hand. They were both looking straight ahead. She smiled. From far away, they heard the car-crusher slam shut on itself. The sound roared through the cars, reverberating under the mountain. Motes of dust rose in front of them and hung in the dead air.

Climbing the Tower

I was on the University of Texas campus in Austin, back in the state where I had sworn never to go again—having flown from Gainesville, Florida, to Atlanta, to Dallas, to Austin—and I was shaking and scared, feeling very tenuous, as though I had somehow become a shapeless floating fog without substance or identity.

There are some days when I feel my own mortality stick in my throat, when I can't swallow it or spit it up. The feeling first started when I was a child, and it always came on Sunday. An evangelist named Harvey Springer saved my soul when I was twelve years old, but before he saved me, he made me smell the sulfur and feel the brimstone of hellfire and know for sure that I was corrupted beyond even the mercy of God. So on Sunday I would feel my mortality—though at that time I did not know the word—plugging my throat like a lump of half-cooked dough filled with finely ground bits of razor blade.

We all, of course, know we are going to die, but none of us, of course, *believes* he is going to die. Like having a deformed child, it is something that always happens to somebody else. But on the ride in the taxicab from the airport to the University of Texas campus, I not only believed in my death, I could also smell the open grave I would someday be lowered into and could even read the little name cards attached to the funeral wreaths sent by friends and relatives. I took a newspaper clipping out of my pocket for perhaps the tenth time in the last two hours and read that in Capetown, South Africa, my last novel had been banned by the Directorate of Publications. Anyone who owned or imported or distributed *A Feast of Snakes* was, the newspaper clipping said, "in violation of the law and subject to heavy penalties." I read it again because it made me feel more substantial to know that somewhere in Africa somebody had actually read my work and reacted to it so violently that he listed me among those the government looked upon with disfavor.

But even that did not help enough, so when I got out of the taxi, before I went over to the office of the man who invited me to the university, I rushed to the library and looked myself up in the card catalogue. And yes, there I was. I left the university library still feeling diaphanous, still feeling the morning terrors and black twirlies, a burden I carry better at some times than at others. I was softly mumbling to myself as I went into the office of the professor who'd invited me to the university to play writer. God only knows why writers do such things, go hundreds, sometimes thousands, of miles to read out of their work the very things that the people in the audience could read just as easily for themselves. If I let myself think about it too much, that alone is enough to give me a bad case of the black twirlies.

The professor greeted me cordially. We left his office immediately because before I gave the reading that night, I was supposed to have a seminar, if you can believe it, in Southern fiction. I was a little late and we had to step lively going across the campus. As we were walking down a long, gentle, sloping hill, the professor turned to me and said casually: "It was right back there where he started shooting."

I looked over my shoulder, and there it was behind me, the Texas Tower, where one Monday morning in 1966 Charles Whitman had shot dead twelve people and wounded at least thirty-three others, after having killed his mother and wife the night before. That mindless slaughter was suddenly alive and real for me, as though it were happening again, and it was all I could do to keep from running for cover. I wanted to tell the professor that I didn't want to hear about it, that I couldn't hear it, but I didn't know how to tell him without sounding a little nuts.

As we walked, he spoke casually, glancing now and again over his shoulder at the tower. "When they first started dropping," he said, "they couldn't tell where the fire was coming from. They started dropping here." He pointed at his feet. "And then they started dropping over in the street and then on the other side."

By now I was concentrated, screwed down about as tight as I ever get, but I managed to continue walking and not to do anything unseemly.

"They've closed off the tower now," he said. "Students started committing suicide off the top of it—jumping."

I tried not to listen. I tried to think of the newspaper clipping and the anonymous whatever in South Africa who had banned my book and tried to remember the little square cards neatly on iron cylinders in the card catalogue.

"But it didn't do a lot of good," he said. He pointed off to the left toward a high stadium wall. "They've started jumping off the stadium now. It does just as well."

In the classroom I rambled on about various novelists and short story writers from the South and elsewhere, saying that I didn't know any storytellers who wanted an adjective—Southern or gothic or ethnic—in front of the word *novelist*. I told them that I was a novelist from the South and that I had no alternative but to write out of the manners of my people. A student raised her hand and asked the question that writers learn to invent convenient lies about: "Mr. Crews, where do you get your ideas?" I began my standard reply, which, of course, is a lie that I won't repeat here. But as I spoke, I saw quite clearly the teenage Charles Whitman, dressed in his eagle scout uniform, standing in the Catholic church where he served the priest as altar boy. And from the other side of the room I saw the same Whitman, now twenty-five years old, with a Marine Corps footlocker full of weapons: a 6-millimeter Remington Magnum rifle with a four-power scope, a .35 caliber Remington pump rifle, a .30 caliber reconditioned Army carbine, a 12-gauge sawed-off shotgun, a 357 Magnum pistol, and a 9-millimeter Luger. It was Monday morning, August 1, 1966, and he was pulling the footlocker across the administration office on his way to the top of the tower where he would become one of the biggest mass murderers in the history of this country. The night before, on Sunday, sometime between 10 P.M. and daylight, he had killed his mother and his wife.

I saw Charles Whitman as a little boy and later at the age of twenty-five after the killings; I saw him there in the seminar room and knew that I was not remembering something or conjuring something, but that I actually saw him. At the same time I knew that he was not there, that he was safely and securely buried in the ground that waits for all of us. I did not feel any contradiction in what I saw and knew. The two mutually exclusive perceptions rested comfortably side by side in my head.

Late that night, when the party was over, the obligatory party at which I obliged my hosts by getting very drunk, I went alone back out to the Texas Tower. I sat in the grass and looked up at it, 307 feet high, and all manner of things ran through my mind. One of the first was Goethe's statement "There is no crime of which I cannot conceive myself guilty." And I thought about the fact that Charles Whitman had told the university psychiatrist that there were days, many days, when he wanted to climb the tower with a deer rifle and start shooting people. How long must he have resisted the temptation? What battles must he have fought in himself before he finally lost it all forever? It excuses nothing and resolves nothing, and this is no defense for him. But sitting there in the grass, I could imagine myself on the perch high above the campus where the streets looked like diagrams laid out for a housing development; I could imagine myself perched there with my Marine Corps footlocker full of death.

As sentimental, romantic, and grotesquely obscene as it may sound, we all know that there are people throughout the world resisting with all their might and will climbing the tower, because once the tower is climbed there is no turning back, no way out of it, no way down except death. It is probably a good thing that the University of Texas officials had closed off the tower because I know that I would have tried to find access to the building, as late as it was, climbed to that perch almost at the top where Whitman calmly and with incredible accuracy shot mothers and husbands and children, shot them dead because it was in him to do it, because his life and everything that made it had taken him there.

Sometime toward morning I got up from where I was sitting in the grass and walked back to my room. When I got back to the room, I dived to the bottom of a vodka bottle and didn't come up.

As it turned out, the vodka didn't help very much because that night I dreamed the circumstances of what I had known and been morbidly fascinated with for years. I'm not proud of saying that I am morbidly fascinated with such a thing, but again, it is only the truth. That night I dreamed of how, less than three weeks before Charles Whitman climbed the tower, Richard Speck had systematically slaughtered student nurses in their Chicago residence, taking them one by one apart from the others and killing them.

When I awoke, I knew that this day was to be worse than the day that preceded it and that I could not hope to get down from where I was, until I was safely home with my books and my typewriter and all the crippled and ruined manuscripts lying about on the desk. I wanted to get back to the place where I had resisted so many things, and failed at so many things, back to the place where even when I succeeded I failed because it was never good enough.

Graham Greene said: "The artist is doomed to live in an atmosphere of perpetual failure." I am very nervous about the word *artist*, not as I have used it, but the way it has been used by so many people who have no right to bring the word into their mouths in the first place. But I know what it means to live in an atmosphere of perpetual failure. I would not presume to think this makes me in any way unique. All of us whose senses are not entirely dead realize the imperfection of what we do, and to the extent that we are hard on ourselves, that imperfection translates itself into failure. Inevitably, it is out of a base of failure that we try to rise again to do another thing.

Finally, with myself more or less intact, I was able to leave Austin and make my way back to Gainesville, Florida. But going home was soured by the realization that I had to go again through Dallas, Texas, that city of doom. I seem to be unable to go into Dallas without getting into some sort of trouble, without having some hostile hand put upon me and some hostile voice accuse me of something which I never have the courage to deny. In that city I always want to throw up my hands and say: "Whatever the charge, I plead guilty." In Dallas, Texas, I *am* guilty.

I did not leave Charles Whitman in Austin. I will never leave him. The autopsy, after he was slaughtered by an off-duty policeman by the name of Martinez, showed that he had a tumor the size of a pecan growing in his brain stem near the thalamus. It was surmised by various psychiatrists that the tumor could possibly have caused Charles Whitman to climb the tower. Although almost all modification of behavior is associated with the frontal lobe of the brain, it is obvious that since it is housed fairly tightly in a bony box, pressure in the brain stem might translate itself through the brain to the frontal lobe. So, conceivably, it could have caused what happened that Monday morning in 1966. How comforting to think that it might be so. But I do not believe that what happened at the University of Texas at Austin was caused by a tumor.

What I know is that all over the surface of the earth where humankind exists men and women are resisting climbing the tower. All of us have our towers to climb. Some are worse than others, but to deny that you have your tower to climb and that you must resist it or succumb to the temptation to do it, to deny that is done at the peril of your heart and mind.

All the way home to Gainesville, I felt that same tenuous diaphanous quality in the way I walked and what I did and what I said. Someone at that moment was climbing his tower, and I could only hope that he would not look down on me. But worse, much worse, I hoped that I would be spared being on the tower myself, because if I believe any-thing, I believe that the tower is waiting out there. I have no answers as to why it is out there, or even speculations about it, but out there some-where, around some corner, or in some green meadow, or in some busy street it is. Waiting.